LIGHTNING CREEK

LIGHTNING CREEK

◆

HOLLY McCLURE

LIGHTNING CREEK
ISBN 1-933523-03-4

Copyright © 2006 by Holly McClure

First Printing: February 2006

Library of Congress Control Number: 2005936613

Printed in the United States of America on acid-free paper.

Book design by Bella Rosa Books

BellaRosaBooks and logo are trademarks of Bella Rosa Books

Dedicated to the Eastern Band of the Cherokee,
especially the Snowbird community.

blank

LIGHTNING
CREEK

blank

QUALLA BOUNDARY

A hawk circled above the beech tree and a fox slinked at the edge of the yard. The white boy watched them stalk their prey. Like the rabbit feeding unaware, the other boys were too preoccupied to take notice. Eyes wide and fixed on the grandfather, they listened.

Two boys, as alike in size and features as if they were brothers, sprawled on the steps. The smallest of the five sat coiled like a spring, his skinny arms clasped around bony knees. The eldest stood behind the grandfather, watching. The white boy kept his distance at the end of the porch, his eyes on the diving hawk. He was different from the others, and not only because of his red hair and freckles. While the other boys hung on every word the grandfather said, he only wanted the story to end. Had they asked, he would have said he wasn't interested, but in truth, he was afraid.

The grandfather saw his fear, but made no concession to it. If the white boy was going to run around with the Copperheads, he'd hear plenty that would scare him.

The eldest boy, not yet in his teens and already the caretaker and protector of the younger kids, went to sit beside the redhead. The boy asked him the question he didn't want to ask the grandfather. "Was it here, Buck? Did he keep it in this house?" The grandfather let Buck answer.

"That was over three hundred years ago, Johnny. The conjuror's house was long gone before the Smokers built this one."

The other boys looked relieved, but not the redhead. He had

more questions the others wouldn't ask. There was a hint of challenge in his voice. "Looks to me like something that could kill us all, ought to have been done away with. Why didn't Kanegwa'ti destroy it before he died?"

The grandfather would answer that one himself. Not for the white boy but for his own grandson. The skinny one. In a voice that summoned up images of a future the boys would rather not know, he said, "It could show a man things to come, Johnny. It showed the great conjuror, Kanegwa'ti, a time when we would face something bad enough to risk using it again. Then, a Suye'ta would come. A chosen one who could harness its power and use it to save us."

Buck had a question of his own, "Why didn't he come during the removal? Our people could have used some help on the Trail of Tears."

The grandfather waited as the white boy watched the hawk swoop down and soar off with the hapless rabbit before responding. Then, looking into the distance in a way that made the boys wonder if he had also seen the conjuror's vision, he said, "Kanegwa'ti saw those times, and watched us survive them. Then the Ulunsu'ti showed him something worse." He rose to his feet, to let them know he was through with them, and then halted. Speaking so softly they wondered if he was talking to himself, he said, "I think I see it coming, boys. The thing the conjuror knew would take the last one of us out of this world. You and all the others could see it, too, if you'd pay attention. It won't be long now. I hope one of you will have the guts to do something about it before it's too late." He looked straight at the white boy for a moment, then went inside. The screen door clattered shut behind him.

The skinny boy called to the old man but his grandfather didn't answer. The white boy laughed a bit too loud. "Come on, Eli. You guys believe that crap? A snake's spirit in a crystal, eating souls and killing everything in sight? Your grandpa's just trying to creep us out."

The others didn't laugh. The two boys on the steps looked

worried. "Why is he telling us this, David? What are we supposed to do?"

"I don't know, Yona," Could be he thinks one of us is the Suye'ta."

Buck, the eldest, straightened and put his hands in the pockets of his faded jeans. He didn't sound very sure of himself when he said, "Couldn't be one of us. The Suye'ta is an outsider. We're all full-bloods, except Johnny." The four boys looked at the white boy, expecting him to say something. He ignored them.

The fox slunk away into the woods behind the old house, seen only by the white boy.

ATAGA'HI

A shovel gouged through rocky soil, breaking silence that had lingered for centuries in the hidden burial ground. The elder stood aside, watching the desecration. Thin rays of evening sunlight filtered through sparse foliage, casting the digger's shadow against the mountainside. The big white man's sculpted muscles rippled as he tossed shovels full of black earth from the grave. A little apart, propped against one of the straggly pine trees that survived at this elevation, the third member of the party watched the digger work.

The elder directed the digger to move further uphill, then bent close to the excavation, straining his eyes to see anything the shovel might unearth. "Easy, easy," he said when he heard the rasp of metal against stone. "Can't risk breaking anything now. Best use the trowel." The years had roughened his voice but when he stood to fetch the trowel, his back was as straight as the digger's.

"It would be in a coffin, wouldn't it?" The digger asked.

"Nope. Didn't use them back then." The elder dropped to his belly and reached down into the hole with the trowel. When a smooth surface appeared, he cleared the soil with his hands exposing an ancient soap stone pot, sealed tightly against the years.

"Here, help me with this." The elder's voice broke, betraying his fear. The digger stepped into the hole with him. It strained both of them to lift the heavy pot free of the grave and set it down on a patch of mossy ground. The third accomplice left the tree and came to peer over the digger's shoulder at their find.

The elder ordered them both to stand back while he squatted beside the ancient pot and cleaned it with a red cotton bandana. He could feel their eyes on him as he ran his finger around the rim until he found a seam. With a hunting knife the digger handed him, he worked at it until he loosened the seal. Laying it aside, he shielded the pot with his body so only he could see inside.

Ancient buckskin, dry and brittle with age, filled the interior. Holding his breath he inched it free of the container and laid it on the ground, then teased the bundle apart to reveal the grave goods the tanned hide and stone pot had protected for hundreds of years.

Centuries of lying buried with the mortal remains of their owner had left the relics in much better shape than he expected. Taking out an ancient war axe, he tested its heft in his hands. It fit his grip like it was made for him. The skill of its creator was evident in the every detail, from the finely knapped stone to intricate markings on the handle.

He heard the greed in the digger's voice. "This is what we're after. Right?"

Ignoring the digger, the elder examined the relics. Lifting them one by one he searched for the marks that would tell him what he needed to know. There were two graves here. One held what they had come for. The other meant nothing. It would have made things easier if they had opened the right one first but it didn't take him long to realize he had made the wrong choice. Their work wasn't done yet. The elder felt sick. He'd hoped this would go quicker and they could get out before dark. He averted his face, so the digger couldn't see how troubled he was. "Wrong grave. Help me put the pot in the ground, then I'll cover up this one and his goods and let him go back to his rest."

When the pot was in place, he told the digger, "Start digging where I showed you, before we lose the light."

The elder stood in the open grave and watched the digger.

The big white man looked like he could dig all night if need be, but he made it obvious he didn't want to. The elder suspected he'd rather be back at the gym, getting his exercise lifting weights. He repeated his order. "Get busy now, boy."

The digger grumbled as he walked uphill to the piled stones that marked the second burial site. "Are you sure this is even a grave? Looks to me like it could be a natural rock formation."

The elder answered, "It was meant to look that way. Two men came here to bury their dead in secret over three hundred years ago. One of them left this mountain alive. The other was in the grave we just opened. Since that time, only one man in any generation has known what they buried here, or why. Start digging now, boy."

The digger gave him a stubborn look, then drove his shovel into the second grave.

When he was sure the digger was too busy to notice, the elder crouched beside the open grave and positioned the relics and buckskin in the pot. When everything was in its place but the war axe, he ran his thumb across the razor-sharp obsidian of the blade. A sudden impulse made him set the axe aside while he replaced the seal on the pot. He climbed out of the grave and went to the canvas knapsack he had left propped against a lichen covered boulder, taking the axe with him. The digger was hard at work on the second grave and didn't see him slip the axe in the knapsack.

The third accomplice came to help cover the pot and saw what he had done. The elder was ashamed, but he didn't try to explain. There was no excuse for it, but what did it matter. He shrugged away his guilt. With the list of transgressions already on his conscience, stealing from the dead was a minor thing.

The elder accepted the offered help and the two of them worked in silence, scraping the loose earth back into the grave and tamping down the soil. Scattering handfuls of pine needles over the raw earth erased the evidence of desecration.

The digger had made progress. The elder picked up a shovel and went to join him, walking slowly, trying to settle his nerves. His hands still shook as he worked. At about three feet down, his shovel met resistance. When the digger spoke, it startled him.

"Must not have buried him real deep."

The elder agreed. He put his foot to the edge of his shovel and leaned into it. Something hard met the blade.

Strange. He hadn't expected this. They worked faster. When it wasn't safe to use the shovels, they troweled away the dirt, revealing a long narrow object. The digger stood back amazed. "Two men, you say?"

The elder grunted an affirmative.

"They must have had the strength of a couple of bull elephants to lug this thing all the way up here." The digger wiped his brow on his sleeve and bent over the grave. Its occupant had been buried in a full size canoe.

The elder inspected it. The canoe had been buried right-side-up to serve as a casket for the man and his grave goods. It had been treated with fire to preserve the wood.

The sun was just a dim glow leaking from behind a distant mountain. Shadows lengthened across the burial ground. The third partner took a flashlight from a pack and directed its beam into the excavation.

The elder worked alone now, not trusting the digger with what he expected to find.

The digger sat on a fallen log, fidgeting so badly it was becoming annoying. The elder suggested he try to settle down.

The digger snapped back, "I'll settle down when we get out off this mountain. Why is this place so damn quiet? This is getting on my nerves." He got up and paced beside the grave.

The elder let him pace. He understood how the white man felt. Every sound they made exploded in the silence like a firecracker at a funeral. He knew why there was no sign of life in places like this, and it still made him nervous. Anywhere else in the Smoky Mountains, there were sounds of birds, crickets, frogs and other noises of nature. Perhaps he should tell the digger about the Nunne'hi and why nothing intruded on the places where they lived, but thinking about it made it even harder to go through with the plan. Now that he was here, it was too late to lose his nerve and reconsider his plan. He kept his mind on the job at hand, glad the digger wasn't pestering him with questions the way he usually did.

The body in the canoe had been wrapped in layers of cured hides and bearskin robes. What was left of them fell away under the elder's careful work with the trowel. When the round dome of a skull appeared, the digger wanted to help. The elder rejected the offer. He had to do this alone.

With the tip of the trowel, he worked the remnants of wrappings away from the ancient bones. The skeleton lay intact in the bottom of the canoe. There had been times in his life when the elder had wondered if the man in the grave was a myth. It was a lot to ask a rational man to believe the stories told about him. He no longer had any doubt.

Beside the bones sat a round pottery bowl, somewhat smaller than the one in the first grave.

The digger saw and grunted an obscenity. The elder ignored him and bent to encircle the bowl in his arms. His whole body trembled with the effort it took to maneuver it to the graveside. In the glow of the flashlight, he wiped away the dirt. His hands felt the markings before his aging eyes could see them. This was the one. In a quaking voice he muttered something in his own tongue that could have been a prayer, or the primal utterance of a man lost in emotion that threw him back to the days before he learned to speak English.

A round disc sealed the mouth of the bowl against the ages. He needed the digger's help to work it loose. As soon as the seal broke, the elder said. "I'll take it from here," and sent the digger to wait beside the grave. The big white man squatted on his haunches, eying the bowl. Even in the dim light, he couldn't hide the greedy look in his pale blue eyes.

The elder lifted out the first bundle, checking for the markings that would confirm what he needed to know. When he found them, he had a fleeting moment when he almost wished he had been wrong. If this grave had held an ordinary man and nothing more, he could call the whole thing off and go home. But this was no ordinary grave, and its occupant, no ordinary man. He had gone too far to turn back.

The elder could feel the digger's intense gaze as he worried the bindings loose from the bundle. Having him see what the wrappings concealed compounded the desecration, but he would have to show them to him sooner or later.

The elder examined each of the relics, glad that both of his accomplices kept quiet. They stayed out of his way as he secured them in their wrappings and laid the bundle beside the desiccated skeleton.

When he spoke, he saw them startle. Even to his own ears, his voice sounded as brittle as the bones. "Bring the bags. This is what we came for."

The third partner brought a couple of crushed canvas bags to the digger. He smoothed them out against his thighs and handed them to the elder. "This is all I could find but if we use them both, there should be room to hold it all," he said.

Distaste evoked an uncharacteristic profanity from the elder. After all the years he had planned this day, he had nothing better than a couple of old gym bags to hold something that would change the world. He'd spent years spying on his closest friends. He had violated the trust of the Snake Dancers, and by bringing his two accomplices together, involved them in something they could never understand. After all that, he'd overlooked the simple detail of appropriate containers. The gym bags would have to do.

When everything was back in the bowl, the digger helped him put the bowl into the largest bag. It filled the canvas, making an awkward, heavy burden. The white man did as he was told and gathered the bones. The elder watched him line the second gym bag with a dingy towel and place the bones inside, glad that he didn't have to touch them. He'd avoided looking at them any more than he had to. It didn't seem to bother the digger. The elder grunted in agreement when the digger commented that they were in good shape considering how long they'd been in the ground. With the towel folded over them, the skull bulging against the terry cloth. It was done.

The third accomplice walked away and bent over behind a pine. The elder understood why. He hated the desecration, but it had to be done. There was no other way. He had no remorse about getting the digger involved. The white man had his own reasons for helping, but the third followed out of loyalty. If things worked out, they would all be better off, but if not, he would take the guilt to his grave.

By the time the bags were filled and ready to go, darkness mingled with the eerie silence to make the old burial ground feel even more threatening. The digger was in such a hurry to leave the silent mountain where no life intruded, that he would have abandoned the scarred earth and the opened grave and hiked back down the trail. The elder handed him a shovel and told him to go to work. They didn't stop until every trace of damage was repaired. The elder worked as hard as the digger.

One more thing to do, then they could leave. It might be a useless gesture but the elder hoped it would relieve the uneasiness they all three felt. He took an abalone shell from his pack and filled it with herbs from a leather pouch, then held it out to the third partner who struck a match to the herbs. When the flame died and fragrant smoke swirled from the shell, he waved it toward his face and around his body, and then held the shell for the others.

The smudging was meant to make them feel cleansed but it didn't. His accomplices waited impatiently while he made offerings of tobacco to the Nunne'hi, who were said to inhabit this mountain. He feared the immortal guardians were no longer around to appreciate his gifts. The silence that lingered around their dwelling places remained but he saw no sign of their presence. If the Nunne'hi were still guarding this sacred site, they would have shown themselves by now. And if they had left this secret mountain where no one ever came, how could he hope they still lived anywhere else in the land?

With sadness so profound it pierced his soul the elder walked away from the graves. He had spied on a friend who was closer than a brother to find this place, and betrayed that friend with theft and desecration, and there was a chance it was all for nothing. He pushed the growing pangs of remorse from his mind with the thought of the vanished Nunne'hi and steeled himself to go through with the plan he had been working on since he came back from the war. It was the only way he knew to save his people. Perhaps he was already too late, but he had to try.

The others followed in silence, staying close enough to give him the benefit of the flashlight's glow in the gathering darkness. An hour's walk through the pathless forest brought them to an old Ford Pinto, waiting at the end of a road that was barely more than two ruts through the brush. The compact car wasn't built for this kind of terrain but it would get them where they needed to go.

The elder held the door and flipped the driver's seat forward so the third partner, the smallest one of them, could crawl into the back seat, then got behind the wheel.

The white man stashed the bags in the back then folded his long legs into the passenger's seat. Slamming the door he asked, "Where to now?"

The elder was bone tired and didn't want to talk to the digger any more, but there were things the white man needed to know in order to do his part. "Home," he said. "We need a good night's sleep. First thing in the morning, I'll do what I have to do at Tatham Gap, and then I'll come for you so we can start the preparations. Tuesday, we'll be ready. Don't eat anything or drink anything but water before that."

"I've been fasting like you told me to," the digger said, then as if an afterthought, "I'll keep the bags with me till Tuesday. They'll be safer."

The elder's eyes were hard and cold in the darkness but the digger couldn't see that. "They stay with me." His voice was as hard as his eyes. The digger didn't know he was a pawn. He had to be kept under control or none of them would live through the week ahead. That's where the one in the back seat came in handy. He couldn't do this alone.

The digger said nothing more, but he didn't have to. The elder could smell the cold clammy sweat that gave away his fear. It had worried him at first, but he'd had come to know the digger's ambition outweighed his anxiety. The promise of power that would allow him to be what he already claimed, was too good to resist. He'd promised the white man a life that wasn't a lie.

The winding dirt road demanded the elder's attention as he maneuvered the old Pinto around the curves. It would be easier once he reached the parkway. Here, the mist that gave the Smoky Mountains their name obscured hairpin turns so thoroughly he had to be careful not to slip off the sheer drop along the narrow shoulder. Later, there would be time to worry about the streak of independence the digger was beginning to show. He was sounding less like an awed pupil and more like he had a mind of his own. That wasn't good. Not for what he had planned.

Down the Blue Ridge Parkway and on the other side of the mountain, he pulled into the parking lot of Mingus Mill. The restored old grist mill attracted a fair number of tourists, even this early in the year. The Sunday crowd had already cleared out, except for a young couple sitting on the footbridge, their feet swinging over the stream. He parked beside the dark green Mitsubishi Montero his passengers had left there earlier.

The digger reached over the seat and shook their sleeping partner awake, then they both got out of the car. "Where do you want us to meet you tomorrow?" He asked the elder.

"I've got some things I need to do by myself." The elder kept his eyes averted to hide the mistrust he knew would show. "I'll get back to you when I'm done." From the corner of his eye, he saw how the white man looked at the bags in the back seat, like he might just take them, with or without permission.

In a burst of anger he shifted into first and stomped on the accelerator.

The white man's yell gave him a feeling of satisfaction. He watched him in the rearview mirror, staring at the Pinto as he wheeled back onto the parkway.

When he was alone he tried not to dwell on what he carried in the two gym bags. It was his responsibility now and he had to go on with the plan. The die was cast. There was no hope that the Snake Dancers would agree to act, and come over to his side. He was on his own, ready or not. This was what he had been planning for years, following the guardians of the relics the Snake Dancer Society protected until he learned their secrets. Then he'd brought the white man in and taught him what he needed to know. The hardest part was the way he'd used their third partner. He didn't like to think about that. All the while, he had hoped the Snake Dancers would come around and realize they had to do something. For as long as he could remember, they talked about the Nunne'hi and their relationship to the Cherokee. They all said the number of the immortals and the number of the Cherokee was the same, and when the Nunne'hi left the world, the Cherokee would soon follow.

The Nunne'hi had lived near the burial ground they'd desecrated at Ataga'hi long before mortals came to the Smoky Mountains. Now all that was left of them was the silence that lingered near the places they had lived. The immortals were leaving the Smokies. Who could blame them? The very air was unfit to breathe and even the rain was poison. Too many people crowded in, trampling through lands where they didn't belong. If this kept up, it soon wouldn't be fit for human beings, much less the Nunne'hi.

It saddened him that the young people thought the Nunne'hi were only mythic beings, kept alive in old stories told by their superstitious elders. He knew better, and so did the Snake Dancers, but they still wasted time talking. While they talked, the places where the immortals lived were desecrated and they left the homeland. His heart ached to think about it.

He drove past flashing neon lights advertising motels with names like Redskin Inn or Warrior Lodge. This whole tourist town was part of the trouble. The Snake Dancers had been entrusted with the power to change it all and take back what rightfully belonged to the Cherokee, but they'd grown soft. Always too afraid of what would happen if things went wrong. Well, it couldn't get much worse than it was already. Time was running out, and they kept saying wait. He'd waited as long as he could. What he had to do would probably kill him but if he had to die he'd go down fighting. It was his nature. His clan had supplied many of the great war-chiefs of old and their blood was strong in him. This Wolf Clan Warrior wasn't born for talking and waiting. He had honored the duty to protect the Ulunsu'ti and the place where it was hidden on Tatham Gap, but the guardianship of the crystal included the responsibility to see it was used when the time came. His ancestor, who first accepted that sacred duty, and all his fathers who followed, would have done it if they were in his place. He was sure of it.

He hadn't expected to be so scared or to taste sickness at the back of his throat. He swallowed hard and spoke aloud into the darkness. "I have to do it, before everything is gone. If I don't, somebody else will. Somebody who's too weak to handle it." He knew who that would be and it pissed him off to think of how the old fool had sided with the others against him, agreeing to wait and see. Well, if Walker Copperhead wanted to wait, let him. He was too old and soft anyway. Couldn't he see that when their generation passed, it would be too late? The Nunne'hi would be gone by the time their grandsons took over. Then, there wouldn't be any Cherokee people to save. When the big white man came to his trailer, willing to learn and do whatever he had to do, it was time to act. He wasn't perfect but he was strong and had the desire. And he was a damn sight better than that lazy-assed weakling of a white boy Walker Copperhead had his eye on ever since he married into the Copperhead family. For a moment, a hint of suspicion teased at the back of his mind. What if Walker was planning something without telling any of the rest? Wouldn't that be just like the old fart? He hated to admit it, but for all their differences, he and Walker were a lot alike.

He drove past the Qualla Boundary sign on 441 and steered the Pinto off to a side road for a few miles, then up a gravel driveway for the half mile to his trailer. The house he had lived in since the day he was born stood behind it, leaning precariously against rotting porch posts. His wife had wanted something more modern to live in so he bought her the trailer. Two years later she had gone and died and he was still making payments. He parked under the big beech tree and went inside.

With the bags stashed under his bed, he stretched out and tried to sleep. It might be his last chance. In the week ahead he had to face a nightmare. The white man was the only one around to face it with him and he couldn't waste any more time worrying about the flaws in the digger's personality. It would have helped if he could figure out what Walker Copperhead was up to. What if he was planning to strike out on his own and do something himself?

Sally, his wife's old cat, cuddled up beside him. He'd gotten used to talking out his troubles with her since Lena walked over. Sally purred while he fretted about an old Snake Dancer who lived on Snowbird Creek, and a white boy who'd married into the family. He confided his opinion to Lena's cat. "If that boy knew what Walker had in mind for him, he'd haul ass out of Graham County and as far away from all them Copperheads as he could get."

An owl hooted somebody's death call outside in the beech tree. It took his mind off the rest of his worries long enough for sleep to overtake him. His dreams were as bad as his waking thoughts. A snake as big around as his leg surfaced from the shadows of a mountain creek and looked straight into his eyes, forcing him to return the gaze. He had no choice but to stare deep into the very human eyes of the serpent and try like hell to wake up.

THE ROUND HOUSE

The door opened, letting the cigarette smoke out and the cool night air in. The man who entered moved like a shadow, his black eyes darting around the room, settling on the fiddle player as he tucked his instrument under his chin and began to play. The first note was akin to the groan that escaped the musician's throat when he saw who followed the big Indian through the door of the Round House Supper Club. She looked harmless enough, petite as she was. The top of her head would barely reach his chin, and she was smiling. It was the smile that froze his blood. So civilized, not even lighting her dark eyes. Those eyes smoldered like black pools of lava that could roll over a man's soul, if a man was fool enough to cross her. He had been fool enough.

The fiddle player kept playing. The woman listened, standing beside the Indian at the door. She still smiled. The Indian didn't, just folded his arms across his chest like a parody from a Western movie, his face impassive.

The fiddle player had to sing. It was his band and he was the lead singer. He lowered the fiddle and tried to remember the words. His voice was way off key at first, but the boys covered for him. They saw who was at the door and knew this would be his last song tonight. The banjo player gave him a look that said, *I'd help if I could but you're on your own tonight, friend.*

He understood. There was nothing anybody could do now. He had to face this tune alone.

"Shady Grove my little Love,

"Shady Grove my darlin',

"Shady Grove my little love,

"Going back to Harlen."

While the mandolin wailed the last few notes, the fiddle player put the fiddle across his knee and reached under his chair. He needed a sip of courage. The unlabeled Mason jar he came up with held the only measure of comfort he could expect to find in this room. His eyes watered as he drank. One sip was all he had time for. He knew better than to resist when the woman came on the stage and took the jar from his hand.

"He won't be needing anymore of this tonight." She handed the jar to Will.

Will put down his mandolin to take the jar, raising it to his lips with the same motion to take as big a drink as a man could stand.

The fiddle player looked up to see the big Indian towering over him, handing him his fiddle case. He took it and began to stow his fiddle. The woman stood over him, too, until he finished and raised his head. She looked him square in the eye with that unflinching gaze. "John, you've got two kids at home that want to say goodnight to their daddy, and a woman that ain't gonna sleep alone tonight. Yona and I think it would be a good idea if you'd come on home now."

Apparently, John thought so, too. Lightning Creek Bluegrass Band lit into playing without the fiddler. It didn't sound near as good, but the audience put up with it. Some even started dancing. Johnny figured it was because without him playing and singing, they'd rather dance than listen. What was a bluegrass band without a fiddle and a tenor?

He was sure they didn't blame him for leaving. They knew his wife well enough that nobody wanted to see her get mad. Faron Copperhead McLeymore could raise some holy hell if he set her off. Then there was her brother, Yona. He was as big as a bear, which was what his name meant in Cherokee. Yona was a good man. Everybody liked him, and he'd been the best friend John had in the world since they were kids but if a body didn't treat his sister right, friend or not, they'd answer to her big brother.

Yona carried the fiddle. John walked with his arm draped around Faron's waist. She smiled up at him sweet as sugar. He breathed easier to see that the danger was gone from her eyes and hugged her closer. She was the best wife a man could have. It didn't take much to make her happy. Just keep the all night sessions to a minimum, like when her mom could watch the kids and she could come along, be a good daddy and not cuss or drink in front of his daughter and son.

For the most part, he toed the line. He shuddered when he remembered the few times when he hadn't. He had been a slow learner but he finally caught on. Will and the other guys in the band had ragged him about it for a while. "You're whupped, man," they'd say.

"Yeah, like an egg-sucking hound." John didn't mind admitting it. He knew Will and every man in the band, hell, in the whole state of North Carolina, would trade places with him in a New York minute if they could.

There wasn't room in the Round House parking lot for Yona's big logging company truck. It was parked across the road. The logo on the door depicted a snake coiled among the words, *Copperhead Logging*. He had helped his brother-in-law design it. Inside the cab he could see a dark form. "Old Walker?" John asked.

"Yeah," Yona grinned. "He wanted to come along to say 'siyo,' brother."

"I doubt it was greeting me he had in mind. More likely he wanted to come along to watch, in case Faron kicked my ass."

"More likely he did," Yona slid behind the wheel.

John climbed in beside Walker Copperhead and lifted Faron up next to him. One good thing about Yona's old truck, it was as roomy as a limo. "Evening, Grandpa," he said, without looking at Faron's grandfather.

"O'siyo, son," Walker greeted him in Cherokee. "How's the crowd?"

"Good crowd tonight. Kinda rowdy, but then they usually

are on a Saturday night." John looked at his watch in the glow of the dashboard lights. "It's late though, after midnight. High time we cleared out and went home. I appreciate you and Faron and Yona coming to pick me up."

"Bullshit," Walker said.

John didn't say anything else, just hugged Faron as she cuddled closer to him. Walker had said all he planned to tonight. Yona never was one to talk much, not even when they were kids. Besides, he had to keep his eyes on the road. Tatham Gap was the shortest way home but the road was not much more than a logging trail, twisting and turning around the mountain.

Near the top, an even more primitive road veered off to the right toward the fire tower on Joanna Bald, reminding John that he'd be coming this way early Monday morning to take supplies and hang out with Eli Smoker for a while.

The lights of the truck fell briefly on a state park historical marker. He didn't need to read it to know it said Tatham Gap Road was a section of the Trail of Tears. Just passing it always made him think of the stories he'd heard all his life about how his wife's people were rounded up and marched away to the west, torn from their homeland and robbed of their homes. How many of the thousands of Cherokee people who died on the trail, lay in unmarked graves on this very mountain?

The three Cherokees in the truck with him said nothing but the silence resonated with unspoken feelings.

It was nearly one o'clock in the morning when they turned into what could loosely be termed a driveway. It was graveled, but weeds grew between the tire ruts. The door on Yona's side scraped against thick huckleberry bushes. He slowed to ease the big truck into the creek and up to the turn-around below the house.

"Need to build you a bridge over that creek, brother," he said.

"Never seemed to need one before," John said. "We've got the footbridge, and it's no problem to just drive through the creek."

"That's okay for your pick-up, but Faron's Chevy sits mighty low in the water." Yona said. "And Kate's Trans Am don't stand a chance. While little brother Charlie's home from school, we'll get to work on it. We'll be over first thing in the morning with a load of lumber and the three of us will build her a good bridge. Should have done it years ago. One of these days, we need to look into paving your driveway, too."

Wouldn't do any good to object. Seemed like one of his in-laws had something in mind for his property every time he turned around. Well, as long as they came up with the supplies and most of the labor, it wasn't such a bad deal.

As soon as the truck came to a stop, Faron climbed down and went to the house. Yona and Walker stayed in the truck, waiting for Mama Kate. She'd been looking after the kids. John took his time. He was in no hurry to face Faron's mom.

Walker scooted over to the door and prodded John in the ribs with his walking stick. "Need to get some rest, boy. Never know when you might need it." He chuckled like what he said was real funny.

"Yeah sure, Grandpa." John followed Faron up the porch steps. She stopped to pat Red Dog on the head. He hadn't even bothered to get up or bark. He knew the sound of Yona's truck well enough not to waste his energy. Black Dog came around from his post at the back door to check and make sure all was well. "Go back to sleep, old buddy," John said. "It's just us." Black Dog trotted back around the house.

Kate was ready to go. Her displeasure at being kept up till the wee hours of the morning showed in her stance and was echoed by the fire in her eyes. "The babies went to sleep on the couch," she said. "I promised them their daddy would carry them to bed if he ever got home."

John tried not to flinch. Having a mother-in-law who was taller than he, and probably outweighed him, was a bit intimidating. By the time he was ten years old, he'd given up on trying to figure out whether Faron's mom loved him or hated his guts. "Thanks, Mama Kate," he said. She patted his arm as she sashayed past him.

"I'll ride over tomorrow with the men when they come to make you a bridge," she said to Faron. "You'll need some help cooking for all that bunch." She didn't say anything to John. Funny how everybody knew about this bridge project but him.

Diamond hardly stirred when John picked him up and carried him to bed. John kissed his son's cheek and tucked the covers around him. He was a big boy for a two-year-old. Took after his uncle Yona, or his Grandma Kate. John watched him sleeping for a moment then went back to the living room for his daughter.

Wren stretched and opened her eyes. Her sleepy smile warmed his heart as she reached her arms up to him. She was as dainty as the tiny bird Kate had named her for, just like her mama.

The kids were tucked in and sleeping. He had time for a couple hours of shut-eye before he had to get up for the bridge building. When Yona said first thing in the morning, John knew that meant well before sunrise.

The stairs to the loft bedroom felt steeper than usual as he followed Faron up. This was another property improvement the Copperheads had decided John and Faron couldn't live without, back when she was pregnant with Diamond. "Need some more room with another kid coming along," Yona had said. The memory of the weeks following that decision drained the little energy left in him.

He was way too tired for a shower, but knew he needed one. Faron would probably kick him out of bed if he came in reeking of smoke, moonshine and fiddler sweat. He made it quick and staggered into the bedroom ready to fall asleep as soon as his head hit the pillow. Faron had other ideas. Every inch of her soft skin shined like the finest warm, coppery silk as she welcomed him to bed. "Looks like I'm not gonna get much sleep tonight," he said.

"Probably not," Faron answered, tangling her fingers in his

red curls and drawing his mouth to hers. Damn! He was a lucky man. Faron set about removing any lingering traces of doubt about his immense good fortune.

When she was through with him for the night, Faron slept the sleep of a satisfied woman while John lay wide awake. Tired as he was he couldn't shake a vague feeling of unease that kept him tossing and turning. Maybe he was just dreading all the work the Copperheads had lined up for him. These projects of theirs had a way of running his ass off and he dreaded it like a toothache. When he finally did fall asleep, just before time to get up, it was with the memory of Walker Copperhead's farewell words. What the hell did the old goat mean by that?

The next day's bridge building went faster than John expected, and once it was finished, he had to admit it should have been done long ago. If it had been left up to him, he never would have found the time. Sometimes a big family of in-laws can get a man motivated. Lord knows, he never would have had near as many ideas about improvements to his property if it hadn't been for Faron's folks.

Sunday supper almost made up for all the work. After he had eaten way too much, and had his mother-in-law bandage the blisters on his palms, he nodded off on the porch swing. The Copperheads took pity on him and let him doze a few minutes. Yet, even while he slept, the apprehension from last night prodded at the edge of his awareness. He dismissed it again. No place in the world was more peaceful than right here on the Snowbird. The Eastern Band Cherokees knew what they were doing when they claimed this secluded site along Snowbird Creek for part of their reservation. He was a lucky man to have married into the Copperheads and found a home here.

Black Dog and Red Dog returned from their check of the perimeters of his land and sat on the porch waiting for Faron's family to leave so they could settle in for the night. John woke up in time to say goodnight and thanks as he stifled yawns. A man was supposed to rest up on the weekend. A few more days like today would just about kill him.

He didn't sleep much that night either. Part of it was all the aches and pains in every muscle and joint in his body. Hard manual labor could do that to a man. John wasn't used to it and didn't want to adjust. But mostly it was the dreams that kept waking him every time he did doze off. Damn. He'd never had such dreams in his life. Might need to talk to Walker about it tomorrow. Being married into the Copperhead family all these years was making him as weird as they were.

Snakes. They'd say it was a sign of something; dreaming all night about snakes. Especially when one of them kept talking to him. Too bad it didn't speak English instead of Cherokee. At least then he could have told Walker what it said. But all he could understand was something about the snake not wanting his grave bothered. That didn't make any sense at all, just left him with the feeling that something bad was going on while he lay there in bed doing nothing about it. Something that was going to cause a lot of trouble.

Sometime before dawn, the snake went away and let him get some sleep—and forget.

QUALLA BOUNDARY

The elder looked through the open window. A thin crescent moon hung over the beech tree. Lena's old cat must have gotten tired of his tossing and turning. She had jumped on his chest to wake him up no more than two hours after they got into bed. He thanked her for freeing him from one of the worst dreams he'd ever had.

He stretched stiff limbs and reached under the bed. Both the gym bags were where he put them. He hated to leave them, even long enough to take a shower. The hot water would loosen up his sore muscles and wash away the dream image that clung to his mind. He checked again to make sure the doors were locked, even propped a chair under each door knob and closed and locked the window as an added precaution. Then he carried the bags with him to the bathroom.

Breakfast would have tasted real good after his shower but he had started fasting a week ago and needed to keep it up until after he *went to water* at sunrise. The ritual purification would prepare him for what he had to do tomorrow when he took the other two to Council House Mound. Once he was cleansed, he hoped he'd feel more in harmony with the Above Beings and with the Nunne'hi who still lived in the area around the mound. He didn't like this feeling of separation from them. It was the worst part of his loneliness, and one he hadn't expected. Another of the consequences of going against Walker Copperhead and the other Snake Dancers.

He brewed a pot of coffee and filled a Thermos, then stuffed a loaf of bread and a wedge of hoop cheese into a paper bag.

That would have to do. It was all he had in the house. Lena always took care of the food before she walked over to the above world. Now, he mostly lived on sandwiches and the few meals he ate when his son's bossy wife or the white girl his grandson married, cooked for him. Or when he went to Walker's house and Kate invited him to stay for supper.

The thought of Kate's cooking tempted him but he couldn't face the Copperheads now. Every one of them could look right through a man and see anything he tried to hide. Kate would probably have one of her feelings about him and pester him to death until he told her something he didn't want her to know. He had too much to hide to risk running into her intuition.

He hated to keep this from Walker, and not only because of their life-long friendship. As a fellow guardian and a principal Snake Dancer, Walker had a right to expect honesty from him, and here he was piling another betrayal on top of years of deceit, following him to find his hiding place. He told himself he had good reasons for what he was doing, but it didn't ease his guilt.

He laid the two gym bags on his unmade bed while he reached into the linen closet for a worn old sheet that he tore into squares. The bowl protected the fragile relics, but it was far too heavy and bulky to carry where he had to go. He removed the grave goods from the bowl and arranged them on his bed. One by one, he wrapped them carefully in the squares of linen. Padding a gym bag with the rest of the sheet, he gently packed each bundle and zipped up the bag.

The guardian of the grave would see its desecration as his own failure. If he learned the bones and relics in his charge had been stolen, the shame would probably kill him. If there was time, he would have to tell Walker Copperhead how many years it had taken him to spy out his secret and commend him on his dedication to the duty the ancestors entrusted to him. It wouldn't help either of them, but he hoped for the chance.

In the back of a storage closet he found an old canvas duffle bag. Both gym bags fit inside it with room to spare. They would be easier to carry like this, and the two other things he needed would fit when the time came.

He dreaded what he had to do at Tatham Gap even more than robbing the grave at Ataga'hi. His grandfather had taken him there when he was a young man, just before he went away to war, and told him about their family's duty to guard the Ulunsu'ti. Nothing on the battlefield scared him half as much as what lay hidden behind that big stone. He'd had a few years to learn about his duties when he returned, before his grandfather died and left him sole guardian of the powerful crystal. It had taken him years to get up the nerve to go check on the place alone. Even though it terrified him, he'd worked hard to measure up to his grandfather's expectations and do a good job of guarding the crystal entrusted to his family.

When he was through at Tatham Gap, he had to go to another hiding place up the Cheoah River. The relic hidden there would be the last thing he needed. Many years ago an Englishman had written about it, calling it *The Cherokee Ark of the Covenant.* The ark held the only thing that could control the power of the Ulunsu'ti once it was awakened. It had been even harder to find than the burial site on Ataga'hi. For years he had believed Driver Wayanettah guarded it and had wasted time spying on him. When Driver caught him following him through a cave on Wolf Mountain, he'd explained the cave was special because it was where his family hid out to avoid being rounded up and marched off to Oklahoma during the removal. It sounded like the truth. The Wayanettahs had managed to stay on in the homeland, even getting some of their land back when the dust settled.

The only Snake Dancer left with the status to be a guardian, was Del Locust. Del was even more careful than Driver had been. When he died and left his grandson in his place, it wasn't much easier. The boy had learned well, but in time, he gave his secret away.

Out beyond the old burial ground called Degal gun'yi, the Locusts guarded the ark, almost in sight of the Council House

Mound. Since that was the only place a sane man would dare wake up the crystal, it made sense to keep it there. Council House Mound was one of the few places left where the Nunne'hi still lived like they did when the first guardians concealed the ark. They would be needed when the Ulunsu'ti came to life. He hoped the big white man was up to his part, but if he wasn't, the intervention of the immortals would be crucial.

With every minute, his dread intensified. The thought of touching the crystal made his gut clinch. In all the centuries it had been hidden away, not one of his ancestors had dared even check to make sure it was actually there. He was certain none of them had given any thought to doing what he was about to do. Not even when their people were on the brink of extinction during the removal did they consider using it to save them. They probably had their reasons, or perhaps they were just like the Snake Dancers of today who wanted to wait and see, or just leave it hidden away forever. If he could have been sure it would stay hidden, he might have been more like them, but he couldn't count on that anymore.

Now they needed the power it could give them more than ever, and he was the only one willing to admit it. He had no choice but to go against them. It wasn't in his warrior nature to accept the end of his people if there was a chance to save them. He'd watched the desecration of the Cherokee homeland and seen what it was doing to his people. The young moved away and forgot who they were. The elders died out taking their wisdom with them. Most families didn't even speak the language, or know the names of the Above Beings, much less invoke them. Worst of all was what was happening to the dwelling places of the Nunne'hi. They weren't protected anymore. Houses and towns encroached on the very doorways to their land. One by one, the immortals were abandoning sacred sites, leaving them silent and dead. When they were gone, his people would be gone, too. He'd heard it said in the Circle that some people believed it was time for indigenous people to leave the world. That their days were up and all over the world they were dying out or being absorbed. He wasn't ready to accept that. Waking up the Ulunsu'ti was a drastic measure, but what did they have to lose? Unless something was done, it was over for them anyway.

He braced himself for the hardest job he had ever done and hefted the duffle bag into the front seat of his Ford Pinto. No more waiting. It was high time to put the conjuror's tools to work, while they could still do some good.

Surely he'd feel better after *going to wate*r in Snowbird Creek where generations of his family had gone for purification. There was nothing that could fully restore him to harmony after what he had done, but the cleansing ritual would help. After that, he'd get the ark.

All the way to Tatham Gap, he drove in darkness. Not a house he passed was lit. All the night owls had turned off their televisions and gone to bed, and the early birds were still asleep. He had the world to himself. Might as well get used to the solitude.

At the top of the gap, he turned up Joanna Bald Road toward the tower, then after a few miles, off onto a new logging trail. It got him to within half a mile of where he had to go. This was what had finally forced his hand. For centuries this place lay undisturbed, the hiding place secure. Now, loggers spread out everywhere. While they didn't clear-cut like loggers did in other old growth forests, they were still all over the mountains.

Sooner or later one of them would stumble on the fact that a niche lay behind that big granite boulder blocking the hollow. If they looked inside, they would find what his family had watched over since Kanegwa'ti entrusted it to his forefather. Then, it would all be over. There were no safe places to keep something as important as the Ulunsu'ti anymore. Any day now, everything would end up in a museum or some pot hunter's private collection, or worse.

If the others could only see it as clearly as he did they'd be helping him now and he wouldn't feel like a traitor to everything he believed in.

He could see the top of the boulder from where he parked the Pinto. It lay right in the path of the logging trail if they should need to cut it in a mile or so further. With the prime virgin timber spread out in that direction it was only a matter of time.

In minutes he was standing beside the boulder, wishing he had never started this. His hands shook so bad he was afraid he couldn't go through with it. His biggest fear—and hope— teased at his mind. What if this was all just a myth? What if the hiding place was empty and the thing didn't even exist? Even as he wished it was only an element of one of the old stories, he knew better. He and all the Snake Dancers had learned just how true some of the legends were. Any doubts they had were erased in the first sessions with their elders after initiation.

A pile of stones and a sapling served as a fulcrum to pry the boulder loose. Inch by inch he worked it aside, enlarging the gap between it and the excavation it concealed. After almost an hour of toil, it toppled forward, rolling down the slope, crashing through the undergrowth and coming to rest against a giant poplar tree. A cascade of rocks and earth followed it, leaving a path of debris in their wake. When the noise died, he dropped to his knees and reached into the fissure that now gaped open, unprotected. His hand met emptiness. Lying prone, his head inside the opening, he shined a flashlight into the dark interior. He had expected the Ulunsu'ti to be waiting for him just behind the boulder, but the fracture was deeper than he anticipated. It took every ounce of determination he had in him to crawl into the shadows. The smell of moist ancient earth comforted him. He closed his eyes and breathed it in, reaching forward.

His fingers touched something smooth and cold.

Things went gray then. It wasn't that he lost consciousness, but his attention shifted somewhere that he couldn't quite connect to. Dreamlike, he drew the crystal into the crook of his arm and wiggled backward out of the hole. Somehow, he reached the Pinto and slumped across the hood. His ears rang, a high pitched tone that vibrated in his head and left him disoriented and lightheaded. He shivered, chilled deep to the core of his body. Staggering to the car, he wrenched open the door and dragged the duffle bag out. With numb hands he opened the bag and dropped the Ulunsu'ti inside. The duffle bag fell against the car when he let it go. Slowly, warmth returned to his hands. He stopped shivering and the ringing in his ears ebbed to a soft whine. His head still throbbed.

He was curious about the Ulunsu'ti. No one had ever told him what it looked like. He couldn't resist the urge to see it, just for a moment. Pulling the neck of the duffle bag open, he peeked in. The ringing intensified, and he pulled away with the feeling something was looking back at him. He tightened the cord and boosted the duffle bag into the front seat.

With his ears still ringing and his head throbbing, he got into the car. The familiar comfort of the Pinto's worn seat gave a measure of ease to legs that were almost too weak to stand on. He had to sit for a minute to regain his strength and get his nerve back. He sucked in a deep breath of the clear, cool air. His insides still quivered. He figured it was from the fasting. Seven days was a long time without food for a man his age. Or perhaps he'd finally come to his senses and realized how foolhardy he was being. To betray the Snake Dancers was to invite their vengeance. All he had was the white man and if his plan was going to work, he had to be managed every step of the way.

He fingered the cord on the duffle bag. Everything he needed was there, except the ark. And he would have it before the day was done. He had reason to be proud of what he'd accomplished, outsmarting all the guardians, doing something nobody had been able to do since the days of Kanegwa'ti. It didn't seem fair that he had to turn it over to a white man who hadn't contributed anything but an evening of digging. But the white man was the outsider. Only an outsider could wake up the Ulunsu'ti.

The wave of possessiveness that swept over him with the thought of the Ulunsu'ti in the white man's hands, caught the elder off guard. It came on so hard and sudden it took his breath away. Why should he turn all this power over to a man who had done nothing to earn it? Why not keep it for himself? If an outsider was required, he was as qualified now as anyone.

His mind played with the concept of what it would be like to be the most powerful man in the world. How would it feel to know anything you wanted to know, from any time? To be able to make things happen the way you wanted them to? He would be like Kanegwa'ti, the great conjuror, so powerful his fame lived through generations yet to come. But that power would go to the white man, not him. The injustice of it began to gnaw at him.

With a start, he realized he had lapsed into the kind of thinking that could get him into real trouble. He had to get these ideas out of his head if he wanted to live through the week. His job was to keep the outsider under control. This was for the good of his people. Not for one man's gain. He counted on purification to help him get a grip on his mind and avoid the kind of temptation that could ruin everything. He needed to get to Snowbird Creek in a hurry.

He turned the key and the Pinto's starter ground weakly. When the engine finally rattled to life he backed up to a wide clearing, turned around, then bounced over the logging trail, heading down to Joanna Bald Road. From Tatham Gap he wound along the narrow road and on to the way that took him to the Snowbird.

The sheltered cove on Snowbird Creek held memories that spanned generations of his people, going back long before the removal. The preparations for his purification ritual were so familiar he didn't need to think.

By sunrise he had finished the preliminaries and stepped into the icy water to begin the seven immersions. He prayed harder than he had ever prayed before, calling on every Above Being he could think of who might still be willing to listen to him, imploring them to restore him to harmony and empower him to finish his task. He called them by name and invoked their presence to comfort him. He went under the cold water, staying down until his lungs hungered for air, praying to beings who had always listened and made themselves known before. Seven times, and they were silent. He was alone. Even when he was a young soldier in the middle of the war to end war, he hadn't been this scared. He'd marched through blood and bombs, earning medals and a battlefield promotion. He had been a hero then, but in those days, other men fought at his side and he was in harmony with the Above Beings. Now there was no one but him.

His seven days of fasting could end when he came out of the water but the thought of eating was of no interest. His insides couldn't handle food. He left the untouched bread and hoop cheese in the knapsack and kept praying as he drove up the Cheoah and on into the hills.

He had told the other two he would pick them up, but disgust at the idea of the Ulunsu'ti in the white man's possession tempted him to reconsider. The urge to leave the white man out of his plan grew stronger, but everything he knew said the outsider was necessary for this to work. What if an old man's body couldn't stand the strain? He'd need the white man's muscles then. He drove to the white man's place, still wishing there was a way to manage without him.

His accomplices were waiting at the end of the drive leading to their cabin. The way the white man eyed the duffle bag through the lowered window was the last straw. The elder looked into those ice blue eyes and saw something that made him want to get the Ulunsu'ti out of his sight. Calling out directions as he shifted into reverse, he instructed them to meet him, then turned the Pinto around and sped away so fast he left behind a smear of rubber the old tires could ill afford to lose. There was a road, of sorts, to the meeting place he had described but as far as the white man knew, the only way to get there was by foot.

He drove even slower than the gravel road required, trying to think of a way out of the partnership he had created. The white man couldn't hide that greedy look in his eyes, and greed meant big trouble for all of them. But there was no way around it now. He couldn't turn back and he needed the white man. They'd work on the white man's motives as a part of purification. Going to water would help set him right.

A few miles back down the road around the Cheoah, he pulled off under the trees to an almost invisible trail through the woods. Although it wasn't much more than a couple of ruts worn into the ground, and so rough it felt like his car was coming apart, it beat walking. When the Pinto had all it could handle, he quit trying to force the spinning tires up the incline and left the old car under a stand of pines. From there he walked about half an hour to the clearing to wait for his accomplices.

He would need to do some rearranging before they came along. It wasn't a good idea to leave the crystal in the duffle bag with the other things. Wishing he didn't have to touch it, he reached in and eased his hand beneath the cold orb. It was heavier than he remembered. Ice spread up his arm. As quickly as he could, he dropped it into his knapsack. It settled beside the war axe. The now familiar chill left his fingers icy. The ringing returned to his ears.

He clutched the knapsack against his chest, fighting an irrational desire to take another peek at the crystal. It scared him that it was so hard to close the knapsack and put it behind him out of sight.

An hour or so later he heard them coming through the woods. He made no attempt to conceal his presence, but even so, the big white man didn't see him till he spoke. The other had stopped a few yards away to wait.

He motioned for the outsider to sit down with him beside the gym bags. Best to see how things went today, then he would decide whether to show him the Ulunsu'ti. When the white man reached for the gym bags, he drew them both closer against his thigh, then slowly opened the first one and pushed it toward him saying, "I've told you what we're gonna do. Now I want you to see what we'll be doing it with."

"Is this everything?"

"There's one more thing. I'll get it later, then first thing in the morning, we have to prepare you."

"What do I do now?"

"Take out the bones."

The white man hesitated. "You never explained to me why we need the skeleton."

"It has to be held in the conjuror's own hands for it to work. We only need his hands, but it wouldn't be respectful to separate them from the rest of him. Find them, and then I'll tell you how it works."

The sound of rattling bones was barely audible but it shattered the stillness of the woods. The elder turned his head while the white man spread the items on the towel that had lined the gym bag. The third partner walked further away and sat under a tree, facing away from them.

"What the hell is this shit, old man?" The white man's face was red with anger.

The elder made himself look at the skeleton lying spread out on a dingy white towel, fragile and ancient. The skull's empty eyes stared accusations at him. A pile of ribs lay stacked beside it. Spinal discs, femurs, tibias, fibulas and feet were there but no hands and no bones that looked like they had ever been hands.

Squatting down beside the pile of bones, he lifted the intact arm bones and examined them in the morning sunlight. They ended abruptly at the wrists. The marks on the bones told the story. The hands had been cleanly severed by something very sharp.

Desperation can cloud the mind, but there are times when it brings clarity. This time it swept away the cobwebs, leaving his thoughts sharper than they had been in days. He understood something that had nagged at the back of his mind for years.

Driver Wayanettah was a Snake Dancer Guardian, just as he had thought, but he wasn't guarding the ark on Wolf Mountain. He hadn't lied about that. He guarded the conjuror's hands in his cave. The hands had not been buried in the grave at Ataga'hi. Driver had them all along, and he'd given up on him.

"We can't do anything without the hands," he told the white man. Come to my house at dawn tomorrow. I'll need your help to get them."

Suspicion clouded the white man's face. "Where are you going?"

"To get the ark. Go on home now, and meet me in the morning."

"And you plan to keep everything with you till then?"

He didn't bother to answer. Ignoring the white man, he gathered the bones and wrapped them in the towel. He put them back in the gym bags, put the gym bags in the duffle bag and hoisted it to his shoulder. Slinging the knapsack across the other shoulder, he turned to go. "Be there around sun up," he said, and walked off into the woods. He could feel eyes on his back until he was well out of sight behind a stand of spruce.

His mind sorted through the facts. The great conjuror had hand picked the first Snake Dancers and prepared them to keep the wisdom of the elders alive through the generations. To the elite among them, he entrusted the guardianship of the Ulunsu'ti and all the tools for waking and using it, then bound them all to an order of power and secrecy. The Snake Dancers all knew each other, but the identity of a guardian was known only to him and his chosen heir. The elder was the guardian of the Ulunsu'ti, but it had taken most of his adult life to learn who the other guardians were and what they protected. After all that effort, he had never learned that the hands were separated from the rest of the body. That part of the Ulunsu'ti's story was not told to all the Snake Dancers. Only the man the conjuror had appointed to take care of the hands knew it. And only the heir he passed the duty down to needed to be told. He had found Driver Wayanettah's hiding place when he searched the cave on Wolf Mountain for the ark. He'd thought tailing Driver was a waste of time better used looking for the ark, but if he hadn't followed Driver, all his work would have been for nothing. He couldn't wake the Ulunsu'ti without the hands, and he knew where they were. It meant a trip to Wolf Mountain to get them, but that wouldn't delay him for more than a day. For once, luck was on his side.

This slowed down things somewhat but not enough to make a difference.

It would be hard to wait until tomorrow to make sure he was right. If he wasn't so tired, he would get the ark and then go straight to check on the hands. But that meant a long hike up the steep rocky side of yet another mountain. His legs already trembled with exhaustion and his back ached. After he went to Degal'gun'yi for the ark, he needed to take it easy for awhile. Whether it was age or nerves, he didn't know, but the strength drained out of him. He would need the white man's muscles on Wolf Mountain.

The Locust's hiding place was easy enough to get to, but he needed to rest before he could retrieve what he'd come for. He sat on a flat rock and ate his meager lunch, finally ending his fast. A nearby stream provided water, and the bread and hoop cheese gave him the energy to go on.

The meal over, he brushed the crumbs from his jacket and started gathering up what he needed for the work he had to do. Too bad he couldn't trust the white man enough to let him do this job. It was almost too much for an old man who was already so tired. He gathered up the tools and set to work. It took all afternoon. When he finished he had added another set of aches and pains to his arthritic joints, a few more blisters to his calloused hands, and another artifact to his collection. This one had been named in legend almost as often as the Ulunsu'ti, but few would have believed it really existed. It had been hidden well, deep in a tunnel and concealed behind a false wall. The hardest part had been opening the mouth of the tunnel. He ached all over from the exertion.

He emerged from the cavity in the hillside and blinked in the bright light. When his eyes adjusted, he examined his find. The ancient buckskin that had protected it through the centuries fell apart in his hands as he pulled it away, revealing the prize he had searched for for so many years. It was smaller than he thought it would be. No bigger than the box his boots came in. He couldn't tell what it was made of but it was beautiful. Some had said the Nunne'hi made it themselves and gave it to Kanegwa'ti to protect the treasure it held. The *Cherokee Ark of the Covenant*, the name fit as well as any. He looked it over, caressing the graceful markings that spiraled the lid. Its intricate beauty alone was enough to give it great value, even if its real importance remained unknown, and he was the first to see it in centuries. He lingered over it awhile, admiring the handiwork of the long dead ancestors who created it, or if the stories were true, the artistry of the immortal Nunne'hi. Curiosity made him look for a latch, or some obvious way to open it. No one knew what was inside, and none of the stories hinted at what it could be. All he knew for sure was that whatever it contained would be needed to control the Ulunsu'ti once it was awake. He resisted the temptation to open the ark. There would be time later.

With the buckskin covering crumbling in his hands, he needed something else to protect the treasured artifact. He removed his jacket and wrapped it around the chest, tying the sleeves to secure it. When he added it to the duffle bag, his load was heavy in more ways than weight.

He trudged back toward his car, grateful for the hidden road that allowed him to drive as close as he had. His legs and back were ready to give out. The worth of what he carried in his knapsack and duffle bag was beyond the imagination of the white man, no matter how much he thought he knew.

Shifting the load to ease the ache in his shoulder, he remembered the feel of greedy eyes on his back. No, the white man couldn't be trusted. Nobody could, and his house trailer didn't present much of a challenge to anyone who wanted to break into it. Besides, he couldn't think of anywhere in the trailer that he could hide something as big as the duffle bag. He looked around as he walked. Searching for a place where he could leave it for awhile. Somewhere nobody ever came.

A cool breeze carried the scent of early blooming wild flame azaleas. Lena always loved those flowers. Their aroma reminded him of coming home to a house full of the smells of good food and wild flowers on the table. He went toward them, just for the comfort they offered.

Beyond the blossoms he spied a big hickory tree uprooted by one of last winter's storms. This would do. He scooped a hollow under the trunk and stuffed the duffle bag inside. When he covered it up with leaves, nothing betrayed the presence of what he had hidden. The knapsack, he kept with him. He couldn't even consider leaving the crystal behind. It was almost comforting to know it was resting there atop the war axe he had taken from the grave.

He was so weary he barely remembered the drive home. The years weighed heavy on him but he had to find the strength to go on. The Pinto coughed a few times on the steep mountain grade like it, too, was aging fast. Maybe after a good night's rest they'd both be ready for another day tomorrow, he thought.

The climb up Wolf Mountain loomed ahead like a threat.

By nightfall he was home, but it didn't seem like a good time to sleep in the trailer. He felt too vulnerable there.

He drove the Pinto behind a tangle of laurel bushes beyond the house and parked it where it would be well out of sight.

The night chill gnawed at his aching bones. He'd need a warm blanket from the trailer. Taking one from his bed he carried it into his old house. It felt good to be there, warm and safe, with memories of good times gone. Thomas, his only son, had been after him to tear it down, saying it wasn't safe. The boy was probably right but he couldn't give it up yet. It wasn't much, but it was a lot more solid and secure than the trailer.

Wrapped in his blanket, he slumped into the old recliner Lena had banished from the living room of her new trailer. The worn brown chair had served him well for many years, even after it was the last piece of furniture in his old house. He snuggled under the blanket like a child.

Lena's old Sally Cat curled up beside him and they both fell asleep.

ƒNOWBIRD

Monday morning came way too early for Johnny McLeymore. Wren woke him. From the smell of bacon and eggs wafting in from the kitchen he could tell Faron had breakfast nearly ready. He unwrapped the gauze from his blistered palms and flexed his fingers. If he could hold a toothbrush, he would probably be able to handle a steering wheel. "No problem," he muttered through a mouth full of toothpaste. His hands still functioned and the pain was well within the range of bearable. Even if it wasn't, he knew it wouldn't do any good to complain to Faron. All he would get from her would be that look that said, "What a freakin' wimp." All compassion, that girl.

He carried a paper bag full of sausage biscuits and a Thermos of good strong coffee to his pick-up truck. Wren was out of school for a teacher's work day and was coming with him. She said she wanted to be a forest ranger when she grew up and was learning from her daddy. Wren had a more substantial supply of food in her school lunchbox. He didn't tell Faron, but he had seen their daughter switch the carton of milk she put in the cooler, for a bottle of Coke.

"Don't let her be climbing up that tower, John," Faron ordered after she had kissed them both goodbye. "And don't hang around with Eli Smoker all day. You know his language isn't fit for a child to hear."

"Don't worry about her, honey. I've always brought her home in one piece before, haven't I? And she's never said a cuss word in her life. Eli knows to watch his mouth in front of a kid. You know that, Faron."

"He'd better watch his mouth."

Faron waved as the Dodge Ram eased up onto her new bridge.

John knew Wren was excited to be going to work with him. Not that she did anything to show it. Wren wasn't the kind of kid to bounce around and carry on like most eight year olds. Her eyes searched the trees along the lake. He didn't blame her. The road to the ranger station went through some of the prettiest country in the world.

She raised her hand for him to slow down; just like her mama did when she saw something she wanted to look at for awhile. He followed her eyes and saw the red-tailed hawk soar up from the shore with something small and furry squirming in his talons.

"He caught him some breakfast." Wren sat back on the seat ready to talk to him. She had seen what she was looking for. Both Wren and Faron liked to catch sight of some special bird at the beginning of what they considered an adventure. It didn't begin until the bird showed up. John thought it was probably because they were members of the Bird Clan.

He watched the hawk soar away and felt the same twinge of apprehension that had nagged him the past couple of days. Is that what Faron and her folks meant when they said they were getting a *feeling* about something? If it was, then he was getting a feeling the hawk foretold more of an adventure than he cared for. He had a sudden urge to turn around and take Wren home. The urge, and the feeling, passed quickly. He chalked them both up to the influence of the Copperheads and their superstitions.

He checked in at the ranger station and exchanged greetings with the few men who were still around. Most were already out on duty. The forestry service truck was loaded with supplies for the tower and ready to go. John scooped Wren up and set her in the seat beside him and drove away quickly. No need to push his luck.

Nobody had ever said anything before about him taking

Wren along once in a while. From the time she started walking
they had called her "Daddy's little shadow." Sometimes he just
didn't want to leave her at home and go to work, so he took her
with him on days he was doing something she wouldn't get in
the way of. Today was one of those days.

He wheeled the truck out onto the blacktop, drove alongside
the Snowbird a few miles, then turned up Tatham Gap Road.
The pavement ran out just before they passed the last house; a
wood frame cottage set back in the woods, hardly noticeable. A
mile or so on he had to pull over to let a dusty Honda Civic
pass from the opposite direction, the only other car they saw.

"Amanda Hooper coming over from Andrews to see her
Mama and Daddy up on Sweetgum Creek," John said. He and
Wren both called "Hello" when she braked to greet them.

"Saw your Mama at the store Friday," John yelled. "She
said she was feeling a lot better after her operation."

"Yeah," Amanda answered. "Doctor says she's gonna be
just fine. She's got a valve from a pig in her heart now. Can
you believe that?"

"Not hardly," John answered, "but you never know what
they'll be doing next. Tell her me and Wren said hey, and if she
and your daddy need us for anything, just let us know."

"Thanks, Johnny." She shifted the Honda into gear and
drove away.

"Wonder why she doesn't take the highway in that Honda?"
he said to Wren as they drove off. "This is a mighty rough road
for a car that small."

"'Cause this way is prettier," Wren said. "And you and
Uncle Yona say its closer. Besides, she didn't seem to be
having any trouble."

He turned off toward Joanna Bald and before long they were
up in the fire tower, sharing the lunches Faron packed with Eli
Smoker and the sleepy rat-sized Chihuahua he carried around
with him everywhere he went. Yippi was a gift from his wife,
to keep him company in the tower.

"Best biscuits I ever tasted," Eli said. "If my woman could

cook like Faron can, I probably would spend more time at home." He poked a bite of sausage into the dog's mouth. "Here ya go, Yippi."

Eli's wife, Hilda was a shapely blonde cheerleader for the Black Knights back when they were in high school. She was still cute but she would top the scales at around one-fifty now. She didn't have any trouble eating her own cooking. Eli, on the other hand, was as skinny as he had been when he and John and Yona were boys running wild in the woods. Hard to believe he was a descendant of the famed Wolf Clan Warriors. Not only was he scrawny, he was an outspoken pacifist and dedicated environmentalist.

"Shouldn't have married out, Eli," John said. "Your grandpa tried to tell you. He knew white women can't cook."

"Faron's mama and grandpa tried to tell her the same thing, didn't they? Not to marry out?" Eli punched John playfully on the arm as he sat down with his coffee. "Wonder what Walker Copperhead told her white men can't do."

"Whatever it was, she knows by now whether I can or can't." A wicked grin spread across John's face. "Anything she ever asked for so far, I've managed to handle. No problem."

Eli laughed. He put down his dog and stroked the skimpy mustache he kept trying to grow. He had a habit of doing that when he was about to get serious. Looked like the light-hearted part of this visit was over. "One thing you're real good at, John, that I want you to check on for me. Come over here. I want you to take a look at something."

"Sure, Eli," John followed his buddy to the row of windows that circled the highest level of the tower. Wren picked up Yippi and followed without a word. Eli was quiet as he pointed the telescope toward the northwest and focused it. "Look here, Johnny, and tell me what you see."

John put his eye to the glass. He could see for miles, nothing but a vast sea of green, the kind of green only seen in spring and early summer. "It's a beautiful sight, man," he said. "You just wanted to show me the scenery?"

"Keep looking right where I've got it pointed. Tell me what you see."

John let his eyes roam across the expanse the glass magnified. He saw dark green stretches where pine and hemlock grew, lighter greens shading into each other among the hardwoods, and then, something that just didn't look right. That must be what he was supposed to see. Eli would have been the first to notice. Years of searching the forests for any sign of fire had made every mile that fell within range of his telescope as familiar to him as the tower room he virtually lived in.

"You see it don't you?" Eli asked.

"Uh huh, but I'm not sure exactly what I see. It just doesn't look like the right color, but not like a die-back or blight or anything. You filed a report on this yet?"

"No. Wanted you to see it first. I figured you could check it out for me. There's nobody else at the station, except maybe Buck Locust, that I'd want to send up there." Eli turned to look toward the place he had shown John, as if he could see it without the telescope. "You know where that is, don't you, Johnny?"

"Well, I'd guess somewhere south of the Cheoah. If it's where I'm thinking, there's not a decent road or trail for miles around. A man would have to do some serious walking to get to it. That's not in the state park system, is it?"

"It's our land. Belongs to the Cherokees. You've heard of it." Eli's voice dropped, as if hearing echoes of the tales they had listened to at the feet of the old people all through their childhood. "Degal gun'yi."

"Sorry, buddy," John rolled the word around on his tongue. "Degal gun'yi." It was familiar but he couldn't remember why, and the words, when he tried to translate them, didn't add up. "I'm not that good with your language."

"Degal gun'yi," Eli repeated. " Means something like, where they are piled up. It's a burial ground. A big one, and old. The kind with mounds."

"That's why you want me to take a look at it, huh. So we don't risk any outsiders finding the graveyard." They both looked toward the Cheoah without the scope. "How long do you think it would take before a bunch of archaeologists started digging the whole place up if word got out?"

"Archaeologists, National Geographic, the Smithsonian. Everybody wanting some bones and pots and stories of the indigenous people." Eli looked like he wanted to spit.

"Tell you what, Eli," John said. "I've got some things to do first, but when I finish, I'll go get my truck at the station and run on up there. I'll talk to Buck about it first chance I get." Buck Locust was John's supervisor, and as good a friend as Eli and Yona. John and his buddies had all gone through a rebellious stage when they were younger. Buck had set them straight before they got too wild. Not that he was that much older than they were, just a few years, but as level-headed as a guy could be, and they'd looked up to him ever since he'd allowed them to tag along when they were hardly more than toddlers.

"Thanks, John." After a thoughtful moment, Eli added, "Take Walker Copperhead with you."

"Hey, man. We'll be walking for an hour at least. Old Walker might not be up to it."

"You tell him where you're going, and why. He'll be up to it." Eli took Yippi from Wren and scratched the dog's head with one finger.

John knew Eli was right about Walker. He just didn't know why it was so important for him to go along. He'd learned that sometimes when dealing with Faron's people, it was best just to do as he was told. That was usually the only way to get any answers. He sure didn't get them from asking questions.

He nodded toward the dog. "Hey, buddy, how long since that mutt's feet last touched the ground? I wonder sometimes if he can still walk at all."

Eli looked offended. Yippi just nodded off to sleep.

John drove in silence back down the mountain, wondering

what could cause the changes to the foliage in just that one spot. Whatever it was, it had to be in the early stages or Eli would have called him sooner. Eli knew John could tell him more about these mountains and their flora and fauna than just about anybody. John grew up in them. His dad, Duncan McLeymore, worked with the forestry service most of his life and took John along even more often than John took Wren. He had learned a lot that way. Then there was his degree—he had actually studied this stuff in college.

Wren interrupted his reverie. "Daddy, what's wrong at Degal gun'yi?"

John was surprised. The only thing he could remember about the mound was that the stories said even the powerful Nunne'hi stayed away from it. "What do you know about that place, honey?"

"I've been there," she answered. "With Uncle Yona and Mama Kate. They take me to a lot of places in the stories. They want me to learn the real history, so I won't get confused by the stuff we learn in school."

There were times when John felt left out when it came to the education of his daughter. She was learning things he never knew. Well, at least Wren could answer his questions. "So, sugar, what did you learn about Degal gun'yi?"

"It's real old, older than anybody knows for sure. Grandpa says it goes back to the days of the Ani'Kuta'Ni." She sounded like she knew what she was talking about.

John hesitated. He hated to show his ignorance to his own kid, but who else was going to fill him in. "And who are these Ani'Kuta'Ni, and what were they doing at Degal gun'yi?"

"Oh, they lived a long time ago, Daddy, but they're all gone now and that's good, cause they thought they were the boss of everything." She was warming to the role of the one with the answers and he didn't interrupt. "They did mean things to everybody cause the people were all afraid of them cause they had all the power and they got it from the Above Beings, cause the Ani'Kuta'Ni thought they were born to be the boss and had magic power."

He wasn't used to his quiet little girl talking this much or this fast, but was glad to get answers. He waited.

After a deep breath, Wren continued, "One day they got what they deserved for all the bad things they did. They made a warrior's wife go with them to their lodge on the top of a mound and did very bad things to her. The warrior got so mad he didn't care about their magic and power so he killed them all dead."

John remembered that story, now that she brought it back to his mind. "Is Degal gun'yi where they killed the Ani'Kuta'Ni?"

His luck had run out. Wren had told him all she knew of the story.

"I guess so." She flipped her black hair back in that way that said, don't ask me any more about it, then added, "What's wrong at Degal gun'yi?"

"I don't know for sure that anything is, honey. Eli just noticed that the leaves were a bit off color around that area. Sometimes that can mean an infestation of borers or other insects, or a blight or disease. Trees can get sick just like people."

"Like what happened to the chestnut trees?" she asked.

"Yeah, like that." John hoped it wasn't at all like what happened to the chestnut trees. He still occasionally ran across the remains of one of the massive trunks, rotting away, the last trace of a forest that had provided a major food supply to the Cherokee people for thousands of years. Now, not one single tree still lived.

"Grandpa Walker will know what to do," Wren said. She quickly added, "and you, too, Daddy."

John smiled at her to let her know he didn't mind. He was used to coming in second to Walker Copperhead. Faron's grandpa probably would know what to do. People were always coming to him for answers, calling him "the conjuror." He hoped at least one of them would know.

The work he had to do took longer than he thought, but it was just as well. He was still on the clock till four. He called Walker from the station to fill him in, and asked him to be the one to call Faron and explain why they were taking Wren along. They needed all the daylight that was left. The half hour it would take to drop the kid off at home was more than they could spare.

He parked the Forestry Service truck, got into the Ram with Wren and drove away without telling anybody where he was going. When they got to the Copperhead place on Little Snowbird Creek, Walker was waiting at the end of the neat, tree-shaded drive to the house where he lived with Kate, Yona and Charlie. He claimed he moved in to look after Kate and his two grandsons when his son, Kate's husband, was killed in a logging accident about ten years ago. It looked to John like it was the other way around. Kate had been bossing and pampering Walker nearly to death ever since. She'd practically taken over running the family logging company.

The Copperhead women were all like that. Faron had learned it from her mother. It was a good life as long as a man didn't harbor any illusions about being the one to make a lot of decisions around the house. The women had things well in hand and didn't like the men interfering. John didn't mind, but his father made it clear to him that he thought it was downright unnatural. Duncan McLeymore was the undisputed head of his house, and couldn't understand why John put up with Faron's ways.

John smiled as he thought of all the reasons he wouldn't change a thing.

Wren opened the door for Walker and scooted over next to John to make room. Walker got into the truck and propped his walking stick between them. The eagle carved on the head of the walking stick rested against her leg. She traced the curved beak with her finger. "He looks like he's alive, Grandpa," she said. "Like he could just fly away."

"Well, he hasn't done it yet, honey. Not in my father's

lifetime, nor his father's, or mine. "He'll probably stay around to keep Diamond company when he's an old man."

John looked at the walking stick and wondered again what it was made of. Walker called it locust wood, but he'd seen some very old locust and this was different. In fact, he'd never seen any kind of wood like that walking stick. As heavy as it was, it was amazing an old man like Walker could still lug it around. It looked like more of a hindrance than a help, but Walker would never go anywhere without it, always kept it within easy reach, even when he slept. John suspected it had something to do with his *conjure work.* He'd asked Walker about it. All he got was some nonsense about how the walking stick came in handy for spirit walking, whatever that meant. It was about as good an answer as he ever got from the old man.

"So, Johnny, how big of an area are we talking about checking out before dark?" Walker asked.

"We don't need to look at much to figure out what's going on," John said. "My guess is it's just some kind of borer. We deal with that kind of sh— stuff all the time. No problem"

"If it covers enough ground for Eli to spot it from the tower, must be a lot of borers," Walker said.

"Lord, Grandpa, Eli could spot just a single one of those pests from his tower," John said. "I don't think he even needs that telescope. The man knows every tree in Graham County by heart. If there's a lick of change in one, those beady eyes of his are gonna spot it."

Walker nodded. "And just as stubborn as his grandfather. If he thinks there's a problem he'll aggravate you to death till you do something about it."

"You and Daddy can fix whatever it is," Wren said. "No problem."

John smiled at her as he turned off the pavement onto the graveled road that edged along the river. The trees beside the road were already ancient when Walker Copperhead was a boy. Their branches met to form a canopy above the truck. Through the open windows they could hear the rushing of the Cheoah beyond the laurels. A few calls came from unseen birds high among the leaves. The only other sound was the crunch of gravel beneath the tires. They rode awhile in silence.

John had adjusted to the quiet nature of Faron's folks, only talking when they had something worth saying. When he spent time with his own family they were always asking him what was wrong, and why was he so quiet. It didn't take long for him to tire of the chatter.

After a few miles Walker pointed to a cut-off John would never have seen. It couldn't really be called a road, just a pair of ruts with not quite as much growing between them as in the rest of the forest. John shifted down to second and eased in.

The window had to be rolled up because the branches slapping him in the face made it hard to drive. He asked Walker how he knew about the road but the old man didn't answer, just leaned over and tightened Wren's seat belt. Even though they hardly topped twenty miles an hour, it was a bumpy ride and she was bouncing around.

John didn't ask any more questions. One of these days, his in-laws might stop thinking of him as an outsider and let him in on a few things. Like why they maintained these roads to nowhere in such out of the way places on their lands. He knew without asking that this one would end somewhere that he couldn't see any reason for going to. He just hoped it would get them close to the die-back before it ended.

"Anything you want to tell me, Grandpa?" John asked, expecting Walker to ignore him like he usually did. He was surprised when Walker answered in a serious, almost respectful manner. "There are many things I want to tell you, son. Troubles and worries you don't want to know about. Soon, John. When the time is right."

John wasn't sure he wanted to hear any more. Walker's manner made him nervous. When the road ended at the top of a steep incline, he wasn't at all surprised to find it went to nothing but the woods. He got out of the truck and looked back the way they had come. He spotted car tracks on the trail but didn't mention it. Walker probably knew about every vehicle that had come this way since the road was built.

Walking ahead while Walker and Wren were getting out of the truck, John scanned the trees for any sign of the discoloration he had seen from the tower. So far, he saw nothing out of the ordinary. A squirrel chittered on a limb above and was scolded by a jay whose nest he was getting too close to.

Wren and Walker caught up with him. When Wren ran ahead, John didn't try to stop her. She knew these woods better than he did. He could see her through the trees in the distance and knew where she was going. The first buds of a bank of wild flame azaleas were a bright orange flash in the underbrush. Faron loved the way their scent filled the kitchen when she put a vase of them on the table. Wren would want to surprise her with a bouquet. They'd be a rare treat this early in the year.

He kept Wren in sight while he and Walker discussed the healthy appearance of the foliage in the area. She was clambering over a fallen hickory tree, heading for the wild azaleas when she stopped, still hanging over the log with her feet on the other side and yelled, "Daddy, come here. Quick!"

John leapt over the log and lifted her down. "What's wrong, baby?"

She dropped to her knees, raking away leaves with her hands. "I felt something with my foot." She cleared the leaves from a mound of gray-green canvas. "See, I told you I felt something." She began to tug at the object but it was jammed in tight and she couldn't get it loose.

Walker stooped beside them and gently moved Wren out of the way. John could feel the old man's tension as he watched him pull an old duffle bag from under the tree trunk. The neck was closed tightly by a draw string and secured by a metal latch. Walker held up the latch for John to see, commenting that there was no sign of rust on the metal and the canvas showed no evidence of exposure to the elements. It hadn't been there long.

"What do you reckon this is, Grandpa?" John asked.

Walker looked grim. "Danged if I know, boy. One thing's for sure. Ain't nobody got any business around here hiding stuff." He set the duffle bag on end and unfastened the latch. Then he untied the cord and opened the bag, holding it while John reached in and pulled out something wrapped in an old windbreaker jacket. The sleeves were tied snug around it. Under that was a black nylon gym bag. A blue one about the same size came next. The three objects looked completely out of place there on the forest floor.

Walker unzipped one of the bags and spread it open. Yellowed linen fabric covered a collection of carefully wrapped bundles of various sizes. "Somebody went to a lot of trouble packing this," he said. "Must be something fragile." He lifted out a couple of the bundles and laid them on the leaves.

Walker gently removed the wrapping from the first bundle, exposing its contents. He looked at it for a moment like he couldn't believe what he saw then said a word he didn't usually say in front of Wren. John didn't think she heard it. Her eyes were wide with shock as she stared at what he had uncovered.

John opened another bundle and thought he understood why Wren and Walker were so upset. "Grave goods?" He asked.

"More than that," Walker answered, opening a package that held an ancient, long-stemmed clay pipe. He laid it aside and unwrapped a turtle shell rattle and a desiccated doeskin pouch, its contents showing through the frayed leather. He took out a small hollow bone with tiny holes drilled along its length. "Eagle bone," he said. "The one who owned this whistle walked over to the other world about the time the first white people started settling around here."

He put the whistle back in the pouch and laid it on the sheet and reached for the package wrapped in the windbreaker. When he untied the sleeves, the jacket fell away from a small rectangular chest.

John barely got a glimpse of it but he saw it was bound with mummified hide and marked with faded symbols. Walker quickly wrapped it up, muttering something in Cherokee that John couldn't understand. Wren's face paled but she didn't say a word.

John resisted the urge to ask questions. Walker motioned toward the other bag and John unzipped it. A dingy white towel wrapped something else. He laid it down beside the rest and pulled away the corners. "God damn," he said.

Wren and Walker both looked like they couldn't move. They just sat on the forest floor, frozen in a moment of pain and anger. Then Walker folded for the towel back over the ancient brown skull and the pile of bones beneath it. "Johnny, zip him up and let's go. We'll have to check on these trees later. Right now, we need to take Kanegwa'ti back over to Swain County where he belongs."

John repeated the name. "Kanegwa'ti." He knew what it meant, sort of. The Water Moccasin. At least that's what he thought. Was that who this bundle of bones used to be? A man, who for some reason, was named for a snake. And how did Walker know?

Wren held the blue gym bag while John zipped it closed. Walker was working on gathering up the grave goods and wrapping them. John and Wren helped finish up and pack the goods back in the black bag.

Walker didn't seem to want them to help him wrap up the chest. He'd covered it with the jacket and kept it close to him and out of sight all the while. John tried to get another look at it but Walker was too cautious. His furtive behavior made John even more curious. Was it part of the Water Moccasin's burial goods? Did Walker want to bury it with the rest in his grave?

Shadows deepened among the trees. Sunset came quickly in the mountains. They had precious little light left to see their way back to the car. John was tired, and figured the day had already been too eventful for Wren. It was time for them to head home.

He pointed out the lateness of the hour to Walker. "Grandpa, I'd say we ought to wait till morning to take this stuff back to the burial ground. Faron's gonna be mad as hell if we keep Wren out much longer."

When Walker stubbornly insisted that they needed to take care of this problem right away, John tried using logic. It didn't usually work with any of the Copperheads, including his wife, but it was worth a try. "We need to see the place in broad daylight, so we can check for any clues that would lead us to who ever is digging up old Cherokee graves. At best, it'll be pitch dark before we even make it to Swain County. Besides, if we put him back in his grave, what's to stop the same guys who dug him up before, from digging him up again. Anyway, I have no idea how to find the burial ground you're looking for after we get there."

"Ataga'hi. That's where we need to go. On Thunderhead Mountain right near the county line. Don't have to be in the same grave, but his bones have to stay in Ataga'hi." Walker drew a deep breath as if to calm himself. "Don't say a word about this to anybody. Either of you. We gotta keep this in the family."

The thing that finally convinced Walker to wait until morning was not logic so much as the dread of Faron's wrath. If they kept her daughter out any later on a school night they would both catch hell. That was John's closing argument, and it worked.

John hadn't expected Wren to give him any trouble but sometimes his kid could be as stubborn as the rest of the Copperheads. Since she was the one who found Kanagwa'ti's bones and goods, she felt responsible for seeing them safely back where they belonged. She started making plans for the trip to Swain County with him.

"You've got school tomorrow, honey," John told her. "Grandpa Walker and I will see that everything gets taken care of, and remember, we don't talk about this to anybody."

Wren came as close to pouting as she ever did. "It's not fair, Daddy. I should go to Ataga'hi with you. After all, I'm the one who found the great conjuror's bones and treasures."

"We'll have to leave that up to your mama, honey." John shook his head to clear the cloud of confusion that was becoming more and more familiar as his daughter got older. The great conjuror, huh. What else did Wren know that he had no clue about?

He dropped Walker off at his house and drove home, still wondering who was the conjuror named Water Moccasin who had died a few hundred years ago. Who would know the location of two of the sacred burial grounds the Cherokee had managed to keep hidden all this time, and why would they dig up a grave in one and bring its contents to another at least ninety miles away? And why did his eight-year-old little girl know so damn much he didn't know? He put that last question to Wren as they crossed her mama's new bridge and parked in front of the house.

"Cause I listen, Daddy," was her answer.

Damn! "So, since you know so much, who was this great conjuror you and your great grandpa seem to know all about?"

"Some people think he was an Ada'wehi," she said.

Well, that helped a lot.

Faron met them at the door. She looked at John expecting an explanation for why he left home before seven o'clock in the morning with their daughter and was just now getting her home when it was already past her bedtime. He was still trying to frame an acceptable description of the day's events when Wren calmly spoke up.

"Mama, we've got a lot to tell you. You wanna listen while Daddy and I eat supper?"

"You two go wash up while I put it on the table," Faron gave them both a quick hug. That meant she was going to reserve judgment until she heard the full story.

Supper was a venison roast Yona had brought over. It took some getting used to, but John had learned to like the sweet tender meat better than beef. But it had to be cooked right, so it didn't taste gamey. Faron knew how to cook it. She let them eat in peace for awhile, waiting for them to give her some answers.

Wren was impatient. "Mama, did Grandpa Walker tell you about why we had to go up to Degal gun'yi?"

Faron nodded. "That's where you've been all evening?"

"Uh huh, and we found a terrible thing there," Wren said.

"Is it like what happened to the chestnut trees?" Faron's expression was grim.

Wren shook her head as John answered, "We didn't get a chance to look at the trees, honey. Still don't know what's going on there. Wren's talking about something she found before we even got to where the trouble is." He and Wren filled Faron in on what Wren had found.

"Is it in the truck now, John?" Faron asked. "I almost wish you had gone on over to Swain County and put everything back in the grave where it belongs. I don't like this."

"Walker didn't trust me with it I guess," John said. "Took it with him. Said he wanted to show the stuff they dug up with the bones to Mama Kate."

Faron nodded. "Yes, Mama would know for sure."

Wren nodded. "Yep. She'd get a feeling if it is."

"Know what for sure?" John asked.

"It's time you were in bed, young lady," Faron said, clearing Wren's empty plate away. "Go tuck her in John, while I clean up in here."

John and Wren both complied. "What will Mama Kate know for sure, honey?" he asked as he pulled the blanket around her chin.

"Whether it really is the great conjuror. But I already know."

"And is it?"

"Oh, yeah. It is for sure, Daddy."

"How do you know?"

"Because of the ark. Grandpa Walker thought he hid it real

quick, but I saw enough of it. It was the ark all right. He knew it, too, cause of what he said when he saw it."

"What was it that he said?" John asked.

"Ulunsu'ti." She cuddled down under the covers, already half asleep. "Goodnight, Daddy."

John went into Diamond's room to say goodnight to his son. He was still awake. "Sorry, buddy, about not getting home before you went to bed." Diamond just reached up to be held. John picked him up and carried him back to the kitchen and sat down at the table. Faron handed John a cup of coffee. He was funny about coffee. Didn't care for it in the morning, preferring to start his day with a cold Coke straight from the bottle. At night he could drink all the coffee he wanted and still sleep like a baby. This was the best. Strong, scalding hot Luzianne. The chicory in it was what made it so good.

Diamond snuggled against John's chest, ready to fall asleep now that he was safe in his daddy's arms.

"Darlin', I kinda need some straight answers here," John said.

Faron put the last plate in the dishwasher and sat down beside him with her own cup of Luzianne. "I thought you might, Johnny. Where do you want to start?"

"Well, let's start with you telling me who the hell is the great conjuror named Water Moccasin, and how Walker could tell those were his bones from looking at the stuff from that grave, and why our daughter knew it from seeing that box thing and hearing her Grandpa say one word when he saw it."

"And what one word did he say?"

John made a stab at pronouncing the word. It was close enough for Faron to understand. "And you didn't guess what that meant?" she said. "Think, John. You spent a lot of time hanging around with me and Yona and Eli and Dave when we were kids. You heard the tales our folks told us same as we did, and you must have realized by now that our grandpas knew things most folks don't."

John cupped his free hand around the hot mug of coffee and

leaned back, looking away from his wife. "I don't think I listened the same way y'all did. I thought they were just telling stories, the same way my folks used to tell me Jack tales. Now, according to Wren, you guys consider them history, and old Walker is acting plumb weird."

"He's got his reasons, and no, not all of them are historical, honey." she rubbed his thigh. It felt good. "There's history in the stories, some of them at least. Some are just tales, like your Jack tales. Some are legends built up around real people and events. A lot of the stories go way beyond history. Those are as sacred to us as your grandma's Bible is to her. You want me to tell you again about the great conjuror?"

Finally, some answers. "I'd appreciate the hell out of that, honey. But first, what category does this story fall into? Was the great conjuror a real person?"

"He was real. That part we know for sure. The rest—well, I believe it's true." She hesitated long enough for John to begin to wonder if she had changed her mind about filling him in. "He lived a long time ago. Back about the time we started seeing a lot of your people settling around here. He was a great man, some people say more than a man."

"Ada'wehi?" John asked.

"Uh huh," she nodded. "You remembered some of what you heard from the old folks."

"With a little help from our daughter," he said. "They were magicians, weren't they? Or supernaturals of some sort?"

"Something like that. We learned the word conjuror from your people. It doesn't do justice to what Kanegwa'ti was, but it's the title he has been given. The great conjuror, they called him, because he was the most powerful man of his day. His power came from the Ulunsu' ti."

"That thing that came from the snake's head?"

"The great crystal from the head of Uktena," she answered. "And yes, he was a snake. A snake so big he could coil around Bald Mountain with his head resting on the top. He was a monster that devoured anything that lived for miles around.

You remember the story about how the Cherokee captured a Shawnee and sent him out to slay Uktena. Many others had tried, but no one was ever expected to succeed.

The Shawnee was brave and sly, and using trickery, he killed the monster. It was Uktena's blood and poison that caused the mountain to be bald. Nothing will ever grow there again."

John hesitated before he asked his next question. "Honey, aren't we getting too old to believe in monsters and magic crystals?"

Faron sipped from her cup and put it on the table. Leaning away from John she looked him in the eye. "Somebody still believes. Somebody believes enough to gather up everything they need to bring the Ulunsu'ti back to life. Then they brought it all to the only place it can be done. I doubt they did it for any childish reason."

"Darlin." John was still trying to adjust to his practical, down to earth wife's belief in the old legends. "If it's been buried more than three hundred years, I don't think it's gonna be real easy to bring it to life. I'm afraid the Ulunsu'ti is just as dead as old Water Moccasin, and if those are his bones in that Addidas gym bag at your grandpa's house, he's pretty dang dead."

She hardly blinked. It was disconcerting the way she could hold his gaze that way. "I hope you're right on both counts," she said. "Kanegwa'ti took a lot of precautions to make sure the Ulunsu'ti slept till we needed it the most, and until there was someone who had the power to control it. We've had a lot of times when we sure could have used it, but there was no one who dared wake it. Looks like there's somebody around here who thinks he can handle it. The Suye'ta, or Chosen One."

"Chosen for what, and who does the choosing?" John asked.

"Chosen to be the master of the Ulunsu'ti. As for who does the choosing, I don't know. Could be the guardians. Could be the Ulunsu'ti himself. Anyway, Kanegwa'ti inherited the crystal from the conjuror who had it before him. He used it wisely and the people respected its power. Those who held it before him never had to fear that someone would try to take it. Native people knew what it could do, but they also knew the danger it brought to a man who didn't have what it took to be its master. In the wrong hands, well, there could be hell to pay."

"Anything with that much power must be real valuable," John said. "How come it ended up buried with its owner? Sounds like one of those things that used to get passed down to the next conjuror in line for it."

"It always did before, but like I said, our people knew enough about it not to mess with it. When the white people heard about Ulunsu'ti, they wanted it. They thought it was kept in the box they called the *Cherokee Ark of the Covenant.* They were wrong. The ark only held the ceremonial objects used to wake it, and control it. Kanegwa'ti had to post guards around his lodge to keep them from taking it, but he knew they would keep trying. They didn't understand the danger of owning a talisman with a mind of its own."

"Wait a minute, honey. It's a piece of crystal, or something, from a dead snake's head." John needed to remind Faron, and himself, that they were talking about an old myth. "My ancestors were sensible types like me and didn't think inanimate objects had minds."

"Well, whether they believed it or not, it did."

She was acting as stern as his third grade teacher. It almost made him feel like he was the one who was being unreasonable. He was tempted to tease her about it, but since that might mean she wouldn't tell him anything else, he kept quiet and let her go on.

"The Ulunsu'ti had a mind of its own, and a hunger. It had to be fed."

"Whoa, sugar. This is getting too weird. The thing was a piece of rock. Rocks don't eat." When she said nothing more he said, "Okay. What did the rock have to be fed?"

"Blood." She dropped the word in his lap and got up to rinse out their empty coffee cups.

"Damn, Faron. Who writes this shit for you guys? Stephen freakin' King?" This was too much. Vampire crystals from a snake's head. And she was the level-headed one in the family.

"You gonna put the baby to bed, honey?" she asked as she wiped the counter top. "He's sound asleep now." John didn't answer.

Finally, when it was obvious she wasn't going to volunteer anything further, he had to ask, though he was afraid he would rather not hear the answer. "Honey, what kind of blood did the rock like?"

She ruffled his curls and kissed his earlobe. "That of skeptical husbands," she grinned. "Preferably cute red-headed ones. Now where could we find us one of those?"

He wasn't amused. "Really, Faron. Did the conjuror give that crystal thing human blood?"

"Of course not, John." Faron was indignant. "He just killed a little bunny rabbit and bled it on the crystal. Once in a while, if Ulunsu'ti had been working hard, he needed something stronger. Then he got the blood of a whole deer."

"And if he didn't get it, what happened? Did he starve to death, and just lie there like, say, a rock?"

Faron's playful mood disappeared. "No Johnny, he didn't. He went out and found him some dinner. When he had to fend for himself, he usually didn't settle for rabbits and deer. People are much easier to catch."

John got a chill down his spine. "Now, Faron. How's a crystal gonna go anywhere, let alone go catch somebody and drink his blood?"

"It's not just a crystal," Faron said. "What they don't tell you in the story is that you can't ever kill the Uktena. He just goes into the Ulunsu'ti to live, but he doesn't always stay there. If he needs to, he can take up residence in somebody's head. Somebody who has touched the crystal. He just needs a taste of their blood to give him strength."

"And they have to do his killing for him?"

Faron nodded. "And once he gets a taste of human blood, he learns to like it better than any other kind. That's why they had to get the Shawnee to kill Uktena in the first place. He was eating up everybody for miles around, not just their bodies, but everything that made them who they were. Their very being— their souls."

"Sugar," John said. "I think I'll go put Diamond to bed now. He's sound asleep."

"Yeah, I know." She stroked the baby's black hair and kissed his forehead then slipped her arm around John's waist. "I'll come with you, Johnny. It's high time you and I got into bed, too."

John was fine with that. He'd had about all the weirdness he could stand for one night. "No problem," he said.

Qualla Boundary

The sound of a car engine coming up the drive to the trailer roused the elder before he got to sleep good. He sat up in the recliner and listened. Lena's Sally Cat lifted her head and listened with him. The knapsack was right there under the chair where he left it, safe.

"I knew he couldn't be trusted," he muttered, then hugged the cat against his side to keep her quiet. Sally Cat understood and froze without a sound.

Loud, insistent knocks rang against the trailer door. The voice that yelled his name was not the one he expected. It was harder then to be quiet because he really would have liked to talk to the man who was calling. Of all the people he knew, this was the one who could probably have been the most help.

He would know what to do, but he had reason to be far angrier than anybody else. Did he know the mound at Degal'gun'yi had been violated? He forced himself to stay still, even when he heard the crunch of footsteps on the gravel behind the trailer where he usually parked his car.

For a moment there was silence. He could almost see the man outside looking around at the empty parking space and the dark windows of the trailer. He didn't breathe until the footsteps were muffled by the grass on the patch of lawn he kept cleared in front of the trailer. Loneliness closed around him as he heard the car head back toward the highway. Sally Cat curled up on his lap and purred him to sleep.

He didn't wake again until almost dawn when the sound of someone pounding on the trailer door roused him. This time, the voice that called his name was the one he expected. He stretched his stiff back, hearing his joints crack and pop. A long nap in the chair was one thing but a whole night's sleep left him twisted and aching all over. He grabbed the knapsack and hefted its weight. A mighty heavy load to carry where he had to go, and the man he was going with wanted it bad. Best stow it away before the digger saw it.

The old well on the back porch still supplied his water, though now an electric pump brought it into the trailer through shiny copper plumbing. He wiggled a loose stone in the well's wall, inching it free to reveal a roomy niche secreted behind it.

Lena had come up with the idea of making a safe there when they remodeled the porch twenty-five years ago. Only the two of them knew about it. It was plenty big enough to hold the few valuables they had. He wished he had let Thomas in on his secret. It was likely he wouldn't get the chance to do it now.

He removed the Ulunsu'ti from the knapsack and slipped it into the niche. It lay atop the deed to his land, the title to the Pinto, a handful of medals and a couple of US Savings Bonds that comprised his life savings. He fitted the stone back in place, slung the knapsack over his shoulder and went to meet his visitors. The stone war axe was a heavy but reassuring weight against his back.

The pounding on the trailer's front door became more insistent about the time he entered the back door. "Coming," he called.

As soon as the door opened, the white man barged in, complaining that he hadn't had his coffee yet. Their partner went straight to the kitchen and started the pot perking.

The elder objected, saying they needed to get on the road.

"Hey, man. You look like you could use a cup, yourself," the white man said as he grabbed cups out of the cabinet like he owned the place.

The coffee smelled good, and with the electric coffee pot Thomas had brought him, it wouldn't take long.

He went to his bedroom and got a faded flannel shirt from

the closet while the coffee perked. The shirt wasn't as warm as his jacket had been but it would help keep out the chill. A cup of black coffee was waiting when he got back to the kitchen. It was strong and hot and he gulped it too fast. It was just what he needed.

Now that he felt more alert, he decided he didn't want to get into the Montero with the other two. He gave them directions as he downed the last few drops from his cup. "Go up Big Cove Road till you come to Lightning Creek Road. Drive as far as you can till the road ends. Turn onto that dirt road that crosses the creek then go about a mile and park. I'll meet you there."

He didn't wait around to argue with them, just ducked out the back door and through the laurel thicket to his car. They were getting into the Montero when he pulled around it and drove down his drive way toward the road. Before they could catch up, he drove behind the Holiday Inn on the highway then watched from the hill above the motel until he saw them go by. He needed nourishment before he could face the hike up Wolf Mountain. McDonald's was just opening for the day.

From the drive-through, he ordered a couple of Egg McMuffins and a second cup of coffee. After a seven day fast, he needed to get his strength back.

The sky was still dark when he turned onto Big Cove. The Pinto was the only car on the road. As a tinge of color announced the first hint of dawn, he angled off to Lightning Creek. A well tended gravel road curved along beside the creek. Folks here liked their privacy. The few houses on the far side of the water were just a glimpse of lighted windows through the trees. In full daylight, most people would never notice them.

He rattled along for a few miles until the road ended abruptly against a thick stand of hemlock.

He pulled the Pinto under the trees and left it. No one would ever guess it was there, so completely did the thick low-hanging branches conceal it.

To his left, a dirt road crossed an aging wooden bridge over

Lightning Creek and curved around out of sight. Less than a mile ahead, the Montero sat waiting. The two inside were completely unaware of him until he opened the back door. "Start driving," he said, climbing into the back seat. "I'll tell you where to go."

Winter had been hard on the road. He was glad they were in the Montero and not his Pinto. Rivulets of spring rain and melting snow had left their mark. He watched the roadside till he saw the remains of an old logging trail disappearing among the trees as it wound its way up the mountainside.

"Turn here," he said. The white man did as he was told. The elder hoped he would be as compliant in more important matters. "Go as far as you can, then park this thing. We'll have to walk the rest of the way."

He didn't know whether to be annoyed or pleased when the driver turned to his companion and asked, "You okay with that?" After all, that was just the attitude he had hoped the white man would have toward their partner. The closer they were to each other, the easier this would be.

A stand of hemlocks once again served as a good place to park when the logging trail petered out. Chances were, nobody would be around to see the Montero. There were only two houses on this road and practically no traffic, but just in case, it was best to leave it out of sight.

He took the lead as they began the climb up Wolf Mountain. There was no path to follow but he had been this way before, trailing furtively behind a man who had been closer to him than a brother. That was back when he thought Driver Wayanettah guarded the ark somewhere on this mountain. Driver was gone now, walked over to the other world like most of his old friends. Even if he was still around, it wouldn't matter. Driver wouldn't want anything to do with a man who could betray the Snake Dancers and everyone else who trusted him.

He slung the knapsack around under his arm and clutched it close to his body, listening to the footsteps behind him. He could only hope that if the white man made a move to take it from him, the other would warn him. He wasn't so sure anymore. There was a time when he had no doubts about the loyalty of the third accomplice, but loyalties have a way of shifting in these matters. Now the two walking behind him were more united than he anticipated. He was the one on the outside now, not the white man.

A couple of times he had to back-track to relocate a landmark he had missed. It had been years since he followed Driver up this way, paying close attention to the terrain and fixing all the details in his mind for later. After he learned Del Locust and his grandson were the guardians of the ark, he lost interest in the cave. Driver's story about how his ancestors hid out there to avoid the removal and the Trail of Tears had the ring of truth. They'd talked about how places like the cave made it possible for a few of the Cherokees to avoid the long march west, or one of the shallow graves along the way, and stay in the ancestral homeland. Yes, Driver had been very convincing.

His accomplices walked behind him without questioning anything he did, even when he got confused and had to double back to pick up the trail. In fact, they didn't talk to him at all; just spoke quietly to each other. That was a change. The white man usually grilled him every minute they were together, wanting to know all the lore and mythology of what he called the "Native Way." What had changed him? He didn't seem interested in learning from him anymore. This worried him.

After a while the trees gave way to a steep expanse of granite interspersed with sparse scrub laurel and boulders. The entrance to the cave he'd followed Driver into lay behind one of the great boulders, but he couldn't seem to remember which one.

His companions stayed close on his heels while he searched, so that when he did find the entrance and step inside, they were right behind him. When they stopped to discuss who would accompany him deeper into the cave, he offered no comment, just waited to see what they would do. They decided the white man would go and the other would wait outside, watching the trail to make sure they were not disturbed.

The white man took the same cheap plastic flashlight they had used on Ataga'hi out of his back pack and pointed it into the cave. It cast a weak light against the darkness. The elder was glad he had brought a better one. He clicked it on and strode into the cave, signaling the white man to follow.

They walked in silence. The flashlights illuminated only a few feet of the cave ahead before the dark stone devoured the light. He heard the white man humming something that sounded like a hymn and remembered Driver had whistled when he followed him in here. That's the only time he'd ever heard his old friend whistle. This dark hole in the mountain probably spooked him, too.

When they were deep inside the cave, the elder decided it was time to explain where they were going. "Up ahead, we'll come to a waterfall. I watched Driver duck into a passage just this side of it and followed him as far as I could without getting caught. I hid in a crevice and he went on ahead, but I never lost sight of his light, and he never got out of hearing. From what I heard him say, I know this is a sacred place to him. We'll find the hands in there."

The big white man didn't answer, just pushed by him and lit out in the direction of the distant roar of a waterfall. The elder fell in behind. The sound of water got louder, just the way he remembered. He and the white man used their lights to search the cavern walls for the jagged cleft he remembered. When he saw one that looked right, he nodded to the white man and ducked inside. The white man had to stoop over to manage the cramped passage.

Many years had passed since he'd followed Driver to the cave, but this fit what he remembered. The ceiling was now so low the elder couldn't walk upright either. The awkward stooped gait sent spasms through his legs. When the cavern expanded into a spacious chamber, he stretched his knotted muscles and went to work. Fissures and crevices marked the granite walls. He remembered how Driver had reached into a crevice, said something about his duty, and come out empty handed. He had lurked in the shadows, watching.

The white man was having trouble breathing. He pulled a white handkerchief from his hip pocket and tied it across his nose and mouth. The close, dry air was tinged with a sharp ammonia odor that stung their eyes and burned their throats. When a swarm of tiny black bats, disturbed by the intruders, poured out of a crevice, it explained the smell.

"Could they be in there?" the white man asked, indicating the hole the bats came from and looking like he would rather go into hell than search the bat roost.

The elder had to acknowledge the possibility. The white man ducked into the filthy crevice and began the search. When he came out, he glared at the elder and accused him of lying. Saying he had probably just used him for the hard work and planned to let some other damn Indian in on the pay off.

The elder didn't respond. For the first time, he was scared of the man he had taken in to his confidence. He went to the other side of the cavern and probed inside a cleft in the stone. The white man went back to work, muttering about damn savages and their double-crossing old men who didn't deserve what he was doing for them.

The elder listened, trying to control his rage. He thought of sneaking out of the cave but the white man wasn't letting him out of his sight.

After a couple of hours, probing every crevice and cranny they could find, even digging through layers of bat guano, they had no more than what they came in with.

The white man had jammed his flashlight into a crack in the stone. Its weak beam shined on the spot where he had just completed a fruitless search of what turned out to be a two foot long fissure in the stone, jammed with bat dung and the crawling vermin that lived in it. His litany of obscenities grew louder and more vehement the longer he worked. His flashlight drained the last ray of light from its batteries, dimmed, and then went dark. He banged it against the cave as if that might bring it back to life. Instead, it shattered the lens and bulb and sent sharp fragments flying. Enough of them connected with his face and forearms to draw blood and further enrage him.

He flung the useless plastic shell down the cavern, shouting incoherent curses at it as it bounced and slid along the stone, then turned his rage on the man who had brought him here. "God damn piece of shit you are. Why didn't I go to Walker Copperhead to start with? He wants an outsider to make into the Suye'ta. I'd be a damn sight better than that lazy-assed son-in-law of his."

The elder's remorse came on so strong it made him tremble. How could he have been fool enough to talk about his people to this mad man. He'd told him how Walker thought John might be the Suye'ta. And all about the Ulunsu'ti and what it could do. To his shame, he had trusted this muscle-bound wannabe and refused to listen to Walker and the Snake Dancers. The white man had come to him with lies and flattery, telling him he had an Indian soul and wanted to do anything he could for the tribe, and he'd fallen for it.

The white man kept looking, determined to find the hands. With a visible effort, he bit off the stream of obscenities and tried to calm down. In a placating tone he pleaded with the elder to forgive him for losing his temper. It was just frustration, and the bad air, he said. He didn't mean anything by his ugly remarks. He'd be the best Suye'ta the tribe could ever want, and they'd make a fine team.

The white man's condescension was harder to take than his insults. This fool must never get his hands on the Ulunsu'ti. Unable to hold back his rage any longer, the elder turned his flashlight full in the white man's face and started filling him in on some facts that would shut him up once and for all. For a start, he could forget any plans of becoming the Suye'ta. The Ulunsu'ti and all that went with it were out of his reach for good. He'd never get his hands on them or the power he wanted. That done, he told the bastard what he thought of him and his ridiculous delusion that he was an Indian in spirit, and spiritual heir to shamanic medicine. When he was through, he spit on the ground at the white man's feet in a gesture that left no room for any illusion of dignity.

At first the white man looked too stunned to respond and too angry to resort to trickery. His basic nature asserted itself and he did what he usually did when he didn't have time to control with cunning. He struck out with a fist the size of a catcher's mitt and caught the elder on the side of the face with a blow that felt like it shattered his skull.

Twenty years ago he might have been able to fight back, or at least he would have done a better job of ducking, but not this time. Too old and slow to do anything but bounce off the cave wall and fall under the crushing blow, he lay on the cold stone where he landed. When the white man picked up the flashlight he had dropped when he fell, and went storming off down the corridor, the elder could only watch helplessly as the glow of the only light in the cave receded into the distance. He struggled to stay conscious and staggered to his feet, leaning against the wall for support.

All the fight was knocked out of him. The rage had died but sickness and shame knotted in his belly. He had failed. Worse than that, he'd desecrated sacred sites, stolen from his people, and turned a mad dog loose with knowledge of things so powerful that even some of the Snake Dancers didn't know it. All he wanted to do was to curl up in a ball and pass out from the pain, but he couldn't do that, not if he ever wanted to see daylight again. He could still see the pale glow from his own flashlight bobbing against the darkness ahead.

He managed to get his feet in motion and stumbled after the light, desperate to keep it in sight. If he could make it out of the cave, there was a chance he could find a way to fix the mess he had created. The thought of what would happen if he didn't, was all that gave him the will to keep moving. He had to keep the light in view, but stay far enough behind that the white man couldn't hear him.

Blood oozed from his mouth and he wiped it on his sleeve. The huge fist had done a lot of damage. On the other hand, it might have knocked some sense into him. He knew what he had to do now, and strangely it lightened his spirits. He actually felt a shred of hope. Nobody but the white man and the one who waited outside, knew what he had done. If he put everything back in its place, and if the white man was out of the way, everything could go back to normal. He had good reason to believe he could trust the one outside, but the white man was too dangerous to be allowed to live.

The white man didn't see the elder come out of the cave a few seconds behind him. He eased over to squat behind a boulder and listen.

"Where is he? Is he alright?" The voice of the one who had waited sounded concerned.

"Doesn't matter," the white man said. "The old bastard doesn't know any more than I do now. I don't need him."

"You know where the conjuror's medicine is? And the Ulunsu'ti?"

The white man laughed. "Not yet, but after he's been in there in the dark a couple of days without food or light, he'll be glad to tell me anything I need to know."

The elder flattened himself against the rock and listened to the white man planning how he would stay and guard the entrance while the other went for supplies. Well, the lying son of a bitch was going to have a long wait, sitting there watching an empty cave.

He listened while the other pleaded with the white man, begging him to go back into the cave and help, threatening to go in alone and search in the dark. The white man had made up his mind. "You know the way back to the truck," he said. "We need lights and food. You have to go for it."

He listened, hoping the white man got his way. He couldn't leave an innocent person at his mercy. Unfortunately, their partner felt the same way. The loyalty he had never really doubted went deeper than he knew.

The white man, enraged that he wasn't obeyed, raised his big fist again, ready to strike.

"Do as I tell you," he said. "I can't leave, so you have to go down for the things we need." He went closer, his voice now a vicious snarl. "Go now or you'll both rot in that cave. Nobody knows you're here but me."

It was all he could do to keep still then. Never before had he wanted to kill another human being. He had done it, of course, but that was war. Now, he would gladly have squeezed the life out of the white man with his bare hands. Only the sure knowledge that he wouldn't stand a chance, and that a challenge meant the white man would likely kill them both, gave him the self control to keep quiet.

He had to hold back until the odds were more favorable. He wasn't the only one he had to protect. He had put another life in danger and it was his responsibility to make up for it. First, he had to get off Wolf Mountain without being seen.

While the white man waited for him to weaken inside the cave, he'd be at home, getting ready to come back and take care of things once and for all. Then, the bastard would wish he'd never met an Indian.

He eased over to a boulder, then toward a clump of scrub brush. Neither of them saw him. They were too distracted by their argument. He was only a few feet away from the cover of a line of brush that would conceal him until he was well on his way. He thought he had it made, until his approach spooked a rabbit already hiding there. The white man turned at the sound and grabbed a jagged rock the size of a basketball from the ground and rushed forward.

The ape-sized fist alone was enough to crush a man's skull. The rock would finish him for sure. All he could do was run. The weight of the knapsack pounded against his side, reminding him that he was not completely unarmed. The weapon he carried had served his ancestor well. Since it was all he had, he could only hope it would at least buy him some time. On his best day, he'd never be able to outrun the white man, and his old legs were about worn out.

He fumbled in the knapsack as he ran. He could hear the white man's boots pounding closer. Saw him strike out at the other who tried to stop him. It was good to know he wasn't alone, but that meant both of them were at the white man's mercy. Even if he could somehow escape, he wouldn't leave an ally behind. Time to stand and fight, like the warrior he was, for both of them. He wouldn't run anymore. His fingers closed around the handle of the axe. It fit his hand like he had used it all his life. It felt good. He turned to face his enemy.

With a cry that would have made his war chief ancestor proud, he raised the axe and took aim. Every ounce of strength he had in his body went into the throw. Time stopped as the war axe arced through the air. He saw the white man duck as the axe whistled past his head.

He had missed.

It felt like he stood there for an eternity, watching. The axe hit the cliff face behind the white man and seemed to gain momentum as it glanced off the stone. What happened next drew a curtain of darkness across his soul. He sensed his own spirit leave him as surely as the spirit left the one the axe struck. He saw blood spatter against the cliff, then watched the one who had trusted him through it all, crumple and fall to the gray stone, motionless.

When the white man knelt beside the lifeless form to feel for some sign of life, he eased forward, hoping against hope that it wasn't as bad as it looked. When he saw the crushing blow the axe had struck, and the bone shards protruding through the wound. He knew it couldn't possibly be any worse. Blood already pooled in the crevices of the rock.

When the white man rose and looked at him, he saw the last shred of sanity leave his eyes. The madness that was left, matched that which threatened to invade his own mind. How had it come to this?

He stood as still as the boulders around him, too numb to move until the white man rushed him. Some innate survival instinct propelled him toward the only escape route available. As fast as his legs would carry him, he sprinted toward the mouth of the cave. He ran with no thought of where he was going or why. Darkness swallowed up the last trace of light and he kept going. The image of the body lying on the rocks filled his mind until he was unaware of the pounding of boots behind him or that his heart hammered from exertion.

When he couldn't lift his feet for another step, he collapsed on the cold stone, gasping for air. His chest heaved and every breath burned like acid in his lungs.

The thud of boots and shouted obscenities came closer, then dwindled off into echoes as the white man passed him in the darkness and continued into the deeper recesses of the cave.

When his panting subsided, he lay still and listened. The soft echo of the waterfall came from somewhere in the distance. He didn't hear the boots behind him. He had escaped the white man but it didn't matter anymore. Nothing mattered now.

Curled into a ball of pain beyond anything a man could endure, he lay still and retreated into a place even darker than the cave. His spirit sank deeper into hopelessness to wander with other lost souls while his body lay unmoving on the cold granite of the cave floor. The elder waited like a hibernating animal. For what, he didn't know.

ʃNOWBIRD

No way to deny it, he was just not a morning person. John rolled over and sandwiched his head between two pillows to block out the murmur of voices drifting up from the kitchen. Since he hadn't opened his eyes, the fact that it was still pitch dark didn't penetrate his sleep logged brain.

He had a few more minutes before Faron or Wren came to wake him. They usually let him sleep until there was just enough time for a quick grooming and breakfast before rushing off to the ranger station. He hoped it was Faron this time. The way she always kissed him awake geared him up for the day.

The footsteps approaching the bed were soft and quiet, but not like Faron's or Wren's, and the hand prodding between his shoulder blades was not near as gentle as theirs. In fact, it didn't feel like a hand at all. He opened his eyes and peeked from beneath the pillow. A carved eagle eye returned his gaze.

"What the hell?" The pillow flew over the foot of the bed as John bolted upright.

"Time to get up, son," Walker said, withdrawing his walking stick. "Can't lay here in bed all day when we've got things to do."

"All day?" John glanced at the night pressing against the bedroom window. "Day won't be here for another five or six hours at least. What time is it, midnight?"

"Nearly five o'clock," Walker said. "High time we got started, Johnny." He turned on the bedside lamp.

The glow from the hall lamp was almost more light than John could stand. He sure didn't need any more. "Five o'freakin' clock. Damn. I just got in bed."

"You got in bed at eleven and slept all night. Faron told me. Now haul ass, boy." Walker turned and left the room.

John smelled coffee. Thank God. It was the only way to handle waking up. With Walker here for breakfast, he knew the Luzianne would be strong enough to float a horseshoe and hot enough to melt one. A cup or two might help him keep his eyes open. He pulled on a sweatshirt and boxer shorts and staggered barefoot to the kitchen, grunting his breakfast order as he collapsed into his chair. "Coffee, darlin', and could I get a biscuit and jelly to get me going."

Faron didn't say anything, though she did give him a sympathetic look, then just sat there sipping her own coffee. John noticed that Yona and Walker were both sitting at their usual place at the table, but without coffee or biscuits. And Mama Kate was there, drinking coffee with Faron.

"You might as well go upstairs and put your britches on, son," Walker said. I'm afraid your belly's gonna have to stay empty for a while longer."

Understanding dawned. "Oh, shit," John groaned. "Please tell me he's only gonna make me do a sweat lodge with him."

"'Fraid not, brother," Yona grinned. "You can skip your hot shower this morning. By the time we get out of Big Santetlah, you're gonna be plenty clean."

He had gone to water before, just to please Faron. The first time was the day before their wedding and then twice more after the birth of their babies. Doing it first thing in the morning was a good-news, bad-news kind of thing. The good news was it wasn't as hard to fast while you were asleep. The bad news was that every river in these hills was cold enough to freeze a man's balls off, and climbing out of the water into the morning chill made him feel like a sack of ice cubes all day. Damn! He hated being cold. Hell had to be a place where they dipped you in ice water on a cold morning. He shivered at the thought of dipping himself seven times in Big Santetlah.

"Grandpa, look. I have a job that I'm expected to show up

at. No reason for me to traipse off with you to that burial ground. And if I'm not gonna be a part of this, no reason for me to go to water."

Walker laughed. "Good try, Johnny, but I already talked to Buck Locust at the station. You got all the leeway you need to handle this. Buck says it's really part of your job anyway. You work for a good man, son."

Why did he even try? And Buck claimed to be his friend. "Thought you said to keep this in the family. How come you told Buck?"

"Buck is family, son. The kind that counts when it comes to this kind of thing," Walker said.

"I'll get you a towel and a blanket, honey," Faron got up and kissed him. "You better go get dressed now."

There was nothing to do but follow orders. He started back up the stairs to the loft to dress.

"John," Mama Kate called after him. "Faron and I will come on over to the river with some breakfast for when you're done. We'll have a fire ready to thaw you out."

Perhaps she liked him after all.

It didn't take long to get ready to leave the house in the morning if he skipped breakfast and showering. Within ten minutes he was slumped in the back seat of Yona's Blazer, feeling like he had completely lost control of his life. It was not a new feeling. Seemed like the Copperheads had been leading him around by the nose since he and Faron were kids. Back around the time she told Kate she planned to marry him when they grew up.

Fog lay so thick on the road that he couldn't see ten feet ahead. Yona had to be driving from memory. The Chevy Blazer was a lot easier to handle than a truck. That's probably why little brother Charlie always confiscated it when he was home from school, leaving Yona no choice but to drive one of the company trucks, or borrow Kate's shiny black Trans Am.

Yona had his window down. The cold didn't bother him but the damp chill cut right through John. It would be a good month before it warmed up enough to get Johnny McLeymore into the river at mid-day. Here it was, early enough in the spring that the mornings were still so cool you needed a jacket, and he was on his way to plunge his white freckled ass into the Big Santetlah River. Walker laughed like he could read his mind. More likely his moaning and grumbling gave him away.

"You know, Old Man, that I'm a plain ol' Presbyterian. We don't have to get dunked in the water. If I wanted that, I'd a been a Baptist, but even then, I sure wouldn't do it on a cold morning. Why in hell do you people put yourselves—and me, through this?"

"For a good reason, Johnny," Walker answered. "We need to be purified before we go messing around with some of the things we're gonna be messing with. If you've got any desires to be the big boss man, better get ready to let them go. Gotta get rid of any cravings for power, or you might get it, and son, you don't want it." Walker was serious now. "Need a clean spirit and a mind on service to the greatest good of the people. Anything that would break harmony has to go."

The mist coming through the windows got colder. "Old Man," John asked, "Is the Ulunsu'ti in that box we found?"

"I wish it was, Johnny." Walker's face was grim. "At least then we'd know it wasn't in the wrong hands. This could get bad."

"The thing Faron called the ark; they used to say that's what it was for, to hold the Ulunsu'ti." John was shivering now.

"Ain't nothing can hold the Ulunsu'ti," Walker said. "Lots of people thought it was in the ark but it never was. The ark just holds some of the tools you need to use it, and it looks like somebody was planning to use it. They had the ark and Kanagwa'ti's bones and medicine bundle."

"Grandpa, if I'm gonna go through all this craziness, I think I've got some answers coming," John said.

Walker looked back at him, his eyes as innocent as a lamb's. "Why didn't you ask me, if you've got questions, boy? You know I'd tell you anything you need to know."

Now it was John's turn. "Bullshit," he said and folded his arms across his chest and went silent. Yona laughed out loud at the perfect parody of his grandfather. The mood in the Blazer lightened.

Yona braked and eased into one of those cut-offs that nobody seemed to be able to see but the Copperheads, then bounced along until the river appeared right in front of the wheels.

"Think you could wait a while for those answers, brother?" Yona asked. "Like after we puke and go for a swim?"

John didn't respond. His stomach was already churning in anticipation when Walker unscrewed the lid on his Thermos. The liquid he poured into the plastic cup was hot and black, but it wasn't Luzianne. He could smell it from the back seat as Yona took it and gulped it down, then hurried away to disappear into the trees. Walker poured again and reached the cup back to John. "You know why you do this, boy. You been through it before. Gotta be clean, inside and out. Hit the woods now and do what you gotta do."

John gagged more than once, but it was not as hard to swallow as it was the last time he went through a purification. If he'd been a woman, he could have skipped this step. Women didn't need to purge.

The black drink wanted to come up faster than it went down, but he gagged it back and ran for the woods. There was an order to this, if he could only remember it with his whole insides heaving. He leaned against a tree and let the draught do its work. He hated puking. This was a hell of a way to start something that was supposed to be spiritual.

When the emetic draught had done its work and cleaned his insides out, he found what felt like the right place under a big oak and addressed the four directions, calling on the guardians of each to help him. They must have heard because it went a little easier. The prayers Walker had taught him came back to his memory without a hitch, and he surprised himself by adding some of his own. He felt thirty pounds lighter, probably because there wasn't a trace of anything left in his stomach. That had to be what made him so light-headed and floaty. Kinda made a man think he was hallucinating sometimes.

Walker and Yona were waiting by the river. So far, there was no sign of Kate and Faron. Walker sat on a flat stone. Flames flickered into sight as he nurtured a small fire to life.

John stopped and waited while Yona disrobed. He wanted to delay that step for as long as possible. When Yona's sweatshirt and pants lay in a neat stack on the rock, he followed and added his own jeans, shirt and jacket to the pile.

Walker stood, wearing nothing but a leather pouch around his neck. He nodded at Yona, then at the mound of green cedar branches beside the rock. Yona picked up the branches and scattered them to enclose the three of them in a protective circle of green, then threw the rest on the smoldering fire. The smoke spread the warding fragrance of cedar up and out beyond the circle. John remembered that nothing evil could cross the cedar circle.

Walker lifted his hands toward the dawning light in the east and began to chant so softly his voice barely reached beyond the fire's warmth. The language was Cherokee, but in an older form, a form that went all the way back to the time when his people were still known as the *Ani'yun Wiya, The Principal People.* John's limited grasp of the language was of no use at all. Yona looked like he didn't understand any more than John did. When the chant ended, only the rushing of Big Santetlah broke the silence. Not so much as a bird call could be heard.

Walker took the pouch from around his neck and opened it. Wild native tobacco was not easy to come by anymore. This must be a special occasion for him to use the precious supply he had. He filled the hollow of his left hand with the crumpled leaves, added some sage leaves, and something John didn't recognize. He then rolled it between his palms until it formed a tight cylindrical bundle. He lit it from a burning cedar twig Yona retrieved from the fire and blew on the bundle till the smoke swirled from it just right. He handed it to Yona and with closed eyes, accepted the cleansing of the sweet-smelling smoke. Yona circled him, directing the smoke to flow over his skin from his feet to his skinny gray braid. Walker took the smoking bundle and repeated the smudging for Yona and John, chanting something in a whisper.

The smoke reached John's face and he breathed deeply, drawing it into his lungs. He felt warmer now, like the smoke itself was a barrier against the chilling mist. Surely he was imagining it, but he could feel it, like something alive, writhing up his body. He could even hear it. No. That must be the river—or the snake. The snake that curled up his legs and around his belly, then across his chest, its fanged head lifting just inches from his glazed eyes. The forked tongue flicked and John stared into the gaping mouth. Cottony white.

The tongue flicked again, then dissolved and drifted upward to float away, followed by the rest of the serpent. Smoke blending into mist. And then was gone.

"John. Time to go, brother." Yona's voice sounded like it came from far away. John watched him wade into the river, and followed without hesitation, stepping over the rocky shore and into the cold water. Strange, it didn't feel all that cold. Without the usual prompting from Walker, he remembered the prayers. Seven times under, and each time the prayer entered his thoughts and was spoken without effort, and more prayers added that Walker hadn't taught him. Well, he had been in the family for nearly ten years. It was about time their Above Beings decided to accept him.

Yona and Walker were waiting on the bank when he came out of the water. Yona had his jeans on and was pulling a sweatshirt over the kind of body some men work out for years to get. Being a logger had its good side.

Walker was fully clothed and dousing the fire. "Put your clothes on, boy, and we'll go get us some breakfast," he said.

John dried off and dressed. The only sign there had ever been a fire was the lingering fragrance of scented smoke on the morning air. He followed Yona and Walker and asked no questions when they didn't head toward the Blazer.

He smelled coffee. Around the bend in the river, Faron stood by her own fire. A smoky old percolator bubbled away over the coals and Faron was stirring something in a big iron skillet. Nothing smelled as good as breakfast cooking on a campfire.

"Hey, Daddy. You done already?"

John was startled to see Wren. The sun was just barely up and the kid had school. He asked her why she was here beside the river, wearing nothing but a blanket with her long hair soaking wet.

"Same as you, Daddy," she answered. "We've got important things to do and we needed to get ready."

"Faron, you wanna tell me what's going on here?" John asked.

"She already told you, honey," Faron speared sausage links with a fork from the smoking skillet and transferred them to a paper plate.

Kate wrapped Wren's blanket tighter around her and sat her down on a rock, then perched behind her with a comb and began to smooth the tangles from her wet hair. "Stay here by the fire and let it dry a while," she said, "then we'll braid it." Wren did as she was told while she sipped on a Coke.

John squatted beside his wife. She added a pile of scrambled eggs to the plate of sausage links and handed it to him. He put it down on the same rock with his coffee cup.

"Faron," he said. "You get pissed off at me if I get Wren home twenty minutes after bedtime, or feed her something that's not on the approved list, or say a cuss word or two in front of her. Now, you drag our little girl out of bed before daylight on a school day and let your mama dunk her in the freezing cold river. Am I missing something here?"

"Eat your breakfast, John." Faron spoke in that soft sweet voice that didn't tell John anything. "You don't want it to get cold."

Across on their side of the fire, Kate and Wren were singing something. John listened, wondering what kind of ritual his little girl was observing now and what prayers she would say. Their voices drifted softly on the mist.

"Feeling good was easy, Lord, when Bobby sang the blues.

"Feeling good was good enough for me.

"Good enough for me and Bobby McGee.

"La te da te da da da da di."

"Could this possibly get any more surreal?" he muttered. "If Janice Joplin herself walked out of that river butt-naked, I'd just hand her a cup of coffee."

"She's dead, you know," Yona said.

John sat flat on the damp ground, his head between his hands.

"Faron, you better get some food into your man," Kate called. "Looks like he might be about to pass out. That happens to the men sometime."

Faron held the coffee cup to his lips like she was feeding a baby. The mischief in her eyes suggested less solicitation than teasing. He sipped, and it did make him feel better. "Here, honey. Eat these eggs now," she said. "Mama's right. You look kinda pale."

"You want some of my Coke, Daddy?" Wren asked, coming around to his side.

"Yeah, Johnny," Kate said. "That might be just what you need. It's got plenty of sugar in it, and you're probably just slightly hypoglycemic." She took the bottle from Wren and held it to his lips. He downed the whole thing then started in on the eggs while the women talked about his habitual early morning lethargy and its possible causes. Yona and Walker just grinned and ate.

John looked at Walker, the grin on his face as wicked as theirs. "I hope you brought a can of that Metamucil with you, Old Man. You know you're supposed to take a dose after every meal. A man your age has to take care of his bowels."

Walker's grin faded instantly. Yona almost choked on his coffee, not daring to laugh, because even he was not immune to the women's preoccupation with the health of their men. John was just relieved to direct their attention away from himself. While they fussed over Walker, handing him a cup of water to mix his Metamucil in, John opened a carton of heavy whipping cream and added a generous portion to his steaming cup of Luzianne. If he really was hypoglycemic, a couple spoons full of sugar was a good idea, too.

His son stirred in the back seat of the Chevy where he was finishing up his night's sleep. John was the only one who heard, since the rest were too involved with Walker's digestive tract. "Faron, honey, I think Diamond is awake. Sounded like I heard him." Guess he owed it to Walker to call them off.

Faron left them to get Diamond. Kate took Wren's blanket and helped her into a pair of jeans and a T-shirt. "Wear these socks, sweetie. You're gonna be doing lots of walking today over some rough ground and you don't want your feet to blister."

"How come she's walking so much today, Mama Kate?" John asked. "They got a field trip at school?"

Kate didn't answer till she had tied Wren's high-topped Reeboks. "She won't be going to school today. She needs to go with you and Dad and Yona." Kate reached for a pair of jeans and unwrapped her own blanket from her ample pair of breasts, then stood there, wearing nothing but her son Charlie's Black Knights football jersey.

Kate looked damn good in that jersey. John couldn't help noticing she had a nice, shapely set of legs. In fact, it was no surprise that she had such a cute daughter. Kate Copperhead was a good-looking old girl. Big as an Amazon, but firm and solid and with a fine shape to her. Not an ounce of fat anywhere. She'd sure be worth consideration if a man was looking.

Damn. He must be under the influence of some kind of herb to be thinking such things about his nearly fifty-year-old mother-in-law.

Faron came back to the fire with Diamond toddling behind,

still wearing his Bugs Bunny pajamas. "Mama," she said. "Spray some of that Deep Woods Cutters on her clothes. I don't want her coming home covered up with ticks and chiggers."

"I don't think there are many ticks around this time of the year, honey. And I know it's too early for chiggers." Kate took the can of insect repellent from her back pack. "But I'll spray some on her clothes just in case."

"Faron, why is Wren laying out of school and traipsing around the Smoky Mountains all day?" John asked, resigned to the reality that the decision had already been made.

"'Cause she had a dream, honey." Faron answered, like it was the most logical thing in the world. "Kanegwa'ti thinks she needs to go along."

He looked at his daughter, not even trying to conceal his suspicion. "So, the great conjuror needs you, huh?" he asked. "And I reckon he told you this himself."

"Sure did, Daddy. I'll let Mama tell you about it. I've gotta put my stuff in the Blazer." She slung her backpack across her shoulder, pulled an Atlanta Braves cap over braids still damp from her own purification and, jumping from boulder to boulder went upriver to where they had parked the Blazer.

"She had a dream?" John asked. "Must have been a hell of a dream to convince you to let her do just what she's been angling for all along. Sometimes I worry that she has too damn much imagination."

Faron and Kate ignored him, and got busy cleaning up the breakfast gear.

John watched his daughter duck through the underbrush and disappear. So innocent. He couldn't see any reason for the pang of apprehension that gripped his gut. She was safe with him. Every living soul here cared more about the safety and well being of his two kids than anything else in the world. They wouldn't let her do anything that wasn't good for her. Could it be that he didn't want her to be around when they buried Kanagwa'ti's bones? She was just too young to have to think of death.

John wasn't worried about Wren's reaction to the bones in the back of the Blazer. They wouldn't scare his daughter. It bothered her that someone had desecrated the grave of one of her ancestors, but she knew the spirit of that old skeleton was gone to the above world.

A vague image from his dreams drifted across his mind. He must be learning to have premonitions like all the rest of the Copperheads because he was getting a real bad feeling about this. There had been a body in his dream. Not just dried out old bones, but flesh and blood.

Seeing that would bother Wren a lot.

ON THE ROAD

"Can you believe we've got a traffic jam on Stecoah Mountain?" Yona came to a dead stop. "This used to be the middle of nowhere."

"People working over in Bryson City I guess," John said. "They have to leave home mighty early to get to work on time."

They moved in spurts, inching along for the next half mile until they came to the source of the hold up; a white mini-bus with a blown out tire that didn't quite make it off the road. A knot of people stood off to the side of the road, watching while the driver changed the tire. Walker read the logo on the side of the vehicle's front door, "Sacred Circle Medicine Way. Bullshh—"

John was pleased to see that he wasn't the only one Faron had trained not to cuss in front of Wren and Diamond. Even Walker knew better than to cross her when it came to the kids.

"I've seen that thing up on the Cheoah a good bit lately," John said. "I take it the Sacred Circle—whatever, is not sanctioned by the tribe."

"Just another bunch of Indian wannabes," Walker said. "Some big blond honcho that claims he's a half-blood Cherokee and the descendant of Shamans on both sides of his family. Brings a bunch of white people up here for what he calls shamanic training and initiation. He's got them convinced there's a power place at the head of the river, and he can take them to it."

Yona laughed. "They came in over at Philip's cafe last

week. Funniest thing you ever saw. Every one of them dressed up like TV Indians with their medicine bags around their necks. One of them asked me if I knew any elders they could apprentice with."

"And what did you tell them?" Walker asked.

"Oh, that my grandpa was a genuine Native American elder who would train them all. Gave them your name and told them how to find your house. I figured you could get with them and dance around awhile and teach them how to make good medicine." Yona acted dead serious until Walker started to raise his walking stick, then he laughed.

Walker put down the walking stick and chuckled. The old man had a sense of humor. "Son, they're just trying to find some way to feel connected to Creator. Their own ways have let them down and they're searching. I hope they can find what they're looking for. I just wish they'd look somewhere other than up on Cheoah. That's getting too close to some places they don't need to be."

"I've seen the blonde guy at the station. He came in one day to ask directions to some of the hidden ceremonial grounds where you guys used to meet when it wasn't safe to do it out in the open," John remembered something else that hadn't seemed important at the time. "A young girl was with him. She looked Indian but I don't think she was Cherokee. Not Eastern Band anyway. At least I've never seen her around here. Buck talked to them."

"Yeah," Walker said. "Buck called me later and told me about that. Said they knew about how we had places where we used to hold ceremony back when it was against the law to practice our religion. The blonde man calls himself Eagle Feather."

It embarrassed John when white people tried to turn Indian. He gave a derisive snort. "Of course that's the name his blonde mama and daddy gave him at birth."

"No. They named him Carl. Carl Johnson," Walker said. "He used to be a Methodist preacher. Now he runs these shaman schools like they ran the old Methodist camp meetings. He has camps set up in Graham County, and one down in Mississippi near the Choctaws, and near the Catawbas in South Carolina."

"Buck Locust told you all that?" John asked. "How did he find out so much about Mr. Eagle Feather?"

"Not much gets by Buck Locust," Walker said. "And we like to keep an eye on these people that show up with their disciples. Most are fairly harmless, but some are not. We need to know who's who."

"And is the blonde Indian one of the harmless ones?" John asked.

"Don't know yet," Walker answered. "But he sure is making a heap of money off of people. And he seems to have a lot of control over them, even after they go home from the camps. Keeps them coming back for the next level of initiation."

"I don't guess we can be too critical of his pigeons," Yona said. "Look at how many of our people pay tithes to Christian churches or send money to television preachers. Like you say, Old Man, everybody's looking for something. It's just funny how so many have trouble finding it in their own ways."

"Count your blessings, boy," Walker chuckled.

"What seems funny to me," John leaned over the front seat, "is that you've got a perfectly happy Presbyterian white boy back here that you've done everything to but appoint head high muckety-muck in your traditional religion. Sounds to me like somebody might be speaking with a forked tongue around here. I've been smoked and smudged and sweated and purged and half drowned for the past ten years and nobody complained about how I ought to be sticking to my own ways."

Walker had the decency to look uncomfortable for a few seconds. Yona just turned on the radio and asked John what station was most likely to play the new version of *Ring of Fire*.

"Damned if I know," John said. "I'm way too purified to listen to that hard core shit."

Wren stirred and adjusted the pillow she had scrunched

under her head against the corner of the Blazer and settled back down to sleep. John could almost hear Faron saying, "Watch your mouth, Johnny." Yeah, he was well trained. He reached behind the seat to get a blanket for her. The blanket caught on the tangled roots of a tree stump packed in beside the tarp that covered the duffle bag. He didn't ask about it. Why bother?

After the traffic eased, they hurried through downtown Cherokee with its ticky-tacky stores selling genuine Indian moccasins with their made-in-China labels and real Indian headdresses and plastic bows and arrows. It was a mercy that it was too early for the live Indian chiefs to be out with their feathers and breechcloths, like they just rode in off the plains. Hollywood did such a good job of teaching people how Indians were supposed to look, that even some of their own people didn't remember that Cherokees wore turbans, tunics and pants while the Plains Indians were in those headdresses.

Walker must have been reading his thoughts again, because before John could comment on what he thought of the whole thing, he broke in, "Lot of people don't understand why we tolerate this, but having a major highway through reservation land was the best thing that could have happened to us. This crap brings in enough tourism money to finance a lot of good things. Long as we educate our kids about who they are, we can live with it."

Yona grinned. "Besides, they won't let us scalp 'em no other way anymore."

Right in the middle of the main tourist trap, Yona made a right turn, like he was going to the bingo hall, or doubling back toward Highway 19 and the brand new casino, then swung left and drove along the Oconoluftee River on Big Cove Road. John had not expected this detour. Thunderhead lay straight ahead off the Blue Ridge Parkway.

"I take it we're going to visit some of the kinfolks in Big Cove," he said. "Is it any of my business who it is and why we're going there?"

"I already asked him that, brother," Yona said. "All he tells me is that he has to get some facts straight."

Walker shifted in his seat, to look at both Yona and John. "Just a few things I need to understand better. Whoever robbed the conjuror's grave knew exactly what he was doing. He knew where to find the ark, and he must have known what it was and what it contained and why it was important."

"Wait a minute, Old Man," John said. "I thought the ark was part of the conjuror's grave goods. How did the grave robber know where to find it?"

Walker had that look he got when he was trying to decide how much he could tell somebody who wasn't a Cherokee. John was used to it, but it still annoyed him sometimes. When Walker made up his mind, he spoke slowly, like it went against his instincts to talk about such things. "The ark was in its own place. Everything was separated long before Kanegwa'ti died. He planned it that way. No one person knew where everything was. One man knew where the Ulunsu'ti was hidden. Somebody else knew where the ark was. Another man was already appointed to bury the conjuror and his medicine bundle in the grave he chose before he died. The Suye'ta has to find all three before he can wake the Ulunsu'ti. We know where the bones and the ark are. Let's hope nobody knows where the Ulunsu'ti is. David Wayanettah can tell us some things we need to know about that."

"Is that why we're hauling around that tree stump behind the seat?" John asked.

"Lightning-struck buckeye," Walker said. "Dave will make something pretty out of that. The man's a hell of an artist. But we're going to see him because he knows more about our history than anybody I know. He can tell us how much of the story of Kanegwa'ti is true and how much is myth built up over the years. He's a purist about our mythology. Strips off the layers laid on to make them more palatable to outsiders and gets to the old way. I want to hear his version of this one. And besides, I'd like to know about some things his grandfather might have told him before he walked over to the other world."

John had more questions but decided to save them for later. He had already gotten more answers than he expected and decided not to push his luck. He sat back to enjoy the drive. Big Cove community was nothing like what tourists would expect an Indian neighborhood to look. No tepees or villages, just ordinary homes set back in the trees or in the middle of grassy lawns by the roadside, a lot like where the white folks lived.

The houses had thinned out considerably by the time they came to Lightning Creek Road. A few miles more and the Wayanettah's house stood beyond a narrow one-lane bridge over Lightning Creek. The bridge rattled and swayed when they drove across. David was waiting for them, standing barefoot, holding the front screen door ajar. His long black hair hung loose and tousled, like he had just gotten out of bed.

John roused Wren from her nap and helped her out of the car. Yona was taking the porch steps three at a time. He caught David in a casual one-armed hug, slapping him on the shoulder. The two big men were about equal in size and still looked as much alike as they had since they were kids. If John hadn't known them all his life, he would have thought they were brothers.

"Damn, I miss you on the crew, Wolf," Yona said. "You get to be such a big time artist you don't need a job anymore, then we don't see you for weeks at a time."

"The price of success, old Bear," David answered. "Just don't have the time to enjoy working like a mule on a logging crew anymore."

Their camaraderie was familiar and comforting.

Walker made a more dignified entrance and Dave stooped to clasp his extended forearm. "Good to see you, Young Wolf," Walker said, using the English translation of Wayanettah. "Looks like you've been plenty busy."

The porch, as well as the living room and the dining room beyond held wood and stone carvings and works in bronze. John admired a carving in the early stages of creation. Under

David's skilled hands, a buffalo was beginning to take shape from a block of white alabaster. All he could say was, "Wow."

Wren wandered around the living room, curious as kitten as she examined each piece. "Come look, Daddy," she called. "It's the Nunne'hi coming out of Council House Mound."

John bent over beside her to get a good look at the wood carving displayed on a corner table. A seven-sided lodge grew right out of the wood, its walls blending into the carved mountainside so well it was hard to tell where the mountain ended and the council house began, or if perhaps they were one and the same. The lithe forms emerging from an unseen doorway were dressed in the old way and carried decorated bows and beaded quivers full of arrows. It didn't look like they walked through the doorway so much as just materialize from the mountain itself. The effect was as if they stepped from another dimension into our own.

"It looks exactly like the real place, Daddy," Wren said. "Except I've never seen them there before. They look just like I thought they would."

"So, that's how you imagine them, too?" David asked. "My great grandpa claimed he saw a Nunne'hi woman there one time. Said she was the most beautiful being he had ever seen."

"There's something familiar about this piece," John said.

"Well, John, You've been all up and down the Cheoah haven't you?" David asked.

"Uh huh. Nearly every mile of it."

"Then you've seen the Council House Mound," David said.

"We were almost there last night, Daddy," Wren said. "When we were going to Degal gun'yi."

Another one of the old myths intruding on the real world. He knew this one. It only went back around five hundred years. The mound was once the council house in the center of a Cherokee town. The people who lived there heard the voices of the Nunne'hi calling on the wind, warning of the coming of strangers who would bring death and destruction and rub out the old ways. A plan was offered whereby the town could survive to preserve their knowledge of the sacred ways. All they had to do was allow themselves to be sealed inside the mountain and become like the invisible immortals who lived there, the Nunne'hi. They listened. At the appointed time, they waited inside the council house.

A whirlwind came and took the whole town inside the mountain where it and all its people still live, but in another dimension. The only evidence that it ever existed is the shape of the mound. It looks just like the old seven-sided council houses.

He told the story to Wren, mostly to let her know that he knew it.

"And the people are still there inside the mound, Daddy," Wren said. "You can hear them if you are quiet and listen. When I'm old enough, Mama Kate is gonna take me there at night so I can go to sleep. Then they can teach me in my dreams. That's why they decided to do what the Nunne'hi asked. To keep the old ways and teach them to their children's children. That's how Mama Kate and Mama know so much. They slept on the mound. So did Uncle Yona and Grandpa."

John had the fleeting wish that there was someone who could teach him how to keep up with his kid. He'd be glad to sleep on the mound for that kind of dream. He didn't say it out loud though, just muttered, "That's good, sugar. You do that," and followed David to the kitchen where Walker was already pouring himself a cup of coffee. Wren stayed behind, examining each sculpture. Her awed comments showed she was seeing in them a visual telling of the stories she had memorized.

David opened the refrigerator and took out a Coke and handed it to John. "The kid knows her stuff," he said. "Kate must be teaching her."

"A lot more than I can keep up with, Dave." John sipped on the Coke while he leaned against the door frame. "I don't know about her sleeping on Council House Mound, though. Sometimes Kate goes too far. It'd be a big disappointment to

Wren to go to all that trouble and not have any of those dreams she's counting on."

"And what if she did have them? Who would be disappointed then?"

"Hey, I don't mind her getting into her culture. I guess it does bother me sometimes when I don't have a clue what she's talking about."

"You know, John, that town you told her about. Where the mound is now. It used to be what your folks would have called a medicine village. It was a place of knowledge and healing, where holy people lived and taught. That's why the Nunne'hi chose it to be sealed off and protected. All the knowledge the elders had then is still there with them. That's what the dreams are about. And its one of the few places around here where the Nunne'hi are still seen."

"You've done it, Dave? And did you dream?"

David picked up the coffee pot, got a cup from the cabinet and strolled over to the table. "Yep," he said.

Yona was seated at the table, admiring the way David had made it from a single round slice cut from the trunk of an old oak that fell victim to the latest road widening project on Highway 441. John remembered that tree. Must have been at least three hundred years old. David had made good use of it.

John tried not to be impatient, listening while they talked about the same old things, like they'd forgotten the pile of human bones outside in the Blazer. David went on about tribal politics and Walker talked about family and mutual friends on the Snowbird.

Yona's only contributions were a few anecdotes about guys who worked for the logging company. He sat bent over his coffee cup like he had something on his mind. John knew what it was. Yona and David's sister, Meredith, would have been married by now if Meredith hadn't decided to get a medical degree and complete her residency and internship before she settled down on the Qualla Boundary. Yona respected her decision and bragged about her all the time but that didn't stop him from missing her.

When Walker got up to put the coffee pot back on the stove, Yona cleared his throat nervously, "Dave. What do you hear from Meredith? She said anything about when she's gonna be home?" John figured they must have had one of the spats they were famous for ever since they were kids.

"That's funny, Bear," David said. "She asked about you in her last letter. In fact, she asks about you nearly every time I hear from her. She said to tell you hello, and ask you if you'd like to drive down to Georgia to see her. Said you know how to get to Atlanta just as well as she knows how to get here."

Yona slumped in his seat and looked like the loneliest man alive. John felt sorry for him but there was nothing he could say that would make the waiting easier. Meredith wouldn't be moving back for at least two years and Yona had a logging business to run, now that Kate had turned most of the management duties over to him. He couldn't go to Meredith and she wasn't coming home.

Yona abruptly interrupted Walker, "Grandpa. You wanna tell David why we're here so we can get on our way? We've got a lot to do today."

"Finally," John said. "I thought we were just going to sit around and drink coffee all day. I took a day off work for this?"

Ignoring John, as usual, the old man sipped long and slow from his cup. "David. I want you to tell me a story. The old version."

"That's the only version I tell," David said. "You won't get the sanitized stuff from me. I think we need to leave in the sex and humor, tell it the way our elders did. And speaking of our elders, Grandfather, I figure you know a lot more about our legends than I do. Between you and Grady Smoker, you must know everything that's happened in these hills since First Man and First Woman lived here."

"Never hurts to get a second opinion, son," Walker said. "I want you to tell me everything you know about Kanegwa'ti, and when and why and how he hid the Ulunsu'ti and the tools for using it. I need to know who's around today that might know about this stuff."

John felt the tension deepen in the room. Nobody said a word, like they were trying to wait each other out. David had his arms crossed over his chest. His expression gave no indication of what he was thinking. Finally, he said, "You ask for a lot, Grandfather. You wanna tell me why you need to know things that according to tradition, only one man at a time ever knows?"

"If you're not one of those men, you don't have to worry about telling any secrets," Walker's face was closed. Each of them suspected the other of holding something back. "Just tell me the story."

Wren stood in the doorway, intent on every word. She had no business being there. John wished he'd stood up to Faron and Kate for a change and left her behind. He shuddered at the thought of what that would have led to.

David got up and went toward the living room. He hesitated at the door, like he wasn't sure he was doing the right thing, then went to a locked cupboard built into the wall. Fishing for a key in his wallet, he unlocked it and swung the doors open. From their vantage point at the table they could see a collection of sculpted figures.

John wondered why they were not displayed like the rest. He had seen some of David's work that had gone to the Smithsonian, and pieces that had sold for more than a forest ranger made in a whole year. These were more intricate than any of them, and more primal. They exuded an energy, a force that could be felt, like needle-fine sleet against naked flesh. David took out a soapstone carving and carried it to the table.

"It's all here," he said.

Walker began to scan the piece inch by inch. The men were all so engrossed in the sculpture they weren't aware of Wren until they heard her awed whisper. "Look at his hand, Grandpa Walker. He's holding it."

It was hard to tell if the figure was a man or a snake. It

appeared to be both. John shivered when he looked into the white-fanged mouth. There was something familiar about it. In his right hand, the man-snake held a knife carved from an antler. At his feet, a rabbit's carcass, hardly more than a crumpled mass of fur, receded into the earth, all essence of life drained away. His left hand held an oval object that filled it the way a basketball would have filled John's hand. Life stirred in the object. John could see it as clearly as he could see the fear in the face of the man-snake. Life, and unbelievable power. John didn't realize he was reaching out to touch it until Walker stopped him.

He heard David say, "That's the only way it can ever be woke up. In the hand of the conjuror. He laid that on it before he hid it."

David and Walker sat looking at the figure, each waiting for the other to speak and neither wanting to say too much. Both of them showed signs they weren't satisfied, like there was something that needed to be said and neither of them wanted to be the one to say it. John lacked the patience to sit around and watch the tension crackle between them. He and his little girl were involved in this, too, and he wanted some answers.

John figured a little information about the snake was a good place to start. "As I understand it, the conjuror was what you call a skin changer. He was a man who could turn into a snake. Right?"

David nodded.

"From what I remember," John continued, "Cherokee skin changers are usually the bad guys. Water Moccasin seems to be a hero. Why is that?"

David paused a moment before he decided to answer, looking at Walker like he expected him to object. Walker didn't say a word. David said, "Well, for one thing, the conjuror wasn't a Cherokee. The Suye'ta never is. The chosen one is an outsider, same as the cottonmouth moccasin is an outsider around here. The cottonmouth is venomous, unlike our local water moccasins. Or like the Shawnee who risked his life

and killed Uktena in the first place. The part of the story that
gets left out these days is that the Ulunsu'ti was a bride price.
The Shawnee loved a Cherokee woman so much he put the
woman and her people ahead of his own safety. She was the
bond that made him the Suye'ta."

This was a part of the story John hadn't heard before.
Walker looked like he would just as soon David ended his
story. Getting actual answers to his questions was heady
business for John so he figured he had nothing to lose by
asking another one. "Why is it that the Ulunsu'ti has to be
brought to Degal' gun'yi to be awakened?"

"It doesn't." David said. "In fact, that's the worst place for it
to be. "It has to be brought to the Council House Mound. It's
safer there."

"Safer?" John asked.

David's smile was cold and completely without humor.
"Yeah, safer, because that's a place of the Nunne'hi. The
Suye'ta has a slight chance of surviving the first few minutes
there."

Out of the corner of his eye John thought he saw Walker lift
his left eyebrow in that signal that he had only recently become
aware of. The rest of the family appeared to know it meant,
"You've said enough." Apparently, David knew the signal, too,
because he stopped talking and became a dutiful host, warming
up coffee cups and offering some bagels from a plastic bakery
bag. When only Yona refused, he sliced three in half and slid
them into the toaster oven on the counter top, then opened a
pack of cream cheese and served it on its own foil wrapper.

Wren stood on a chair in the pantry and took out a jar of
homemade blackberry jam and brought it to the table. "I bet
Meredith made this jam from the blackberries she picked with
me and Mama last summer," she said.

Yona reached for the jar and smeared some on one of
Walker's bagel halves that he had now decided to confiscate
for himself. "Your sister makes some good jam," he said to
David, and his mood visibly lightened.

When they finished the last crumb, John helped carry the cups to the sink and clear away jars and wrappers and bottles. Wren had returned to the living room. He watched as she stood in front of the open cupboard doors, gazing reverently at the sculpted figures. Dave came to his side and nodded at Wren. "She understands what they are," he said. "She's okay. Now, let's see if we can get Walker to tell us why he's here."

Walker looked like he was ready to talk. When David asked him what was on his mind, Walker stood and walked toward the door, like it was his idea in the first place. "Come out to the car, son," he said. "I want to show you something."

The three men followed him to the Blazer and stood aside while Yona lifted open the back. First, he took out the stump and handed it to David. "Lightning-struck buckeye," he said.

"Grandpa found it down on Snowbird," Yona went on. "We thought you might like to have it for your art work." They watched while David examined it; wondering how he could see things in stone, wood and even an old tree stump, that nobody else could.

David held the stump up, turning it so he could get a closer look at all its surfaces. "Looks like a beautiful lady in there to me. I think the lightning just parted her hair. I'd say she's one of the Nunne'hi. We'll see if Wren thinks so when I'm finished bringing her out of the wood." He walked to the porch and put the stump down and came back to the Blazer. "I don't think you guys drove all the way from the Snowbird on a work day to haul a tree stump out here. Now, you want to tell me what's going on?"

A piece of tarp covered the two gym bags. Yona removed it and handed one bag to Walker. Walker opened it and gently removed some of the linen-wrapped objects and laid them on the carpeted floor of the Blazer. He unwrapped the first one, an ancient rattle, and gave it to David so carefully that it didn't make a sound. David ran his finger along the old terrapin shell. It gave off a soft rustle as he turned it, examining every inch of its surface.

"It's his all right," David said. He pointed out the carving of the open-mouthed snake that coiled around the handle. John noticed the snakes then. Walker opened another bundle and lifted out a pipe and held it up for them to see. It was fashioned in the form of a snake, its open mouth serving as the bowl.

John watched as Walker unwrapped the other relics and displayed them. It was the first chance he'd had to make a close inspection. Every item Walker laid out was marked in some way with a serpent. A soapstone medicine bowl looked like it had just been made. The color had hardly faded. John leaned into the Blazer to get a better look at it. A painted snake encircled the bowl, coiling around it from the base to the lip. Its vivid cottony-white mouth opened wide. Chills crept up John's legs. He didn't want to see anymore but Walker wasn't through yet.

One more thing remained, wrapped in a nondescript old blue jacket. Walker sat it down beside the rest, but he kept his hand on it. They waited for him to unwrap it, but he just stood there. He made a move to untie the sleeves, then pulled them tighter. When it was obvious he couldn't make up his mind, David asked, "Is it the ark, Grandfather?"

Walker nodded.

"Have you looked inside it?"

John had never seen Walker look so confused, like he didn't know how to answer. He would start to speak, then stop. When he finally got his words out, it made them all uncomfortable.

He stuttered, "N-no. I figured I needed another—another elder around. But who? I can't find Grady Smoker. He's not answering his phone and nobody's seen him. I had to talk to Kate about it. Some folks won't approve of bringing her into this, but I had to. She didn't feel right about me going to Grady."

He wiped his forehead with his handkerchief. With the morning chill still lingering, he couldn't have been sweating. John suspected he was stalling. They waited.

Walker put the bundle back into the Blazer. He lowered his

voice when he continued like he was afraid of being overheard. "Dave, I've got a bad feeling. A real bad feeling something's going on that's serious trouble."

"What do you want us to do, Grandfather," David asked worriedly.

Walker said, "This is something we've never had to deal with before. David, I wish your grandpa hadn't walked over. If Driver was still alive, he would have been the one to handle this. Could be that's why me and Kate both felt so strong about coming here to talk to you."

David reached into the Blazer and lifted a fold of the jacket away from the ark, just enough to reveal a corner. He looked at it thoughtfully, then covered it up and said, "Pack it all up good. This is not the place. Be ready to go when I get back." He turned and bounded up the steps and into his house.

John stepped back out of the way and let Yona and Walker repack the duffle bag. This was not his problem and he didn't want to have anymore to do with it than he had to. He wanted out before it went any further. Even Walker didn't understand what was going on or what to do about it. Why should he hang around? He certainly didn't want Wren involved. This was some kind of creepy Indian mysticism and he was way too white to understand. For that matter, his daughter was half white. This looked more and more like a problem for the full-bloods to deal with.

He was working up the nerve to call Faron and insist that she come get him and Wren to take them home when David reappeared in the doorway. He wore heavy hiking boots and a backpack hung across his right shoulder.

Wren was with him, looking like she knew what David had in mind and was intent on going with him. John heard her ask, "So, where are we going now David?"

John gave up on calling Faron. It wouldn't make any difference. Faron would side with Wren and he would be overruled. For all he knew, they had talked on the phone and agreed on the decision. He was in for a hike.

David lifted Wren into the back seat of the Blazer before he answered her question. "Honey," we're going to a place I never took anybody before. We're going to a cave half way up Wolf Mountain."

Walker climbed into the front seat beside Yona. John and David got in the back with Wren between them. The Blazer felt crowded.

David directed Yona to drive up the narrow dirt road that curved along the back side of Lightning Creek and wound its way toward the foot of Wolf Mountain.

John hugged Wren to him and wished they were in Faron's Chevy going back to the Snowbird. Wolf Mountain rose ahead, its peak covered with clouds. "Half way up" sounded like a hell of a climb. He felt Wren tremble as she cuddled against him.

LIGHTNING CREEK

They rode in silence past three small houses. John knew David's relatives lived in all of them. A fourth house had an air of emptiness that reached all the way to the road. Two months ago, he'd come there with Walker to say Goodbye to David's grandfather, Driver Wayanettah. Driver had died the next day. Now, an owl perched on the peak of the roof, standing guard.

David turned his head away as they passed the lifeless house. "Yeah, Grandfather. I wish Grandpa Driver was still here, too. And not just because I miss him. I need him for several reasons. You know what I mean?"

Walker nodded. "Yeah, I think I do, son. Me and old Driver danced to the same drum."

"He told me" David said.

John wasn't sure what that exchange meant, but he had a feeling Walker and David were communicating on a different level, passing more information between them than the words alone revealed. He could tell Walker was calmer when he looked across at David and almost smiled.

"I thought Driver might have had a talk with you," Walker said.

Whatever it was Walker had needed to know, his question had been answered. It showed in the way he relaxed against the seat, a measure of tension gone from his body. Nothing else was said but Walker looked more peaceful. That made John feel better, too.

The road ended about five miles beyond Driver's deserted house. Yona kept driving up a path. The tires struggled to make it a few more feet up the slope, leaving the smell of burnt rubber on the morning air. When the underbrush got so thick the Blazer couldn't go any farther Yona turned off the engine.

"Hope everybody's wearing good walking shoes," David said. "We've still got a ways to go, and it's mostly uphill."

Wren was solemn as she climbed down from the vehicle. She held Walker's walking stick until he joined her. "Are you up to this, Grandpa Walker?" she asked.

Walker tweaked the bill of her cap. "Don't worry about me, sugar. I reckon you can tote me if I can't make it."

She giggled and said he was much too heavy. John was glad to hear her laugh. She wouldn't laugh if she was scared.

David got the duffle bag from the back of the Blazer and packed the gym bags in it. When he started to put the ark in with the gym bags, Walker objected.

David said, "We don't have to worry about all these things being together. As long as the Ulunsu'ti isn't here, too, we're okay."

David rearranged the contents until they fit just right then tightened the cord and slung the bag across his shoulder. He hoisted his backpack and was ready to go. It looked heavy. John briefly considered offering to carry it, but changed his mind. He might have to go along on this hike, but he'd be damned if he would lug around baggage. Why should he make it any harder on himself than it already was. Besides, David didn't look like he needed help.

"Where to now, Youngwolf?" Yona asked. He didn't offer to carry anything either.

"To a hiding place," David said. "A good one. My great-great grandparents and all the family hid out there during the time of the removal. That's why their descendants are Eastern Band now and not living out in Oklahoma." He looked around at the mountains rising to meet the smoke-like mist that veiled their peaks and gave them their name. "We're the lucky ones. This is where the spirit of our people lives. Like my grandfather, I'll do whatever I have to do to keep it here."

"Your grandpa would be proud, David," Walker said. "You're doing the right thing, just like Driver would have wanted."

"Nothing else I can do, Grandfather," David's jaw had a determined look. "We need to be sure at least one of Kanagwa'ti's hiding places is still holding up. The grave goods, the bones and the ark have already been found. The only thing missing is what my family looks after, and Ulunsu'ti himself."

Walker stopped short. His knuckles whitened around the walking stick. "You don't have the Ulunsu'ti? I—We—always thought— What else? Dave, what else is there?"

John felt the chill of apprehension that had begun back in David's yard creep higher up his spine. What the hell was wrong with Walker? He hoped the old man wasn't as freaked as he looked.

He glanced at Yona and Wren and saw that they had noticed it, too, and were just as uncomfortable with Walker's unease as he was. Walker should be the one with all the answers. As the elder, they expected it of him. John found himself wishing Kate had come along.

"We've got some walking to do, Grandfather," David said, picking up the pace. "We'll talk later." He took long, easy strides up the incline. Yona was right behind him. John and Walker walked with Wren. When they lagged behind, David slowed to let them catch up.

John hadn't noticed when Wren slipped her hand in his, but now she gripped it like she needed to hold onto her daddy. They brought up the rear. Wren kept her eyes on David, careful not to let him get so far ahead that she would lose sight of him. She didn't say anything, but she seemed to feel more secure with John than with Walker. John felt a perverse sense of satisfaction. He walked taller, his little girl's hand in his.

It was a good thing they had gotten an early start because they had a fair distance to cover and no trail that they could see. A few times, John wondered how David found the way at all. Once, when they stopped to let Walker lean on his walking stick and rest, John asked, "Hey, man, do you know where you're going? Looks to me like we're just wandering in the woods."

David fixed his eyes on a place high up on Wolf Mountain where Lightning Creek began as a pond, bubbling up and spilling over the falls. "Yeah, John. I've been there a few times. I just don't ever go the same way twice. It was Kanagwa'ti's idea, not to wear a trail that could be followed." He wiped his brow with his sleeve and walked through some scrub laurel. His boots cleared a slightly easier path for them to follow.

Wren left John's side and walked beside Walker, her hand now tucked in his. John guessed it was more for Walker's comfort than Wren's. He saw her stumble and realized she was getting tired. Before he could pick her up, Yona stooped and swept her up to his shoulders.

"I can almost see clear over the mountain from here," Wren said. "I hope I grow up to be as tall as you, Uncle Yona."

"Well, your grandma Kate nearly did, honey," Yona laughed back. "But I don't think you're gonna take after her."

"I wish she'd a come with us." Wren's wish was one nobody else had expressed aloud, but John, at least, had thought it. Everyone was very quiet after that.

Later in the afternoon when they were all tired, David stopped beside the creek and sat down and began pulling stuff from his backpack. He took out a brown paper bag and laid it beside him then brought out a loaf of sourdough bread and began slicing it with his hunting knife. "Not much time to pack a lunch but I did the best I could," he said.

Wren opened the paper bag and found two jars. She couldn't have been more pleased. Crunchy peanut butter and strawberry jelly on sourdough bread was her favorite sandwich.

It would have felt good to rest by the creek after their picnic, but David only gave them time for a long drink of cold, clear creek water before he had them on their feet again for the steepest part of the climb. Before long they had left the tree line behind and trudged up a steep rocky incline.

The mountain changed as they went higher. Granite protruded through sparse soil until the only dirt left had accumulated in pockets where scrub laurel and brush grew. An occasional pine found purchase and grew tall and gaunt. Giant boulders littered the landscape.

David stopped again. "Wait here. I need to check on something before we go any further." He took off around a big boulder and disappeared from sight before they could ask him where he was going. They sat down on the sun-warmed rocks to wait.

It didn't look like there was a place for him to go. They were half way up the mountain and as far as they could see, there was nothing but rocks and scrub brush the rest of the way to the top. It was quiet, too. The kind of quiet not found much in the Smokies. Like there weren't any birds or crickets or any of the scads of critters that make so much noise he'd learned to block it out. John mentioned it to Walker, who just nodded and grunted.

Wren said, "Daddy, do you think this is a place where the Nunne'hi live? It looks and sounds and feels like it could be."

The now familiar chill crept between John's shoulder blades. "I wouldn't know, honey." What else could he say? He'd always thought of the Nunne'hi in the same way as he thought of fairies; just a story you tell your kids. But this place had a weird feel about it. From the look on Walker's face, he felt it, too. If the Nunne'hi did live here, David would need to get their approval before bringing visitors into their territory.

Wren got up to look around. If there were any supernaturals in the area she was bound to find them, invisible or not. John didn't want her to wander off alone, but as long as he could keep an eye on her, it wouldn't hurt to let her explore a bit. "Watch out for snakes, sugar," he called. "And stay where I can see you."

"I don't see any snakes, Daddy," she shouted from behind a heap of boulders. "But there sure are lots of ants. Their trail goes down behind these rocks."

Well, an ant trail couldn't hurt her. John sat back down beside Walker. With Wren out of hearing range, now was a good time to ask a few questions and hope for an answer here and there. "Just where is David going, Grandpa," he asked. "And what in the world does he need to check on way up here in the middle of nowhere? Does he think there really are Nunne'hi around here?"

Walker fiddled with the head of his walking stick. "Could be," he said. "I know bringing us here wasn't an easy thing for Dave to do. This might be as far as we go. At least I hope so."

Walker actually looked scared. His apprehension must have been contagious because John jumped like a rabbit when a lone pine dropped a dried up pine cone on the rocks. "Why are you so nervous about coming here? You look like you're waiting for the hangman," John said.

Walker didn't answer. He kept looking in the direction where David had disappeared.

"What if David comes back and takes us—wherever he is now. Would that be so bad?" John asked.

"It would be very bad," Walker said. "It would mean there's no reason to keep Kanagwa'ti's hiding place a secret any more. That there's nothing there to hide"

Yona stood up and stretched his legs. I'm gonna go see about Wren. Don't want her following her ant trail too far."

It was then they heard her scream.

Tuesday
WOLF MOUNTAIN

The white man couldn't see it in the darkness, but he could hear the waterfall somewhere nearby. He slowed to a walk, his hand against the cave wall to feel his way, thinking he must have lost his mind. Why else would he have chased that old goat into the darkness, leaving his flashlight outside? Following the sound of running footsteps had led him this far. Now, he didn't even have that. He wondered if the roar of the waterfall masked the footfalls. No matter how hard he listened, he heard nothing that sounded like another human being.

It would have been so easy to pick up the flashlight before he tore off into the cave. It was right there on the rock. He remembered putting it there, still shining. The sensible thing to do, now that he had calmed down, would be to turn around and find his way back to the entrance. He thought he must still be in the main chamber so all he had to do was retrace his steps and be careful to avoid places where the cave branched off into secondary caverns. Hugging the wall, the white man walked slowly in what he hoped was the direction he had come.

Over the noise of the water, he heard another sound. He flattened his body against the granite and listened. Footsteps echoed off the cave walls. They were coming his way. He could see a light. The dim glow in the distance was getting closer. Feeling along the wall, his fingers encountered a cleft in the rock. He squeezed inside a fissure just big enough to keep him out of sight.

The light grew brighter and spread down the cavern. Had the old fool somehow escaped him and gone back for the flashlight? He waited, watching the approaching light.

The light passed by, silhouetting the dark form of a man in its glare. He couldn't see who it was but this man was bigger than the one he had chased into the cave, and appeared to know where he was going. That made him worth keeping in sight. He followed as close as he dared. The sound of rushing water got louder, obscuring the thud of boots on stone, his and those of the man ahead. He felt spray on his face.

The man with the light bent over to enter a cavern that ran deeper into the mountain. The white man hung back for a moment, then followed, walking stooped like the man ahead.

The sound of the water receded, and he wondered just how far they were going into this narrow tunnel. The passage was getting smaller. When it squeezed down to a size that no longer allowed him to walk, he crawled on hands and knees until he saw the other man lie on the floor and wriggle inside an opening barely big enough to accommodate his wide shoulders.

The white man could see him stretch full length and reach for something. When he found it, he brought it out, mumbling something about Kanagwa'ti's hands being safe, then squirmed back inside to replace the object.

He forgot all about the body outside, and the one who threw the axe. They didn't matter anymore. He had it now. The last piece of the puzzle was his. He eased backward in the passage until he found a crevice big enough to conceal his body and stayed there till the light passed, then followed it back to the waterfall. Now that he knew what to look for, he could easily find the hands.

He had to follow the light back to the main cavern. From there he could find his way out and retrieve the flashlight. Everything was going to work out for him after all. Somewhere in this cave was the man who knew where the duffle bag was, and he could be made to give it up, one way or another.

He followed the light to the angle where the cave branched off into what he figured was the main cavern. His shoulder scraped against the wall causing a shower of loose pebbles. He ducked into the shadows just in time to avoid being caught in the beam of the flashlight when the man swung it toward the noise. After that, he held back farther. When the light disappeared around a bend, he wasn't worried. He could catch up. All he had to do was follow the upward slant in the floor. The entrance had to be close now.

When he saw the light again, he kept it in sight. Good thing, because he was farther from the opening than he thought, and there was a turn he had forgotten. It scared him to think of how easy it would be to get lost. The cave must ramble all through the heart of Wolf Mountain. No wonder the old man hadn't been able to find the hands before. He paid close attention to every detail outlined by the light ahead. As soon as he got his pack and flashlight, he'd be back. He had things to do in the cave.

It wasn't quite as dark up ahead. The cave entrance had to be close. Just a little longer, as soon as the man he'd followed was out of the way he could ease out to where he had left his pack and the flashlight. He watched the man silhouetted in the narrow opening. Voices reached him from outside. They weren't alone on the mountain.

He stayed back in the shadows of the cave. A shrill scream came from outside and echoed behind him into the darkness. The man ahead bolted from the cave.

He made his way toward the entrance. The people outside would be too busy to see him now. He kept to the shadows until the last moment then dashed out to the rocks near the mouth of the cave. His pack was where he left it. The flashlight lay beside it, still glowing weakly.

The voices faded behind him as he ran back into the cave. His heart raced with excitement. He was going to have it all. The pieces were falling into place like it was meant to be. Perhaps it had been preordained to happen this way. If he was the Suye'ta, it would all come to him. The Ulunsu'ti would be his, along with everything that went with it. Now, he would have it all to himself without some crazy Indian calling the shots.

He knew what he had to do. As soon as he had the conjuror's hands, he'd find the old fart and force him to reveal where he hid the duffle bag. As the Suye'ta, he had the power to demand cooperation.

The flashlight cast a weak glow against the gray stone. He decided not to waste the few minutes of juice the batteries had left. He could manage without the light for a while. He knew the main cavern well enough now that he could find his way with a hand against the wall until he felt the floor sloping downward. Besides, there were forces on his side that would get him where he needed to go. He would save the light as long as possible. With it off, the darkness was complete. A surge of primal fear of the dark tempted him to turn it back on but he resisted and felt his way along the wall.

When his hands met emptiness where the cave angled off, he used the light long enough to get his bearings. He counted his steps back down the narrow corridor, carefully measuring out the distance from the angle to the branch that led to the waterfall. From there, he would follow the sound of the water until he could feel it on his face. He remembered exactly where that was, and how it felt and sounded. He must be getting close to it by now. He stood still, listening. In the silence he could hear his heart pounding and another sound he couldn't identify. When he realized what it was, he was amazed that he could actually hear his blood rushing through his body. He listened to it until the roar of the water eclipsed it.

It seemed farther to the opening than he remembered. He turned on the flashlight and searched the cavern until he found it in the weak beam. It appeared as a deeper blackness in the dark cave. He would never have noticed it if he hadn't followed the other man. Surely the guardian of the conjuror's hands had been sent to reveal them to him. The Suye'ta could count on getting help when he needed it.

His confidence grew as he walked stooped over down the narrow tunnel. When he was flat on his belly reaching into the hole, he knew what he would find. He felt around until he touched a ledge, and then the hard roughness of something round. Slipping his hand under it, he carefully drew it to him and backed out with it clutched to his chest. His heart pumped so hard against his prize, he could hear it echoing like a drum beat in the hollow vessel.

As soon as he reached an area high enough to stand, he tore away the rough hide wrapping. He had to chew through a thong tie. When he was done, he shined the fading light on an ancient clay pot. The image of a snake marked it, coiling around from base to rim, its head resting on the sealed lid.

The pot wasn't very impressive, its only adornment the snake but he had learned enough to know this was what he was looking for.

The next step was to find the elder who could take him to the Ulunsu'ti and the duffle bag. He was somewhere in the cave, waiting. The old coot might resist at first, but when he understood that he was dealing with the true Suye'ta, he would have to do as he was told. The worm had turned.

With the pot tucked inside his jacket he made his way back toward the main cavern. The flashlight died before he got there. He had hoped it would get him back to the entrance, but even the darkness didn't dampen his confidence. The powers that had brought him this far would get him out of the cave. He still had a book of matches in his pack to use when he needed to get his bearings. He was confident that's all he would need.

He took measured paces in the dark, counting each step until he thought he had arrived in the main cavern that would lead him to the surface. The sound of the waterfall faded. He walked on in silence. So far, so good. All he had to do was keep going until he saw daylight. Once outside, he'd gather some pine pitch for torches, then come back and find the elder and convince him to turn over the duffle bag. His confidence grew by the moment.

Pain thudded up his arm when his outstretched hand met rock. He must have gotten turned around. No problem. It was a good time to use one of the matches in his pack. It would give him just enough light to get oriented, that's all he needed.

The brief flame flared, then died, leaving him shaken and confused. He struck another match. The cavern soared higher than the match's light could reach. The wall at his back was the only one he could see. Nothing looked familiar. He guessed he was in a chamber he hadn't been in before. It was much bigger than the one that led to the opening. Fear began to nibble at his confidence. He kept walking, carefully feeling his way.

After what felt like hours, wandering around with one hand to the wall, he had struck enough matches to determine he was in a dead-end cavern, like a big stone room with no way out but the way he came in.

He tried to retrace his steps, but now he couldn't even be sure he was going the same way. He struck another match, then another. Soon the paper matchbook from Phillips Café was empty. He dropped it on the floor and inched his way forward. The darkness was total now. Not a sound reached him except the pumping of his heart, his labored breathing and the hesitant tread of his own footsteps.

He had no idea how long it had been since he last heard the waterfall, and not once had he seen the light of day. For all he knew, night had fallen. He had lost all track of time. He strained his eyes in what he hoped was the direction of the entrance, looking for a hint of moonlight. He tried calling on the powers that had helped him find the hands but the Above Beings weren't listening. He began to doubt they even existed. As he stumbled in the darkness, an even greater fear worked its way into his mind. What if the Cherokee deities were real, and what if they were out to get him?

The craving for light gnawed at him like hunger but not a ray reached the depths of the cavern. Darkness had become a weight that crushed his spirit as he staggered into one dead end after another.

The floor began the upward slope that led to the outside, but by then, he didn't perceive it. He collapsed on the floor of the main cavern, too scared to go on. He babbled to himself, or to the great conjuror, or anyone who would listen, but he knew no one heard. Whether he lived or died was up to him. He had to get hold of his emotions or he was lost. Perhaps if he rested for awhile, he could calm down and think more clearly.

He sat on the cold stone, feeling the chill seep into his bones. Taking the pot from his jacket he cradled it in his lap. Darkness pressed against him, roaring in his ears like the voice of something alive. Something that caused him to whimper like a scared child and wonder if the cave was to be his tomb.

Tuesday

On Wolf Mountain

The fear John had tried to suppress all day surfaced with a vengeance when he heard Wren scream. He was the first to reach her. She stood, frozen to the spot, staring at something behind the rock. A red stain on the stone led his eyes to the girl lying sprawled like a broken doll on the rocks. Blood matted her dark hair around a crushing wound. Her eyes stared at the sky, dull and lifeless.

John picked up his daughter and pressed her face against his chest, murmuring something dumb, like, "It's okay, baby. It's okay." He couldn't take his eyes off the girl. The only two things he knew for sure at that moment was that nothing would ever be okay again and that the girl was dead.

He hung onto Wren, stroking her hair, trying to comfort her and wishing he had never brought her to this place. Why hadn't he called Faron like he wanted to? She would have come to David's and they would be home now, back on the Snowbird where his baby would be safe.

Walker and Yona checked the girl and saw there was nothing they could do for her. They came and stood beside John, looking helpless and saying the same sort of dumb things to Wren that he had already said.

David came out of nowhere and stopped long enough to see that Wren was safe. Walker showed him the girl. David knelt and gently pressed his fingers against her throat in a vain search for some sign of life.

"Thomas Smoker's daughter," David said. "Dead, but hardly even cold."

Yona made a visible effort to pull himself together and knelt at David's side. "She was here a while before she died, looks like. Probably bled to death." He stared at the blood, pooled in the hollows of the flat expanse of granite she lay on. It was just beginning to coagulate.

John looked over Wren's head at the girl's face. There was something familiar about her. With a sickening jolt of recognition, he remembered her. "That's the girl who was with Eagle Feather when he came to the station that time."

Nobody seemed to hear him. They were too stunned by what David had said. When it hit John that David had called her Thomas Smoker's daughter, he stammered, "Who did you say she was?" John had known the Smoker family all his life. Eli Smoker had been one of his best friends since they were boys. He would have known if Eli had a sister.

Walker was confused, too. "You're not making any sense, Dave," he said. "Eli is the only young'un Thomas has. If Grady Smoker had a granddaughter, I think I would know about it."

David stood up and turned away from the dead girl. "I'm sorry, guys," he said. "I should have said something before. I've seen her around with Eagle Feather. Buck found out who she was and told me yesterday. He's been trying to find Grady and see what he knows. Sorry I didn't mention it to you, Grandfather, but Buck thought we should keep it quiet. I'll tell you more later, but first things first. We've gotta report this and get Wren out of here." David went over to his backpack. He unzipped a side pocket, rummaged around and pulled out a cell phone.

Walker stopped him before he could finish dialing. "Whoa, David. You're gonna have people all over this mountain. What are they gonna find? Have you thought about that?"

"Doesn't matter, Grandfather. The most they could find is an empty cave."

Walker's shoulders drooped. There was a tone of sick finality in his voice. "So they found it? Whoever killed this girl, has got it all. It's over."

David spoke quickly. "No, Grandfather. The cave's been searched, and good. Somebody even dug holes in the floor, but they didn't look in the right place. We're safe." He finished dialing and looked toward the cave while he listened to it ring. "There are miles of cave in there, all the way to the heart of Wolf Mountain. You'd have to know exactly where to search to find what the Wayanettahs guard. Nobody has found it in the last three centuries. I don't think we have to worry about that."

John sat down on a rock, cradling Wren like she was still a baby. Walker leaned on his walking stick beside them. Wren wriggled free from her daddy's arms and reached over and patted her great grandpa's hand. "Don't worry, Grandpa Walker. He won't let anything happen. He's looking after everything."

Walker perked up. Wren had that effect on him. "You're right, honey. I never would have thought of bringing along a cell phone. Good thing David did."

"No, Grandpa. Not David. The conjuror will know what to do. He's the only one now. David doesn't know about everything. Some stuff has been forgotten by everybody, even you."

John heard what she said, and it scared him in ways he didn't understand. He didn't want her to talk about the conjuror anymore, but he had to find out what she knew. He asked as gently as he could, "And how would you know that, honey? If everybody forgot, even Mama Kate couldn't have told you. So who did?"

"He did, Daddy. Nobody else would listen to him."

John couldn't take anymore of this. Now his little girl was claiming to communicate with a man who had died centuries before she was born. Lord help him, he almost believed her. That scared him even more. "That's it, Walker," he said. "I don't want her involved in this. She's just a kid."

Walker ignored him and caught Wren's hand between his. "You've got to let her talk, son. She might be right. The rest of us are getting old. We thought we knew everything. We wouldn't listen to anything or anybody. Maybe it takes a child to pay attention to what he needs to say. A child would listen. We have to let her talk, John. It could be our only hope."

"It's true, Daddy," Wren said. "The conjuror needed to tell us stuff and nobody could hear him. I wasn't scared of him."

John knew when he was out-gunned. If Wren and Walker both thought Wren had some answers, he had to let her tell them. But he would be the one to control how far it went. He asked her, "What did the conjuror tell you, baby? And how did he talk to you? Have you seen him?"

"Thank you, Daddy." Her attitude showed she was more annoyed at his resistance than grateful. "I saw him, but only in dreams. He was a big snake at first, but then he was just a man. I thought he was Grandpa Driver cause he had just walked over, and the conjuror looks a lot like him, but he told me his name."

"His name was Kanegwa'ti?"

She talked so fast John couldn't interrupt. "Uh huh, Daddy. And he said Grandpa Driver gave David something important. You have to have it to wake up the Ulunsu'ti. The conjuror doesn't want the Ulunsu'ti to wake up. He's really scared of that."

John was shaking. He looked into his little girl's innocent dark eyes and realized he couldn't even imagine what was going on behind them. He didn't want to hear anymore. Even Walker had heard enough.

David stuffed the phone into his backpack and zipped it closed. He turned to John, "I have to wait here, but y'all need to take Wren home. I'm gonna show you a way that will get you to a logging trail about an hour and a half away. I called my Aunt Marge and she's gonna pick you up and take you to my house. Stay there, and don't talk to anybody till I get home."

Walker crossed his arms over his chest and kept his seat when the others got ready to leave. "Dave," he said. "I don't like to argue with you, son, but I don't feel like I should leave."

"We could be stuck here awhile," David said. "And there's no way off this mountain that doesn't include a lot of walking. It's gonna be pitch dark before we head down."

"Yeah, I know," Walker remained seated on the boulder. It didn't look like he was going anywhere.

"On your feet, Old Man," John said. "Faron and Kate will both skin me alive if I leave you here. Don't get stubborn on me."

Walker still didn't move. "I reckon they would tell you that the most important thing is to get Wren off this mountain and safely back on the Snowbird. Besides, boy, I've made up my mind and you can't change it for me."

John appealed to David, who just shrugged and said, "Don't waste your time, Johnny. You know better than I do how stubborn he is. I'll look after him. Just get Wren out of here before dark."

Yona made a stab at persuading Walker to come along. He didn't relish the idea of facing Faron and Kate and telling them he'd left his grandpa on Wolf Mountain with a dead girl. Walker held his ground and told them they better get started if they wanted to make it down the mountain while they could see the way.

"Well, we tried, John," Yona said.

John gave up on persuading Walker to go. He nodded toward the duffle bag, "You want me to take this with me?"

He was relieved when David said, "Just leave it here. Me and Walker will take care of it."

David walked with them around the boulders. Pointing out landmarks, he gave them directions for the quickest way down to the place where they were to meet his Aunt Marge.

"Now get going," David said. "Or else you'll be trying to find your way out of here in the dark."

Wren was tired and scared. John was mad as hell that she had been subjected to such a nightmare. It was his fault. If he had called Faron when he had the chance, they wouldn't be in this mess. He offered to carry her down the mountain, but she shook her head. Taking her bearings from the landmarks David had described, she set out in the lead toward the logging trail. His daughter was made of tougher stuff than he was. His stomach was still in a knot from the sight of Thomas Smoker's dead daughter, but it seemed Wren had put it aside to focus on getting home.

There was no discernable path, but as long as they watched for David's landmarks and stayed lined up with a rock formation he'd pointed out, jutting from a peak in the distance, they knew they were going in the right direction. After nearly two hours of walking with no rest stops, they saw the logging trail below. Aunt Marge Wayanettah's Jeep Wrangler was there waiting.

John greeted Aunt Marge and thanked her for coming to get them. He lifted Wren into the back seat and was about to climb in with her when something caught his eye. In the stand of hemlocks a few feet away, the setting sun sent a shiny reflection shimmering through the dark branches.

"Hang on just a minute, Aunt Marge," he said. "I think there's a car over there."

Yona followed him. For once, Wren was content to stay where she was. She had seen enough for one day.

The hemlock trees provided good camouflage for the dark green Mitsubishi Montero. If the reflection off the rear window hadn't given it away, they wouldn't have seen it.

Yona pulled the branches aside and looked the vehicle over. He knew who it belonged to. "Wonder if Mr. Eagle Feather was making an attempt to hide this thing or just trying to drive as far as possible," he said.

"Well, he couldn't get it much farther than this, even if it does have four-wheel drive," John said. "Must have been trying to keep it out of sight. Don't know why, though. Not likely anybody else would come around here."

They didn't notice that Marge had followed until she spoke. "I don't know who this thing belongs to or why he hid it, but from what David told me we'd better go call Nathan Axe and tell him about it. This is the sheriff's business."

John and Yona agreed. They all got into the Jeep and Marge headed toward her house, and the nearest telephone. Only David had thought to bring along a cell phone. Half the time cell phones didn't work in the mountains anyway, unless you had one of those fancy satellite phones like David's.

They got to Marge's house a lot quicker than expected. Apparently, Marge wasn't afraid to drive at top speed on the narrow road. The Wrangler was airborne a good part of the time, launched by the boulders and runnels left by a bad winter.

She wheeled up her driveway and left the motor running while she ran inside to make the call. She was only gone a couple of minutes and her face was set in an annoyed scowl when she came back. "Nathan wasn't in," she snapped. "They said at the sheriff's office that we should wait till one of them gets here. We're supposed to keep an eye out to see if anybody comes around, or drives off in the Montero." She shifted into reverse and backed out to the road and drove back toward the hemlocks and the hidden Montero.

John hugged Wren close and held on for dear life. His butt was already bruised and battered from the trip to Marge's house. The combination of hard seats with skimpy padding and a high-speed ride over what barely passed for a road, made for a punishing journey.

They bounced along the rutted road for the five miles back to the hemlock trees, None of them were in the mood for conversation least of all Marge Wayanettah. She parked behind the Montero and they sat in the Wrangler without a word, waiting for somebody from the sheriff's office to arrive.

John held onto Wren, just in case she might get bored and want to go explore again. If there was anything else to find, he didn't want her to be the one who discovered it.

Their wait was mercifully short. Within twenty minutes, Sheriff's Axe's deputy, Jimmy Hanks drove up. John and Yona got out of the Wrangler and pointed him to the Montero. They were telling him how they found the car when Marge gave an impatient beep on the horn. She glowered at them from where she sat hunched over the steering wheel. John didn't blame her for wanting to be done with this whole mess and get back to her peace and quiet. Apparently, Jimmy didn't either. He apologized for keeping her waiting and told John the sheriff would want to talk to him and Yona later.

John and Yona got in the car. "Let's go, Aunt Marge," John said anxiously.

Marge spun the Wrangler around and tore off down the road, adding a few more bruises to John's butt. It didn't seem to bother Marge and Yona. Either the front seats had more padding, or Marge and Yona supplied their own. Marge came close to matching Yona's weight and most of it was in her backside.

At David's house, Marge didn't drive across the bridge. She dropped them off at the roadside and was gone before they could thank her.

Wren was so tired John would have let her go to sleep on David's sofa if he hadn't been concerned about her nutrition. The peanut butter and jelly sandwich she had for lunch must have worn off long ago. When she went to the kitchen, he figured she was looking for food. He was wrong.

"I've gotta talk to my mama," she said. Perching on a stool at the counter, she reached for the phone and punched in the number. Her brave front disappeared the moment Faron answered. She cried quietly as she told what had happened. "I was so scared, Mama. She was hurt so bad, and we couldn't do anything." She dried her eyes with a paper napkin and listened. "Mama, I can't come home yet. David said we should stay here till he comes. We have to tell the law people about the girl. I don't want to, Mama. Can you and Mama Kate come? I'm really scared."

John listened to Wren's end of the conversation while he made her a bologna and cheese sandwich. He wanted to cry, too. She was fairly calm as she hung up the phone and climbed down from the stool. "Mama and Mama Kate will be here as soon as they can," she said. "What have we got to eat?"

John put the sandwich on a plate and gave it to her. She found a bag of Doritos in the pantry, and, ignoring the glass of milk Yona poured her, grabbed a Coke from the fridge and went straight to David's easy chair in front of the TV.

John followed, watching as she settled her food on a hassock. She found the remote control, turned on the television, then clicked through channels, stopping on one of her favorite shows. This was good. It was the episode where Bart falls in love with Reverend Lovejoy's daughter. He'd watched this Simpsons' rerun with her more times than he could count. Now, she could enjoy her dinner.

When he came back to check on her, The Simpsons' episode was half over and the sandwich barely touched. Wren was too tired to finish either of them. John put a blanket over her to let her sleep until her mama came.

THE CAVE

Walker watched John walk away with Wren and felt easier, knowing his great granddaughter would be safe. This whole thing had gotten out of hand. He needed Driver and Grady, but Driver had walked over and he couldn't find Grady. He had an nervous feeling at the pit of his stomach every time he thought about his old friend.

There was a time when he would have had a choice of elder Snake Dancers to call on, but most had walked over, leaving grandsons to take their place when they had them. He knew of two elders who had nobody to take over for them. Fortunately, they weren't guardians. He wondered if the day would come when the Snake Dancers would all die out and be forgotten. When even the guardians would be gone.

Driver Wayanettah had been the oldest one in the Circle and the Principal Snake Dancer. When he walked over, the job fell to Walker. The responsibility weighed heavy on him, even before things started falling apart. Now, he needed help, and all he had was a young dancer just brought into the Circle. He was glad it was David. Driver had believed in educating grandsons early and was proud of the way David took to it. Walker hoped David had learned enough to help deal with the fix they were in because the two of them had to talk about things they weren't supposed to tell a living soul. He had to trust David, and if David returned that trust, they might stand a chance.

It was hard to ask a Snake Dancer to break the rules, but he had no choice. "Son," he said, "You and me, we're in a mess I don't think any Snake Dancer's ever been in before. We've both got information we're not supposed to have. That's a burden I don't like, but we're gonna have to carry it."

David agreed so fast Walker suspected he had been wanting the chance to talk. "Driver said things were gonna be a lot different for me than they had been for any of the other guardians. Said I'd have to learn to adapt. Me and all my generation. I guess this is where it starts."

"Yeah, we talked about that, too, him and me," Walker kept his eyes on a straight pine tree at the edge of the cliff. "We talked about how it would be hard to keep people away from places they don't belong. There's just too many people. They've built a subdivision just a mile away from one of the last places where the Nunne'hi still live. That boy Eagle Feather set up a camp on the edge of a site that's more important than he can imagine." His voice dropped to a whisper, like it hurt to say it out loud. "The Nunne'hi are leaving. Driver knew it. Once they're gone, we're not far behind."

David echoed Walker's pain. "I know, Grandfather. I know." He hesitated. "Driver told me to trust you . . . but not anybody else. Not another Snake Dancer. Not even the other guardians."

Walker's eyes never left the pine tree. "He hinted something to me, son. I think he knew things he didn't want to say."

David sat silent for a moment. Walker gave him time to think things over.

David stood, paced, then came back to his seat. He'd made up his mind. "Grandpa Driver trusted you, and he said I should talk to you when the time came. He said I'd know when." He opened the duffle bag and pulled out one of the gym bags. "This the one with his bones?"

Walker nodded and said the Cherokee word for "yes," which sounded like a grunt.

"Why would somebody want this old skeleton?" David asked.

For a moment, Walker thought he might have overestimated

how much David knew. "Dave, you know how it goes. The Ulunsu'ti can only be awakened in the conjuror's hand. I figured we were thinking the same thing. That they dug him up to use his hand."

David lifted out the bundle of old bones and folded back the edges of the towel to expose them. He used a corner of the towel to sort out what had once been Kanagwa'ti's lower left arm, then the right. "Take a good look, Grandfather," he said.

Walker bent over the bones. He saw what David wanted him to see. His chest tightened, it was hard to breathe. When he finally got his voice, he said, "Gone. They kept his hands." He looked closer. "Cut off. You can see the marks on the wrist bones. Cut off before the bones dried out. Who did this, David?"

David's answer shocked him more than the sight of the severed wrist bones.

"He cut off the left one himself just before he died. Wanted to be sure it would get done. That's the one the Ulunsu'ti has to be held in for it to work. His son, the one he left the guardianship of his hand to, cut off the other one just to be sure, then he preserved both of them. Only he and those of us who inherited the guardianship after him, knew about this, until now. You're the first one outside our family to hear this part of the story."

Walker couldn't speak. This brought everything he had ever believed into question. From the time old Tsali Copperhead turned his guardianship over, he had thought the hands lay in the grave with the conjuror. That's one of the reasons the Copperheads had guarded the grave with such dedication. Not once had he ever suspected that the hands were not there with the rest of Kanagwa'ti's remains. Nothing Tsali taught him had prepared him for this. He gripped the head of his walking stick and leaned his head on his hands for a moment until he reigned in his emotions. When he spoke, his voice sounded so calm one would never know how this new information had rocked him.

"That's what Driver looked after—Kanagwa'ti's hands? I

figured he guarded the Ulunsu'ti."

"He thought you had it, till just a few months ago," Dave said. "When he found out who really had it."

"He knew who watched the Ulunsu'ti?"

"Yep. And he told me. He said I should tell you. When the time came."

Another surprise. Walker stared David in the eyes, the way it was impolite to do without good reason. "Has the time come, David?"

David didn't look away. "Yeah, Grandfather. For the first time, there will be at least three of us that know who holds it, and you and I know where the other keys are. Scary, huh?"

Walker turned his gaze back to the pine tree, took a deep breath and exhaled with a sigh. "I've been scared shitless since Monday night, son. When I saw the ark, and the conjuror's bones and grave goods right there within half a mile of Degal'gun'yi."

"I've got a feeling it's gonna get worse, Grandfather. When they start killing off a Snake Dancer's family, that's a bad sign. Especially this dancer."

A commotion on the rocks where the girl's body lay got their attention. A couple of crows were getting too close. Walker picked up a pebble chucked it at the crows. They scattered momentarily.

"Grady? He guards the Ulunsu'ti?"

"That's what Driver said."

"And you watch the hands?"

David answered yes in Cherokee. "Were you the bones or the medicine or the ark?"

Walker tossed another pebble at the crows. "I watched his grave. His bones and medicine were both in it. I always thought the hands were, too."

David nodded. "I figure Buck Locust for the ark."

"Good man, Buck. We're lucky to have you and him in the Circle. He's covering for Johnny to be off as long as he needs too. Said he'd check on that die-back over at Degal' gun'yi himself."

"Grandfather," David tossed a rock at the more persistent crow. "Do you think it's time for Suye'ta?"

Walker felt sheepish, like a dark secret he'd tried to hide had been discovered. "I reckon if some damn fool managed to wake Ulunsu'ti, we'd sure need a hell of a lot more than we've got."

"They say only Suye'ta can wake it," David said.

Walker stirred the pebbles around with his walking stick and found a good big one. The crow squawked and backed off when he scored a fair hit. "They say only Suye'ta can control it, but the truth is that anybody with the keys, and with enough knowledge and stupidity to try can wake it up. If that happens, only Suye'ta can keep the shit from hitting the fan. I figure we'd be better off if we called out a Suye'ta of our own. Somebody we could guide along."

They stopped talking and watched the crows, who had been joined by a couple of relatives.

After a few minutes David said. "If Faron knew what you had in mind for her husband, she'd kick your ass all the way back to Graham County."

Walker tried to grin, and almost made it. "Why do you think I'm so scared, boy?"

David laughed. "Yeah, what's some unleashed demon compared to the wrath of a Cherokee woman?"

The laughter died before it began. Only the squawking of the crows broke the grim silence as the sun sank lower behind Thunderhead. Walker threw a handful of pebbles at the flock that had gathered, but it didn't even faze them. David stood to pick up some bigger rocks. He was getting good at this since he stopped aiming to intimidate and started going for blood.

One by one the crows retreated to the big pine tree to quarrel among themselves.

David tossed the last stone he had and turned back to Walker. "Axe will be here in an hour or so. We need to decide what to do with the conjuror's bones and the rest of the stuff.

Any suggestions?"

Walker threw a couple more rocks to make sure the crows wouldn't return. "The bones and medicine have to go back to Ataga'hi. We don't have a choice there. They have to rest in the conjuror's grave until the Suye'ta comes. As for the ark, I guess we have to talk to Buck about that. But you're right, Dave. We've got to do something. We can't keep toting it around in an old duffle bag."

"How much of a hike is it to Ataga'hi, Grandfather?"

"About an hour more than it took us to get here. I don't know about you, but I don't think I'm up to it tonight."

Dave walked over and picked up the duffle bag. "Come on, Grandfather. We're gonna stash this where it won't be found unless somebody blows up this whole damn mountain. We can take it where it belongs later."

Walker used his walking stick to pull himself slowly to his feet. "If you got that good a hiding place, I guess you're right. I won't feel easy till he's back where he told us to keep him, but we gotta do something, and I can't think of anything better. Lead on, boy."

David led him through the scrub and rocks. The ground and foliage was undisturbed, like nobody had ever set foot there before. Walker hoped they were too high up on the mountain for snakes, because this was a perfect habitat for rattlers. He hummed the song that was supposed to let them know he was a friend, just in case, as he followed the younger man through the sparse brush, the only sign of life, other than the crows.

He wasn't sure what to expect when David climbed up to an overhang and disappeared under it. Walker followed and saw that the boulders concealed the mouth of a cave. It was so well hidden he could have stood six feet away without seeing it. David motioned him to come on in. Walker tried not to think of how much he hated places like this. David pulled a flashlight from his backpack and shined it ahead into the darkness.

After a few steps, the cave curved inward to the heart of the mountain and began a gradual downward slope. Walker stayed close on David's heels, trying not to think of how dark and damp the place was, and how much he disliked the whole idea of caves. The deeper they went, the less he liked it. A breeze touched him, light as a feather. Walker thought of it as the cold damp breath of the mountain. It must be coming from the water he heard somewhere in the distance.

When he complained that they must have been in there an hour, David told him it had only been about half that long. He had to shout to be heard over the roar of the waterfall. David swung the flashlight around and even Walker had to admit it was worth a walk underground to see the way the light sparkled off the clear water cascading over the walls of the cave and splashing into a deep crystal clear pond. They couldn't see where it went after that. It looked like the pool was the end of it, but when Walker listened carefully he could hear echoes of another waterfall far below.

"Lightning Creek," David said. "This is where it starts."

Walker stretched like his back hurt from the weight of the mountain over him. "I hope it ain't far to where we're going, boy, cause I'm not one for being underground any longer than I have to."

David didn't say anything. Walker kept quiet and let him think. Finally, he turned around. "Grandfather. I've got a real important question. Kanagwa'ti's hands are not far from here. Driver told me the conjuror had his hands kept apart from the rest of him so he could stick around to keep an eye on things. That if his hands and body are united, he's free to go on to the above world. If we get them too close to the rest of him, does that mean he's free to walk over if he wants to, or that he has to go whether he wants to or not? Or is the whole thing a load of bullshit?"

"Son, we've always believed Kanegwa'ti haunted Lightning Creek. Remember a few years back when that bunch of great white hunters from Atlanta came up here to kill them a wild boar. They were diving in the pond down the mountain, the headwaters of Lightning Creek. One of them died from snake bite. The other three swore the biggest cottonmouth water moccasin they'd ever seen, got him. Folks didn't pay any attention to them, cause no cottonmouth could live this far north. I wondered about that."

David got the duffle bag from where he had laid it on an outcropping of rock. "Weird shit, huh? But being who we are, I guess we gotta believe. It's probably best that we don't get the rest of him any closer to his hands than we have to. We might need us a skin changer's ghost before this is over." He doubled back to another almost invisible passage and was gone a few minutes.

"It will all be safe there for the time being," he said when he reappeared. "If you want to go see where it is, just duck down that way. It's in a niche in there."

"I'm ready to get out of here, if you don't mind," Walker was already heading for the entrance. "This place puckers my ass." He needed to see the light of day again. Underground darkness was an almost tangible thing.

David laughed. "Aren't you supposed to be the head Snake Dancer now, Grandfather? I didn't think us conjurors, especially you elder guardians, were supposed to be afraid of anything."

"With what we know, son, we ought to be too scared to function most of the time. Who's got a better reason to be afraid than us?"

"You got a point there, Grandfather."

The light was fading when they emerged under the overhang at the mouth of the cave. They heard voices and listened long enough to identify them. Somebody had bashed in that poor girl's head, and if her murderer was back, they didn't want to run into him. They didn't have to worry. Sheriff Nathan Axe had arrived. They dreaded having to talk to anybody with all the secrets they had to keep but it helped that it was Nathan. He was one of their own.

They told Axe what they had to, which wasn't nearly as much as he wanted to know. The sheriff didn't look too happy when David suggested that Walker needed to get started home. After all, he was old and tired, and faced a long hike back to the Blazer. Walker obliged by acting as old and tired as he could until they were out of sight, then set a sprightly pace for David to follow. The walk down went fast.

Tuesday
Back In The Cave

The elder fought the spark of will that stirred him awake but it was a losing battle. Consciousness returned with a sharp stab of pain that began in his head and worked its way down his body. He tried to stand but that only made it worse. The taste of old blood brought back the memory of the big white man's fist. He staggered and fell against cold stone.

Physical pain was nothing compared to the despair that engulfed him, weighing heavier than the utter darkness of the cave. How long had he been there? An hour or a day? He had no way of knowing and didn't want to care. He longed to lie back down on the cold granite floor and wait for his spirit to ebb away, but something in him kept fighting, struggling to clear the fog from his mind. He had to think. Something had happened that he needed to remember. It hung over him like the darkness.

An image of a sweet young girl flashed across his mind. She had trusted him. Now she was dead. The agony of the memory left him breathless. He slumped back down on the floor. Dying would be the easy way out, but another recollection teased at his mind. Something even harder to face than recalling how he had killed an innocent girl who had stood by him till the end.

He struggled back to his feet. He had to find a way out of the cave. His people would be lost if he didn't, and it would be his fault. He'd set into motion a chain of events that no one could stop but him. Somehow, he had to change it. Then he would be free to die.

He faded again and fought his way back from the fog. In the

distance, the roar of the waterfall helped him get his bearings. If he walked away from the water, and not into one of the caverns that meandered off the main cave, he would find the entrance.

His mind cleared as he stumbled in the dark. He even began to form a plan. The duffle bag was safe, miles away under the hickory tree. He would leave it there for now. Walker Copperhead would take care of it when he knew where to find it. He would call Walker after he turned the Ulunsu'ti over to his grandson and made him the new guardian. When he filled him in on things only he could teach him, Walker could do the rest. And he might do a better job.

He leaned against the wall, massaging a cramp that seized his leg. He heard footsteps. Was it the white man? He flattened his back against the cave wall and trusted the darkness to hide him. He couldn't survive another beating, and he needed to stay alive a few more days.

The sound of the footsteps came closer. If it was the white man, he had brought help. He could hear two sets of footsteps heading straight for him. He held his breath and pressed harder against the cold wall.

Just before their light reached him, the footsteps stopped. Familiar voices echoed in the cave. He didn't move a muscle or make a sound. The cramp in his calf made it hard to be still but he toughed it out and listened. These were men he could trust. He toyed with the idea of going to them and asking for help but there were too many reasons not to. Yet, it was comforting to hear them talk. It helped him focus his mind and made him feel less alone. And he needed to hear what they were saying.

In the glow of a flashlight, he could see what they carried. How could that be? The duffle bag was supposed to be under an old hickory log near Degal'gun'yi. He stifled the urge to rush out and claim it. Then he heard what they were saying.

He didn't have to worry about the duffle bag and all the relics it held. It was already where it belonged, with men who took their duty as seriously as he once had. The only thing he needed to retrieve from it was the ark. He had to take it back to the Locust's hiding place. Then, he would perform his last obligation as a guardian. He wouldn't be free of his sworn duty to the Ulunsu'ti until he turned it over to his grandson and revealed to him the secrets that a guardian had to know.

Before he could restore the ark to its rightful owner, or turn over the Ulunsu'ti to his grandson, he had a more urgent problem. Somewhere in this cave, the white man was waiting, and he knew enough to destroy them all.

He watched the two men, David and Walker. When David took the duffle bag he followed him, staying in the shadows and taking careful note of where he went. He watched him stash it in a niche back near the waterfall. Everything in it but the ark belonged with them. That was the property of Buck Locust.

He followed David and Walker to the mouth of the cave, staying close enough to keep their light in view. Outside, he could hear them talking to someone. He crept close enough to see Nathan Axe kneeling on the rock beside the girl. He prayed that Nathan would say she was still alive, that they needed to take her down the mountain for help. Instead, his worst fear was confirmed. The girl was dead. Thomas would never get to meet his daughter.

A wave of anguish came too swiftly to suppress. He couldn't live with it much longer. The pain was too much to endure. He had to find the strength to bear it until he repaired the damage he had done and earned the right to end his misery.

Nathan Axe's voice echoed in the recesses of the cave as he cursed the soul of the monster who could do a thing like that to a poor little girl. The sheriff's words hit him harder than the white man's fist, their impact a blow that sent his spirit reeling into the void between the world of the living and the land of the dead. He felt nothing now. His senses dulled. He was aware of the pain, but it lacked the tormenting sharpness that made it unbearable.

He was no more than a shadow, creeping now, steeling

behind boulders and scrub laurel away from the cave and down the slope. One last look back at the girl's body, one quick prayer for her forgiveness, then on to the bottom of the mountain to the hemlocks where the Pinto waited. It offered sanctuary scented with gas fumes, age and the lonely odor of fast food eaten on the run.

His strength was gone. Labored breath burned in his lungs. A sharp pain knifed through his chest and settled into a crushing ache under his ribs. Fighting for enough of a grip on his soul to make him care, he willed himself to bear it long enough to set things right.

Weakness lowered his guard, allowing images to drift across his vision. The axe as it flew toward its mark, the moment of impact. Her eyes as their light faded and died.

Nathan's curse was no more than he deserved. Death was too good for a man who had done what he had. He wouldn't fight it. When his spirit drifted free of his body, to wander within that gray emptiness beyond this world, he let it go.

In an old yellow Pinto under a hemlock tree, an aged body slumped over the steering wheel. From a gray place between the worlds, the spirit it had housed more than eighty years, watched, taking on the anguish that would have rendered the old form useless and willing strength into the empty shell.

The elder sat up behind the wheel of the Pinto. The guilt and grief lifted, leaving his mind clear. Everybody on Lightning Creek Road or Big Cove knew him and his car. They would be looking for him by now and he couldn't afford to be seen. He had time to wait under the hemlocks and rest. Later, when folks were in bed, the Pinto would be just the rattle of another old car in the night. Possibly some kid coming home from a date.

It was dark when he turned the key in the ignition. The familiar grinding of the starter almost brought him out of his trance, but he willed the numbness back and tried the starter again. When the Pinto sputtered into action he shifted into reverse and backed out of the shelter of the hemlocks.

A few miles down the creek, he turned off the headlights

and parked just before the bridge to the Wayanettah place. A soft pool of light from the porch illuminated a black Chevy Blazer in the yard. A lamp burned in the living room window. He knew that room well, but there would be no comfort there for him tonight.

He continued on toward his home in the woods. Again, consciousness threatened to return when he found himself remembering Lena, wishing she had been there to keep him straight, regretting that he had ever left his trailer that morning.

He was surprised that the knapsack was still around his shoulder. He slid it off and left it lying on the threadbare seat. He would need it later to carry the crystal he had hidden in the niche inside his well.

He hurried past the houses along Lightning Creek, hoping no one saw him, trying not to think of the times he'd sat in those rooms sharing coffee and talk.

He was a dead man now, with no place among his people. The only thing animating his body was the determination to right the wrongs he'd done them.

There was one thing he could never undo, but the memory of that was so far away it had no power to hurt him. The image of the girl passed so briefly through his mind he barely perceived it.

He drove slowly through the town of Cherokee. All the shops were closed, the streets dark and deserted. Neon lights cast an eerie half-light that only accentuated the darkness. An occasional vehicle went by, its occupants in such a hurry to get home they paid no attention to the faded yellow car. Would they have wondered why he wasn't home in bed like he usually was at this time of night?

He drove on, barely aware of the road. With the exception of the time he was away during the war, he'd never lived anywhere else. If need be, he could have made this trip in his sleep, which was a lot like what he was doing. His mind was occupied, working out what he had to do, and his spirit was so far away it wasn't even part of him.

He could sense that dreaded place of wandering lost souls. He was halfway there already and had to fight the desire to give in to its pull. The despair of the below worlds held less fear for him than the life he had to endure long enough to set things right.

The days when he could face his people with an open heart, free of shame were over. Now he slunk home like a fugitive, afraid to be seen by people who had been close as family.

He left the neon lights and souvenir shops behind. When he came to the highway, he drove into oncoming traffic without a glance. The angry shouts and blaring car horns barely pierced his awareness. Nothing mattered but keeping his wits about him long enough to finish this last obligation to his people.

First, the white man had to die. It was the only way to keep him from doing anymore harm. With a stir of anticipation, he made the decision and plotted how to do it. Even if there had been another way, he'd still want to kill him. The girl's death was an accident. This would be cold blooded murder, something he never thought himself capable of. Now, he relished the thought. There were some people the world would be better off without. The white man had deceived him, had played him like a trout on a hook, and taken away everything that mattered. He needed killing.

He almost missed the turn into his drive. The tires squealed when he stomped on the brake. Anticipation of what he was going to do had taken his mind off driving. It drew him closer to the darkness that hovered so close. How easy it would be to let go and slip away. The gray world lurked at the edge of his mind, promising oblivion and peace. In the emptiness he would be free from it all.

The headlights caught the beech tree in their beams. He barely remembered the drive home. Parking under the ancient tree he sat in silence for a moment, recollecting, and saying farewell. He wouldn't be back this way again.

The plot of land he brought Lena to on their wedding day had made a good home for them. Thomas could tear down the old house now, like he had wanted to for a year or more. Nobody would have any use for it when he was gone. Thomas or his boy would probably want to build on the land. Eli had always loved the place. Memory tugged at his spirit but he resisted. He couldn't let anything make him feel. Not now.

The night was wearing on and he had work to do. He wiped his eyes with an old red bandana and got out of the car, then reached back for the knapsack. He'd need it to hold the Ulunsu'ti. And some ammunition.

DAVID WAYANETTAH'S HOUSE

John and Yona both went to the door as soon as they heard Faron's Chevy drive onto the bridge. It had been less than an hour since Wren called her. Sheriff Nathan Axe's car wasn't far behind. Kate waited to walk in with the sheriff, greeting him warmly with a lingering hug. John could see him blush from the door.

Faron was in a hurry to see about Wren. John held the door open for her and led her to their daughter, curled up in David's easy chair sound asleep. Faron didn't wake her, just went over to get a closer look to make sure she was comfortable, then she went back out on the porch with John.

"How did she take it," she asked him, "seeing that poor girl like that?"

"Not so good at first. She was shaking like a leaf when I picked her up, but she calmed down and handled it as well as the rest of us."

"Probably a little better than some of us," Yona said. "Made me sick as a dog to think somebody would hurt a girl that way and just leave her there alone to die."

"Oh, John, I just hate it that Wren had to see something so awful." Faron pressed her forehead against a porch post. "Mama Kate still insists we had to let her go with you, but I don't know."

John put his arms around her and held her close, for his own comfort as much as hers. "Honey, I don't know what's going on. Somebody murdered that girl. At first I thought she might have fallen, but she didn't get hurt like that from a fall. And what was she doing way up there anyway? We should never have let our baby go there today, no matter what she thinks her dreams said. Hell, I don't want to be out there anymore myself."

Sheriff Axe and Kate stopped at the top of the steps. "He's right, Faron," Kate said. "Nathan just told me. That poor girl was murdered. Hit in the head with one of those old stone war axes like they have at the museum. They found it in the rocks with blood all over it."

"Who did that to her, Sheriff?" Faron asked. "And where's my grandpa and David Wayanettah?"

John and Yona greeted the sheriff. Axe tipped his hat and turned to Faron. "Evening, Faron. Walker and David should be here soon. They claimed they told me everything they knew about the dead girl, then they took off down the mountain. Said they'd walk down to Yona's car and drive straight back here"

"Was Grandpa all right?"

"He looked tired, but he seemed to be in good shape to me," Axe said. "I got a feeling he and David had something to do they didn't want to tell me about. I'll let it go for now, but I'm gonna need to talk to them later. If I didn't know them both as well as I do, I'd wonder what they were up to."

John echoed Faron's question, "Any idea who killed the girl?"

"Maybe," Nathan said. "That big old SUV Marge called us about is registered to those Sacred Circle people. Back before they bought those mini-busses to haul their . . . *students* around in, they used that Montero. They were having meetings in the Holiday Inn on Highway 19 then. They'd drive the students off into the woods early in the morning and come back at night. Now they have those camps and a lot more people. I think Eagle Feather uses the Montero himself. Jimmy Hanks is checking it out."

John stroked Faron's hair. It was soothing to both of them. "Nathan," he said. "I've seen that girl before. She came to the station one time with that Sacred Circle man,"

Faron stepped out of John's embrace and turned to Kate. "Mama, is she the same girl you saw with him in town that day? Remember, we wondered who she was."

"You know, I bet she is the same one." Kate said.

"You saw the dead girl, with Eagle Feather?" Nathan asked.

"It must have been her," Kate said. "I tried to talk to her but Mr. Sacred Circle rushed her off before I could find out anything. I think she's Cherokee though. Just not from around here. She was as pretty as could be, just like a little doll."

She had Nathan's full attention now. "Real young?" he asked. "Say around eighteen or nineteen? Small frame?"

Kate nodded. "And I doubt she was more than five-feet-two. Tiny thing, and quiet as a mouse. I don't think she said a word."

"Sounds like the same girl," Nathan said. "I'm not sure how Buck Locust found out who she was, but if there's anything going on anywhere in our community, Buck's gonna know it. He called me a couple of days ago and wanted to talk about her. The weirdest thing is, he said she belonged to Grady Smoker's son, Thomas. Says he got worried when he saw a young girl with that weirdo and started checking on her. Buck ain't gonna let some flake take advantage of one of our kids if he can help it."

"I don't see how she could be Thomas' daughter," Kate said. "I've known Grady Smoker and his whole family all my life and I would know it if he had a granddaughter. Thomas is a real horse's butt, but he's the only child Grady and Lena had. Thomas and his stuck-up wife didn't have any kids but Eli. You know how Grady dotes on Eli. He'd be unbearable if he had a granddaughter."

"I doubt Grady knew anything about her, Kate," Axe said. "Buck went over to Murphy yesterday and talked to Thomas. Seems like Eagle Feather told Buck who the girl was and he went to check it out. Grady's boy 'fessed up and said she could be his kid, because back when he worked construction down in Mississippi, he took up with a Choctaw woman. Lived with her for nearly a year, till the job was up, just coming back home to his wife on the weekends. When he finished the job, he came home and didn't go back anymore. Never knew she had his kid till Buck told him about her."

"I always said that boy of Grady's was a sorry no-account dog. Now I know he's worse than that." Kate wasn't one to hold back her opinions.

"Buck never has trusted Eagle Feather," the sheriff said. "He was afraid he would get to Grady and try to use the girl against him somehow. He went to Grady's house last night to talk to him about her, but nobody was home. Didn't see any sign of his car or anything. I sure wish Buck had found him. If only he'd had a chance to meet his granddaughter before—"

The sheriff took off his hat and ran his hand through his hair. "I should have done something. Maybe if we'd tried to get the girl away from that man, she might still be alive."

Sliding her arm around Nathan's waist, Kate snuggled against him. "Don't feel bad, Nathan. You couldn't know this would happen."

John interrupted. "How do you reckon Eagle Feather met the girl?"

"He's got those camps down near the Choctaws," Nathan said. "He probably met up with the girl or her mother and they told him about Thomas. It's my guess he had his own reason for bringing her up here. I never trusted him any more than Buck Locust did, but he isn't doing anything illegal as far as we can figure. The girl was young, but she was legal age."

Kate rubbed Nathan's arm. He had some difficulty breathing for a minute. John rescued him, whether he wanted to be rescued or not, with the suggestion that they go inside for a cup of coffee. He didn't much like the look Kate gave him as Nathan disentangled himself.

"I could use a cup, John," Axe said. "And I need to use the phone to call Sheriff Dorsey over in Graham County. He was gonna send somebody to look for Eagle Feather and to check around and see if anybody has seen Grady. I'd like to know if they've had any luck."

Faron said, "I'd sure hate to be the one to tell Grady about that poor girl and the way she was killed. It's going to break his heart, especially since he never even had the chance to get to know her."

John had every intention of making the coffee himself, but Kate took over. The sheriff sat on a stool at the kitchen counter, talking on the phone and jotting notes on a pad he had pulled from his shirt pocket.

Kate worked quietly. It would appear she was being courteous, trying not to disturb Nathan. But John could see she was taking in every word of the conversation on his end. By the time the pot was perking on the stove, she had given up any pretense of not paying attention and stood across the counter from the sheriff, openly listening. Nathan didn't seem to notice.

"You talked to anybody that's seen him since Saturday?" he paused. "What about Buck Locust over on Snowbird? Anybody talked to him?"

Axe listened for a while, a worried frown forming on his forehead. "When did Amy call you?"

Yona and Faron got out cups and brought them to the table. John added a carton of milk and the sugar bowl. They heard the sheriff ask a few more questions then thank Dorsey for his help. He came to sit with them at the table to wait for the coffee to perk. "I don't like this a bit," he said, shaking his head. "People just aren't where they're supposed to be . . . where they always are. It just beats all."

"Who's not where they're supposed to be, Nathan?" Kate asked.

Axe turned to John. "You didn't go to the station today, did you?"

"I had some things to do with Walker," John said. "Buck gave me the day off and said he would handle the work I had lined up for today. He went up on the Cheoah to check on a die-back Eli saw from the tower. I was supposed to be up there all day but Buck took over."

The sheriff looked at John for a moment. John didn't like the suspicious expression on his face.

"Where on the Cheoah?"

"Over on the south side, way off the road."

"Were you anywhere near that Sacred Circle camp, John?"

"Maybe," John said. "I'm not sure just exactly where the Sacred Circle camp is, but I reckon it's in that general area. I think Eagle Feather would set up close to a road though. I doubt the folks who come to his camps are gonna want to hike in."

Nathan nodded thoughtfully. Nobody said anything. Kate brought the coffee pot over and filled the cups. Axe added liberal amounts of cream and sugar to his and took a long sip. After he'd savored the coffee for a moment he said, "I called Dorsey and told him about the Montero y'all found. He went out to Eagle Feather's place to talk to him, but he wasn't there. Nobody knows where he is. He didn't show up at the camp today and his pigeons are worried. He was supposed to teach them to make medicine or something. Dorsey said they were standing around with their hands full of crystals and dyed chicken feathers, looking like lost sheep."

"That's just pitiful," Kate said. "If he's gonna charge those poor people an arm and a leg and drag them up here to the mountains, he ought to at least show up and give them what they paid for. If he isn't the biggest charlatan in the state, he sure runs a close second."

John cleared his throat. "Well, Mama Kate. Like Walker said, they're just looking for some connection to Creator. If they can't get people who know something to teach them, like you for instance, then they have nobody to turn to but the charlatans. Ever think about that?"

Kate gave him a look that would freeze molten lava. It was what he expected. He knew she wouldn't acknowledge his comment, but before she could make a show of ignoring him, lights from the Blazer beamed in the living room window and they heard the engine shut off in the yard. It had to be Walker and David.

Kate and Faron ran to the door, anxious to reassure themselves that Walker was alright. Yona followed more slowly, but he couldn't hide the fact that he was as relieved as they were that his grandpa was safe.

John waited at the table. He didn't want to talk to Walker. Somehow, the old man had something to do with this, and it made him mad as hell. Even so, he was worried enough to take a good look at him to make sure he was in one piece. Walker looked fine, if a little tired and worried. But it was easy to see that he wasn't at all pleased to see Nathan Axe.

"Sheriff Axe," David said with a nod. "Glad to see you made yourself at home. Sit down and finish your coffee."

Axe waited where he stood while David hugged Kate and Faron and responded to their inquiries about the health of his various relatives and told them how Meredith was doing in medical school down in Georgia, then they all calmly trooped to the kitchen, except for Walker.

John followed him to the living room where he was bent over Wren, listening to her breathing. John softened toward the old man. Walker wouldn't ever do anything to hurt his little girl. He thought the world of his great grandchildren.

"She's okay, Grandpa," he said. "Just tired out."

Walker tucked the blanket around her shoulders. "I just want to know my grandbabies are all right. Where's Diamond?"

John realized he hadn't even asked about his son. He and Walker went to the kitchen and sat down to the coffee that was waiting for them. He sipped and asked Faron who was looking after Diamond.

"Bonnie Locust is watching him for us," she said. "She's real good with the kids for a girl who's just turned thirteen. And her mama's close by if she has any problems."

Nathan put his cup down. "Faron," he said. "Amy Locust isn't at home. She's in Dorsey's office right now. Buck was supposed to be home around five. When he didn't show up, Amy called the station to see if anybody had heard from him.

Nobody's seen or talked to him since he left the station early this morning. Eli Smoker and some of the men went up on Cheoah to look for him. Eli found his truck off up in the woods, but no sign of Buck. Amy's real worried."

Faron reached for her car keys on the counter top. "Honey," she said to John. "Go get Wren. We've gotta go home."

Kate started to object, but when she saw the look on Faron's face, she just gave her a quick hug and told her goodnight. "You drive carefully, honey," she said.

John asked Kate, "You want to ride home with Yona and Grandpa or come with us?"

"I'll stay and make us some supper while Walker rests for awhile. I think he could use a hot meal before we head for home," Kate said.

Faron rushed out the door without saying goodbye. John heard the car start before he could pick Wren up from the chair where she was still sleeping. She didn't stir as he carried her out. As soon as they were in the car, Faron backed across the bridge, wheeled around and took off for home. The people along Big Cove Road probably wondered who was in such an all-fired hurry when they heard her Chevy speeding toward the parkway.

John had never seen her like this. She knew as well as he that something was going on that she had no control over and she didn't like it a bit. From the way she was driving, John could tell she needed to get back to their house on the Snowbird quickly. He didn't try to slow her down. He was as anxious as she to get home.

Wren was wide awake now, secure in her seatbelt in the back seat. "Mama, it'll be okay," she said. "Mama Kate will take care of Grandpa and Uncle Yona."

"I know, baby," Faron said, in a tight controlled voice. She wouldn't rest easy till she knew they were all back where they belonged.

John understood that. Sanctuary. That's what they had found in their little corner of the world on Snowbird Creek. A place of refuge from the frightening things that happened to people beyond the protective circle of the Smokies. Out there young girls got murdered and old men went missing. Women had to worry about their husbands not making it home. But not in their house. Not on Snowbird, at least not until now.

Buck and Amy were like family. Now Buck was missing and a girl was dead. A young girl who was one of their own, and they didn't even know her.

John put a hand on Faron's thigh and felt it tremble. She was scared to death. Something bore down on them, getting closer and more threatening. He could feel it, too, and he had no idea what it was.

Faron never was one to cry much, but he could see unshed tears on her lashes. She held them back. She wouldn't want to scare him and Wren. He felt helpless in the face of her fear, but it was her stoicism that reduced him to complete impotence.

The knot in his belly tightened. He had been scared all day and his fear was growing by the minute. But that wasn't the worst part. Seeing Faron hurting and being unable to do anything to help was killing him. If she was the kind of woman who'd cry in his arms and let him hold her, it would have made him feel like he was taking care of her.

"You okay, honey?" John asked her.

"Sure, darlin." She smiled a tight smile and reached to squeeze his hand. Her hand was cold as ice. "No problem," she said.

DEGAL GUN'YI

Buck Locust hadn't told anybody the truth about where he was going Tuesday morning. He left a message for John McLeymore, saying he was going to check on the die-back before going to the station. That was partly true. He would be in the area Eli Smoker showed John from the tower, and while he was there he would take a look, but he had a more urgent reason for his pre-daylight trip to that isolated corner of tribal land. Well before sunrise, he was already driving along the Cheoah.

Ever since Walker Copperhead told him about the duffle bag, Buck had fought off the compulsion to go as fast as he could to a mound beyond the old burial ground. When Walker said that some unknown intruder had not only been there, but had robbed other places nobody was supposed to know about, his gut had twisted into a tight knot. He knew it wouldn't ease up until he saw for himself that no one had disturbed the site the Locust men had guarded for generations. As the hereditary guardian of the Cherokee Ark of the Covenant, it was his responsibility now. Walker wouldn't tell him what the duffle bag contained, but he had to be sure it wasn't the ark.

He eased into the well camouflaged turnoff as the first hint of daylight filtered through the leafy canopy. The road went a few miles into the forest but its condition made for a slow, rough ride.

The crushed weeds in the ruts and tire tracks in the damp earth didn't surprise him. John's Dodge Ram would have left their mark when he came to check on the die-back last night.

But when he reached the rise at the end of the road, a second set of tracks brought him up short. Buck parked his truck and got out to take a look. John's truck didn't leave this trail. It would have climbed the incline easily and not left torn up earth as evidence of spinning wheels. The second set of tracks were narrow, made by small tires, like on a compact car.

He bent over to examine them more closely. The tires that left these marks were so bald there was hardly enough tread to leave an imprint.

Of all the people he knew who drove compact cars, only one came to mind who would know about this place. That would explain why Grady Smoker wasn't at his trailer last night. But what would he be doing in these woods?

His unease refused to be suppressed any longer. Buck Locust was very, very worried. He had been in these woods alone so many times he could find his way in the dark, but this time something unfriendly permeated the shadows. He wished John was with him, but according to Walker, John had more important things to do. More important than coming to work. Besides, John couldn't go where he had to go. This was something even his best friends couldn't know about. It had to be his secret alone until he had a male heir to bring into the Circle.

Walker Copperhead needed John but wouldn't explain why. He just said some of the things the Snake Dancers guarded had been found hidden in a duffle bag and he needed John's help to set things right. Why John? The knot in Buck's gut twisted tighter. Fragments of conversations about Suye'ta and outsiders flashed through his mind.

He got the pick-axe and shovel out of the back of his truck and walked south through the trees. The old burial ground they called Degal'gun'yi, where the Ani'Kuta'Ni were buried, lay in that direction but he wouldn't be stopping there. He needed to go a couple of miles further, to a small mound even fewer people knew about. If his grandfather hadn't explained what lay under that mound, he would have thought it was just another hill, covered with pine trees and scrub brush.

The mound looked intact as Buck approached, no different from the way it had looked when Del Locust brought him here the first time. His grandfather had taken him to the far side of the mound and pointed out the stone that blocked the entrance to the hidden tunnel. That day, Del told him how the great conjuror had directed the first Snake Dancers to prepare the tunnel and shore it up with stout timbers, then entrusted the Locust men to guard it. That was all Buck was told then, except that it was a secret he must never reveal to a living soul.

Four years later, when he was eighteen, he learned the reason for the tunnel. It was the hiding place for the Cherokee ark, and his family had inherited the responsibility to keep it safe. When he learned the job would fall on his shoulders when Del Locust walked over, he didn't know whether to be proud or terrified.

Buck was honored that Del trusted him enough to bring him into the Circle at a younger age than usual for a guardian. It made his resolve even stronger never to let the ancestors or the Snake Dancers down as long as there was breath left in his body. He rounded the base of the mound, dreading what he might find on the other side. There was no path through the last stand of pines between him and the tunnel. He hurried past the trees and stood at the foot of the mound, near the spot where Del Locust had explained the role of a guardian. He looked up the slope and saw the worst thing imaginable.

The mouth of the tunnel he had guarded so carefully since his grandfather entrusted it to him was a gaping hole in the hillside. The great round stone that had sealed it lay among moss covered rocks at the foot of the mound.

There was a chance the ark was still safe. His ancestor had taken precautions against the possibility that someone would discover the tunnel. He sank down on the big stone with his head between his hands to wait for his trembling to subside and tried to bring his thoughts under control.

Del had told him there was a false wall at the end of the

tunnel. The ark was hidden behind it, sealed with earth and stone that gave the appearance of a dead-end. A collection of grave goods and the bones of a dead relative were left to explain the existence of the tunnel, in case an invader made it that far. He should have been the only one alive who knew that the big stone concealed an opening into the mound, but somehow, someone else knew about it. The extra precautions his elders had taken had seemed unnecessary when Del described them. The tunnel was well hidden and carefully guarded. The tribe owned the land and the Snake Dancers had always maintained enough power in the council to make sure it, and other sites, remained undisturbed.

Now, he was very grateful for the added precautions of the false wall and the burial. He uttered a desperate prayer that it had worked.

He examined the ground at the foot of the mound for clues to the identity of the interloper. His mind was already preoccupied with possibilities for a new hiding place for the ark.

Among the dried pine needles, a flash of red caught his eye. He picked up a sticky triangle of red wax. A quick sniff confirmed it to be the wax rind from a wedge of cheese. It didn't tell him who rolled the stone away, just that he had taken time for a picnic. It wasn't much, but it gave him something to go on. He looked at it for a moment then slipped it into his jacket pocket with his cell phone and pager.

A layer of leaves and pine needles covered the rocky soil, a poor surface for footprints. The only thing that looked out of place, other than the cheese rind, was a stout maple sapling. Its bark was skinned and scarred in such a way he knew it had been used to pry the stone away from the tunnel.

Buck removed his jacket and spread it over the stone that had been rolled away from the tunnel's mouth. He couldn't delay any longer. Taking up the pick-axe, he climbed the hill and strode into the darkness. If the ark was still there, as he prayed with every step that it would be, he couldn't leave it. He would need to devise a better hiding place.

He could see nothing until his eyes adjusted to the dark. The man-made cave was no more than four feet high, forcing him to inch forward in an awkward crouch that produced cramps in both his thighs. But he had to keep going and try to get it over with as quickly as possible. When all light was gone, he used the Mag-Lite on his keychain. Deep inside, he passed the ancient bones of a forgotten ancestor that lay undisturbed among pots and artifacts. A carved effigy stood in a niche on the wall. If the trespasser had been a pot hunter, it would have been gone. The pots were intact and undisturbed. The bones, blackened and crumbling, had not been touched.

On the walls he saw fresh marks in the earth between the ancient timbers that shored up the excavation. Someone had known to search for something more than the pots and bones. Beyond them, a pile of rocks and dirt littered the floor. Over that, high on the side, a jagged opening lined with mortared stone ran behind a massive log. He shined the light inside.

Empty.

The ark was gone.

Generations of his family had kept this place secure, and on his watch it was all over. His mind refused to accept that possibility. The ark had to be here. Somewhere behind the logs or beyond the niche they concealed, protected by yet another of the conjuror's clever deceptions, he would find it.

He swung the pick-axe as hard as he could in the cramped quarters, smashing through rotting timbers and mortar. His attack revealed nothing but the packed earth behind them. Splintered logs and broken mortar littered the floor.

He dropped the pick-axe and leaned against the wall. The bones of his ancestor crunched under his feet.

He couldn't give up. As long as he was alive, he was the guardian. The ark was his responsibility no matter where it was or who had taken it. It was his job to find the thief and retrieve it. He willed his mind to clear, taking deep breaths of stale air to settle his nerves.

It was quiet in the tunnel. He could think without distractions. He considered the tire marks on the trail. The wax cheese rind. He thought of discussions among the Dancers about the troubles of his people. Of the fear that the Nunne'hi were leaving and the need to do something before they were gone. He had agreed, for he believed the legends of their coexistence with his people. When the Nunne'hi were gone, the Cherokee would follow.

Absorbed in contemplation, he did not notice the first deep rumble far back in the mound. It had started when he used the pick-axe on timbers already weakened by centuries of erosion and decay. They creaked and groaned until the noise broke through his distraction. By the time he realized what was happening, the rumble became a roar. Overhead beams shattered releasing an avalanche of packed earth and rocks.

Buck scrambled toward the tunnel's mouth. With a roar like a freight train, the roof collapsed behind him, filling the tunnel at his heels and sending plumes of dust and rubble toward the sunlight. He ran, desperately trying to stay ahead of it. One end of a falling timber thudded across his back and knocked him off his feet. He kept his eyes on the light ahead and crawled for all he was worth. When he was only a body length from safety, pain shot through him as a beam fell across his lower back, pinning him to the ground. He clawed at the earth, trying to drag himself that last few feet.

A second beam cracked and fell, striking a glancing blow on the side of his head. Blood oozed warm down his face and neck. For a moment more, he struggled, then faded into unconsciousness.

Buck didn't know how long he had been lying there when pain roused him. The throbbing ache in his head brought on an instant awareness of the danger he was in. The weight of the beam across his back pinned him to the ground. He flexed the muscles in his legs and wiggled his feet. The cramp that shot through his calf hurt like hell, but at least it signaled an intact spine. He was able to turn his head and move his upper body. It could have been worse.

He spit out dirt, wiped grit from his eyes and tried to drag himself free of the beam. With his teeth clenched against the pain he twisted toward the light at the tunnel mouth. Only a few feet to go and he would be out in the sunlight.

He did a push-up that lifted his head and chest off the ground, shoving his body up against the timber. A groan echoed above him and deep in the hillside. Panic gave him strength to push harder. The beam shifted.

He couldn't see what was happening above him, but he didn't have to. He heard enough to know the beam on his back was somehow connected with the last intact supporting structure of the tunnel. He weighed his choices. He could try again to get free and make a dash for the opening, or he could lie still and wait to die. The opening tantalized him with its nearness.

Focusing all his strength on the task at hand, he braced his feet against the ground and stiffened his arms under his chest. If he had to drag the whole hillside with him he would, but he intended to make it out alive. With everything he had, he lurched toward the light. He moved less than a foot when the beam above him sagged and released a shower of rocks and dirt. The rumble resumed, resonating through the hill and releasing a cascade of rubble. Buck cradled his face in his arms and lay still while the wreckage of the tunnel supports thundered down around him.

When the cave-in stopped, he lay in the dark afraid to move. The weight of the beam across his back was heavier, pinning him firmly into place. Very carefully, he raked debris from around his face.

He could still breathe, but for how long? He tried to judge the space around him with an outstretched arm. He guessed there was about two feet that wasn't full of dirt. That would give him possibly two hours of air, then he was done for. If he was going to live, he had to get out soon.

In the pitch darkness, Buck felt the weight of the mound crushing down. He shifted slightly. Even that small movement brought the supporting beam down by an inch or so, decreasing the air space.

Before he could control his panic, he yelled at the top of his lungs, calling for John or Eli, even the great conjuror himself, to come help. The mouthfuls of dust he inhaled convinced him of the futility of his shouts. He was only using up his meager ration of oxygen, a senseless waste since there was nobody within miles to hear him.

He dismissed the fleeting thought that a quick death in the initial cave-in would have been better than what he had to look forward to—trapped, alone in the dark, waiting for suffocation or thirst to kill him.

Panic almost got the best of him. It required every ounce of willpower he had to calm himself down and think. As long as there was life in his body he was still the protector of the ark. He didn't have the right to die until he had exhausted every means to live up to that obligation.

If Walker and John had the ark, Walker would know what to do. And John and Eli knew he was going to check on the die-back. They'd come looking for him when he didn't get home on time. If he could stay alive until they got close enough to hear him yell, he might survive. He lay still, trying to make the air last as long as possible.

He counted minutes in his head. It helped settle his nerves. He was still breathing long after he'd expected to run out of air. If anything, the air quality was getting better. The dust had settled, and it didn't seem to be as dark. A pinpoint of light filtered through the rocks. Not enough to see by, but it gave him hope. If light could get in, so could air. This increased his chances of staying alive until John and Eli came looking for him. If he didn't die of thirst first.

He imagined he could hear the creek at the foot of the hill, taunting him with the sound of clear clean water. Thirst was becoming a real problem. And it would be a long time before John came. He had the day off work to do something with Walker. And Eli was in the fire tower.

Buck closed his eyes and tried not to listen to the sound of the creek.

DAVID WAYANETTAH'S HOUSE

Walker closed the front door as the tail lights of Faron's Chevy disappeared around the bend. He looked every bit as tired and old as he had the last time Nathan Axe saw him, up on Wolf Mountain. Only this time, he didn't have to pretend. He felt as bad as he looked. He went over to Dave's easy chair and sat, clutching the blanket that still held Wren's warmth. Axe came and perched on the arm of the couch.

"Mr. Copperhead," he said. "I don't think you and David had anything to do with killing that girl, but I know you can tell me more than you have. I need you to help me out. I'm just trying to make sure that nothing like that happens to anybody else's little granddaughter. I want you to tell me what the hell ya'll were doing way up on that mountain today. Something's going on, and you know what it is if anybody does."

"I reckon so, Nathan. But they're reasons I can't tell you much more than you already know. You're one of us. You know how it is," Walker said.

Nathan Axe looked very uncomfortable. "Look guys," he said. "I don't like this any better than you do, but I'm just trying to do my job. I don't know much about our spiritual ways. I leave that to my mother. I've been a Baptist since I was twelve, and our church doesn't approve of it. That works for me, because I like things that make sense, and let's face it, our old ways defy logic. I might not believe, but I respect your belief." His voice softened. "Mr. Copperhead, my job is to find a murderer. I won't talk about it to anybody unless there's no other way. Anything I learn here tonight, I'll follow up on my own."

Walker leaned his head against the back of the chair and let the blanket drop across his lap. Axe was watching him expectantly. He could hear Kate in the kitchen. Familiar homey sounds that usually made a man feel comfortable, but tonight it didn't have the same calming effect. David and Yona waited, like they expected him to know how to handle things.

Walker was well aware that the sheriff's patience was wearing thin. Tradition, and a lifetime of respect for the secret mysteries of the Snake Dancers Circle, determined how much Walker could tell the authorities, even Nathan Axe who was a member of the tribe.

Finally, Walker grinned like this was just a friendly visit from an old family friend and said, "Nathan, you know us elders have a lot of old fashioned ways you young men don't think much of. That's all it is. These boys just try to humor me sometimes. That's the only reason we were up there."

The sheriff didn't buy it. Walker's explanation just made him mad. "I hoped you would do better than that," he said. "You might pull something like the superstitious elder bullshit on Dorsey, but I thought you had a little more respect for the son of one of those elders."

Walker held his temper. He'd watched Nathan Axe grow up in one of the most traditional families on the Qualla Boundary. The boy knew enough to understand when it was best to leave things alone. Couldn't he take a hint? He tried turning the questions aside with small talk. "Speaking of your mother, Nathan, how's she doing these days? Mighty fine woman Maddie Axe is. You tell her how much I appreciate how she's taught Kate ever since she was just a girl."

"You see my mother at least once a week, Mr. Copperhead. You know how she's doing as well as I do. Now, no disrespect intended, but let's cut the crap. Tell me why you three just happened to be in a place you had to hike three hours to get to and you find a dead girl there. Then tell me why you think it is that two of your good buddies and a weird-assed white shaman have turned up missing."

The sheriff had gone too far. Walker was pissed off now. His voice dripped ice sickles. "Nathan, like you said, you're the son of an elder. You know there are some things we'd be better off not airing to the world. I suggest you settle for what I tell you. Just accept that we were teaching Wren a history lesson. David was helping us out by showing us the place where some of our people hid out during the removal. You've done the same thing yourself for some of the kids. It makes it more real to them."

Nathan leaned toward Walker. "That's the story I'll put on the book if you want me to, but only if you tell me the truth, as much of it as you can. The sooner we work this out, the better it will be for all of us. I doubt that you want this to drag on with a lot of people prowling around the crime scene."

That put a damper on Walker's anger and made him apprehensive. He glanced at David. "Boy, what do you think Driver would have said about this?"

"He already said it, Grandfather. Things are a lot different now. We have to find our own way."

Walker stared at Nathan a while and then grinned a little. "I reckon you'd have to answer to Miss Maddie if you didn't keep your mouth shut."

Nathan nodded. "Talk to me, Mr. Copperhead. I've got a lot to do before I can get any sleep tonight."

Walker didn't see any way out. An innocent young girl was dead and whoever killed her was out there . . . somewhere. And Wren wasn't far away. If telling the sheriff enough to help him catch the killer would protect his granddaughter, he had to do it. At least Nathan Axe was a Cherokee. That made it easier.

First he spoke to Yona. "Listen up, boy. You're gonna need to know this, too." He told the story in the same way it had always been told it to the kids. How the Ulunsu'ti was taken from the head of Uktena by the outsider. The way it was used by the conjurors of old until Kanegwa'ti, the Water Moccasin hid it to await the Suye'ta who would use it again to help the

Cherokee people. Neither Nathan or Yona interrupted. When Walker finished, Nathan said, "We've heard the story before. What does it have to do with that girl getting killed?"

Walker asked, "Have you ever heard about a society made up of the descendants of the conjurors of old? A society that's responsible for looking after certain objects that could give a man the same kind of power the old conjurors had?"

Axe said, "I've heard rumors."

"The rumors are true," Walker said. "I'm a member of that society."

"I figured you would be," Nathan turned to David. "And, your grandpa must have been in it."

David grunted a yes. "So were two of your missing men. And I hold Driver's place, since a while before he walked over."

Nathan asked again what all that had to do with the dead girl. Yona said, "Go on, Grandpa. I'd like to know that, too."

"I'm getting to it," Walker said. "It could have something to do with the things the society was organized to protect. They were powerful objects, well hidden by the first guardians long before the removal, each in its own place, each with it's own protector. Nobody knew the whereabouts of anything except the thing he was responsible for. Yesterday, that changed. We found a duffle bag full of almost everything we've been watching over for nearly four hundred years. All of it in one place."

Nathan leaned forward. "You've seen them, and know for sure they're real? I thought that was just another old story."

David was quick to let the sheriff know what he thought of that remark. "These old stories are the only way we have of passing our heritage down. Everything our ancestors put in writing has either been destroyed or stashed in a museum, where none of us will ever get our hands on it. The little we have left is encoded in the stories we tell. People like you, who've turned more white than Indian, might be surprised at how much truth the stories have in them when they're told right. If you'd a listened to your mother, you'd know that. Miss Maddie knows."

Walker was proud of the boy. Driver had left his place in the Circle in good hands.

The sheriff looked sheepish. "Sorry, David. In my line of work, you tend to get a little cynical." He turned back to Walker, all business now. With notepad and pen ready, he said, "Now, Mr. Copperhead. Tell me what was in that duffle bag."

"Put that away, Nathan, or I won't say another word about anything," Walker said. "None of this has ever been written down and I aim to keep it that way."

Axe reluctantly put the notepad back into the inside pocket of his jacket. "Okay, Mr. Copperhead. Have it your way, but I need to know what you saw and why it's such a big deal."

Walker had already told him more than he wanted to. Only the thought of the dead girl, and the need to help Nathan catch the man who killed her before he hurt anyone else, made him go on. He leaned forward. "Nathan, would you understand what it meant if I told you that duffle bag was filled with Kanagwa'ti's medicine, his bones, and the Cherokee Ark of the Covenant? And that it was within a couple of miles of the Council House Mound?"

"I'd appreciate it if you'd go on and tell me what it means, Mr. Copperhead."

"It means, at the very least, that somebody robbed the conjuror's grave. And that they stole the ark from where it had been safeguarded for generations, then they brought everything they stole to the only place it can safely be used to wake up the Ulunsu'ti. It means they might also have the Ulunsu'ti and they are just waiting to get their hands on the only other thing they need to wake him. That last thing is just a few yards away from where that girl got killed. If they have that, we can just stick our heads between our legs and kiss our asses goodbye."

Walker sat back and looked the sheriff in the eye. "You wanna write all that down in your little book and tell it to the folks down at that church you been going to? Wonder what they'd have to say about your superstitious Indians then, Nathan."

Nathan stood and walked to the window and looked out into the darkness for a moment, then came back to his perch on the end of the sofa. "Is the Ulunsu'ti real, Mr. Copperhead? Can it really do what the stories say it can?"

Walker wished he could say no. "Yeah, son. It's real, and it can do more than you ever heard about. If it gets into the wrong hands, and the wrong person tries to use it . . . Well, we don't want that to happen. Kanegwa'ti went to a lot of trouble to prevent it."

"Don't they say that somebody is supposed to come along and be able to use the Ulunsu'ti's power for the good of the tribe?" Nathan asked. "Could it be that he's the one who gathered up all the stuff you found?"

"If the Suye'ta was here, the Snake Dancers would be the first to know. We would have spent a lot of time preparing him and making sure he didn't bring on more harm than good. No, Nathan, it's not the Suye'ta, but it's somebody who knows a lot of things they shouldn't. That, or . . ."

"Or what, Mr. Copperhead?" Nathan asked.

Walker couldn't bring himself to say it.

David answered for him. "Or one of us has gone crazy."

"One of the Snake Dancers?" the sheriff asked.

Walker nodded.

David said, "Most of my generation had a hard time believing what we were told when we were first brought in. Doesn't take long to be convinced though, once you've seen a few things you never thought possible. But those things have always been enough to keep us on the straight and narrow. It's possible they didn't make that big of an impression on everybody. Could be that somebody hung around to learn all they needed to know to—"

"No, Dave." Walker couldn't let him say such things. "In all these centuries, that never happened. I know all the others. Not a one of us would even think about it. Somehow, somebody found out. It had to be an outsider. No Cherokee would dig up the conjuror's grave."

"I know it wasn't easy for you to tell me all this," the sheriff said. "But it'll help me figure out who killed the girl and I'll keep it to myself."

Walker nodded his approval. "I appreciate that, Nathan." The sheriff knitted his fingers, stretched his arms out and cracked all his knuckles at once. "Mr. Copperhead," he said. "Tell me about the Suye'ta. If I remember right, he would be an outsider. Right?"

"Yeah, he would. But we've always believed he would be someone we brought in. Someone we had to bribe with a prize that made the well-being of the tribe more important to him than his own safety. He would be like the Shawnee who killed Uktena so he could have the Cherokee woman he loved."

"What if a man wanted the power of the Ulunsu'ti the same way the Shawnee wanted a Cherokee wife?" Nathan asked. "What if that power was important enough that he would put it ahead of his own safety? There are lots of people like that in the world, possibly even in your society. I hate to do this, Mr. Copperhead, but I'm gonna have to ask you to give me the names of the other members."

David jumped to his feet, but Walker raised his hand in a quieting gesture before he could say anything. He was as mad as David, but anger wouldn't accomplish anything. Walker stood and pointed to the door. "Nathan. You'd best be getting to work. Like you said, you've got a lot to do tonight, and you've got all you're gonna get around here."

Nathan didn't have time to object. Kate was suddenly at his side, all smiles. "Nathan, honey, I do wish you had time to eat some supper with us, but I understand." She took his hand and began to lead him to the door. "I cooked almost everything David had in the house, too, even if it was just a few trout from the freezer and some frozen french-fries. You'll have to come over to Snowbird real soon and I'll make it up to you. How does next Sunday sound? You could bring Miss Maddie over for dinner with us. Would you like that?"

She was practically purring. Axe was so busy blushing and fidgeting with his hat, he hardly noticed when she edged him out the door.

"Why sure, Kate, but I do need to talk to Mr. Copperhead just a minute longer."

Kate laughed. "Lord, Nathan. You men will have plenty of time to socialize later. Right now, Grandpa needs to eat and get home to his own bed. You run along now, and we'll see you Sunday." She kissed the air at him and shut the door.

"Supper's ready," she said to her men folks. Walker motioned to Yona and David and they followed Kate to the kitchen. A woman like her was handy to have around.

Supper was good, although dark thoughts kept Walker's mind occupied as he ate in silence. He was surprised that he could eat at all, but he finished every bite. As soon as the last morsel of crisp fried trout disappeared from his plate, Kate cleared the table.

When she got to the sink with a load of dirty dishes, Walker spoke in a near whisper, "Boys, we've got some talking to do, but I need to think awhile first. Why don't you take over and clean up, so Kate can go home. If she's gonna be on the road by herself, I'd like her to head out soon."

"She kinda figured on you and me going home with her, Grandpa," Yona said.

"I know she did, son, but we've got too much to do right here on Lightning Creek. Dave, hope you don't mind if me and Yona stay the night with you."

"Sure, Grandfather," David said. "I've got plenty of room here since I've been living alone. Yona, you're familiar with Meredith's room. I doubt she would mind if you bunked in there."

Walker grinned at Yona. "So, you've been coming over here to hang out with Dave, huh? I noticed you haven't been over here much since Meredith went back to Atlanta."

"Lay off, Grandpa." Yona reddened. "If I'd said anything to you, you would have had us married and cranking out grandbabies by now if it killed you. Meredith's not ready for that."

"When do you reckon she's gonna be ready, boy?"

"When she's ready, Grandpa." Yona grunted. "You ask her when that'll be." He carried the rest of the dishes to the sink. Kate came to the table and planted a loud kiss on top of Walker's head. "I need the keys to the Blazer," she said. "I guess David can bring you home when you and Yona finish whatever you've been whispering about."

"You're not gonna fuss about it or nothing?" Walker asked.

"Would it do any good?"

"I reckon not, Kate," Walker almost wished she would insist that he come on home, or just tell him he was way too old to go trudging around through the Smoky Mountains. Regretfully, he watched her walk out the door. It sure would feel good to be heading home to his own bed.

It was some comfort to know she would be safely on Snowbird within an hour. Faron and John and Wren should be almost there by now. He didn't have to worry about Wren any more. Tomorrow night he'd be there with them—if things went well. If not, then who knew if he would ever be back home.

Sound echoed as if through an empty house. The closing of the door. Kate's footsteps on the porch. The rattle of the bridge under the Blazer's wheels. The resonance of things unsaid, hanging in the evening silence.

Walker sat in David's easy chair, listening to the clatter of dishes while Yona and David cleaned up, and thought about what he had to do. By the time they joined him, he was ready to talk.

"Boys," he said. "You've heard how the stories say the Suye'ta has to be an outsider. I think you know what I had in mind, don't you David?"

David nodded. "About John?"

Walker looked at Yona. "How about you, son? We've talked about Suye'ta being an outsider with a strong connection to the tribe. David caught on that I had John in mind and was rightly pissed. How about you?"

Yona stopped pacing and faced his grandfather, "I know something's been going on, but I don't know what. Reckon you could fill me in, Grandpa? I'm getting a little pissed myself. Just following along, keeping my mouth shut when I don't know jack-shit about what's up. You been throwing me hints as long as I can remember. Don't you think it's about time you— bring me in, or whatever?"

"Whoa, boy. Don't get ahead of yourself." Walker hadn't expected that.

David leaned back in the chair across from Walker. "Grandfather," he said. "I don't see that Yona is getting ahead of himself. Driver claimed if you had your way, you'd try to hang on till Diamond gets old enough to take over for you. I'd say we can't afford to take that chance. With things the way they are, Yona needs to be able to step in if anything happens to you."

"Does it look like I been holding back on Yona? He's heard a lot in the last two days."

"He's heard next to nothing, considering all he's gonna have to learn. Grandfather, the last thing Driver said to me was that he wished he hadn't waited so long. He walked over knowing he wouldn't have time to teach me all the things he needed to. I'm looking to you to take up where he left off. Yona and I will have our hands full. We need to work with you as long as we can, and you're not getting any younger. Buck's grandpa brought him in early. They had years in the Circle together. I wish I'd had that with Driver."

Walker tried to come up with some sort of objection. He was losing control of a situation that he thought he had very well planned.

Yona stood and stretched to his full height. "It's late and I'm wore out. Grandpa, why don't you get some rest now? You and I have to get up early in the morning and take the conjuror's bones and medicine back to Ataga'hi. That's a good place to start I reckon. We can do what we need to do then. It's about time I was a Snake Dancer." He went to Meredith's room without a backward glance.

"Looks like it's been decided, huh, Grandfather," David said.

Walker didn't answer. The boys were right. It was high time he got started on preparations for Yona's initiation. Why had he waited so long? True, it did make him face his own mortality, but then at his age that was unavoidable. He'd talked about it with Grady. They both had grandsons ready and waiting, but for some reason, they both stalled.

He could hear Yona getting ready for bed. He would be glad when Meredith Wayanettah finished her residency so she and Yona could have him some more grandbabies. But Yona needed to stay alive for that.

It's like Grady had said when they talked about Eli and Yona. The Snake Dancers would be right in the line of fire. That was a hard place to put somebody you loved, especially now that it looked like the very thing they feared had come true.

This generation of Dancers was going to have their hands full, and the elders wouldn't be around to help much longer. He and Grady were both too old. Driver Wayanettah and Del Locust had already walked over. Walker leaned back in the chair and said a prayer for the grandsons. It would all be up to them soon. Very soon.

QUALLA BOUNDARY

There was nothing comforting about the trailer. Even the old house was just a hulking shadow against the darker shade of the mountain. He didn't bother to hide his car behind the laurels this time. The only one he feared was back in the cave, probably still searching for the conjuror's hands, or for him. Next time they met, he would be the hunter, not the prey. He was tired of running from a man who had already cost him everything that mattered. The chance to undo the harm he had done was all he had left. He wouldn't let that go.

Time was running out and he had a lot to do before he was free to walk over to the other world. With the Pinto parked under the beech tree, he walked to the old house. He stopped for a moment on the front porch and leaned against one of the sagging posts. Memories of better days flashed through his mind. Faces and voices of people he would never see again reminded him of all he had lost. At the edge of his mind, the darkness drew him in. He slipped into it, away from the pain.

He could think better this way. His mind was sharp, as long as he stayed in that place where pain and remorse couldn't reach him. It was strange to watch his worn out old body from that gray empty void, to see it wander through the memory-haunted rooms of the house and out to the back porch. To watch it stoop down and wiggle the stone loose from the well.

His hands reached in and lifted the crystal from the safe and cradled it against his body. The weight of it drew him back to reality. It was heavier than he remembered. It filled his arms and compelled him to look into it's core. Did he imagine a fiery radiance awaking there? With an act of will, he turned his eyes away and dropped the crystal into the knapsack.

Opening the back door of his old house, he breathed in the smells of age and decay. The house no longer held the welcoming sense of home, only the echo of a life that belonged to somebody else. The man who had lived here couldn't have killed, no more than he could have betrayed his people.

Memories flooded his mind and wrenched him back from the shadows. The weight of all the generations he had dishonored bore down on his soul. He couldn't blame anybody but himself and his own foolish pride. If he had gone to the other Snake Dancers, they would have stopped him, but he thought he knew better than his brothers.

How could he have listened to the flattery of a man who only wanted to use him? He could see it now, but now was too late. One person was already dead and he was the murderer, all because of a web of lies and flattery. His own conceit had made the lies sound believable.

He didn't linger in the old house. What he needed wasn't there. He hurried through the house, across the yard and into the back door of his trailer. In the kitchen the coffee pot still sat on the stove, the grounds emitting the smell of stale coffee. He tried not to think of the gentle trusting girl who had poured his last cup of coffee from that pot, but the memory washed over him before he could stop it. Grief knifed through him until he found his way back into the gray world. There, the pain numbed, he could think again. He remembered an extra flashlight in the pantry and took it to replace the one that had been stolen from him in the cave. He put in a couple of fresh batteries. He grabbed a second flashlight from his bedside table. With all that was at stake, he didn't dare risk getting stranded in the dark again.

It had been a long time since he had gone hunting. Not since he was a boy, when game sometimes meant the difference between hunger and a full belly. It never was something he enjoyed, so he didn't have fancy rifles like his son. From the bedroom closet he pulled out what he did have. The old double-barreled twelve-gauge shotgun hadn't been fired in years, but he kept it polished and ready. Living out here in the woods, he never knew when he might need a gun.

There were only two shells left in the box. They were old, but they would have to do. He put them both in the knapsack and went back to the car, shivering in the damp air.

Just before dawn he pulled out onto 441. Thick dark clouds hung low in the sky and made it feel more like the dead of night. He cranked up the heater to try to dispel the bone-deep chill in his body but it didn't help, just fogged up the windows. He turned it off and drove on, back up to the head of Lightning Creek.

He needed to see if the Montero was still where they left it yesterday. As he crossed the bridge, the Pinto coughed like it was ready to give up. He looked at the gas gauge. Empty. With everything he had on his mind, he had forgotten to fill up. With the remaining few drops of gas he managed to get the car off the road, beside the creek. It coughed one last time and died. He had hoped to make it to the thicket where it would be better concealed, but as long as nobody saw it and came looking for him before his work was done, it was good enough.

Slinging the knapsack over his shoulder and cradling the shotgun in the crook of his arm, he set off back up Wolf Mountain. The ache in his jawbone made him wonder if it was broken. He ignored the pain and kept walking. Nothing he could do about it anyway. A damp cold wind blew against him, slowing his steps and chilling him to the bone again. He shivered and considered it small penance for what he had done.

His discomfort helped to keep his mind focused on the task at hand. When he was so tired he didn't think he could take another step, he willed his legs to keep moving.

Near the crest, he'd gone as far as he could, but by then, the boulders that marked the entrance of the cave were in sight. He could afford to rest a few minutes, but not out in the open. For all he knew, the white man was lurking somewhere up there in the rocks waiting to finish him off. He sunk down under a clump of scrub laurel and rested long enough to catch his breath and regain some strength in his legs.

There was one more thing to do before he was ready to meet the white man again. Breaching the shotgun, he loaded both barrels. Wherever the bastard was, he'd be ready for him.

He made it to the overhang at the mouth of the cave, but before entering, he looked around. There was no sign of anyone else. That could mean the white man was sneaking up behind him or that he was still in there, wandering around in the darkness.

He took a flashlight out of his knapsack. The shotgun was in the other hand, his finger on the trigger. A few feet past the entrance, he stopped and listened, flashing the light ahead. Nothing but his own labored breathing broke the silence. Adjusting the knapsack across his shoulder he plunged ahead. The Ulunsu'ti's weight pressed heavy against his body.

He heard the white man's voice before he saw him staggering toward him at the edge of the light, calling out like he was glad to see him. The fool would have been glad to see the devil himself if he brought light into the cave.

The white man hurried toward him, talking fast in that oily, smooth voice. "I found them. We can do it now. Just like you planned. It will work."

He couldn't listen. The white man would stop when he saw the shotgun. He swung the barrel up and rested the stock against his shoulder. His finger gripped the trigger.

The white man kept talking. "I have them. Look." He reached inside his fringed jacket and brought out the bowl, holding it out to the elder like a gift. "See. We have everything we need now. I *am* the Suye'ta." His voice was low and sincere, but his eyes were on the knapsack.

The elder shouted at him to stop, but the white man eased closer, saying the girl's death would be in vain if they didn't go on. They had to do it for her. She would want them to.

The sound of her name in the white man's mouth was a

sacrilege he couldn't bear. He gripped the trigger and nestled the stock against his shoulder, pointing the long barrel at the white man's head. It didn't stop him. His finger tightened on the trigger. The explosion that followed reverberated in his head. The force of the recoil slammed the gunstock hard into his shoulder and knocked him off his feet, sending him reeling against the cave wall. A sharp protrusion in the rock caught him high on his back, tearing through muscle and flesh.

He sagged to the floor and lay limp, afraid to open his eyes. Echoes of the blast resounded in the deep recesses of the cave and died away. He called the white man's name, straining to catch any sound. The silence was absolute.

He had dropped the flashlight. The shotgun was gone, too. His right arm felt numb. He checked the shoulder that had taken the brunt of the shotgun's recoil. It was bruised, and hurt like hell, but the skin wasn't broken. Still, something that could only be blood, spread warm and wet through his shirt.

A diffused glow illuminated a spot a few feet away. He pulled himself to his feet and took a couple of halting steps toward it, only to trip over the knapsack. He fumbled inside for the extra flashlight. It shook in his hand as he searched the nearby floor. He needed the gun. If the white man came for him, he had to be prepared. When he found it a few feet away, he clutched it under his arm, his finger on the trigger ready to fire. He panned the light around, searching for the white man.

He saw the blood first, and followed the trail to its source. The white man's smooth talking tongue was no longer a problem for him or anyone else. Its influence was gone, along with most of his face. The flashlight still glowed eerily under the body.

The elder stared down at the body, feeling only relief that one of his problems was solved. Now, he was free to finish what he had to do without worrying about the white man interfering.

His shoulder was beginning to really hurt. Blood trickled down his arm and soaked his sleeve. He remembered falling against something sharp. The gash in his upper back was bleeding too much to ignore. He pulled a red bandana from his pocket and fashioned a makeshift bandage, applying pressure to staunch the flow of blood.

He swung the light to the shards of pottery beside the body. A bundle wrapped in deerskin nestled in one broken half of a bowl.

The white man had said he had the conjuror's hands.

He picked up the half of the bowl and inspected the bundle, hoping it was anything but what the white man claimed it was. If it held the hands, that would complicate things. Walker and Dave would know what to do with everything in the duffle bag, but how would he get the hands back to David.

He peeled away the protective wrappings, one layer at a time, hoping against hope that the white man had lied. That this was just another one of his tricks and the hands were safe where they belonged. When the last layer was removed, he saw that for once, the white man had told the truth. The ancient, mummified pair of hands lay there in the broken bowl, so well preserved they could have been the shriveled aged hands of a living old man.

The hands had to go back to David Wayanettah, not necessarily to their original hiding place. If he put them in the duffle bag with everything else, Walker would make sure David got them. He had to hurry. Pain and blood loss were taking a toll, leaving him weak and dull witted.

He eased the hands into the knapsack. Something flashed in his mind, something about why he shouldn't have done that, but he couldn't think about that now. He had a lot to do while he was still able. He slung the knapsack over his wounded shoulder, ignoring the pain its weight caused. It was lighter than the shotgun, and he needed that in case anyone tried to stop him. There was one shell left in the chamber. If he still had it when he finished what he had to do, it would come in handy to end his misery. He staggered down the cavern toward the sound of the waterfall where David had stashed the duffle bag.

The duffle bag was still there, tucked under the crevice where he'd watched Driver's grandson hide it. It wouldn't do any harm to take one last look. He propped the flashlight on a ledge and pulled the duffle bag out and opened it. The ark was still there, right where he had put it. How beautiful it was. The power of it vibrated in his hands. He had gone to a lot of trouble to get it out of the Locust's tunnel. Buck had been careless to let him find it. A man who couldn't take better care of his guardianship than that, didn't deserve the job. Buck Locust couldn't be trusted with something as important as the ark. And David had let the white man find the hands. Could he handle the responsibility of the hands that could revive the Ulunsu'ti.

He opened the first gym bag. The medicine pouch was right there on top of the rest. He wanted to look at it, but something was wrong. Touching it made him shiver. The pouch felt dangerous, like it could hurt him. He didn't want to touch it anymore. The sense of threat lessened when the pouch was back in the gym bag.

He put the gym bags and the ark back into the duffle bag. Now, all he had to do was leave everything there but the Ulunsu'ti, and go. David and Walker would take care of it. And he could give the Ulunsu'ti to his grandson and be done with it all. But he was tired now. Too tired to make it down the mountain.

He clutched the knapsack against his bleeding shoulder and leaned against the cave wall to rest. His mind was beginning to clear. Perhaps there was a better way to handle this. He had proven that he could outsmart the Snake Dancers. He'd outdone all the guardians and had everything they had been so careful to protect. And the white man who thought he was so smart, was dead now. Only he was left, and he had the Ulunsu'ti and everything he needed to wake it. He didn't feel weak anymore. He was thinking clearer than he had in years. The duffle bag didn't feel so heavy when he lifted it to his good shoulder. He hugged the knapsack against his side, picked up the shotgun and set out toward daylight.

The white man was still sprawled where he had left him, his body outlined in the darkness by the flashlight he had fallen on. He stopped and looked down at the body for a moment, searching for some emotion that would tell him he was still human enough to feel remorse. The sound of a brief harsh laugh startled him until he realized it came from his own throat. He moved on, troubled that he had found pleasure at the sight of the dead man.

His shirt was wet. Blood had soaked it and was seeping into the knapsack. The bandana had come loose. He needed to make a better bandage before he went out into the weather. He could hear the rain as he approached the cave mouth. He unburdened himself and stripped down to his undershirt. Tearing strands of plaid flannel from the tail of his shirt, he fashioned a dressing. It was awkward work with one hand, but he applied it the best he could, then secured it with strips of flannel. It would do for now. He put what was left of his bloody shirt back on, gathered up the duffle bag, knapsack and shotgun and started outside.

Someone was there. He listened to the familiar voices, torn between asking the men outside to help, and hiding from them. When two of them came into the cave, he ducked out of sight and pressed his body against the wall. This would have been a good time to call out to David. And to give him the hands, but he kept quiet. He wasn't sure why, until he thought of the Ulunsu'ti. What if they wanted it, too? It belonged to him, and his grandson. Nobody else could be trusted with it.

When the two men had disappeared into the recesses of the cave, he stepped outside. The smell of smoke stung his nose. Through the cloud of smoke, an old man huddled by a smoldering fire, calling his name. He could stop now, leave the duffle bag and go on his way. It was over, and he was free. That's what he had intended to do, but the old man was on his feet now, looking at the knapsack, just like the white man did.

He crept away from the fire, but Walker Copperhead followed him, still eying the knapsack. He wanted what was inside it. Not just the relics that belonged to him, but the crystal, too. He wanted it to give to the white boy his granddaughter married.

He tried to get away, but the old man kept coming at him, grabbing for the knapsack, prodding him with his walking stick. He snatched the walking stick from the old man but he wouldn't stop. He swung the shotgun and felt it connect. The old man crumpled to the ground.

Remorse hit him with the force of a blow. What had he done? First the white man, now this. It was one thing to kill an enemy, but this was a friend. He left him lying in the rain and staggered away.

The voice in his head whispered that the old man deserved what he got. Anybody who got in his way would get the same thing. He liked what he heard. The voice got louder. The elder, who had only wanted to help his people, listened and knew he was lost. There was nothing he could do now, not in the body of a man who could strike a friend. He let his spirit slip away, into a gray, hopeless world far beyond Wolf Mountain.

From the shadows of that world of the lost, he watched an old man stumbling down the trail, clutching the bloody knapsack to his side. He remembered a time when he had been a good man. A man everybody trusted. Now, the wounded, worn out old body that crept away was all that was left. The good man who had walked in it for more than eighty years was gone now, watching from the gray world where he could do no more harm.

LIGHTNING CREEK

Morning broke gray and way too cool for this time of the year. Walker must have been really tired, to sleep in long enough to let the boys get up before of him. He heard them in the kitchen. The smell of coffee motivated him to join them. David poured him a cup when he got to the table. A pan of bacon sizzled on the stove and Yona scrambled the last dozen eggs he had in the fridge. He had half a loaf of buttered bread toasting in the oven and a jar of Meredith's blackberry jam waiting to be smeared on while the bread was good and hot. The day was getting off to a good start.

Walker let Yona and David serve him, one of the privileges of being the old man of the family. He hurried through breakfast but David and Yona took their time, like they planned to linger over coffee and enjoy the morning. They would need a nudge if they were going to get on the road early.

"Boys, I'd like to get on the trail as soon as we can," he said. "I want to put things back where they belong. Kanagwa'ti's bones and medicine ought to have a good resting place before nightfall."

"As soon as we finish breakfast, Grandpa," Yona said. "Then, Dave and I will go back up Wolf Mountain to get the stuff we left there. You can wait here while we do that. Then I guess you and I have to go to Ataga'hi alone. From what I've heard, I figure we'd have to kill Dave if he knew where we dug the grave."

Walker didn't laugh. Yona needed to learn not to joke about such things and he told him so.

"Well, Grandpa," Yona said. "To be honest, I wondered if it was true. The way you guys talked, sounded like you'd do just about anything to protect your secrets."

Walker sipped his coffee and didn't say anything.

David chuckled. It sounded strained, like he was worried he might end up dead if he learned the Copperheads' hiding place. "No problem. One mountain a day is enough for me to climb. You two are on your own when we get back from the cave. I'll be busy finding a new place to hide the hands. I don't think it's a good idea to leave them in the cave."

"I don't guess you need our help for that?" Yona said.

"I better do it by myself," David said. "Can't have you Copperheads knowing where they are. A tough old dude like Walker would be mighty hard to kill, but I reckon I'd have to do it somehow. Snake Dancer rules."

Walker got up and carried his plate to the sink. "Forget it, boys. You're not leaving me here. I'm ready to go. No reason for me to hang around the house doing nothing all morning."

Yona and David exchanged glances. Yona shrugged in resignation. "Well, Dave. We tried."

David looked for a moment like he would argue, then echoed Yona's shrug and finished the last of his breakfast.

They left their dishes in the sink and piled into David's pick-up. The closest route to the cave was the path off the logging road past Aunt Marge's place. The ride would give Walker time to start Yona's education. He had finally admitted to himself that it was long overdue. There was plenty both of the boys needed to know, about the history of the Snake Dancers and what their duties were. It would all be in their hands soon.

He told them about the Ulunsu'ti, not the stories they had heard but real things it could do and how it could be used. And the truth about Kanegwa'ti. Of how he had been an outsider adopted into the tribe. He was the Suye'ta of his day, risking possession by Uktena, the serpent spirit of the Ulunsu'ti, in order to use its power for the good of the people.

"With the white people taking everything else, Kanegwa'ti knew it was only a matter of time before they found out about the Ulunsu'ti and wanted it, too. You boys are part of a long line of Snake Dancers Kanegwa'ti appointed to protect the Ulunsu'ti and its medicine. You're descendants of men who hold the knowledge of where each object is," he said.

Yona said one word under his breath. "Damn."

David grinned in sympathy. "Hang in there, Yona. It's a lot to ask modern guys like us to accept, but I've learned enough to believe it's all true."

"You sure this isn't a load of bullshit, huh, Dave? He's not just putting me on, like some sort of initiation or something? Is he just testing me to see how gullible I am?"

"No, man. There's more, and it gets weirder." David answered.

Yona was quick to point out that he didn't know where, or what anything was. "I've been kept in the dark until now, when things are all messed up."

It was rare for Walker to apologize, but he owed it to Yona. "I was wrong to keep things from you for so long. I don't know why I did. Me and Grady talked about it once. He never told Eli anything either. We had a feeling this generation was going to have a hard time, and we hated to put that burden on our grandsons. Now, if we can't find Grady, we'll have to take Eli in, too."

There wasn't time to fill Yona in on the details of his guardianship before they reached the trail. David parked his pick-up near the hemlocks where they had found the Montero.

David slung his backpack across his shoulder and picked out a path toward the cave. Walker tried to keep up with the younger men, but he didn't feel as strong as he let on. The rain that had been a drizzle when they left home, came down in heavy cold drops now. He wore a plastic poncho he'd found in a hall closet at David's house. Judging by the powder blue color, he figured it was one Meredith had left behind. It gave him better protection than the windbreakers and baseball caps

Yona and David wore. He'd tried to warn them, but they'd been so sure the rain would let up. The weatherman on TV said so. They'd learn.

The wind picked up, leaving them all chilled. Walker couldn't stop shivering under the poncho. When he lagged behind, David and Yona waited for him to catch up. Now his teeth were chattering. David and Yona looked worried.

"When we get to the cave, we'll build a fire to thaw you out," David said. "It's not far now. Can you hold out a little longer?"

Walker lied and said he was fine. A fire would feel good. That motivated him to find the strength to speed up a little. By the time they were in sight of the rocks where Grady's granddaughter died, he was chilled to the bone.

The granite overhang at the mouth of the cave sheltered them from a fine cold drizzle that looked like it could go on all day. Walker hunkered down against the rock. "Where's that fire you promised me, Dave?" he asked. He was shivering and every joint in his body was stiff with cold. He clenched his teeth, trying to stop their chattering.

A few crows still crouched forlornly in the tall pine tree. He watched David take a nine-inch hunting knife from his pack and go at an old stump beside the tree. The boy should be able to hack out enough pitch to start a fire. It would burn even if it was wet. Yona gathered up some dead branches and hurried back to him.

Walker sat hunched over under the poncho. It didn't offer much warmth. His shivering was getting out of control. Yona dropped the branches on the ground and looked him over. "I don't like the way you look, Grandpa. Dave, what do you think?"

David looked up from the wood he was trying to light. "He's turning kinda blue. I think we better get him warmed up. He can rest awhile before we head back. If the rain lets up it won't be so bad." Walker huddled against the rocks, drawing the poncho around him.

"Too much easy living, Grandfather," David said. "In the old days, a man your age would still be in his prime. Here you are, shivering like you're gonna freeze to death." He laughed, but the laugh was strained.

"Yeah, I'm getting soft from easy living. Just get the fire going, boy, if you don't want to tote my carcass back down the mountain." Walker tried to laugh, too, but started coughing instead.

David coaxed a flame from the damp pine pitch and watched it crackle to life. Yona's hands shook as he piled on the wet pine twigs. Walker wasn't the only one who was getting chilled to the bone.

Dark, pitch scented smoke spiraled up toward the crack in the rocks and disappeared out into the drizzle. Walker leaned toward the fire and watched David take a Thermos from his pack. The boy thought of everything. He accepted the coffee David offered and cupped it between his palms, enjoying the warmth. His teeth had finally stopped chattering.

"You think you gonna make it now, Grandpa?" Yona asked.

"I reckon I just might, son. I'd sure like to dry out some, though. I can't remember it ever being so cold this late in the year."

They passed the coffee cup around, all taking a swig, then David refilled it.

"Hey, Dave," Walker said. "Any chance of you pulling a helicopter out of that knapsack of yours? You seem to have nearly everything else. I could use a ride down this mountain."

"You had your chance to stay home warm and dry, Grandfather. Reckon you'll have to make it home on your own two feet, just like the rest of us." David put the Thermos down beside Walker and stood up. "You stay here and get warmed up. Me and Yona will go get the stuff. If I recall, the pucker factor is a bit too high for you in the cave anyway."

Walker leaned back against a rock and tried to get comfortable. He poured the last of the coffee into the cup and sipped. "You're mighty right, son. I'd just as soon stay here."

He waved them off and watched them go, Yona following Dave into the cave, hoping they were as strong as they looked. It wouldn't be long now before their generation would be on their own. He and Grady were the only elders left and they were both way too old to handle a guardian's duties. If he'd had any doubts about it before, he didn't now. The exertion and cold had left him so weak he wasn't worth a crap. He was practically dead on his feet, right in the middle of the biggest crisis the Snake Dancers had ever faced.

If he ever made it down off this mountain, he would have to find Grady Smoker. It was time to turn things over to the next generation of Snake Dancers. He hoped they were up to it.

BACK INTO THE CAVE

"Damn, man. What is this? Journey to the center of the earth?" They were less than fifty yards inside and Yona had already decided he didn't like it much.

"Still got a long way to go," David said, laughing. "You don't like this any better than old Walker does, do you, brother?"

"Let's just say you're right about the high pucker factor," Yona answered. He started to say something else, but when David suddenly stopped and knelt on the cave floor, there was something in his attitude that said, "Be quiet." Yona stopped and kept his mouth shut till Dave waved him to his side. David pointed to the cave floor. A wet footprint stood out against the gray stone.

"You think it's yours? Or could it be Grandpa's from last night?" Yona asked.

"Wasn't raining last night. It would have been gone now anyway. Somebody's been here recently, within the last few minutes I would say." David spoke in a whisper, but his words echoed in the stillness.

He stood and cast the light ahead finding several more dark spots on the dry stone. He didn't take time to check them out, just signaled Yona to feel his way to the cave wall then snapped off the light and started walking.

Yona could barely hear Dave's footsteps even though he was right behind him, trying to walk just as softly, and not to think about the possibility that someone else lurked ahead with his own light turned off. Darkness closed around them so thick he swore he could feel it, like cold water. He reached for David and held onto his shoulder. David was the one who knew his way around in the cave and Yona didn't want to risk getting separated.

It felt like they had walked for miles. Yona thought they had begun a slight descent, as if the cave floor sloped downward, deeper into the mountain. It unnerved him. He stumbled against David. David reached back to steady him, then kept walking. Silence hung as thick as the darkness.

When a small ray of light appeared in the distance, Yona thought it must just be his brain's way of giving him some hope when he had stood all he could of the total absence of light. But if he was hallucinating, David was, too.

"Do you see that?" David's whisper was barely audible.

"I think so," Yona whispered back.

They inched forward, hardly daring to breathe. The light was getting closer but not much brighter. Yona could hear his heart pounding as they got nearer. He stepped away from David and focused on the light. It was at his feet when he stepped on something that felt so out of place in the cave he yelled before he could stop himself. He knew it was a body. Nothing else would give quite that way under a hiking boot.

David clicked on the flashlight then yelled louder than Yona had. "He's dead."

"Shit!" It wasn't the most appropriate thing to say, but it was all Yona could get out at the moment.

"What the hell have we got ourselves into, man?" David said.

"A damn sight more than I signed on for. Shit!"

There wasn't much left of the face. A shotgun blast from close range could do that to a man. It didn't matter though. They both knew who it was. Hell, most anybody around here could have identified him even without a face.

David got his wits about him enough to keep his voice down. "Looks like we need to let Nathan Axe know he can stop looking for this guy."

A thick blond braid, tied with a beaded leather thong, trailed in a pool of blood. In the ear that remained, a silver feather hung from the lobe on a stud shaped like an eagle.

"Shit!" Yona yelled.

David flashed the light away from the bloody mess and began to shine it around the cave. The light fell on an empty shell casing lying a few feet from the body. Yona bent over and looked at it, remembering not to touch it. It was evidence. He recognized a spent red shotgun shell.

Beyond the shell, shards of a broken pot lay scattered on the floor. David went to one that was almost half of an ancient clay pot. After he examined it, he swung the flashlight around, like he expected to find something.

"What are you looking for, Dave?" Yona asked.

David didn't answer. He had bent over a wadded pile of old deer skin that lay discarded just beyond the dead body.

Yona asked again, "Dave, what's wrong."

David stood up with the deerskins in his hand, tearing through their brittle folds. Then he dropped them at his feet and started acting like he had lost his mind. Yona had never heard David use that kind of language or yell the way he was yelling as he tore off down the cavern, taking the flashlight with him.

Yona was left in the darkness, alone, with the dead man. He had to follow David and find out what was wrong, but the echo of footsteps resonated deeper into the cave. He needed light. The glow from beneath the body didn't illuminate much more than a bloody fringe hanging from the sleeve of the white shaman's buckskin jacket. He didn't want to touch it, and he knew he shouldn't disturb evidence, but he couldn't take standing there in the dark with a dead man. The only way to get the flashlight was to roll the body off it. He bent over and pushed. It was all he could do to keep from puking when the white man's blood oozed between his fingers, but he hung on till he could reach the flashlight.

He wiped the flashlight on the dead man's pants to clean as much blood off as he could. He was through with the worst part. The mingled odor of blood and gun powder hit him hard when he stood up. A wave of nausea caught him off guard and he lost his breakfast a few steps away from the body.

If the killer was hiding somewhere in the cave, he already knew he wasn't alone. There was no need to worry about being quiet now. Every living thing on this mountain had already heard them. So much for the myth of the stoic Indian. Yona ran after David, bellowing his name as loud as he could. When David didn't answer, he kept running, straining his eyes ahead into the darkness hoping to see David's flashlight.

"Shit!" He didn't know why he kept saying that. It didn't help. Maybe it's the one thing you can say when you're so scared your brain turns to jelly. He said it again, a few more times, then fell silent when he saw a speck of light in the distance. Hoping it was David, he waited until it got close enough that he could be sure. "Just don't be the man with the gun," he prayed under his breath.

David wasn't running any more. In fact he looked like walking was too great an effort. He still held fragments of buckskin in his hand.

"Yona." His voice was hoarse. "They got the hands. The hands and all the rest. It's all gone."

Yona didn't know what to say. He reached out and David gave him the buckskin. He searched through them trying to find the conjuror's hands among the ancient, brittle folds. The dried fragments crumbled. He handed them back to David. David kept looking through them, as if he couldn't believe the hands weren't there.

"Dave. We gotta find whoever did it. We'll get Nathan Axe and anybody else who can help, and tell them anything they need to know. We gotta find him, and the hands. It's our job now."

He had to get David moving. They couldn't stand around the cave doing nothing.

He watched David reign in his emotions, impressed that he could do it after the shock he'd had.

"We need Buck. He's been a guardian for awhile. He'll

know what to do." David sounded almost calm.

Buck was missing, too. What if they didn't find him? He couldn't keep his worry to himself. "What if Buck's somewhere with *his* face blown off? And Grady, what if he's gone? Eli ain't got a clue about what's going on. He won't be any help. What are we supposed to do, David?"

"Take good care of your grandpa, for a start. He's the only one we've got who might know how to handle this. We gotta look after him good now." David picked up the fragments of buckskin off the cave floor and stuffed them into his backpack, then started back the way they had come. Yona was right behind him.

David was right. Walker was alone outside, and someone with a shotgun had already killed one man a few feet away.

They hurried past Eagle Feather's body, trying not to step in the blood.

It was well behind them when David yelled, "Oh shit."

What the hell had gotten into David now? He was pointing the light down at the floor, running back into the cave toward the body. Yona ran after him. David was pausing every few steps to get a better look at a trail of footprints. They were dark and perfectly formed, like tracks of boots just in out of the rain. But it wasn't water that wet those boots, and the tracks were not going into the cave, but toward the entrance—where his grandpa was waiting.

"Shit!"

This time it was both of them, and they were both running and yelling at the same time, remembering with horrible clarity the marks on the floor near the entrance. Not more than fifty yards from the only guardian they knew to still be alive.

David kept the light trained on the trail of footprints. They became less definite the farther they went from Eagle Feather. Halfway to the entrance, Yona slowed and knelt beside a dark stain.

"Hey Dave, wait."

David came back and squatted down beside him.

"Look at this," he said.

With obvious distaste, David touched a finger tip to the stain. "Still wet," he said, rubbing his finger on the stone to wipe the blood off it. The wet blood framed a partial print of a boot heel.

"It's fresh," David said. "Like he just stepped in it. But Eagle Feather is way back there."

Yona looked closer. "Looks like the blood is pooled up beside his shoe. Like it just dripped down and he stepped in it."

"You think it could be the killer's own blood?" David asked. "Maybe Eagle Feather did some damage before he got shot."

"Whatever happened, he's still on his feet, and Grandpa's out there by himself." Yona was already trotting toward the opening.

David caught up with him, pointing out every few feet, another splotch of blood, sometimes with a bit of boot print. They could see the light from the cave mouth when the prints veered toward the wall.

A spent flashlight lay there among a few shreds of plaid flannel. Wet blood stains marked the cave floor.

"The man who killed Eagle Feather," David said. "He must have stood here and bandaged his wound, and it wasn't long ago. The blood is still wet."

Yona's heart beat like a hammer. An armed man, who had already killed once today, had been just a few feet away from his grandpa, one of the last guardians alive. At least, he was alive when they left him. He ran toward the entrance, yelling for David to hurry.

At the entrance, the fire still smoldered. The empty coffee cup and Thermos sat beside it. But there was no sign of Walker. Yona ran out into the misty rain. Something blue lay crumpled on the rocks near the tall pine. He yelled for David as he bolted toward it, afraid of what he would find.

David was with him when he knelt beside Meredith's blue poncho. There was no movement under it, but the form it covered was unmistakable.

"Grandpa!" Yona cried.

He heard David on the cell phone, asking for Nathan Axe. Since Nathan wasn't in, he left a message he knew would bring help right away. "Walker Copperhead's down with a bad head wound. Eagle Feather is dead with his face shot off, and somebody is running around up here with a shotgun." He stuffed the phone in his backpack and began helping Yona try to revive Walker.

Yona swabbed at Walker's temple with the corner of the wet poncho. With the blood wiped away, he could see an ugly purple lump. Walker moaned and opened his eyes. He started to struggle, then recognized his grandson. "Grady," he mumbled. "Get Grady," and pointed weakly toward the trail down the side of the mountain, then he slumped in Yona's arms.

David reached for his wrist. "His pulse is faint and thready, but he's got one."

"Help is coming, Grandpa. We'll get you out of here." Yona was afraid he was going to break down and cry like a baby. He cradled Walker in his arms and pleaded with him to hang on. "Who did this to you, Grandpa?" Walker's head lolled to the side.

Yona looked helplessly at David. "What kind of person would do this to an old man?"

David said, "The same kind of person that would split a young girl's skull with a stone axe, or shoot a man in the face with a shotgun."

He looked closer at Walker's wound, dabbing at the blood with the sleeve of his shirt. "Somebody hit him hard. Probably with the butt of the same gun that killed Eagle Feather. He might have a concussion, but he's not bleeding. This isn't his blood."

"Damn. Whoever's blood it is, my grandpa's hurt bad. We can't just sit here, Dave. Call Nathan back and tell him to send Cherokee Rescue Service up the way he came last night. We can carry Grandpa down and meet them on the way. We gotta get him to a hospital, fast."

David got out the phone and dialed. Jimmy Hanks answered this time and David filled him in on Walker's condition and where to send the rescue team. When he hung up, they didn't waste any time. Yona already had his arms around Walker, lifting him to carry like a child.

"Wait, man," David said. "Remember that fireman's carry we learned? "Let's do it like that." He put an arm around Walker's back and Yona shifted his hold to conform to the position they had learned when they joined the volunteer fire department. This was much better. He was surprised to find just how much Walker weighed. He wasn't a big man but he sure was solid. With Walker between them, they set off down the mountain in a near trot.

Once, Walker stirred and opened his eyes. "Go get Grady," he mumbled, then went limp. With his head against Yona's shoulder, he passed out again.

"Yeah, Grandpa. We'll find Grady as soon as we get you to the hospital," Yona said.

"Grandfather," David pleaded. "Stay with us, man." Walker just moaned. "Well, at least you don't have to walk back down Wolf Mountain. You got your way there."

They had been on the trail almost an hour when the Rescue Squad met them with the litter.

The steep, rocky trail was hard to negotiate, even without the dead weight of a semiconscious man between them but they'd made good time. Walker hadn't opened his eyes more than a couple of times. When he did stir, he seemed more concerned about Grady than his own well being. They were more than glad to turn him over to the rescuers with the litter.

Nathan Axe wasn't far behind. He'd made good time after he received David's message. He was as worried as they had ever seen him. "Wait here a minute, boys," he said. "Mr. Copperhead's in good hands. I need to talk to you right now and I don't want any bullshit."

"You won't get any from us, Nathan," Yona said. "David

and I are way out of our league with this one. We're ready to tell you anything we know."

"Let's start with what you were doing up here, and where exactly you found the body."

"We're here because there was something hidden up on the mountain that we couldn't allow to fall into the wrong hands," Yona said. "If it does, we could all be in a hell of a lot more trouble than a few murders. We were trying to prevent that from happening because—because it's our job."

"We tried to keep it from happening, but we failed," David said. "The stuff is gone. The man who has it is probably the same guy who blew Eagle Feather's head off. The only ones who might know what to do now are Walker, Grady Smoker and Buck Locust. Walker is out of the picture. Buck and Grady are missing. If you got any suggestions, Sheriff, we're listening."

"Damn! You're telling me two people have already been killed because of something out of an old story. I don't want to hear that bullshit. My job is to figure out who's killing people and I expect you to help me do my job by telling me the plain, down to earth truth. You Snake Dancers are welcome to handle the supernatural stuff. I want you to, but you've gotta fill me in on everything you know about what's happening right here and now."

They told him, and didn't hold back anything. The story tumbled out with both of them talking so fast Nathan had to ask them to slow down. He was getting information quicker than he could scribble in his notepad.

When they got to the part about Grady's dead granddaughter, Nathan interrupted. "We don't have to feel bad anymore about Grady not getting to know the girl. According to Martha Waits at the bank, he's been sending a check to the girl's mother on the first of every month for years. Sounds like he knew about her long before Thomas found out he had a daughter. Martha said Grady even sent her money for a bus ticket to come up here."

Yona was to stunned to respond. That news should have made him feel better, but it didn't. One look at David's stricken expression and he knew it hit him just as hard. This could be bad news for so many reasons, most of which he was just beginning to understand.

Nathan wasn't through asking questions. They had to come up with some answers. Yona told him all he knew. He'd never been so scared in his life, and he still hadn't learned enough to comprehend what it was he feared.

Nathan closed his notepad and slipped it back into his pocket, satisfied they had told him all they could. He had a bit of information for them that eased Yona's mind. "I called Mr. Copperhead's house to let Kate know what happened. She's gonna go tell Faron, then head over here. Now, if you'll tell me how to find the dead man, you can go on and catch up with Walker."

The cave held no more secrets. There was no reason to hide it anymore. David told Nathan how to find the entrance. From there, all he had to do was follow the trail of bloody footprints.

Nathan set off up the mountain behind the men who had already passed him, on the way to check out yet another dead body on Wolf Mountain.

Yona and David hurried to catch up with the litter bearers that carried Walker. Yona was so anxious to see about his grandfather, he didn't detect the smear of fresh blood that marked a laurel leaf off to the side of the trail.

"Yona, wait," David called. "Your grandpa's in good hands with the rescue squad. They'll take care of him. There's a trail here and we need to follow it."

Yona was impatient, urging David to come with him to catch with Walker, until he saw the blood. He took one last look down the trail to a flash of color through the trees. Cherokee Rescue could do a lot more for Walker than he could. He had to trust him to their care and find the man who had hurt him. He plunged into the wet laurel thicket behind David.

The hunt was on.

SAFELY ON THE SNOWBIRD

The house on Snowbird had never been a more welcome sight. His wife and kids were safe here, but where was Buck? John couldn't get him off his mind.

Bonnie came to the door before Faron's Chevy came to a stop. "Diamond's asleep, Aunt Faron," she said. "I've gotta go home now."

John wanted nothing more than to go inside with Faron and his kids and lock the door, but he and Faron both knew he couldn't do it. Buck was in trouble. He sent Bonnie to wait in his truck and kissed Faron and Wren goodbye. "You know I've got to go look for Buck, don't you, honey?"

Faron didn't try to stop him. She wasn't one to show it when she was scared, but he could tell. She and Wren both clung to him for a long hug then let him go. "My mobile phone's in the truck. I'll keep in touch." He kissed them again and left.

Bonnie climbed into the Ram without a word. The poor kid was worried about her daddy, and with good reason. Buck had never been late getting home in his life, at least not without calling, and here it was nearly midnight and he hadn't been seen or heard from since before daylight that morning. John tried to reassure her, but he wasn't very convincing. They both knew it would take something serious to keep Buck from calling home.

Amy Locust was waiting for them on the porch. Faron had called to let her know they were on the way, and that John was going to look for her husband. Hugging Bonnie close, she thanked him with tears in her eyes.

"Hell, Amy, you know he'd do the same thing for me." John promised to call as soon as he knew anything.

He drove as fast as he dared, straight up the Cheoah to the place where Eli had found Buck's truck. Eli would be somewhere around there, too. He could count on that.

It was a stroke of good fortune that Walker had shown him that cutoff. It meant he could drive a lot closer to Degal'gun'yi and save himself a long hike. Strange how Eli and Buck both knew about it. Sometimes he wondered just how much they knew and couldn't tell him. He'd learned a great deal since Wren found those gym bags. Perhaps a thing or two that even Buck didn't know.

The Council House Mound wasn't far away. He wondered if Buck and Eli had slept on it, and if they'd had dreams like David did. Maybe he'd try it himself one of these days. It might help him keep up with his kids.

The slope under the pines was beginning to look like a parking lot. There was Buck's pick-up truck. Eli's truck was behind it, then there was a Bronco marked with the Graham County Sheriff's Department logo. He pulled beside the Bronco and parked.

His mobile phone and pager were on the seat beside him. He clipped the pager to his belt and put the phone in his jacket pocket. Eli and Buck both had the same equipment, issued by the forestry service. He didn't bother calling Buck's number. Surely somebody had already tried that. But if he could get in touch with Eli, he might know something by now. He punched Eli Smoker's mobile phone number in and almost instantly heard a frantic, "Hello," at the other end, along with the yip yip of the Chihuahua.

"Where are you, man?" John asked.

"I'm just east of the burial ground. You know the one. Degal'gun'yi."

"Anybody seen any sign of Buck? I just left Amy and Bonnie and they're about worried to death."

"Ain't seen hide or hair of him, Johnny. I found a partial

footprint back a ways. It might have been Buck's. I don't know. Dorsey wants to wait till morning to start a search. Says we can't see to hunt for him in the dark, but I think we need to keep looking."

"You're right, buddy, but the sheriff's probably smart not to get a search party out tonight. Any tracks Buck might have left would get destroyed. I'll head your way. Keep in touch, and hey, if that barking rat you've got in your pocket ain't scared to get his little feet dirty, see if he can sniff out a scent or something."

So, Eli was troubled, too. John had a real bad feeling that tomorrow might be too late. They needed to find Buck tonight. Then they could look for Grady Smoker. Come to think of it, Eli probably didn't know about the dead girl, or that Grady was missing. Amy said she had called Eli first, as soon as Buck didn't answer her page, and sent him to look for her husband. He'd been in these woods since around six-thirty.

Scanning the ground for footprints and the bushes for signs of disturbance, John made his way toward the burial ground. It felt like the right direction. Eli must have thought so, too. He didn't know where the owner of the Bronco was, but at least somebody from the sheriff's department was out searching.

Making sure to orient himself with landmarks that would lead him back to his truck, he headed into the thick growth of pines. Wouldn't do any good for him to get lost, too. Here and there he came across a broken twig or a scuff mark on a patch of moss, but not much else to indicate anyone had passed this way. There was no mistake, though. The trail was leading him toward Degal gun'yi.

He was examining what he thought might be a heel mark when his phone buzzed against his hip. He answered as quickly as Eli had.

"Hey, John, where are you?" Eli asked before John could even say hello.

"Heading toward you, I think. You still around the burial ground?"

"Yeah. And somebody's been here recently. You know this ground ain't much good for holding tracks, but I've found a couple of fairly clear ones. I think they might be Buck's."

"And I'm following a trail right for you. You wanna stay where you are and I'll catch up with you?"

"No problem," Eli answered. "I'm not too crazy about being in this old graveyard by myself in the middle of the night. Gives me the creeps. I could use some company."

John didn't bother looking for tracks anymore, so he made better time. If Eli had already tracked Buck as far as the burial ground, no need for him to track him there, too. Within half an hour he saw a light ahead. Eli must have gotten spooked and was coming back to meet him. John didn't blame him. There was something about this place that made him feel wierded out even in broad daylight. In the dark—well, he just tried not to think about it.

When Eli called out to him, he nearly jumped out of his skin. After so long in the dark with no sound but the nightlife, a human voice came as a shock. John couldn't remember ever being so glad to see somebody. He would have run the distance between them if he hadn't been sure he would trip over a log and break his neck.

He'd be cool, though. After all, they were both big strong forestry service men, and should act like it. Trouble was, they both knew they were just acting. They would have laughed out loud with relief to see each other if it wasn't for the fact that they were seriously worried about the best friend either of them had ever had. Neither would feel like laughing until they knew Buck Locust was safe.

"How far have you trailed him?" John asked.

"Me and Yip looked around some since I talked to you. We found two prints just beyond where Degal gun'yi slopes off into the woods. There's a narrow stream that runs by there and it looks like somebody jumped over it. They're two real good prints in the mud, one on each side. I figure they're Buck's tracks."

The bloodhound duties must have been a real strain for the Chihuahua. John saw his little round head and forepaws hanging over the pocket of Eli's jacket. The poor thing was trembling like he was scared to death. He wasn't usually *that* nervous.

John followed Eli for a while, debating with himself whether he should say anything about the duffle bag and what was in it. Walker had said not to talk about it to anybody but family, but the Smokers seemed like they were the kind of family that really mattered, like Buck was. With all that had happened he didn't want to keep secrets from his friend. Besides, if he talked about this first, he could stall about other things he had to tell Eli. Like, that there was a young girl in the Swain County morgue who was his blood kin. And that nobody knew where his grandpa was.

John kept his voice as casual as he could. "Eli, what do you know about a blood-drinking crystal called Ulunsu'ti, from a big snake's head?"

Eli slowed down. "Are you asking just because you remember the stories we grew up on, or do you have some other reason?"

"Let's say, some other reason. So, what do you know about it?"

Eli was trying to decide just how much he should say. John had lost patience with all the secrecy. "How about it, Eli?" he demanded.

Eli spoke slowly. "For some time now Grandpa has been dropping hints about telling me something important when the time comes. His hints were broad enough that, combined with some snooping and keen observation, I figure I've learned more than anybody suspected."

When he clammed up again, John prompted him, "Care to let me in on it?"

Eli stalled, then gave one of the half-assed answers John had learned to expect. "I probably know more than I'm supposed to but not as much as I need to. Why are you so interested in something that might not even exist outside of legend?"

John decided not to hold anything back. After all, nobody had sworn *him* to secrecy. "Because, yesterday evening just before dark, when I came up here with Walker and Wren to check on those trees you were worried about, Wren found something hidden under a log that freaked her and Walker out. They said it was all the stuff that was needed to bring the Ulunsu'ti back to life, and the best place to do it was at that mound that looks like an old council house, which was very close to where we found the stuff."

"Good God, man," Eli said. "Who all knows about this? Has Walker told my grandpa?"

"Well, buddy, that's something else I wanted to ask you about. When's the last time you talked to your grandpa?"

"Not for a couple of weeks," Eli said. "I don't know what's going on with him lately. Buck told me he's been hanging around with that weirdo white man who claims to be a shaman. The one with those camps all over the place where he rips off other white people. He says the white man's taken up with a Choctaw girl he met at one of his camps down in Mississippi, and she seems awfully young. Buck didn't like the looks of it. You know how he is. He won't rest until he finds out every detail."

They kept walking toward the stream where Eli and Yippi found the footprints. John hated to say anymore about what had happened up on Wolf Mountain and why Grady might be hanging around with the girl. Eli would have to know sooner or later, though. Might as well get on with it.

"Eli, did you know I didn't go to work today, and that's why Buck was up here checking things out instead of me?"

Eli grunted an affirmative and kept walking.

"Well, I didn't go to work because I went with Walker and Yona and David Wayanettah up to a cave on the side of Wolf Mountain. I don't understand why we had to go, but Wren found something else up there that was real bad. Worse even than what we found here in the woods."

"Yeah? Sounds like your kid's real good at finding bad things, John. What did she find this time?"

"That girl you were talking about. The one with the white man. We found her body. Somebody killed her and left her lying there in the rocks."

Eli stopped short and almost dropped his flashlight. "Damn! From what Buck said, she wasn't much more than a kid. Who'd do a thing like that?"

"I don't know who did it. Nathan Axe is trying to find out. There's more, Eli. Something you should know."

"Go on."

"Okay, buddy. But it's bad. You ready?"

Eli nodded, obviously impatient.

"Buck found out who the girl was. He talked to Nathan Axe and David Wayanettah about it. It started back when we were kids and your dad went to work on that construction job down in Mississippi and was away so much."

"That was nearly twenty years ago," Eli said. "What's that got to do with the dead girl?"

John realized he had to just spit it out. There was no way to make it easy. "Seems like your dad took up with a woman down there, and she had a kid. Somehow, the white guy met up with the kid."

Eli stopped him. "You can't be saying—No!"

"Damn, Eli. I wish it wasn't true, but it is. It's her. The girl that was killed belonged to your dad and the Choctaw woman."

Eli's arms dropped limp to his side and the flashlight fell from his hand. He walked off into the darkness. John grabbed the light and went after him. "Wait," he called. "I'm sorry, man. Just slow down."

Eli stopped and leaned against a tree. When John got there, he had Yippi snuggled under his chin. The dog whimpered and licked his face. John wasn't sure what to say, so he just waited until Eli was ready to talk.

After a couple of minutes, Eli asked, "When did you find this out, John?"

Eli sounded calm, like it hadn't sunk in yet, or he realized he didn't have time to get emotional. He'd just learned he had a sister, and that she was dead. But he also had a good friend who was lost and in trouble. That had to come first.

"I didn't know till this evening," John answered. "Seems like it started when Buck checked on the white guy and the girl. David knew, too. They traced her down to Mississippi. That's how they found out about your dad. Buck told David he had talked to Thomas yesterday. Buck went to tell your grandpa last night, but Grady wasn't home and nobody had seen him. Buck got worried about your grandpa and called Nathan. Seems like nobody knows where Grady is."

"I wouldn't be too worried about Grandpa," Eli said. "He's gone off on his own before, but he usually lets somebody know. Soon as we find Buck, we'll look for my grandpa."

"I'd feel better about it if Buck was here to help us," John said. "I hate to drop all this on you and then tell you to get over it until we have more time, but that's what we gotta do. We can't leave Buck wherever he is much longer. I have a gut feeling our buddy's in big trouble."

"You've been living with the Copperheads too long, John. You've developed a sixth sense, just like the rest of them. And I think I might have picked it up from you, because I know you're right. Knew it the minute Amy called me. That's why I dropped everything and took off out here. Amy said he was going to check on that blight, or whatever, for you."

They reached the stream and Eli searched along the bank with the flashlight and found the tracks he had told John about. A broken branch on a honeysuckle bush a few feet away and some weeds that had been trampled, indicated they were on the right trail.

"He's somewhere close, Eli," John said. "I know he is."

Eli shouted Buck's name as loud as he could. There was no answer.

"What if he's hurt and can't answer?" John asked.

"Then we gotta find him, John. Let's go."

John pulled the cell phone out of his jacket pocket. "You know, Buck always has his phone and pager with him. He liked to keep in touch with the station, and with Amy and Bonnie." "We've all tried calling him and he doesn't answer," Eli said.

"Don't expect him to answer," John said. He dialed Buck's cell phone number and started walking quietly, listening. They followed an ill defined path through trampled weeds, toward a hill that looked out of place.

Eli dialed Buck's pager number. Somewhere in the distance came the soft sound of ringing and beeping.

They ran toward the sounds. Around on the far side of the hill their lights found a scattered pile of rocks. At the bottom of the hill lay a big round stone. Draped across it was a jacket they both recognized. The beeping and ringing was coming from the pocket.

"He's around here somewhere, John," Eli said as he picked up the coat.

John swung the flashlight around, looking at the pile of rocks and on up to the hillside. Something had happened here. Suddenly he knew what. He started yelling Buck's name and tossing stones away at the same time. He stopped to listen when he heard a muffled voice call his name.

"Buck! Where are you, man?" Eli yelled.

John already knew where Buck was and intended to get to him fast. He attacked the pile of rocks with renewed vigor.

"Easy," Buck yelled. "Nothing holding this hillside off me but a rotten timber. Don't blow it for me."

"Jesus!" Eli said. "He's inside there. How are we gonna get him out?"

Buck hollered his answer. "Very carefully. This thing's been trying to fall in on me all day. By the way, think you could get some light in here so I can see what's happening?"

Eli played the beams from his flashlight across the landslide, hoping to find a place where the light could leak through to Buck. He steadied the light when Buck called out, "There you go. Now hold it there."

John had his phone out again. The only number he could remember at that moment was his own. That was good enough. Faron could get help here as fast as anybody, and she would know exactly where they were. All John had to tell her was, "Come to that funny looking hill out east of Degal'gun'yi." He put the phone in his pocket and called to Buck, "How does it look?"

"About as bad as it gets. I'm in a hole here with a beam right above my head that's holding up the roof, and it's bent almost double. Wouldn't take a hair's weight more to break it. If that happens, I'm in big trouble."

"Think it would help if you had something to support that beam?" John asked.

"Sure couldn't hurt. But how you gonna get anything in here?"

"We'll figure it out," John said and turned away with his light. Eli followed him.

"Damn. It's dark in here," Buck called.

"We need the light more than you do right now. Chill out," John called, then on second thought he said to Eli, "See if you can find exactly where the light was getting in. Try to make a bigger opening there without caving in the place."

John left Eli at work creating an opening and went to search for something to shore up up the beam over Buck's head. He needed a tree branch or sapling that was sturdy enough and yet not too big to maneuver into the tunnel. He found one that looked promising and was trimming branches with his pocket knife when Eli came running. "John," he said. "I don't know how we're gonna do this. Looks like a big log laying right across his back.

John dropped the branch and climbed back up the hill. Eli had found the minuscule crevice between the stones, then carefully eased away one stone at a time till he could look in. The light was propped to shine in on Buck. John's heart almost stopped when he saw the fix he was in.

Eli's desperation was contagious. "He's gotta be hurt bad, John. What are we gonna do?"

John pushed him away from the opening. No need to let Buck know how scared they were. "Keep calm. We've gotta do something in a hurry. Help me find something to shore that hole up till we can drag him out."

Their combined weight was enough to break a couple of limbs from a maple. They stripped the branches off as best they could, ending up with two rough looking poles.

"John," Eli said just before they were in Buck's hearing range. "What if his back is broken, and we pull him out. He could be paralyzed."

"And if we don't, he could be dead," John said.

John carefully enlarged the opening until he could stick his head inside. Then he said as calmly as he could, "So tell me about it, Buck. What are we dealing with here?"

"Well, it's like this." Buck copied John's forced casual manner. "I've got this big heavy thing laying across my back. I think I could get out from under it and dig out of here myself, only it must be holding the beam over my head in place. Every time I try to wiggle free, the roof falls down a little."

John said, "We're gonna hand some saplings in to you. See if you can use them to prop up the roof beam. Think you can manage that, man?"

"It's better than anything I've come up with all day. Give them to me one at a time. I'll see what I can do."

It was pure torture, easing the poles in so slowly when they knew every second counted. But one mistake and Buck would be under tons of earth and rocks. They'd never get him out alive.

All they could do was shine the lights in and listen. They heard a dull creak, then the old beam sagged and splintered. Falling earth and timbers rendered the light useless. A curtain of dust cut Buck off from sight. Sick at heart, John counted the seconds. Beside him, Eli was already digging carefully with his bare hands.

When the noise of falling rubble abated, they listened. Buck's muffled, "I'm still alive so far," was music to their ears.

"You got the beams propped up yet?" John yelled.

"I'm working on it." Buck grunted with exertion. "Got the second one up. I think it's gonna hold."

John pulled Eli away and shined the flashlight through the cloud of dust. Buck had the last sapling in place. The supports looked like tooth picks bending under the big beam above his head. The beam creaked and groaned, releasing another shower of earth. A rumble came from deep inside the mound.

"Now or never, Buck," John yelled. He reached in as far as he could. "Let's go."

Buck gave a mighty grunt, straining to break free of the timber that held him down. The beam above him shifted and settled against the poles. They bent under the weight. One cracked and splintered, useless now.

John reached deeper. He heard Eli yelling, "Oh, Jesus," as he got a firm grip on his ankles. His fingers connected with Buck's. With a yell, Buck lurched toward him and latched onto his arms. He gripped Buck as hard as he could and yelled to Eli, "Pull!"

Thunder rumbled inside the mound. One last desperate heave, and the three of them were hanging onto each other, tumbling down the hillside in an avalanche of rock and earth.

When they came to a stop, John stumbled to his feet. His body ached in a hundred places, but he could stand. Eli lay across Buck a few feet away. John helped Eli sit up. Buck groaned and turned over. He needed help to stand, but as soon as he was on his feet, he stumbled to the creek.

Before he reached it, they heard shouting from the edge of the woods.

Eli said, "Hey, Buck. We're okay now. The pros are here to rescue you."

Sheriff Dorsey and a deputy were running toward them, wanting to know if Buck was hurt.

Buck said, "Don't have time to talk to you now, guys. I'm

gonna go drink that creek dry."

John and Eli helped him limp to the stream. When they let him go he dropped down on his belly with his face in the water. John jumped across the stream and gave Dorsey a terse account of what had happened. He used the excuse that he and Eli wanted to get Buck to the emergency room to have his injuries looked after. One look at him was enough to make that sound believable. He had abrasions and contusions on his face and his torn shirt revealed a bloody laceration.

Dorsey offered to take him.

"Tell you what, Sheriff," John said. "If you'll get in touch with Amy and let her know Buck's okay, Eli and I will look after him. We need to go now. It's gonna take him awhile to get to my truck. Buck's walking kinda slow." He didn't mention that they had cell phones and could have called Amy themselves.

John bent down beside Buck and made a show of helping him to his feet. "Let's go guys," he said.

Buck leaned on him heavier than he expected. John supported him while they walked out of Dorsey's hearing. Unless Buck's injuries were life threatening, there was no time to go to an emergency room. When he was sure they were alone, he stopped and propped Buck against a tree. "We've gotta talk, Buck. Wanna tell me what you were looking for in that hole?"

"What makes you think I was looking for something?"

"Well, for one thing, if you came up here to check on those trees, I don't think they were under that hill. For another thing, I know Walker told you what we found Monday night. I figured there was a good chance you might be worried about that."

"Did you figure I might wonder about an old hide-covered box?" Buck asked.

"That's what you were looking for, huh?" John asked. "Would it make you feel any better to know it's safe? That Walker and David Wayanettah have it?"

Buck seemed to forget all about his wounds. "You gotta tell me everything. Walker wouldn't give me any details. Did you see what all he found?"

John told him to lower his voice. Dorsey and his deputy weren't far away, checking out the cave-in at the mound. Speaking barely above a whisper he said, "I just know enough to confuse the hell out of me. Walker and David are keeping something from me and Yona. I saw a pile of bones. Walker said they belonged to Kanegwa'ti. Then there was a whole shit-load of medicine stuff, like a bowl, a pipe, rattle, whistle and other stuff like that. Everything had a snake on it in some way. Then there was the box. Walker grabbed it before I got a good look at it, and said something about that crystal thing."

"Where's the ark now, John?"

"Last I saw of it, Walker and David had it up on Wolf Mountain. That's where we went today."

"Did Walker get in touch with Grady?"

John figured Buck must still be worried about Grady, since he couldn't find him last night. Eli answered for him. "No. Seems like nobody knows where Grandpa is. I'm uneasy about him, after what John told me earlier." He looked at John. "Tell him about the girl. I don't think I can."

John didn't know where to start. He plunged in, "Nathan Axe says you were checking up on Eagle Feather and the Indian girl with him."

Buck interrupted. "Wait Johnny, there's something I need to talk to Eli about before you get into this."

"No need, Buck," Eli said. "John already told me who she was."

Buck forgot to keep his voice down. "Something's wrong there. I don't trust that Eagle Feather. I wanted to talk to Grady about the girl. I don't like her hanging out with that creep."

"You don't have to worry about that anymore, Buck," Eli said. "John can tell you that part, but if you don't mind, I'd just as soon not listen to it again." He started walking ahead. Buck would have gone after him, but John caught him by the arm.

"Let him go. He's just now learned about the girl. He didn't even have time to get used to the idea of her being his half sister, before she got killed."

Buck swore. "The girl's dead? Damn, man. What happened?"

"We found her body today up on Wolf Mountain. Somebody split her head open and left her to die. David called Nathan Axe and he met us up there. They found an old stone axe near the body. It was all bloody, so he figures that's what they killed her with."

"She was a kid, man. Damn. Did Nathan pick up that Eagle Feather guy? He had to be the one that did it. Son of a bitch."

"Can't find him," John said. "Dorsey sent a man up to his camp looking for him and he wasn't there. Nobody's seen him all day. Can't seem to find Grady, either. I told Eli we'd go looking for him as soon as we saved your ass. You up to it?"

Buck stood there, thinking. "John, what if Eagle Feather killed the girl and Grady found out? If he knew who the girl was, do you think he would be out to get the man that killed her?"

"I don't know, man. I figure Grady for the kind that would have come to somebody for help. He never was one to go out on his own with anything. Grady would have called on Walker. He always came to him when he had troubles."

"And Walker hasn't heard from him?"

"Not a word. I've been with him all day, and he didn't know where Grady was. We left him at David's house this evening. He was gonna ride back with Kate after supper. I'm sure he's at home now. In fact, I bet he'll be back at your truck along with Amy waiting to see you when we get there."

Buck was walking better now. "If he is, I need to talk to him bad. Him and Grady."

John had to hustle to keep up. It was a wonder Buck could walk at all with what he'd been through, but in spite of a limp and an awkward gait, he set a demanding pace. Every muscle in John's body ached from moving the rock pile, and he had

more than a few bruises and scrapes from the landslide that
followed, but so did Buck and Eli. It didn't seem to be slowing
them down. He resisted the urge to complain.

Amy came running as soon as she caught sight of the
flashlights through the trees, crying with relief and hugging her
husband until he had to pull away to protect his battered body.
She wanted to take him straight to the emergency room of
course, or at least take him home and get him cleaned up, but
he wouldn't hear of it.

Kate rescued him. She had brought Amy and kept her calm
while they waited, so Amy wouldn't run off into the woods,
looking for her man. "Honey, if Buck was hurt all that bad, I
doubt he would be on his feet. He looks fit enough to me."

John wondered why the women were there alone. "Where's
Walker?" he asked.

"Last I saw of him, he was at David Wayanettah's house. I
left him and Yona there last night," Kate turned to Buck. "If I
was you, I'd go on over there and see what they're up to. Far
be it from me to poke my nose in your business, but I figure
you're in this up to your eyeballs."

Amy objected. Kate put an arm around her shoulders and
walked with her toward the car. "Johnny and Eli will go with
him. Don't you worry about your man. They'll look after him."

Buck kissed his wife and reassured her that he would be
okay. She made him promise that he would be careful and left
with Kate.

Lights approaching through the woods announced the
arrival of Dorsey and his deputy.

John's truck was the easiest to get to. They made a run for
it. Dorsey had checked out the tunnel and would have a lot of
questions about how Buck got himself trapped in it, and how
John and Eli managed to find him. They didn't have time for
that. They left right behind Kate and Amy, making sure that by
the time Dorsey got there, all he saw was two sets of taillights
disappearing down the trail.

John's truck had better than half a tank of gas. That was a

good thing, since there wasn't an open gas station for miles. After all, it was the dead of night, or to be more accurate, the wee hours of the morning. The dash clock read 4:28 A.M. John thought how much he wished he was snuggled up beside Faron in bed. He had to settle for giving her a call to tell her he was heading back to David's house.

She was awake. He knew she would be. She didn't object when he told her they were going back to Big Cove, but she couldn't keep the worry out of her voice. "Make sure Grandpa is okay," she said.

He told her to try to get some sleep, even though he knew she wouldn't close her eyes until he came home. He thought he heard Wren in the background, asking if that was Daddy. He hung up before he decided to bail out and go home.

The town of Robbinsville seemed sound asleep when they drove through. Of course it never was wide awake. Most of the businesses were closing or moving out to the strip mall. They drove through town in silence and for the second time in twenty-four hours, John found himself driving across Stecoah in the dark.

"Let's go by Grandpa's place first," Eli said. "Maybe he's home now. I'd sure like to know he's okay."

"You and me both, buddy," Buck said. "Grady might be able to settle my mind a whole lot if I could talk to him. You know, he was seen with Eagle Feather more than once lately. I'd like to know why. If he knew about the girl, that would explain a lot. He could have been spending time with her. I'd feel better about that than to think he had taken up with Eagle Feather."

"If he knew about her, looks like he would have told Dad and me. We had a right to know," Eli said.

"Maybe he kept it to himself because of your mom. She'd bust your dad's head if she found out," John said. "He wouldn't want to cause trouble between your folks, but no reason for him not to tell you that you had a sister. This whole thing is weird."

There was plenty of time on the drive over Stecoah Mountain to talk and speculate about what was going on with Eagle Feather, the dead girl, and their elders. Yippi snoozed in Eli's lap, worn out by his night in the woods. The atmosphere in the truck became tense when Buck started asking John a lot of strange questions that got even stranger every time he answered one.

Buck wanted to know if Walker had told him the story of the Suye'ta, and how he had to be an outsider. Then he asked if Walker had mentioned that the Suye'ta would wake the Ulunsu'ti, because something, or someone, in the tribe mattered more to him than his own safety.

John thought of all the times he'd wondered if he was reading too much into what Walker said. All too often lately he'd had the feeling there were things Walker was hinting at but not saying directly. He was already as uncomfortable as he had ever been when Buck mentioned that everybody knew he loved Faron and his kids enough to do anything for them. He made it sound like a compliment when he remarked that for an outsider, John was real connected to the Cherokee people.

John was beginning to catch on and it pissed him off. "Hey, wait a freakin' minute! I've done a lot of things I don't understand. And my own family says that I'm more of a Copperhead than a McLeymore, but if you think that I'm gonna have anything to do with some crazy-assed plan to rule the world with a damn blood-drinking crystal, think again, man!"

Buck tried to backpedal, telling John to calm down.

John wasn't about to calm down. "Don't think you're gonna drag me into this shit. I'm already way more involved than I want to be. Soon as we find Grady, I'm out of this superstitious hogwash." He was driving much too fast for the curves, and only occasionally wandering into the proper lane. Buck and Eli had to do some smooth talking to get him settled down.

"John, I'm not asking you to do anything, especially that," Buck said. "It's just that I have reason to suspect Walker might be thinking about it. My grandpa told me one time that Walker brought it up to him."

"Jesus, Buck!" Eli said. "Your grandpa walked over four years ago. You mean they were talking about this way back then?"

"They've been talking about it for years, ever since Fontana Dam got built," Buck said. "People will never know what was buried under that lake. Since then, it's been one thing after another. They say there won't be any sacred places left if things keep going the way they are. And we need some of those places more than most people will ever know. Even the homes of the Nunne'hi have tourists crawling all over them. The immortals are mighty scarce around here these days, and the elders say once the Nunne'hi are gone, we're not far behind. Some of the men feel like the Suye'ta and Ulunsu'ti are the only way to stop it."

"Well, they can damn sure do it without me," John said.

"Don't blame you, man," Buck said. "It's not the way to go anyhow. The time for conjurors is passed. We need to handle things in a different way now. To tell you the truth, I've been kinda worried that Walker might talk you into something crazy. I should have come to you about it a long time ago, but—well . . ."

"But you Snake Dancers aren't supposed to talk to outsiders about your private mo-jo," John said.

Buck and Eli both were stopped by that. "Walker told you about the Snake Dancers?" Eli asked.

"No, but all day long I've been listening to him and Dave and Yona talking some weird shit. I reckon Grady must have told you, Eli."

Buck was surprised by both of them. "Hold on," he said. "Last I heard, neither one of you knew anything about the Snake Dancers. There's been some complaining about how Grady was waiting too long to bring you in, Eli. And John, according to the way I was taught, you never were supposed to know, unless you were the Suye'ta."

"It's not like I give a rat's ass. I could have lived my whole life without knowing any of this crap, but looks like Walker's been hauling me in behind my back. He even dragged me down to the river about twenty-four hours ago. God only knows what that was all about."

"Walker took you to water?" Buck asked. "The whole deal. With the puking and praying?"

"And the fasting, and the freezing my balls off in the cold water. And that was after the funky smoke that gave me hallucinations of a cotton-mouthed water moccasin crawling up my legs. Damn. That was spooky."

"John," Buck said. "You know we don't use hallucinogens. If you saw a snake, it wasn't from the smoke."

John was suddenly very subdued. "I would rather just go on believing it was the smoke if you don't mind, guys. That was the weirdest thing I've ever experienced. It could be a carry-over from all the snake dreams I keep having—that is when I get a chance to actually sleep."

"Jesus! I hate snakes more than Indiana Jones does," Buck said. "If I'd thought there was a chance of snakes being in that tunnel, it might have saved us all a lot of trouble. I don't know that I could have gone in there. How long have you been having these snake dreams?"

"Ever since I married into a nest of Copperheads," John snapped. "And the head Copperhead started trying to turn me into the living dead or something. Don't you reckon that might be about enough to give a man nightmares?"

"Yeah. That would do it for me," Eli said. "You see now why I married out. There's something to be said for dull in-laws. Hilda's folks are just as happy not to get me too involved. Wonder what they'd do if I offered to start going over to Murphy every Sunday to the Episcopal Church with them?"

That mental image brought a laugh to all three. It helped John's stress level. "Don't do it, man," he said. "They just might take you up on it and you'd be stuck. Of course, they'd want you to cut your hair and get a suit. Think you could go that far just so you could get white man's religion?"

"Oh, I might look sharp in a suit. Might even try it some day, but the hair stays. Hilda likes it just the way it is. Besides, we got married in that church. I figure I've been there enough."

The talk kept John alert for the rest of the drive. Thin brief streaks of lightning intermittently flashed across the gray morning sky, disappearing so fast he couldn't be sure he really saw them at all.

"Looks like it's gonna rain," he said.

"Good day for a drive in the Smokies, huh, guys," Eli said.

Buck stretched and complained of the pain in his back. "Yeah, if I'd listened to Amy I could have spent the day in a nice, warm, dry emergency room."

They were quiet after that, and watched as the rain commenced a steady drizzle on the windshield. After a while Buck broke the silence. "You sure it was the ark, John? And you know it's safe with Walker and Dave?"

John was glad the conversation had picked up again. In the silence, it was hard not to think of the dead girl, or worry about Grady Smoker.

"Wren seemed sure of it, and she knows more about this stuff than I do," he said. "Last I saw of it, it was all in a big duffle bag that Walker hung onto like it was welded to his arm. I think you can rest easy about it. He ain't gonna let anything happen to your conjure crap."

Buck said, "I can't rest easy till I have it in my hands. I have to find a place where it will be safe. It's my responsibility until I have a male heir to turn it over to. Besides, I want to get it away from Walker before he manages to turn you into the Suye'ta."

"Damn, man. Don't even joke about that," John said. "Makes me want to kick Walker's ass for even thinking about it."

Buck didn't laugh. "One thing I agree with Walker about. If we wanted to bring in a Suye'ta, we couldn't do any better than you. When this is over and everything is back in its place, we have to leave you out of all the Snake Dancer business. I kinda hate that. None of us ever kept secrets from each other, except this. I'm glad you understand why it has to be this way."

John hunched over the steering wheel. "Don't let it worry you one bit, ol' buddy. Feel free to leave me out of as much of this bullshit as you want to. I've had about all of it I can stand."

"That's fine for you, John," Eli said. "But I've been left out long enough. As soon as we can find my grandpa, I'm gonna drag as much information out of him as I can. I know enough to understand that the Snake Dancers need me now."

Buck agreed. "We'll both be needed in the Circle, Eli. We've gotta find Grady."

For some reason, John stopped thinking about the dead girl or worrying about Grady Smoker. All he could think of was Walker. This had to be another one of those *feelings* like the Copperheads got. He was getting a bad one about Faron's grandfather. He tried to put it in the back of his mind and concentrated on driving.

Visibility was poor. A steady, cold drizzle settled in well before they reached Grady's trailer. Early spring was a traitorous time here in the mountains. One day it would feel like summer had arrived, then cold wind and rain would dash that hope and make you think winter would stay forever.

This was one of those winter days.

He parked under the beech tree and they ran to the trailer's front stoop, huddling in its shelter while Eli knocked and called. When there was no answer, he tried the door. "I'll be damned," he said when it opened. "Grandpa never leaves the door unlocked."

They trooped in while Eli kept calling, "Hey, Grandpa. You in here, Grandpa?"

The trailer felt empty, like nobody had lived there in a long time. They had been here when it smelled of hot gingerbread and chicory coffee. Now, the coffee pot was cold and there didn't appear to be anything to eat in the kitchen but what was left of a round of hoop cheese on the countertop. Buck looked at it, trying to remember something, then reached in his jacket and pulled out a red waxy piece of cheese rind.

He showed it to John, then called, "Come look at this, Eli." The three of them looked at the cheese rind, waiting for Buck to tell them why. He laid it down next to the round of cheese. "Think it matches?" he asked.

"Man, are we gonna look for my grandpa or stand around playing games with cheese?" Eli said as he turned to walk away.

"Wait a minute, Eli. You want to know where this rind came from?"

"I figured it was laying there with the cheese," Eli looked concerned. "Where did it come from, Buck?"

"Yesterday morning, when I got to the hill where you found me, this was lying there on a rock. It wasn't mine, because I sure didn't take time for a snack. My guess was that somebody had a picnic out in the woods."

John understood. "Probably the same person who opened up the tunnel and stole the ark."

Eli looked like he had been kicked in the belly. "Guys, I can't listen to this anymore. When we find Grandpa, he'll explain. We've gotta find my grandpa." He ran out of the trailer. John and Buck followed him to the front porch of the old house.

Eli was sitting on the steps, his back against a sagging post. They squatted beside him. "Remember how we used to sit out here listening to Grandpa tell us stories?"

John remembered, "Used to scare the crap out of me. I only came up here with you guys because of all the cookies and gingerbread your grandma used to make us."

Eli looked up. "It was a beautiful view, before they put the trailer there. When I'd stay over, we'd sit out here and watch the sunset. It was peaceful, listening to Grandma and Grandpa talk in our language. Made me feel good."

They sat, quietly talking about the old days. They were interrupted by a commotion in the side yard. Expecting the worst, they eased around the corner. Lena's old cat was crouched over her kill, spitting at them. She didn't like it when her breakfast got disturbed. The chipmunk she was ready to dine on would have appreciated it if they had come along sooner. Eli braved her teeth and claws to pick her up and carry her back to the trailer's kitchen. John and Buck followed. They helped him search through cabinets and found one lone can of cat food. Eli dumped it into her dish. She was generous enough to share it with Yippi.

"That lazy cat never hunted in her life," Eli said. "They always fed her canned cat food. She must have been half starved to go kill a chipmunk."

John said, "Grady's not here, Eli. He would at least have fed his cat if he was." Let's look around the place. Then I think we should go talk to Walker."

They spread out to search the grounds. Back near the laurel thicket, Buck bent down to check out a set of tire tracks in the soft soil that were made by narrow and nearly bald tires.

John stooped beside him. "You know something, don't you Buck?"

Eli came around the clump of laurels. Buck said, "I'll tell you about it later. Let's go to David's and see if they've heard from Grady."

Eli heard the last part. "I don't know where Grandpa is, but I'm afraid he's in some kind of trouble. If it has anything to do with that Eagle Feather creep, I want to be ready for him when I see him."

John didn't know what he meant by that, but Eli was running toward the trailer. He and Buck followed.

Eli went to Grady's bedroom and opened the closet door. After he rummaged around a while he announced, "It's gone."

"What's gone, Eli," John asked.

"Grandpa's shotgun. He always kept it here."

The three of them stood staring into the closet like that might make the shotgun reappear, until Eli closed the door and hurried out to the truck. John and Buck climbed in after him.

Again, John drove much too fast for the rain slick mountain

road. He knew Eli and Buck were thinking the same thing he was; that Grady had gone after Eagle Feather for what he did to the girl. They needed to find him first. They would talk to Walker and David and then call Nathan Axe and tell him about Grady and the shotgun.

The ride up to David Wayanettah's house was quiet. John had things he wanted to say, but he didn't want to talk. Nobody did. Hell, it hurt too much even to think.

Eli broke the silence when he couldn't take it anymore. "Eagle Feather. He killed the girl and Grandpa found out. Eagle Feather was probably using her to control Grandpa. My grandpa wouldn't do what you're thinking he did."

"Grady Smoker is as good a man as I've ever known, Eli," Buck said. "All I'm thinking is that he's in trouble and we need to find him and see what we can do."

John wanted to comfort his friend, but he was having enough trouble dealing with his feelings about Walker. The old goat had no right to suck him into something as weird as that Suye'ta business. And he was going right along with it, just like he did with everything the Copperheads came up with. Well, not anymore. When he got hold of Walker Copperhead, he'd let him know just what he thought of his plans.

Even as he relished the thought of verbally ripping Walker a new one, a sharp stab of concern shot through him. He'd sure hate to see anything happen to the old man. He was suddenly in a bigger hurry to get to the Wayanettah place and make sure Faron's grandpa was okay. That bad feeling was getting stronger every minute.

David's driveway was empty. Buck got out and knocked on the door to make sure, but they already knew nobody was in the house.

"Where do you think they went, John?" Eli asked.

"I don't know why, but I figure they went back up there where we found the girl. If not, I'd say they took those bones and grave goods to Ataga'hi." John was already shifting into reverse when Buck climbed in. "We'll go see if David's truck is parked up on the trail. If it's not, we'll go to Thunderhead."

Marge Wayanettah was standing by her mailbox when they drove by her place. She waved them down and John reluctantly stopped. Might as well, just in case she knew something. More likely she wanted to find out more about the girl's murder. Marge liked her privacy but if anything was going on in her neighborhood, she wanted all the details. She didn't wait for any of the usual polite exchanges. As soon as Buck rolled down the window, she started yelling questions. "What in the world is going on around here this morning? Between the Cherokee Rescue people and Nathan Axe and his bunch, looks like everybody in Western North Carolina is tearing up and down my road."

John leaned across the seat and yelled back, "I guess Nathan's looking into what happened to that girl. You seen David go by here this morning?"

"I haven't seen anybody but the sheriff. I came down here when I heard the rescue boys with their siren wailing, like anybody around here needed to hear that. Nathan went by about the time I got to the road. But I heard a couple of cars go by early this morning. There's been more traffic on my road the last two days than I usually see in a week. Body might as well just move to town, with all this racket."

John's bad feeling really kicked in when he heard about the rescue squad. The sheriff must have gone back up the mountain to continue his investigation, but who needed to be rescued? His last shred of anger toward Walker melted into a sick dread that Faron's grandpa might be the one in trouble. He pulled away, yelling out the window, "We'll go see what's happening, Aunt Marge, and let you know something later."

"Something's wrong, guys," he said. "Bad wrong."

Buck and Eli agreed.

"They might have found my grandpa," Eli said. "If he's hurt, that would explain why he's missing."

It made sense. And with Cherokee Rescue Squad there, they figured he was still alive. John couldn't talk about it any more.

He'd stopped worrying about whether or not they ever found Grady Smoker. He needed to know Walker was okay.

The tire tracks on the muddy logging trail told them they were not the first to drive up it this morning. That was confirmed when they saw three other vehicles parked ahead. David's truck was first, then a Cherokee Rescue vehicle. Behind that was Sheriff Nathan Axe's car.

"What the hell?" John said, braking to a stop.

Buck jumped out of the truck. "Surely they're not all here to bring the girl's body down. They would have done that last night."

"I'm sure they did," John said. "We brought Wren down before the authorities got there, but I don't think they would have left the girl up there all night. It wouldn't be respectful."

"No, they're here for something else," Eli said.

They set off up what was now a well defined path.

John forgot all about being tired and ignored the aches and pains in his bruised body. Buck and Eli had their work cut out for them just to keep up with him.

When he saw men up ahead with a litter, he left the others behind and ran. "Oh, Jesus," he said when he saw Walker lying there, eyes closed, still as death. The men carrying him stopped so John could get a look. He felt Walker's neck for the carotid artery, then choked back a sob of relief. The pulse beat weak but steady against his fingers. Whatever made that big purple lump on Walker's head had not killed him. John had never felt so grateful. As long as the tough old goat was still breathing, he would pull through. He had to.

Something was missing. Walker didn't have his walking stick. John lifted the blanket and looked on the litter. It wasn't there. Walker would never have left it behind willingly. If he didn't have it in his hand, he always made sure it was close by. John couldn't remember ever seeing him without it.

"Where's his walking stick?" John asked.

One of the men answered him. "He didn't have it when we got to him. And we didn't have time to look for it. They're waiting for him at Swain County emergency room. Sheriff Axe is up the hill. He can tell you what happened. Ask him about the walking stick."

John bent close to Walker, "Hang on, Old Man. We'll take care of things now." He waved the litter bearers on, then with Buck and Eli in tow, trekked up Wolf Mountain. Within half an hour, they spotted Nathan and a couple of men ahead.

The sheriff was annoyed at the delay, but when Buck called to him, he waited.

"What happened to Walker?" John asked, panting from exertion when they reached the sheriff. "Was he up here alone? Have you seen David and Yona?"

Nathan didn't try to hide his impatience. "Mr. Copperhead was here with David and Yona. Somebody knocked him in the head. He couldn't tell us who it was because he was out cold. We think it was the same person that blew Eagle Feather's head off in a cave up there where the girl was killed. You got anything to tell me that might help me find out who that was?" He looked straight at Buck.

"Eagle Feather's dead?" Buck asked.

"Considering the shape he was in, he's better off that way," Nathan said. "I hear he took a shotgun blast from close range, right in that pretty face of his."

Eli made a choking sound like he was trying to say something, but John didn't give him time to get the words out. "Anybody know where Grady Smoker might be?" It was probably better not to mention Grady's shotgun to the sheriff.

"I've got Jimmy looking for him. Yona told me Mr. Copperhead asked for him right before he passed out." Nathan cocked his head, looking suspicious. "Seems to me Grady's taken off without saying jack-shit to anybody for years, and nobody thought a thing about it. Now he's gone a couple of days and folks are worried. Is that because he was seen with Eagle Feather, or does it have something to do with the Snake Dancers?"

That question surprised John. From the looks that Eli and

Buck exchanged, they hadn't expected it either. Nathan shouldn't know about the Snake Dancers. They glanced at each other, then back at the sheriff. Since they couldn't think of an answer that would help without giving away something they weren't supposed to reveal, they said nothing.

John watched the three of them trying to stare each other down as long as he could stand it. "Nathan," he said. "I don't know about all that crap. I just know Walker is hurt and I'm gonna have to face Faron and Kate sometime today and tell them what happened. What can I tell them?"

"I've called Kate to let her know about Walker. She'll be here to meet him when they get him down the trail. All I could tell her was that Yona and David found him at that cave with a knot on his head. By the way. Why didn't you ask Yona and David about the walking stick when you met them on the trail?"

"What do you mean, met them on the trail?" Buck asked.

"They stopped long enough to tell me what had happened, then took off like scalded dogs to catch up with Mr. Copperhead and the rescue team," Nathan said.

John didn't wait for anything else, just yelled at the sheriff to keep an eye out for Walker's walking stick and started back down the mountain. Buck and Eli ran to catch up to him. Buck shouted for him to wait but John didn't slow down. When they were close enough to talk, John said, "Where were they, guys? We know David and Yona weren't with Walker, but it would take a damn good reason to make them leave him when he was hurt. I aim to find out what that reason was."

Buck had to admit John was right. He and Eli scanned the trail side for some sign of where David and Yona might have veered off. Even Yippi sniffed the air like he could smell something he didn't like. Buck was first to see the splotch of blood on the laurels. From there it was easy. David and Yona had left a well-marked trail. The rain softened soil made for easy tracking. When John spotted the first blood stain on the muddy ground, the search took on added urgency.

"They can't be far ahead," he said. "Whoever they're following must have been important to make them leave Walker. It has to be Grady, and he's hurt."

"What's happened to my grandpa?" Eli said.

"We'll know when we catch up with David and Yona." John hurried to a rock outcropping that would give him a view below. When he spotted movement through the foliage, and recognized his brother-in-law's form, he gave a whistle he knew Yona would recognize and broke into a run.

Yona and David halted to wait for them. John and Eli barely got a greeting. Buck got all the attention. They clapped him on the back, hugging him and telling him how glad they were to see him.

"Jesus, Buck," Yona said. "We were afraid the guy with the shotgun got to you, too. And man, we needed you to be alive. We're in way over our heads."

"The same guy who shot Eagle Feather? Do you know who he is?" John asked.

"Don't know yet. Haven't seen him, but he's hurt. He's been bleeding since he was in the cave," David said. "He's gotta be the one who shot Eagle Feather and slugged Walker. But it's worse than that, John. Lots worse."

The words came out strangled, as if Buck could hardly speak. "Did he find what he killed for?"

"Everything that was in the cave. And that was all but the Ulunsu'ti. If he has that, he can do anything he wants, if he lives."

Buck propped against a tree and rubbed his bruised hip. He stared at the ground to keep from looking at Eli. "If it's who I think it is, he's had the Ulunsu'ti for years. Since his grandfather turned it over to him. I'd just like to know how he got hold of the rest."

David said, "Walker and I thought it would be safe in the cave. We stashed the medicine and the ark, and even Kanagwa'ti's skeleton. I hid everything myself where I thought nobody would ever find it. Yona and I went to get it this morning. We built Walker a fire at the mouth of the cave and he stayed out there trying to warm up. We found Eagle Feather dead in the cave. The things we hid, and what I guarded—all of it was gone."

"What you guarded?" Buck asked.

"The hands of the conjuror. They weren't buried with Kanegwa'ti. They've been in my family."

Buck's whole body slumped, as if the life had just drained out of him "So a man who's killed two people, and tried to kill Walker Copperhead, has the Ulunsu'ti and everything he needs to use it."

John listened as his friends talked. All he could think of was Walker and the dead girl, alone in the rocks with her head split open. Somebody killing and hurting people, and they were worried about some old relics. Let them worry. He wanted to find out who killed the girl and hurt Faron's grandpa. He wasn't going to stop until he made sure the killer never hurt anyone else.

They didn't see him leave. He could move quietly when he wanted to. He heard them calling as he ran into a stand of pines but he kept going. He had a better chance of sneaking up on the man than if all four of them tried. He was lighter on his feet than they. Odd that the lone white boy in the bunch was the best at stealth. His Indian buddies never had got the hang of those stereotypes.

John didn't need a trail. He no longer even looked for one. Somehow, he knew he was on the right track. Following only his instinct, he closed in.

When he first caught sight of the man, all he could see was a shadowy form moving between the tree trunks. He knew who it was, even before he saw his face, and all he could think about was how Eli would take it.

Careful not to make any noise, he closed the distance between them. The man ahead had already killed once, and with the twelve-gauge shotgun he carried, he could easily do it again.

He got as close as he dared, torn between self preservation and the disconcerting impulse to help, when the man stumbled and almost fell. After all, this was one of the elders he'd looked up to since childhood.

The elder stumbled again under the weight of that heavy-looking duffle bag, or the knapsack that looked like it was saturated with blood. The shotgun probably weighed a few pounds, too.

John watched him lean on the walking stick to steady himself. He got so mad when he saw that, it was all he could do to keep from rushing the old bastard. He'd know that walking stick anywhere. The eagle was smeared with blood, but that didn't hide the fact that it was Walker's walking stick. Son of a bitch. He choked back his outrage and kept out of sight. If Grady Smoker was crazy enough to knock Walker out and take the walking stick, let alone shoot Eagle Feather, he was deranged enough to shoot him, too.

He followed quietly, waiting for his chance, and until he decided what to do when that chance came.

Grady picked up the pace. He walked much steadier now. John got a good look at the knapsack and wondered why he had thought it was bloody. It didn't look bloody now, and neither did Grady's shirt.

It got harder to keep up. He was getting tired but Grady was moving like a twenty-year-old athlete. John had to run to keep him in sight.

Grady seemed to know where he was going. His stride was purposeful and straight ahead, directly toward the pond where Lightning Creek began.

The waterfall cascaded down to form a crystal clear pond. John crouched behind a clump of boulders when Grady stopped and left the gun leaning against a rock. That was the chance he had been waiting for. Grady was unarmed, but even without the gun, there was something dangerous about him.

John hung back and watched. Grady put the duffle bag down and took out the gym bags. He lifted out the bundle John figured was the ark, still wrapped in the jacket he'd seen in the back of Yona's Blazer.

It was all there. Everything Walker had planned to take back to the conjuror's grave. Surely he wouldn't have any problem overpowering Grady. Hell, he could even get the shotgun and hold it on him until the guys got there to take over if he had any doubt. Instead, he crouched behind the rock, and waited.

The truth was, he wasn't certain he could handle Grady by himself. This wasn't the same nice old man he had known all his life. The way he moved, the way he lifted the duffle bag like it didn't weigh as much his cat.

John stayed out of sight, and listened for the guys to come up behind him, wishing they would hurry. What the hell was keeping them? He was counting on Eli to know what to do about his grandfather.

When he heard voices on the creek bank below, he stood up before he could stop himself. Kate and Wren stepped into the clearing and looked into the pond, unaware of Grady.

Grady didn't seem surprised to see them. He called to them like it was the most natural thing in the world for the three of them to meet halfway up a mountain where few people ever came.

John resisted the urge to run to protect Kate and Wren. It seemed smarter to ease back behind the rocks out of sight. There was no reason to think Grady would hurt them, but somehow he knew they weren't safe. Maybe he was getting another one of those famous Copperhead feelings because he knew they were in more danger than any of them could imagine.

He forced himself to stay behind the rocks and wait. If he didn't handle this right, Kate and his baby were going to die there at the head of Lightning Creek.

∫NOWBIRD

Wren lay still, her eyes closed, but Faron knew she wasn't asleep. Just pretending for her sake. Diamond snuggled beside her in the big king-size bed, where John should have been. She had needed her kids close, where she could watch over them all night.

Wren stirred. "You awake, Mama?" she whispered.

"Shhh baby. Go back to sleep,"

"It's too scary, Mama. The dream's too real. Like the man-snake is right here in the room. He says Daddy needs me and I should go to him."

Faron rolled out of bed and drew Wren into her arms. "Let's go downstairs, honey," she whispered. "We don't want to wake Diamond." She felt Wren trembling.

They tiptoed down the stairs.

"Where's Daddy?" Wren asked. "Has he called any more?"

Faron spoke sharper than she meant to. "Daddy's with Eli and Buck, looking for Grandpa Smoker. You heard what he said when he called. Let's not worry. He'll be okay."

"Mama. The conjuror talked to me again, like in a dream. He's afraid for Daddy, too. He says I should go to him. I think Daddy really needs me."

Faron opened the kitchen window curtain. It was daylight outside and she hadn't even closed her eyes. "Daddy's okay. You'll feel better if you eat something." Faron didn't need a dream to know John was in trouble. And some long dead conjuror giving her daughter nightmares was only making things worse. She poured two bowls of cornflakes and sat down and pushed hers around with her spoon till they were soggy. Wren wasn't eating either. Faron gave up on breakfast and dumped both bowls into Black Dog's dish on the back porch.

Wren had opened each of them a cold bottle of Coke when she got back to the kitchen. They sipped from the bottles. At least they would have something in their stomachs while they talked. "Okay, Wren, tell me what's on your mind."

Wren put her Coke down. "Did Daddy say where they were going to look for Grandpa Smoker? Because I think he's at the creek where Kanegwa'ti lives."

"I don't want to hear another word about the conjuror." Faron had all she could take of the Kanegwa'ti. This was something the men had let get out of hand, and now her family was paying the price for their mistakes. Before the words were out of her mouth, she regretted raising her voice to her daughter. "Kanegwa'ti has been dead hundreds of years. Daddy probably went to Grady's house to see if he was there yet. Or he's talking to some of the Smokers or their friends. There's no reason he'd be way up on Lightning Creek. Where did you get such an idea?"

Wren didn't back down. "From the conjuror. I know he's supposed to be dead, but even if he is, he's still at the creek. He can't leave as long as he's responsible for the Ulunsu'ti, and I think he will always have to watch over it."

This wasn't something Wren learned from her or Kate. Faron tried to deny it. "Honey, remember how the story says the conjuror turned the Ulunsu'ti over to his descendants to guard. Whoever his living descendant is, has to take care of it now. It's out of the conjuror's hands."

"No, Mama," Wren said. "He was responsible for it till he turned it over to somebody else. He never did, so he's still tied to it."

"Why do you say that, honey? The stories all say he gave it to his grandson who was the war chief of his day, and his family is still watching it."

Wren shook her head. "No, he just gave them the crystal.

The thing that lives in it and makes it strong, is the spirit of Uktena. That's what gave the conjuror his power. He never turned Uktena over to anybody. That's why he still lives at Lightning Creek. You have to cross over it to get something important. You can't bring Uktena's spirit to life without that important thing, and the man-snake is supposed to keep anyone from getting it."

"How do you know this? Did Grandpa tell you?"

"No, Mama. I just know it. I think I might have learned it when I dreamed about the man-snake. I think he's the conjuror. Anyway, he's the one that said I should go find Daddy."

Faron didn't know what to say. She couldn't let Wren go back up there. Not where the girl was killed. But what if John did need her? She got up and wiped the spotless countertops with a sponge. John was in danger. She had known it even before she left David's house. That's what scared her so much. And not just for John. For her little girl, and Walker, too. In the pit of her stomach she knew she could lose all three of them, and she was completely helpless. She needed Kate's help with this.

"Wren," she said. "I don't understand any of this. Let's hope your grandma knows what to do. We'll call Mama Kate."

Wren nodded and handed her mother the phone.

Faron dialed and Kate answered on the first ring, her voice strained and anxious.

"You're already up, huh," Kate said, "You'd think we'd all be asleep, since it was nearly daylight by the time we got to bed."

"Mom," Faron said. "I'm scared. I haven't heard a word from John since they left for Grady's house, and I've got a bad feeling about Grandpa. To make it worse, Wren's had another dream about the conjuror. Now she says he wants her to go look for her daddy. I don't know what to do. Something's happened, something bad. I can feel it, and I just can't let Wren go back up there."

For a moment there was silence on the other end of the line

then Kate said, "You're not the only one who has a bad feeling about John and Walker. I've had one for the last two days. And honey, when I get a bad feeling, you can take it to the bank."

"What are we going to do, Mom? Do you think John is in danger? Is that why Wren's having these dreams?"

"I don't know, but my gut's kicking in real heavy about him. Strangest thing is I can't seem to get any sense at all about what's going on with Walker. Walker and John aren't blood kin to me, but we're close enough that I usually know if they're in trouble."

Faron asked, "How about Grady Smoker. Any idea about what's going on with him?"

"Not the slightest," Kate said. "But I'm not surprised that my instincts don't pick up anything on him. He's not really family. But Walker's different. I'm worried to death about him. Only thing I know to do is to pay attention to Wren's dream."

Faron felt betrayed. "You can't mean that, Mom. Wren's already been through too much. I want her left out of this from now on. She's staying right here with me, and we're not going to talk about this to her. She's only eight years old."

"Listen, Faron," Kate said. "I called Maddie Axe the minute I got home last night. I was hoping she could help us out, but she says there's not much we can do. It's something the men have to handle, but they've screwed up. All we can do now is just look after our men and kids, like we've always done, and we need to use whatever we've got to do it with. Right now, all we have to go on is Wren's dreams. If we can get some insight from them, we have to listen to her."

Faron was more conflicted than she was before calling Kate. Wren was in danger. She knew it. And Kate wanted to get her more involved. But what if it would help John? Sometimes she envied the McLeymores. If they couldn't see and touch something, it didn't exist. They would just dismiss Kate's feelings as woman's intuition at best. And Granny Mac would have treated Wren's nightmares with a cup of chamomile tea. It wasn't such a bad idea to call John's mom and listen to her.

Granny Mac wouldn't send her granddaughter out on a wild goose chase where one girl had already been murdered. She was tempted to hang up on Kate and dial the McLeymore's number, but of course, she didn't do it. Like everybody else in the Copperhead family, up to and including Walker, she listened to Kate.

Kate ended the phone call with instructions. "Get Wren dressed. I'll be right over and we'll talk about what we're gonna do."

The relief that usually came when her mother took charge wasn't there. Faron was still pacing and worrying when Kate's Trans Am roared over her new bridge twenty minutes later.

Kate marched in, dressed for business in a sweater and a pair of jeans that fit like a glove. Sturdy hiking boots and a leather jacket completed her outfit. Her long hair was stuffed through the back of a baseball cap. She entered with news that couldn't wait. "Nathan Axe called just as I was walking out the door. Grandpa's been hurt."

Faron dropped down on the nearest chair, her knees suddenly too weak to support her. "How bad?" was all she could say.

Kate hugged her. "Nathan has talked to John, and he's okay. And Cherokee Rescue is bringing Walker down off Wolf Mountain. I want to be there to meet him."

"What's wrong with Grandpa?" Wren had heard every word.

Kate opened her arms and Wren stepped into her embrace. "Nathan didn't see anything but a lump on his head that didn't look all that bad. The paramedics say he's out cold. They suspect he had a concussion. They'll take good care of him."

Wren choked back tears. Kate tried to comfort her. "Grandpa's gonna be okay," she said. "He's in good hands with the Cherokee Rescue Squad. They'll get him to the hospital in no time. I'm gonna leave now and be there to meet him. I'll make sure he's taken care of."

"I'm going with you, Mama," Faron said. "We'll take Wren

and Diamond by the McLeymores. Granny Mac will look after them."

"No, honey. Somebody needs to stay here in case John tries to call. I'll let you know as soon as I lay eyes on Grandpa."

Wren got her yellow slicker and kissed Faron's cheek. "Bye, Mama," she said. "I have to go with Mama Kate."

"No, Wren. Absolutely not. I can't let you go back up there."

Wren's lip trembled. It wasn't easy for her to defy her mother but she continued to put on her slicker and get ready to go.

Kate bent down to help her. "You know I'll take care of her. We'll be home as soon as we see about Grandpa. We're just gonna meet him and make sure he gets to the hospital all right. I'll call you from there."

Wren looked far more grim and determined than any eight-year-old little girl should. "We better get going, Mama Kate," she said.

Faron tried one last time. "Mom, please."

Kate gave her a quick goodbye hug. "Don't worry. She'll be fine. You just call Amy Locust and tell her what's going on, and try to keep her calm till we can get her man home."

Faron knew it wouldn't be that simple. She sent Wren to get into the car. When she and Kate were alone, she asked, "Mom, do you know what's going on with the men? Is John a part of it now?"

Kate said, "Honey, you know I've suspected Walker was keeping something from me. Not just the Snake Dancers. That's none of my business. But there was something else he didn't want me to know. I know it involved Johnny, and that worries me. That husband of yours gets on my nerves sometimes, but he's your man, and he's good to you. If that old goat does anything that gets him hurt, I'll put another knot on his hard old head."

Faron let them leave, then stood on the porch with Diamond in her arms, waving as Kate drove across her new bridge. It felt like months ago when it was built, and it was only last Sunday, just three days. Strange how her whole world had changed in such a short time. She didn't like the changes at all.

Shivering in the cold, she watched the Firebird until it was out of sight, then went inside and held Diamond a little too tight while she fed him his morning oatmeal.

LEAVING SNOWBIRD

Wren was so cold she felt like it was still the dead of winter. She asked Kate to turn on the heat.

Kate set the heater on high. "It is awful chilly for this time of year, isn't it? The thermometer says fifty degrees, but it feels more like thirty. It's probably the dampness that makes it seem so cold."

Wren was shaking, whether from the chill or the way Kate took the last curve, she didn't know. Her grandma was driving so fast the wheels squealed on the turns. She wasn't used to that. It was scary, but she didn't mind. They would get to her Grandpa faster. When she warmed enough to stop shivering, she asked, "What did Mr. Axe say about my daddy?"

"I told you, sweetie. He's with Buck and Eli and they were all just fine. They look out for each other, so don't worry."

But Wren did worry. In her dream she didn't see anybody looking out for her daddy. He was on his own. The only one with him wanted to hurt him, and she didn't understand that at all. She had always thought Grady Smoker was a real nice man. He and Miss Lena used to bring her frosted cupcakes when they came to visit. She liked them. It was a dumb dream. Perhaps Granny Mac was right, and dreams didn't mean anything. Worrying about her daddy had caused it. She was trying to convince herself of that when Kate asked her about that nightmare.

"It was really scary, Mama Kate. Mr. Smoker was hurting people. He was big and strong and Daddy was afraid. The snake tried to help him, but it couldn't."

"The snake?" Kate asked.

"Yeah, but it's not always a snake. Sometimes it looks sort of like Grandpa Driver, but it isn't."

"Wren, Sheriff Axe will help us take care of your daddy. I don't know what your dream means, but Grady Smoker wouldn't hurt a fly. He's like one of our family."

Wren had always paid attention to what was said even when the grown-ups didn't know she was listening. Sometimes, she surprised her elders. This was one of those times. "If he's like one of the family, how come we didn't know about his granddaughter until she turned up dead?"

Kate didn't try to answer.

Wren leaned her head against the back of the seat and closed her eyes. She was scared, and the scariest thing was that even Mama Kate didn't understand what was happening. Her daddy was in trouble and Mr. Axe couldn't help him. He hadn't kept her grandpa from getting hurt or the girl from getting killed. If Mama Kate had come sooner she could have helped the girl and protected her grandpa. She was better at looking after people than the sheriff.

Wren glanced up at her grandmother. Mama Kate looked like a woman who intended to take care of her family, and she could do it, too. If Grady Smoker or anybody else messed with her, he'd be sorry. But Mama Kate was scared, too. The way she gripped the steering wheel and drove so fast, wasn't like her. But she was trying to act brave, waving at people she recognized as they drove through Cherokee. There weren't many people out, probably because of the rain.

They went through the main drag without any traffic problems. "If only it could stay like this" Kate said. "In a couple if months, this place will be crawling with summer tourists."

Wren knew about the tourists. A blessing and a curse, Grandpa called them. They brought their money and left their pollution. He didn't like the casino or the bingo hall. She didn't either.

They left the town behind and turned onto Lightning Creek Road. The porch light was still on at the Wayanettah house, but that was the only sign of life. "David's car is gone," Wren said. "Nathan said he saw it parked on that logging road past Aunt Marge's house," Kate told her. "He figured David brought Walker and Yona up there." Then she added, "Those two had better have a damn good explanation for why they let Walker get hurt."

Wren wouldn't want to be in Yona and David's shoes when Mama Kate got hold of them.

"Looks like the rain is letting up," Wren said.

"That's a mercy," Kate said, easing the car onto the bridge over Lightning Creek. "Now if it would just get warmer. I hope they don't let Grandpa get a chill."

Something caught Wren's attention off the side of the road. A flash of dull yellow in the bushes beside the creek. "Mama Kate, stop the car." She raised up on her knees to get a better look. "Somebody ran off the road."

Kate pulled over to the side of the narrow dirt road and stopped. Wren jumped out and ran through the weeds. She heard Kate calling but kept running. Kate sloshed through the wet weeds after her. They both recognized Grady Smoker's car. He'd been driving the same old yellow Pinto for more years than Wren had been alive. It looked like an abandoned wreck with both front wheels almost in the creek. They looked inside. The keys were still in the ignition, and a few fast-food containers lay crumpled on the floor. Other than that, the car was empty.

"Mama Kate, where's Mr. Smoker? Do you think he's hurt?"

"I don't know, honey." Kate looked around for signs that Grady might be injured somewhere in the bushes. "I don't understand how he could have accidentally run off the road there. My guess is that he finally got tired of this old wreck and just drove down here and left it."

Wren wasn't listening to her grandmother anymore. She had

a feeling, the strongest one she had ever had, that the snake was calling her. The feeling got even stronger as she walked over to the creek. When its head came up through the water, she wasn't afraid. Now Mama Kate would have to believe her. The snake was real. "Look Mama Kate," she called.

Kate came to stand beside her, looking into the water. The snake ducked its head under the surface. Wren pointed to a dark, undulating form beneath the water. He blended so well with the shadows he was nearly invisible until the snake lifted its head to stare at them unafraid. Fangs, longer than Wren's fingers gleamed in his cottony mouth. His thick body whipped wavelets in the creek. Wren bent over close to the water. Kate tried to pull her away, but Wren needed to see the snake. She struggled, but Kate was stronger. Her grandmother picked her up and set her down a few feet away from the creek. "That's not natural," Kate said. "This creek is too cold for him, and there's no sun to warm his blood. Cold blooded reptiles can't live like that. What's he doing here? He should be holed up in his den or at least so sluggish he wouldn't have the energy to move like that.

"He's got plenty of energy," Wren said, and slipped out of Kate's grasp and ran alongside the creek, looking into the water for the snake.

Kate yelled for her to stop.

Wren didn't want to disobey her grandmother. She never had before, but this time she had to. She needed to follow the snake. She could see him now, just beneath the surface, swimming against the rapids.

She was glad Kate stayed on her heels. Wren wasn't scared of the snake. In her dream, he was the one who tried to help. It was the bad man who wanted to hurt her daddy. She wanted Mama Kate with her if she saw him.

"Slow down, honey," Kate called.

Wren was out of breath, too. It was a hard climb over the rocks and boulders that lined the creek. But there was no time to slow down. "Please, Mama Kate. We have to go with the snake. He'll take us to Daddy."

She reached back and took Kate's hand and felt it trembling. It would have been easier if Mama Kate was brave.

"Stay close to me, baby," Kate said, and let Wren lead her over the rocky banks toward the pond at the head of the creek.

Mama Kate would know what to do when they found Daddy. They were both gasping for breath by the time they heard the waterfall at the head of the creek.

It was peaceful on the creek bank. Without the rain, the air felt warmer. The snake waited up ahead, his huge head protruding above the water. Wren could feel him urging them to hurry. She pulled on Kate's hand, telling her to run.

Kate held back. "Wren, we're supposed to meet the rescue squad with your Grandpa. Can't we come back later and look for the snake?" she said.

"Come on, Mama Kate," she shouted. Her grandmother gave in and scrambled over the rocks behind her.

She lost sight of the snake in the rocks where the water spilled from the pond and rushed down the mountainside. Kate tried once more to get her to turn back. Wren didn't have time to explain why they had to keep going. She knew where she had to go. The snake was calling her.

When they broke through the thick green bushes beside the pond into a rocky clearing, they were not alone. Grady Smoker stood there like he was waiting for them. She'd never been afraid of him before. There was no reason to be. He was a friend. Almost family. So, why did he seem like the scariest thing in the world.

Wren didn't understand. Why was he out on such a cold wet day with nothing to keep him warm but a ragged old flannel shirt. Something was wrong with him. His unblinking eyes stared right through her. And Mama Kate was scared of him, too. Wren could tell by the way her hand turned so cold. Mama Kate should have scolded him for not having on his coat, but she didn't say a word. Grady grinned at them, like he knew a secret they didn't know. But his eyes weren't smiling. They looked dead.

Mama Kate grabbed Wren and ducked behind a boulder. Wren pressed her body against the rock trying to keep out of Grady's sight. She was trembling so hard she couldn't be still.

"Why didn't I listen to your mother and leave you at home?" Kate whispered in her ear.

"'Cause, I had to come," Wren said.

Minutes passed and Grady hadn't made a sound. Kate signaled Wren to be quiet and eased out from behind the rock. Wren had to watch. She peeked from behind the boulder, wishing she could pull her grandmother back. Grady was standing there, less than three feet away. He still had that weird grin on his face.

She looked away from his face, to his chest and thought she understood what was wrong with him. He was hurt. His shirt was torn away from his shoulder. When he turned away, she saw a gash so deep it probably went to the bone but there wasn't any blood. It should have been bleeding but the wound was so white it looked like all the blood was already gone. The bandage had slipped off. Grady needed help.

Mama Kate took a step toward him. He turned to stare at them again and Kate stopped. Her grandmother always helped people who had been hurt, but Wren didn't want her to get any closer to Grady. She didn't like the way he stared at her—like a hungry dog at a pork chop. And he didn't act like his hurt bothered him. In fact, he looked like he felt real strong. She couldn't leave Mama Kate alone with him. She inched from behind the boulder and went to stand beside her grandmother.

"Why is he so blue?" Wren asked.

"Oh, Lord. He sees you," Kate said, and tried to push Wren back behind the boulder.

Wren clung to her grandmother's jacket and choked back a whimper.

Grady came closer and they backed away. He was a good man. Everybody said he was. But now it felt like he was horrible. He wanted to hurt them. Wren looked toward the pond, hoping the snake would come to help. If he was there, she didn't see him. She and Mama Kate would have to manage alone, if Grady Smoker didn't kill them.

"Do you think he killed that girl, Mama Kate?" she asked.

"I'm afraid he did." Kate said.

Uncle Grady Smoker was the bad man in her dream. The one who was trying to kill her daddy. He looked like he wanted to kill her and Mama Kate, too.

THE FIRST WORLD BELOW

Walker Copperhead hadn't moved a muscle all the way down the mountain. A couple of times, the men who carried the litter stopped to make sure he was still breathing. Once, when they couldn't find a pulse or see any sign of respiration, they thought he was gone.

They talked about how they hated to face Kate Copperhead at the foot of the trail, and how to tell her Walker was dead. Then Walker groaned out loud, like he was in bad pain, and they almost dropped him.

It would probably have scared them even more if they had known that while they carried his inert body on their litter, another part of him wandered far from Wolf Mountain, in a gray, cold place where a man could get lost and never find his way home. He had been there before, but long ago and never alone. That first time, Driver Wayanettah had waited to guide him back into the world of light. Driver wouldn't be there to rescue him this time. If he failed, he and Grady would both be left to wander the wastelands. Two lost souls trapped in the first world below.

As far as he knew, there wasn't another spirit walker alive since Driver Wayanettah walked over. He and Driver were the last of their kind. Walker's grandfather, Tsali Copperhead, had taught them both to walk the worlds below and retrieve lost souls. Tsali had honored his grandson with the title, Ai'da, when he proved adept at navigating places where living men seldom choose to go. It meant *spirit walker*, but Tsali shortened it to Walker. Only he and Driver knew what he had endured to earn the name.

He advanced with great caution, trusting the rescue team to take good care of his body back on Wolf Mountain. The thread of life that connected him to his physical form was all he had to draw him back to the living world. If it broke, he and Grady would both be stuck here. Not just a lifetime, but as far as anyone knew, forever. The first world below was the last place anyone would want to spend eternity.

When he last walked the void, rescuing the spirit of a boy more dead than alive from a drug overdose, his body was still young and strong enough to pull him back even without Driver to guide him. Now, the frail old form had so little claim on him he couldn't find it. Grady had even less of a tie to his flesh and bones. He'd fled so far from it he probably didn't realize what kind of a fix his body was in.

Old Tsali's teaching laid a duty on him and Driver. A spirit walker had to venture into this land to retrieve spirits lost before their time. It was their job, and they'd both done it when it was called for, but only when there was no other choice. Nobody wanted to enter the worlds below. That's why so few were trained to travel there.

With no one to come for him, his only insurance was the walking stick. He hoped Grady had hung onto it and could keep his wits about him enough to remember what it was and why it had been thrust into his hand. It offered a beacon to draw both of them back to the physical world, if somebody could manage to put it into his flesh and blood hand. If not, he and Grady would be spending a lot of time together. Damn, he hoped Grady would be better company than he had been the last time he saw him. Otherwise, eternity was gonna be a son-of-a-bitch.

He called Grady's name, the one they knew him by in the Circle. He'd have to answer to that, even if he was controlled by something that might benefit from keeping him here. When there was no answer, he called again, but still there was no reply. He reached out and felt for his walking stick, cupping his palm as if to take hold of it.

When he felt a slight pull, he moved toward it, walking because that gave him more control of where he was going. It would have been quicker to just drift, letting the shadow of the walking stick draw him to it, but that would make it harder to see what else traveled through the wastelands with him. Tsali had described what that might be, and he had no desire to meet the denizens of this world face to face. It was best to stay alert and ready to defend himself. He trudged on. The surface of the gray land sucked at his spirit legs like wading through knee-deep mud.

He called again when he could feel the walking stick getting closer. Something answered, but it wasn't Grady. He didn't call out anymore. He'd rather not draw the attention of whatever traveled near him. It could be something that would love to go home with him. That's another reason he hoped Grady had hung onto the walking stick. He'd know he had the real Grady Smoker if he carried the walking stick. Nothing else here would want to touch it, even if it was just the shade of the real thing.

Thick viscous mist swirled around his face, making the visibility almost zero. Forms moved in and out, blending with the mist until he couldn't tell which was which. The part of him that walked the first world below was of less substance than the mist. Navigating it made him think of better times spent wading against the rapids of an icy trout stream but this was harder to do and far less fun. If he was going to get anywhere, he needed a stronger presence, even if that meant withdrawing even further from the shell of himself he'd left behind on Wolf Mountain.

His body on Wolf Mountain grew cold and still as his spirit drained away to the first world below. Even the weak beacon of energy he counted on to guide him back was almost gone. If someone didn't put his walking stick in his hand when the time came, he'd have nothing to guide him home. He reassured himself with the thought that Grady would know to give it to him. If he survived.

His family would find a way to get the walking stick into his hand if Grady didn't make it back. They might not understand why it was important but they knew he would want it. Years of humoring him had conditioned them to do whatever they figured would please him. In some ways, he carried almost as much weight as Kate.

Grady was close. He could almost feel the well-known shape of the carved eagle against his palm. He called again, softly. In answer, an agonized scream tore through the darkness.

Screams were not uncommon here, but this was more than the silent cry of the disembodied who wandered these hopeless lands. In the world of doomed souls, the cry of physical pain carries a shattering force. The sound told him that even here, Grady couldn't escape what was happening to his body in the world of form and substance.

Walker Copperhead waded toward Grady's voice, trying not to think about the agony that could make one of the toughest old soldiers he'd ever known yell like that. He couldn't hope to save Grady's life, and it was getting harder to stifle the fear of what would happen to his soul if he couldn't reunite it with his body long enough for them to part naturally. He had to try. If he succeeded, Grady would be free to walk over to the above world. If he failed, his old friend would be stuck in the below world without hope.

He wanted to rescue Grady from his self imposed hell, but there was a more important reason to bring him back. Grady had to do his part, or they didn't stand a chance of lessening the harm he had done.

The oblivion of the first world below was a merciful alternative to the horror that awaited Grady, but facing it was the price he would have to pay for betraying the guardians.

Walker turned his will toward the physical world on Wolf Mountain, searching for the substance of the walking stick he had thrust in Grady's flesh and blood hand. It was still there, but with the first brush of his mind against it, scorching heat ran through him, seeking out his body and driving his consciousness back into the world below.

He couldn't risk any more contact. Even his spirit walker form was not safe from the being who inhabited the body of Grady Smoker. He was afraid to think what it might do to his old carcass on the litter.

Back on the mountain, the Cherokee Rescue Team picked up the pace. They'd better get this old guy to the hospital before it was too late. They'd thought he was dead for the past half hour, and suddenly he was howling in pain. Whatever was wrong with him, it had to be more than that lump on his head. That wasn't enough of a wound to make a man yell like that.

They would have broken into a full run if the terrain had allowed it.

LIGHTNING CREEK

Grady Smoker wasn't thinking about his problems anymore. He was at peace in some dark, empty place. Emptiness, where only cold reached him was far better than the searing pain he fled. The throbbing ache in his back no longer tormented him and his mind was at rest. Even the dead girl didn't matter. She existed in his thoughts, still alive, his only granddaughter.

Memories didn't hurt anymore, so he allowed his mind to drift across the years, remembering when the girl's mother came to Robbinsville to look for Thomas Smoker. She had found Grady first, the baby girl in her arms. How Lena's face lit up when she held their granddaughter, but the child's presence was a threat they couldn't ignore.

If Thomas' wife found out, she'd take Eli and go back to her folks in Oklahoma. The Choctaw woman only wanted what was best for her baby, so she listened to them. A father, married to another woman, offered less than a pair of loving grandparents who looked after them both.

He would have done anything, even keep their secret from Thomas, to prevent his daughter-in-law from taking Eli away. The next guardian of the Ulunsu'ti needed to stay in the homeland where he could learn his duties. His education had to begin early, with stories that prepared him for the real mysteries.

Even in the void, remorse touched him with the memory of how he had told Eagle Feather about his granddaughter. He'd trusted him to look in on the girl and her mother when he went down to Mississippi. In truth, even then he had been thinking of the Shawnee who was willing to hunt down Uktena because he loved a Cherokee girl. He had to admit, his plan took form at that time. Eagle Feather was an outsider who wanted to be Cherokee, and he seemed so fond of his sweet, gentle granddaughter. Fond enough to bind him to the tribe and make him a candidate for Suye'ta.

If Grady had known then that the white man looked at Thomas's daughter the way a man looks at a woman, and had managed to worm his way into her affection, would that have stopped him? He wanted to think it would but he knew both he and Eagle Feather had used the girl for their own purpose. He needed a Suye'ta and the white man needed a Cherokee wife to give him credibility with his followers.

Lena would have seen through Eagle Feather. Grady was the one who had been the trusting fool. In a way, he was glad his wife wasn't there to witness the mess he'd made of everything. But then, if she was alive, it probably wouldn't have happened. She would have managed to stop him before he lost his way.

Grady remembered calling Walker Copperhead a crazy old coot for suggesting John McLeymore could be the Suye'ta. Why didn't he see it was even crazier for him to trust a stranger who had nothing going for him but a lying tongue?

Somewhere beyond the fog, a voice broke through his reverie. His name echoed in the darkness, compelling him to answer. Shame gave him the strength to resist but it was fear that made him flee deeper into the mist. He knew Walker's voice, and remembered swinging the butt of the shotgun at his head. Even if the blow had killed him, it didn't explain his presence in the first world below. Walker had earned a better rest. He could only be here to bring the vengeance of the Snake Dancers to the one who had betrayed them. Not even in the below world could he hope to escape them. They had sent the only spirit walker in the Circle to get him.

The voice called again, speaking the name he couldn't ignore. Walker was close now and drawing closer. For the first time, Grady was aware of the walking stick he had in his hand.

Walker had made him take it, back on Wolf Mountain. It would give his presence away even if he didn't answer. Though just a shadow of the real one, its power still connected the worlds. He couldn't hide in this world or any other. The spirit walker would find him.

Before he could answer Walker's call, another hand joined his on the eagle's head. There was no anger in the voice that spoke to him, and no pity, but there was a power he couldn't refuse. Walker commanded him to do what he most feared and refused to allow him to protest. He was a warrior, ordered to look at his own mortal form and see the evil that lived in it. Then he must begin the last battle of his life, to fight against an enemy who inhabited his body.

Speaking his warrior name, the name he had to heed, Walker said, "Look and see."

He was bound to observe what he was becoming in the body on Wolf Mountain. Shadows in a shadow world, they stood side by side, watching an old man staggering through a grove of pine trees. Even as they watched, the old man stood taller and walked with firmer steps. Strength flowed into him from the knapsack on his wounded shoulder. But it was a dark strength that writhed through him, eating into his mind. It was almost more than he could bear, even from a world away. But what Walker wanted him to do was unthinkable. To reclaim the wounded form, with all its guilt and pain, and share it with the thing that snaked through it now, was beyond him. He couldn't do it.

"You must," the shadow beside him said. "You must see with your mortal eyes and hold a part of your spirit in your mortal form."

He watched, imagining how it would feel to walk once more as that man. How strange to look through the mist to see himself so solid and real, holding the eagle-headed walking stick in his flesh and blood hand. Walker's voice was like cobwebs against his mind, urging him closer to the body that walked on the mountain, yet holding him in the shadow.

He reached out with a thread of thought and let it touch the mind of the man on the trail. Serpent hunger snaked through him like fire through his soul. An alien consciousness touched him when he tried to pull away. It held him there with an intensity that trapped him in a body that was no longer his own. He could feel it worming through his memories, seeking the way into all he knew.

Walker's voice held a trace of kindness when he said, "He won't like the walking stick, but don't lose it. It will take us home." He took comfort in that. There was a way home. That's why Walker had made him take the walking stick back at the cave. He wasn't alone anymore.

Grady could feel his body now. The movement of his legs. The weight of the duffle bag and the gun. And the thing that lived with him in the body. A cold, hungry mind snaked against his, tasting his presence. It wanted him there, but promised nothing but pain if he stayed. He could feel it exploring his memories and relishing his fear. Walker still whispered in his mind, helping him hold on when fear threatened to overwhelm him.

The walking stick. The serpent spirit didn't like it. It wanted him to leave it beside the path. Walker made him close his hand tightly around the eagle head and hold on, even when it burned into his flesh. He felt the pain, and still held on. His attachment to his body was stronger now. He saw the trail through his mortal eyes. Blood still oozed from the wound on his back and ran down into the knapsack. That stirred a vague fear. There was something important he must remember, but the serpent mind swept away the thoughts of the conjuror's hands cupped around the crystal in the bloody knapsack.

Walker's voice spoke his warrior name, the name only he could hear. "He wants to go to Degal'gun'yi, where he is safe from the Nunne'hi. Think of that and nothing else."

He emptied his mind. No more thoughts of the pool at the head of Lightning Creek, where the immortals were strong and Kanegwa'ti waited. Thinking only of the mound of the

Ani'Kuta'Ni, he made himself see the image before his eyes, and said aloud, "This is where we are going."

He felt satisfaction from the serpent mind. It liked the image. There, where the Ani'Kuta'Ni were buried and the Nunne'hi never came, he could wait and gather strength.

From the shadows of the first world below, he and Walker guided Grady's body to the head of Lightning Creek. Only a day before, he still thought he could go to the Council House Mound and feed the Ulunsu'ti just enough blood from a rabbit to give it life, but not enough to bring it to full power. The tools in the duffle bag would help him control it, and the eagle bone whistle would call the Nunne'hi if the serpent spirit became too strong. Now, the crystal feasted on the blood of a Wolf Clan warrior, and the Council House Mound was far away in Graham County.

The waterfall at the head of Lightning Creek lay ahead. No bird or insect sang there, and no sound other than the water and the wind could be heard. The doorway to the world of the immortals was a silent place.

Holding the image of Degal'gun'yi in his mind, he watched his body emerge from the pine grove and walk toward the waterfall. His mortal eyes saw only the image he held before it of the burial mound at Degal'gun'yi.

The thing in his head was pleased.

More than eighty years of living in his body should have made him feel as if he belonged there, but it wasn't his anymore. The gash on his back that had caused him so much pain no longer hurt. He still carried the knapsack, but it was almost clean, the last traces of blood drained away. Fresh tendrils of life spread from it into his blood. He could feel it, eating into his mind and seeking out his soul. He couldn't bear it any longer. His body was a trap that held him for the serpent to feed on. Walker spoke the name that made him listen, and ordered him to stay, telling him to look at the thin shining cord binding him to his body. It made him part of all that happened to it as long as it lived. That could be a very long time if they failed. As long as the serpent needed his body, it would still walk and breathe, and Grady Smoker would always be there with him.

When fear weakened him, Walker's voice painted a picture of Degal'gun'yi, in his mind. He used all his will to build up the image and keep it in the Serpent's thoughts. His body walked toward the falls at the head of Lightning Creek, but the serpent saw the mound of the Ani'Kuta'Ni. It urged him to hurry.

Tentacles of fire writhed from the knapsack and into his veins. Without Walker's commands to hang on, he couldn't have endured the pain. When agony weakened him, Walker gave him the strength to keep walking toward the falls and keep the image of Degal'gun'yi strong.

Walker's voice spoke his warrior name, calling him to stand for his final battle.

In the shadows of the first world below, the spirits of two old Snake Dancers watched Grady Smoker's body laboring under the heavy load he carried.

Grady couldn't tell anymore whether he observed the trail from his shadow form or from his physical eyes. His body was getting stronger. Age and weakness dropped away. He stood straight and strong and strode down the mountain like a young man. He felt excitement and power, and not the slightest twinge of the remorse that had driven him to the dark world of lost souls. Even the memory of the dead girl, laying on the rocks brought no anguish, just a vague stirring of hunger.

Grady stopped struggling to distance himself from his body and settled into his familiar form. He wasn't this strong, even when he was young. Sensations surged through him that he had never known, and he liked them. Something nagged at him to fight it, but he didn't want to.

Why had he been so repelled by the Ulunsu'ti? He had never actually looked at it before, and he couldn't remember why. Gazing deep into its core, he saw the glow of life. Fire danced through it, consuming the blood it drew from the

knapsack. He watched the last traces disappear into the living
fire. It was a good and proper thing. Strange, reptilian beauty
made him reach in and caress the surface, as smooth and warm
as flesh.

A serpent whisper told him this was all he needed. Walker's
voice also whispered in his thoughts, reminding him there was
still work only the guardian of the Ulunsu'ti could do. He
ignored it until it called the name he had to heed. Walker made
him struggle against the tendrils of serpent mind that threaded
through his thoughts. Uktena walked in his body, but he must
fight to hold his mind and spirit free.

He and Walker kept the image of Degal'gun'yi before his
eyes. The serpent, pleased with the vision, seemed unaware
that Grady walked straight toward the waterfall at the head of
the creek. Grady listened through ears as sharp as when he was
a boy, but there were no noises. Not a sound, as if every living
thing had fled or gone to ground.

Like a hunter with senses alert for game, he observed the
world. Long unsatisfied hunger stirred in his body as he
scanned for anything that moved. Not so much as a bird flew
over. His eyes looked out on a strange land. The contrail from a
jet overhead didn't register as familiar, and his clothing felt
odd, as if he was unaccustomed to wearing them.

Grady walked on toward the image of Degal gun'yi'. There,
the duffle bag and all the hateful things it held could be
destroyed. The weight of it slowed his steps and clouded his
thoughts. It was dangerous. The old conjurors used the things
inside it to make him weak so they could hold him prisoner.
When they were gone, he would be free of them forever. Then,
neither the Nunne'hi nor the conjurors could control him.

He was aware of the walking stick he carried. It was even
heavier than the duffle bag, and almost as much of a threat. He
would have left it beside the trail, but a voice in his mind said it
should be taken to Degal'gun'yi to be destroyed with the rest.
He held it and walked on.

In the below world, his shadow hand gripped the shade of

the walking stick. Walker held it with him, giving him strength to bear the fear, forcing him to view everything that happened, and get ready. The two old Snake Dancers watched through the mist as the one who used to be Grady Smoker walked toward the head of Lightning Creek.

The serpent saw only the mound of the Ani'Kuta'Ni before him and grew stronger with each step. The tentacles spreading through the body pushed aside the little of Grady Smoker that still inhabited it. He could hear it exulting in the knowledge of imminent freedom. He tasted the memory of how it had lived before the Shawnee warrior came with his fire.

The image of Degal'gun'yi held true, rising before him real enough to touch. He climbed to the top of the mound and opened the duffle bag. First, he took out the gym bag that held the bones and shook them out atop the mound. How shattered and dry they had become, as if they would soon be no more than dust. He felt the serpent's fear when he opened the other bag. His body shuddered when he reached in and lifted out the medicine bowl.

For only a moment, the serpent's hold on his mind lessened. Grady Smoker seized the chance to crack the cover of the medicine bowl against the stone. The pungent fragrance of a powerful preparation of herbs and tobacco spread through the clearing, but the serpent spirit didn't detect it. He was occupied with placing something even more threatening to him on the pile. The medicine pouch held the eagle bone whistle. It wasn't capable of hurting someone as powerful as he, but it would call beings who could.

The rattle was next. He was careful not to allow it to make the slightest sound. The ark, he left in the duffle bag and set it beside the boulder out of his sight. He didn't dare deal with it until everything else was destroyed.

When the conjuror's medicine lay stacked on top of the bones, he put the knapsack beside the pile. It wasn't bloody at all anymore. Grady saw the last trace of red disappear into the glowing thing inside, feeding a burst of heat that built and spread through the clearing.

The knapsack glowed red then flames consumed it, leaving nothing but ashes. Within the ashes, the Ulunsu'ti lay, a pulsing, glowing mass of life. The dried, ancient hands of the great conjuror curved round it while white fire licked at them. They remained whole, until the crystal drew them inside itself.

The heat increased until it seemed the mound would catch fire and burn.

From the shadow world, the two Snake Dancers fought to hold the image of Degal'gun'yi, enhancing it with the vision of the fire. They couldn't let themselves think the truth, that the bones and relics lay untouched on a great boulder beside the creek. The effort of holding the illusion weakened them, but they couldn't rest yet.

The serpent mind was satisfied. The hated tools of the conjurors would soon be ashes. The crystal that held the power to make him whole, lay amid the flames.

Grady reached into the fire. The Ulunsu'ti was his, and now he could claim it. The illusory flame had no power to burn him but the touch of the Ulunsu'ti seared his flesh. His agonized cry echoed through the worlds below. He struggled to draw his hand away from the crystal. but the efforts of the two most powerful conjurors in the world couldn't resist the will of Uktena. He had grown strong, and his power increased with each moment that passed.

Grady's body was no longer under his control. In spite of the pain, his hand plunged deeper into the molten heart of the Ulunsu'ti. It was the serpent's will that lifted the crystal high above his head in triumph. He could only watch helplessly as his hand moved inside the Ulunsu'ti, struggling to escape the pain.

Grady had no more fight left in him. The Serpent controlled his body and devoured the last of his will. His struggle ceased. His mind and body belonged to the serpent. In the shadows of the below world, the odor of charred flesh added its stench to the mist. The wall between the worlds posed no boundary to the evil that had claimed Grady Smoker. It was at home in all dimensions.

The fire that consumed Grady's flesh feasted on his mind. Serpent thoughts spoke in his head and tormented him even more than the fire. It delighted in his pain and fear, and gloated that it would consume his being as it had his blood. Memories surfaced as Uktena drew them from him. The serpent devoured them and knew all that he had ever known.

The battle was over. He had lost. Grady's eyes still looked out at the world, but the serpent chose where those eyes would stare. They saw through rocks and trees, far into the world beyond the mountains, looking in wonder at all they observed.

He could see the woman and child, staring at him from behind the rocks where they had retreated. He saw John, silently closing in behind them, and other men beyond in the trees. He knew them well. They had once been important to him but now they were nothing. He watched them, savoring the taste of their fear.

Why did Kate and Wren stand there watching him? Did his face betray his agony? Could they see that he was on fire inside. If they did, they couldn't imagine how the fire strengthened him, burning power into his flesh and swelling his mind until it encompassed all things and all time.

Blood flowed from him into the Ulunsu'ti and back through his heart as they became one being. His memory awakened to all Uktena had known. He felt its rage against those who had enslaved it, and the rage was his own. Hunger born from centuries of sleep imprisoned in the Ulunsu'ti gnawed in his belly. He was aware that someone fought against the force within him even as it grew, telling him to move away from the boulder.

For a moment Grady Smoker found the strength to stumble away like a man wading against a swift current. He clutched at the trunk of a water willow in all its new spring greenery. The tree burst into flame at his touch and in seconds was just a pile of ashes.

He wouldn't struggle any more. His surrender was complete. The new mind that thought with his brain held full sway. Memories not his own flowed in his blood, promising him all things. Whatever he wanted was his. There was no one who could stop him. Not this time.

He felt Uktena's hunger gnawing through his body. Hunger, as painful as the fire. The blood and being of one old man was enough to awake the crystal, but not enough to sate centuries of deprivation. The woman and child were not what he needed, not after so long a fast. They offered no more sustenance than the rabbits and woodchucks the old conjurors fed him while they enslaved him.

He remembered warriors, strong and powerful in their blood lust. There was a time when they came to him in great numbers, but that was before his last sleep, when he had to subsist on nothing but those frightened animals. Just enough to give him the strength to do what they asked of him and no more. Now, he was free of them. The last one who could bind him was gone.

He watched John lurking behind the boulders. The others who followed him would be here soon. He could wait awhile longer. What was a few minutes when he had already waited centuries?

The child stepped from behind the rocks and walked toward him as if she was completely unafraid. She hid her fear well, but he saw through her pretense at courage. He smiled at her. No need to further frighten the little girl.

"Mr. Smoker," she said. "Kanegwa'ti won't like what you've done. You're gonna be in big trouble if you don't put his Ulunsu'ti back where it belongs."

She was no threat, or of any use, but the man hiding behind the boulder wouldn't want his child to come to harm. No man fought more fiercely than when he battled for the life of his child. This was good. A warrior's blood to give him strength.

Did John McLeymore think he could hide from him? His thoughts were as loud as his labored breathing. He could hear him wondering how an old man could withstand such heat and not be consumed. Grady relished the taste of fear that came with thoughts of the little girl. A father who would die for his child. Yes, this was good.

He watched John walk toward him, trying to act casual, like it was not unusual for him to meet up with his daughter and an old man in the middle of nowhere. Kate couldn't hide her thoughts, either. She was scared, not as much for herself as for her granddaughter. Wren had surprised her, stepping out into the open that way. Some part of him remembered that Kate was like family to him, that part was almost too small now to hear. It had been swallowed up, as another mind laid claim to all he had been before, and drank him up, just as it had drained the blood from his body.

The spark of Grady that clung to consciousness felt the power of the awakening Uktena as it marveled at the knowledge it tasted in his blood. Its memories from centuries ago, of warriors who came with spears, bows and arrows, and even the one who had slain its serpent form with fire, paled against images Grady had spent a lifetime trying to suppress. It knew he had been a warrior, too. The weapons in Grady's memories were powerful beyond anything it had ever known. It feasted on visions of war that laid waste to whole lands and left multitudes slain. A war that had touched the entire world.

The serpent's hunger grew. It savored the first taste of what it was becoming and poured strength into the body it claimed. The old warrior was still strong, but his spirit wandered in the below world where it offered no resistance. Soon, he would absorb the last spark of Grady's life, just as he had absorbed the being of others before the conjurors enslaved him.

Thoughts and images flowed within the blood it now shared with the old warrior's body. A strange and wondrous world had come to be since he slept in the darkness. He craved that world and all the wonders it promised.

Drinking deeply of Grady's mind and memories, the serpent tightened his grip on Grady's being. Something pushed against him, trying to keep him from going any further. The old man lacked the power to resist on his own. Someone was interfering. Someone who gave Grady strength to defy him. He couldn't allow that. A thread of consciousness connected Grady to his source of strength. The serpent followed the thread to the warrior he had sensed. There was nothing to fear from him. He was even older and weaker, lying like a dead man, his mind closed and unreachable. The serpent could have snuffed him with a touch, but this one was a warrior, too, with more knowledge, like that of the one whose memories he had tasted. There were men who carried him. They could bring him to the serpent.

The men from the Cherokee Rescue Squad didn't know why they veered off the path to the logging trail and carried Walker Copperhead toward the falls. Walker didn't move or show any sign of consciousness. The serpent drew them closer. Weak though it was, he sensed a spark of life in the old warrior.

The serpent turned his attention back to John. Something in his thoughts disturbed him. He thought Grady should have known better than to show himself with Walker Copperhead's walking stick in his hand. It meant nothing. The serpent dismissed the trace of fear the thought aroused.

John, Kate and Wren, all pretended nothing was wrong. They would be amusing for awhile, until he had come into his strength.

"Morning, Johnny." Grady said. "You picked a bad day to take Wren for a hike, with all the rain we've had." He had his left hand behind his back out of sight.

"Yeah, Grady, I guess I did," John said. "Where have you been keeping yourself? Eli's been worried about you."

"Eli?" That stirred a memory. "Eli? My grandson? He's worried, is he?"

John came closer. "Yeah, Eli's been looking for you. If you'll come with me, I'll take you to him."

Grady didn't need to take his eyes off John to know that Kate was reaching for Wren, planning to pick her up and run away. He heard John silently urging her to hurry. His desperate hope that she would take his little girl to safety was stronger than his fear for himself.

The serpent watched them through John's eyes until Kate had Wren in her arms, then he turned to her and smiled as if he was still Grady, her trusted friend. She faced him, still trying to pretend she believed him. The strength he sensed in her tempted him. She was strong, too, and a warrior in her own way. She would fight for the child as fiercely as the man would. He studied her as she clutched the child in her arms.

"I'd better get Wren home now," she said, even managing a smile. "I don't want Faron to worry."

He lifted his left hand so they could see. The child didn't pretend any more. She screamed loud and long. Yes, she understood about the crystal. She knew it could make Grady do anything it wanted him to. Kate called Grady's name, begging him to break the crystal on the rocks and free himself.

Grady stepped toward her, his hand still raised. John ran at him behind his back, almost reaching him before he turned around. "Leave them alone," John yelled. "Can't you see you're scaring them?"

John held a tree branch in his hand, raised to strike. Grady touched it with the crystal and it burst into flame and turned to ashes in an instant.

John was pleading now, begging him to let Kate take Wren home.

Wren whimpered aloud, unable to control her fear any longer, but the serpent sensed something in her thoughts that worried him. She was scared, but she wasn't giving up. He could hear her, trying to remember a dream. Grady was in the dream, and John. Another image surfaced in the child's mind. The last one who had enslaved him spoke to her. The one who had made him sleep. Was the conjuror still alive?

A trace of fear weakened him.

Kate reached for Wren but she pulled away and shouted, "I have to find the thing that will stop Uktena. The conjuror wants me to give it to Daddy."

The fear faded. There was nothing that could stop him. All the conjuror's tools were ashes now. There was no one to come against him but old men and frightened weaklings. He was Uktena again.

John yelled at Kate. "Take Wren and get the hell out of here. Go!"

Wren struggled out of Kate's grasp. Kate just stood there watching while Grady got closer. Kate kept pleading, "Grady, try to get free. Please."

Wren had reached the big dome-shaped boulder. She screamed, "Daddy, I can't find it."

"Wren, go with Mama Kate," John yelled, but she ignored him. He almost sobbed with relief when Grady turned his back on Wren and Kate, but when he advanced on him, John stopped in his tracks. This wasn't Grady Smoker. It was a bloodless mockery of the old man he had known all his life. Heat poured from him, so hot it scorched John's face as he got closer. It emanated from the thing that encased Grady's hand all the way to his wrist, like a basketball sized diamond. Its facets shimmered and flowed with life. Inside it, John could see Grady's hand, blackened and shriveled but still moving.

Grady appeared to know what John was looking at. He held the crystal out for him to see better, then extended it toward a boulder that towered over his head. The boulder melted like lava and flowed down the slope. John could do nothing but watch and wonder if his mind was playing tricks on him. He'd heard of sleep deprivation insanity, and he had been awake since five o'clock the day before. After all, this was just Grady Smoker, a nice old man who was almost like kin.

When Wren screamed again, he knew it was no dream. Wren begged Kate to help her. Kate didn't move. She stood like stone, staring at Grady. There never had been a more protective grandmother. John couldn't believe she would let

Wren run around scared to death, and make no attempt to protect her.

"Kate," John yelled as loud as he could. "Look after Wren." Kate didn't hear him. His child was on her own. He didn't dare go near her. He had a feeling she would be safer if he kept his distance. That thing on Grady's hand could burn his little girl to a crisp. And Grady, or whatever it was that possessed his body, looked like he would enjoy watching her die. It was observing him, moving every time he did. Now he understood how a helpless mouse felt under a cat's paw. Grady toyed with them, waiting.

Wren ran to the creek. She leaned over the water and called out something in Cherokee. The only word John could make out was, Kanegwa'ti. Did she think the conjuror would hear her and come to help? Every instinct he had cried out that he had to get her away from here, but he didn't know how.

Grady looked past John into the thick undergrowth on the slope, John knew he was looking at David, Yona, Buck and Eli trying to sneak up. A heard of buffalo would have made less noise.

Only Yona broke through the bushes. John tried to keep the fear out of his voice. "Yona, take Wren home."

Yona took one look at Grady and walked toward the creek where Wren was still bent over, calling for the conjuror. He was halfway to her when Grady stopped him, greeting him as pleasantly as if they had just met on the main street of Robbinsville. "Si'yo, Yona. Where's the rest of the Copperhead family? I doubt Walker is far away."

Yona seemed to forget all about Wren.

John raised his voice. "Yona. Wren needs to go home." Yona didn't move. He was staring at Grady, spellbound.

"What have you got there, Uncle?" Yona pointed at Grady's hand.

Grady held his crystal encased hand up, wriggling his fingers as if he didn't understand how they got there. The sleeve of his shirt had burned away, leaving the smell of scorched cloth mingled with the odor of seared flesh.

Something changed about Grady's face. His eyes blinked and cleared. This was the real Grady. The man John remembered. The familiar features contorted in agony. His lips cracked open when they parted in a scream. Then the mask slipped back into place.

That brief moment was enough to release Yona from the serpent's control. He rushed to John's side. Wren ran from the creek to the big dome-shaped boulder. Kate dove for her and pulled her out of sight behind it.

But Wren wouldn't stay there. She scrambled among the rocks that littered the ground at the base of the boulder. John watched, trying not to draw Grady's attention to his daughter. He heard her crying, "Mama Kate. I don't know what to do. He's gonna hurt Daddy and I can't find the ark."

John yelled, "Kate, get her out of here." He and Yona might stand a better chance if they didn't have to worry about Wren. "Go call Nathan."

He heard Kate plead with Wren, "Come on, baby. We need to get help for your daddy."

"Go with Mama Kate, Wren," John yelled. "Go get help."

"No, Mama Kate," Wren cried. "We have to take Daddy the ark. It's his only chance, just like in the dream."

Kate knelt down beside Wren. She was giving in. John knew neither of them would listen to him now. They were both scared to death, but they had decided to stay, and there was nothing he could do about it.

Grady was circling Yona now, making odd comments about how strong Yona looked. Yona backed away and Grady followed until they were far enough away that John could get close to Kate. Her heard her say to Wren, "Okay, baby. What's in the ark and why do we need it?"

"I don't know," Wren said, "But it's something that will help Daddy."

"Then, we have to find it." Kate hissed, "John go help Yona." She took Wren's hand and ran.

He could only watch and hope they found the ark. Something in it was supposed to control the Ulunsu'ti.

Wren went behind the boulder. Kate was at the base of the boulder, looking up toward the top of it. He followed her gaze and saw thin tendrils of smoke and fragments of charred canvas scatter in the wind. If Grady had burned the duffle bag, the ark was burned with it.

Grady had turned his attention on Yona, tormenting him with a parody of conversation. John joined Yona, feigning interest in what Grady was saying. If they could keep him distracted until Wren and Kate found the ark, there was a chance they could figure out how to use it to control the thing on Grady's hand.

Grady was rambling on about his days as a soldier in World War II. He'd never talked about those days before. When they were boys, they'd begged for war stories and he refused. Now, his descriptions of death and devastation were so graphic it made John shudder.

Grady Smoker wasn't a big man, and he was well into his eighties. John and Yona were both in good shape. They shouldn't be afraid of an old man. If they could just talk to him about the crystal attached to his hand, he might listen to reason. He was a Snake Dancer. He knew what it could do. If they could make him remember his duties as a guardian, he would know how to escape what it was doing to him. It was worth a try.

"Uncle," John said. "Do you know what's happening to you? I want to talk to you, Grady Smoker, the Snake Dancer. Can you hear me?"

"I hear you just fine, John." It was Grady's voice, but he seemed distracted, like his mind was somewhere else.

John came a step closer. It wasn't quite so hot now. Grady was definitely preoccupied. John was shaking like a leaf for fear he'd say the wrong thing and rile him up again, and risk getting melted like the rock. Damn, he wished Walker was here. He'd know how to handle this.

"He's on his way," Grady said. "Ought to be here in a few minutes."

John froze. "What? What do you mean?"

"Walker Copperhead, he's on his way."

Yona lost it then. "What do you know about my grandfather?" He demanded. "He's nowhere near here."

"You are right, and you are wrong," Grady said. "He's as close as I am, and as far away."

John was afraid to ask him what he meant by that. When he heard footsteps on the rocks, he wondered if David, Eli and Buck had circled around and were trying to sneak up on Grady. His heart almost stopped when he saw the men from the rescue squad step into sight with Walker.

Grady didn't look surprised. He motioned for them to put Walker down and they obeyed. He stooped and looked Walker over like he had never seen him before. When he reached out to touch Walker's face, John's reflexes took over. He lunged at Grady, determined not to let him near Walker. One of the men from the rescue squad must have sensed danger, too. He put his hand on Grady's shoulder to push him away. Grady lifted the Ulunsu'ti to push back. The man opened his mouth to scream but no sound emerged. Within seconds, there was nothing left of him but ashes piled around the smoldering soles of his hiking boots.

The crystal pulsed and glowed brighter. The other men turned and walked away, like they were walking in their sleep, leaving the litter and the unconscious Walker Copperhead.

John heard Wren scream again. She had seen everything and still she wouldn't leave. The urge to pick up his daughter and run almost overwhelmed him. But where would he go? Was there anywhere they could be safe? If Grady could make them bring Walker here, he could find them and bring them back. The Ulunsu'ti could give him that power if the old stories were true. He no longer doubted that they were.

"Don't let him touch Walker," Kate yelled at him.

What was he supposed to do? Why didn't Buck or David

come to help? They could at least buy some time. John had never felt more alone and helpless.

Grady squatted down beside Walker. Walker didn't stir or show any sign of life.

John bent down and closed his fist over a smooth round rock. Not much of a weapon against a man who could incinerate him with a touch, but it was all he had. He inched closer, talking softly. "He's your friend, Uncle. You don't want to hurt Walker."

Grady bent closer to Walker's inert form and called an unfamiliar name. Walker's warrior name? When it brought no response, Grady looked annoyed and prodded Walker in the ribs with the walking stick. He didn't get a chance to withdraw the walking stick. Walker came to life so fast it caught them all off guard. He had the walking stick in his hand, brandishing it like a weapon. Even Grady was startled. He stepped back, then pasted a distorted smile on his face.

So relieved he almost cried, John leapt to Walker's side, still holding the rock in his upraised fist. "Don't trust him, Walker. It's not Grady."

"I know who it is," Walker shielded them both with the walking stick and shouted out a name. Grady went still.

"Call this name, John. It'll give Grady the strength to fight the serpent." Walker yelled it again.

John tried to fit the unfamiliar syllables to his tongue, shouting it with all his might. For an instant the Grady Smoker he knew looked at him and pleaded for help. "You are the only one who can take it off me, John," he groaned. Then the serpent took control.

"Stay close to me John," Walker said. "Until he gets his full strength the walking stick is one of the tools that can still hurt him. Don't let him near you. He'll want a stronger body than Grady's when he's ready."

The voice that spoke through the parched lips was a travesty of Grady's. "I hear what you're thinking," it said. "It's good that warriors still come to me. One has a body that will serve me well, when I am ready." He extended his crystal encased hand toward Walker's chest. Walker swung the walking stick, shouting Grady's warrior name so loud it tore through the air with the force of a blow. The walking stick sliced the air, connecting with the charred arm that wore the Ulunsu'ti. The cry of pain was Grady's, not the serpent. Walker raised the walking stick to strike again. Grady cowered in agony.

This was the old man who told them stories on the porch under the beech tree. John caught Walker's arm. "No, Walker," he yelled. "You'll kill him."

Walker pushed him away in a fury that made John fear the old man would turn on him with the walking stick, then spoke through clenched teeth. "Killing him would be a mercy. If I could do it I would. Uktena will keep him alive as long as there's enough flesh and bone left to serve his purpose. Grady will be the one who feels the pain."

He heard Grady's agonized voice begging for release, and knew Walker was right.

Walker yelled, "John, we need Kanagwa'ti's medicine. You've gotta find it before Grady loses his hold."

Walker kept talking to Grady, calling him by his warrior name and urging him to hang on. John rushed to the boulder where the relics were. He saw Wren climb up to the pile of ashes and crumbling bones. Frantically she dusted away the ashes to find the ragged medicine bag and tossed it to him.

"Give it to Grandpa," Kate said. "He'll know what to do."

John ran to Walker with the ragged medicine bag.

David, Buck and Eli picked that moment to break through the underbrush. They joined Yona and Walker to form a circle around the pitiful specter that once was Grady Smoker.

Eli pleaded. "Please, Grandpa. Tell us what to do."

Grady's features twisted in an effort to speak to his grandson, then the mask of Uktena slipped back into place.

Buck shouted at him, "No, Eli. It's not your grandpa anymore."

But it was, for a few seconds at a time, before he was

absorbed into the hunger that was Uktena. He appeared to hear when Eli called to him, "Grandpa. How can I help you? Please, talk to me." Grady's mouth worked like he was trying to speak but the only sound that escaped was an anguished moan.

John came close enough to Walker to slip the medicine bag into his hands. It almost fell apart when Walker opened it to take out the eagle bone whistle.

"Now," Buck yelled. "Blow it."

Walker brought the whistle to his lips and blew. John heard a thin sweet note, so soft it drifted away on the wind. He didn't wait to see what happened. Wren was standing atop the boulder. She tossed a rattle to him and called, "Here, Daddy. Take this."

He took the rattle back to the circle around Grady. Walker was still blowing a barely audible tone from the eagle bone whistle. John did as Walker told him and raised the rattle and began shaking a rhythm from it. The sound it produced was as soft as the whistle. He didn't know whether to stop shaking it or to shake harder when Grady screamed.

Grady pointed his crystal encased hand at Eli. It glowed white hot. Walker blew the whistle and John followed his lead and shook the rattle harder. Eli covered his face against the heat and yelled, "No, Grandpa."

It was Grady who answered him, his whole body convulsing with the effort to pull the crystal away from his grandson. "Run, Eli." His voice was a whisper. He groaned with exertion as he drew the Ulunsu'ti against his chest. What was left of his shirt flamed and burned away from his charred and blistered flesh. His features twisted in a struggle against the serpent's grip on his mind.

Eli stepped away a bit then stopped and stood his ground. "No, Grandpa. I can't leave you." Grady stumbled toward him.

John yelled, "Get the hell out of here, Eli, before he burns you to a cinder. That thing is using you to get to him."

Eli didn't move. John lunged toward him, intending to shove him away from the crystal that now was only inches from his face. Before he got close he was brought up short like a dog on a leash. He couldn't even lift a finger. Heat from the crystal raised blisters on his skin. He tried to back away but paralysis held him where he stood. He heard Buck yelling at Eli to get out of the way. He tried to tell Buck that he and Eli were both trapped, but he couldn't speak. He felt the life draining out of him and remembered the man from the rescue squad and how quickly he'd burned to ashes.

A shadow passed between John and Grady, breaking the invisible bond that held him fast. He lurched forward, crashing into Eli. Eli crumpled to the ground and lay there, still and cold. John shook him and he flopped like a rag doll.

A strong hand closed around his arm and lifted him to his feet. He thought at first it was Buck, until he saw Buck standing a few feet away. David and Yona were with him. Eli lay motionless at his feet. The man who had lifted him knelt down beside Eli. When he stood up, Eli stirred and opened his eyes. In a few seconds he shook himself and returned to his place in the circle.

The strange man turned to Grady. John had never seen anyone like him before. He stood as tall as David and Yona, but his build was slender. He wore buckskin leggings under a beaded tunic. A strip of sky blue linen, wrapped like a loose turban around his head, hung across his shoulder. Though his skin was smooth and unlined, there was something about him that said he was older than they could imagine, and the heat from the Ulunsu'ti had left no mark on his skin though it was only inches away. John had no doubt he was in the presence of one of the immortal Nunne'hi. He had seen enough to become a believer. A week ago he would have said his kind were no more real than dragons and fairies, but this one was not a myth. This was a Nunne'hi, come in answer to the call of the whistle and rattle to help their people in time of great need. He watched, expecting the Nunne'hi to take the Ulunsu'ti off Grady's hand and set everything aright. The immortal did nothing but stand between them and Grady.

Grady howled in agony, fighting to hold his spirit in what was left of his body. The Nunne'hi made no move to intervene. "Help him," John yelled. "He can't take it much longer."

"You have to act fast, boy," Walker said. "Grady's trying to help, but Uktena can drink up his soul if we don't hurry. Then he'll be too strong for us."

"I don't know what to do," John said. Was he supposed to try to kill Grady? The look of helpless terror in the old man's bloodshot eyes, told him Grady was still alive in the pitiful husk of his body.

Eli saw it, too. He tried to get close enough to his grandpa to ask him what to do. Smoke rose from his hair and clothing. John pulled him away for fear he would burst into flame. The crystal was a blazing white orb, driving them all back behind the rocks. The immortal stood his ground.

Buck and Walker were both calling Grady's name, pleading with him to hang on. From blackened lips Grady's voice croaked, "Free me."

The Nunne'hi looked straight at John, like he expected something of him. But what? Everybody here knew more about these things than he did. What could he do? He was the outsider. But then, only an outsider could control the serpent force that inhabited the Ulunsu'ti. In spite of the heat emanating from the crystal, charring trees and bushes for yards around, he felt chilled to the bone.

"Walker, we need the ark," he yelled. "You said it would control the Ulunsu'ti."

Before Walker could reply, Kate shouted, "John, it's here."

He saw Wren dragging the duffle bag from behind the rocks. "Give it to Mama Kate," he yelled. Wren whimpered in fear, and kept stumbling toward him, the heavy bag in tow. Kate caught up with her and picked up both Wren and the duffle bag and ran to John. John looked inside the duffle bag. Grady's jacket was the first thing he saw. He took it out and untied the sleeves. The ark was old and fragile. How could it be used against something as powerful as the Ulunsu'ti?

"Now you get out of here," he told Wren. "I mean it. You've done all you can."

Kate held Wren tight and ran. A weight lifted off John when they disappeared through the underbrush. He rushed back to the Nunne'hi holding out the ark. The Nunne'hi ignored him and continued to speak to Grady in an older version of the language.

Walker said. "You have to do it, son. You're the only one who can."

Do what? Why couldn't Walker, or Buck or David, or Yona handle this? They looked at him like it was all on his shoulders, even the Nunne'hi.

He sank down and put the ark on the ground in front of him. With shaking hands he felt around the edges until he found a protrusion under the ancient hide binding. Something inside was supposed to be the answer.

He pressed down hard on what he hoped would open the box. When he felt it give, he worked his fingers under the crack that appeared and forced the lid open.

When he looked inside, he groaned in despair. "Oh, God, what do we do now?" Somebody must have taken the weapon that was supposed to be there, because he didn't see anything. The ark was empty.

Walker squatted beside him and pulled the lid back so he could see under it. From a slit in the doeskin lining, he drew a knife. The five-inch-long pale ivory blade was thin as paper and looked too fragile to cut hot butter without breaking. John's desperation deepened. He laid the knife across his palm and showed Walker. "What the hell are we supposed to do with this?"

"Save Grady and send Uktena back to sleep," Walker said. "You'll have to figure out how. It's Awi Usdi's antler. That makes it stronger than it looks."

Awi Usdi. The little white deer he had always thought was as much a myth as Santa Claus, and he was supposed to use a sliver of his antler to control the thing that was burning Grady

Smoker alive. This had to be a nightmare.

John shook so badly he could barely walk. The Nunne'hi stood a foot or so in front of Grady, but didn't touch him, or do anything except shield the rest of them from the life-sucking heat of the crystal. He looked at John, like he was waiting for him to do whatever it was he was supposed to do. John tried to get closer to the Nunne'hi, so he could ask him what to do. A dart of heat from the Ulunsu'ti touched him and weakness shot through his body. The Immortal passed his hand between John and the crystal and broke its hold. John's legs trembled with weakness. The Nunne'hi spoke two words to him in English. "Do it."

The miniscule knife balanced weightlessly across John's palm. He looked for Wren, afraid that she had escaped Kate and come back. His daughter had seen things that could scar her for life. He didn't want her to see him die. The Ulunsu'ti would surely kill him if he threatened it with the sliver of antler he held.

The Nunne'hi wanted John to come closer, to stand beside him, there where the thing in Grady's body could reach him. The thought of it turned his insides to jelly. Walker urged him to go on, to do what he had to do. John edged toward the immortal.

"Go on, John," Walker said. "It's up to you now."

John raised the knife. Oh, Jesus. They wanted him to kill Grady. He couldn't do it.

In a hoarse whisper, Grady begged for release. "Now, John. Please. I can't hold on any longer."

Choking back his horror, John brought the knife down across Grady's throat and felt it connect, slicing cleanly through flesh and bone. When he staggered away, he thought it was done.

Walker shouted, "Look out, John!"

John turned. Grady lurched toward him, pulled by the crystal. The bloodless gash across his throat had done nothing but cause him more pain.

Heat took John's breath away until the Nunne'hi stepped between him and the crystal. The fire died when it touched the immortal, leaving him unscathed. The Nunne'hi moved away and John stood alone. No trace of Grady remained in the body that advanced on him. The serpent was in full control. He raised the knife to defend himself but the Nunne'hi signaled him to stop, then called out Grady's true name.

The scent of burning herbs wafted from the boulder. Kate was there alone, fanning smoke toward them with her jacket. John hadn't seen her light Kanagwa'ti's medicine bowl. Something about the smoke strengthened him and gave him courage.

Grady halted and breathed deeply of the scented smoke. The voice that spoke through the charred lips belonged to Grady. "Now, John. Hurry."

The Ulunsu'ti glowed even hotter. John watched it and saw something slither within the flame. It coalesced into a dark writhing mass as smoke from Kanagwa'ti's preparation in the medicine bowl drove Uktena's spirit back into his prison inside the crystal. Grady drew in deep rasping breaths. The Nunne'hi called his name, speaking to him in the old tongue. Whatever he said gave Grady the will to hang on. Uktena still fought him and raised the crystal for one last attack. Grady grasped the Ulunsu'ti in his right hand, drawing it down to send the heat into the ground. John saw the hand inside it blacken.

"Free me, John," Grady croaked. "Please. Use the knife."

John looked at the open gash on Grady's throat. Pale, bloodless flesh and bone showed through. It was more than enough to kill a man, yet he still lived. What would it take. He looked at the Nunne'hi for guidance, but whatever the immortal said was of no use to him. He could understand enough Cherokee to know that was the language he spoke, but the old form he used meant nothing to him.

Walker shouted a translation. "Cut him free, John."

John looked at the crystal. The writhing shape inside it took a serpent form. Smoke from the medicine bowl was thick around them now. Grady inhaled deep gasps of herb scented air. With each breath, the form in the crystal grew, becoming darker and more solid.

Understanding dawned. John choked back nausea and dove for the Ulunsu'ti with the knife. Scalding blood poured over his arms, gushing not from Grady's severed wrist, but from the crystal. Heat and life poured onto the scorched soil. Within the blood that drenched the ground, a black and shriveled hand twitched and then lay still. For a moment Grady kept his feet, then swayed and collapsed in a heap, face down beside the Ulunsu'ti.

John heard himself crying and didn't try to stop. The blood that soaked his shirt and stained his hands belonged to Grady Smoker, a good man who was like family. And he had killed him. "I'm sorry Grady. I'm sorry," he kept repeating, knowing Grady couldn't hear him.

The Nunne'hi man stood impassive, watching. He held the Ulunsu'ti out to John, expecting him to take it. A wave of rage cut through John's grief and guilt. "Get that damn thing out of my sight"

The Nunne'hi lowered the Ulunsu'ti and said something in Cherokee. Walker translated, "You killed the Uktena. The crystal belongs to you now."

The Nunne'hi spoke again. John understood one word. "Suye'ta." He looked at the antler knife in his hand, then threw it at the immortal. He caught it easily, and tossed it to Buck.

They had used him to kill Grady. The blood still drenched his shirt and stained his hands. He swallowed the nausea that rose in his throat and swore at the Nunne'hi, at Walker and all the Snake Dancers, blaming them all for Grady's death and for what it had done to him and his family. Not one of them said a word, just listened like they were humoring him.

With an outraged yell, John made a run for the pond and lunged into the icy water. He tore off his shirt and watched it drift away, leaving red stains in its wake. The water eased the pain in his scalded hands. He rubbed hard enough to break blisters and scour away tender skin, disregarding the pain. He had to cleanse away the blood. When he was clean enough to face his daughter, he swam toward the creek bank. All he wanted now was to find Wren, go home, and forget all about the Ulunsu'ti and the Suye'ta business.

The Nunne'hi waited, squatted beside the pond, talking to someone John couldn't see. He followed the immortal's eyes to the water and saw the snake. The water moccasin whipped his enormous body in a graceful motion and came to John. The cotton mouth gaped wide as the serpent curled around John once then slid away into the creek and disappeared.

He heard the Nunne'hi tell the snake goodbye.

The immortal waited for him to get out of the water. John faced him. "Why didn't you save Grady?" His rage was gone but someone owed him an answer. "You had the power. Why didn't you save Grady?"

The Nunne'hi spoke in English. "Only the Suye'ta could save him. I shielded you and the guardians until it was done." He turned and walked away.

"That's not an answer," John called. The immortal disappeared into the hillside without looking back.

Wet and cold now, John stood alone on the creek bank. Kate came through the underbrush. "Wren?" John asked.

"She's okay, waiting for me down the trail. I'll take her home. You look after Walker and make sure he gets back to Snowbird." She left him to go take care of Wren.

John sloshed back to the others, bare-chested in soggy jeans. The hardest thing he had to face now was Eli. What could he say? He lost his nerve when Eli came toward him. At first, they just stood there mute, staring at each other.

"I'm sorry, Eli." Hollow, empty words that couldn't possibly convey the depths of regret John felt. He had killed Eli's grandfather. He could never atone for that.

Eli was crying as he said, "Walker said you freed him. He was dead already."

John felt warm tears on his face.

Walker cut short their exchange and drew their attention to the pines beyond the rocky clearing. Flames leapt through the trees. "The Ulunsu'ti set fire to the woods trying to get to us. We've gotta clean up and get out of here."

John wasn't worried about the fire. It wasn't likely to spread. The rain-drenched woods were too wet, but the smoke would attract fire fighters. They couldn't leave the conjuror's medicine and Grady's body for them to find. "What now, Walker?" he asked.

Walker handed him the sleeping Ulunsu'ti. "It would have gone to Eli. Now I guess you have to decide what to do with it."

"Don't start that Suye'ta shit with me again, Old Man." John handed the crystal to Eli. "Your grandpa would have passed it on to you. Figure out a good place to hide it, and look after it like you're supposed to."

Buck and Yona hurried over, both carrying bundles wrapped in shirts and jackets scented with the herbs from Kanagwa'ti's medicine bowl. Walker instructed them to take Eli to the truck and sent John back to help David.

Smoke was thick now. John bent low to the ground to stay below it and went to Grady's body where David was waiting. "Do we have to carry him down the trail," John hoped there was another way.

David said, "We'll leave Grady in the creek till we can come back for him. His body needs to be in a grave with his medicine. The Snake Dancers will keep doing what we've done since the conjuror started the Circle."

They wedged the body among the rocks under the creek bank to protect it from the fire. David picked up the blackened hand, wrapped it in his handkerchief, and put it in his jacket pocket. "I'm still the guardian of the last hands to hold the Ulunsu'ti," he said.

Kate waited alone at the road. "Wren needed her mama," she said when John asked about his daughter. "Marge Wayanettah is taking her back to Snowbird. I wanted to make sure you and Walker were okay." He thanked her, and Kate hugged him hard.

"You're one tough old gal, Kate," he said.

Kate had no more time for John. She was too busy fussing over Walker, insisting he get in her car so she could take him home.

Walker was firm. "I can't leave yet. I'll try to be home tonight. You have to go now, Kate."

It surprised John when she agreed. "Faron and I have to do payroll anyway," she said. "Loggers work hard for their wages and they'll want to get paid, no matter what else is going on." She turned to John. "You'd better not let anything happen to the old man."

They watched her wheel the Trans Am around and take off for Snowbird.

John looked back up the mountain where black smoke still rose above the trees at the head of Lightning Creek.

"The fire service is already on the way," David said. "The fire will probably die out before they get here. If anybody asks, lightning started another fire. They'll figure that's what killed Grady, too."

John didn't mention the man who had died trying to protect Walker Copperhead from something he didn't even understand. There was nothing left of him to discover but the soles of his boots, but he, for one, would always remember the man's courage.

He wondered about the other men from Cherokee Rescue Squad. Walker said, "I doubt they have any memory of what happened after Uktena got into their heads and made them bring me here."

They walked to their trucks at the logging trail in silence. John didn't expect them to discuss the hurt they all felt. It wasn't their way. He had his own dark thoughts that would be with him for the rest of his days. He'd have to learn to keep them to himself. This was only the beginning of something that would go on for generations yet to come.

For the first time in his life, he really wanted to *go to water*. Not just to please the Copperheads, but because he needed to be clean of all the evil and pain. He couldn't wait to get to the cleansing flow of Big Santetlah.

He even asked Walker if they could go straight there. Walker said, "I don't think we need to wait that long, son. I've got something closer in mind" As soon as they reached the trucks, Walker got them organized. "Boys," he said. "There's a place on the Oconoluftee where we can purify ourselves and figure out some things. John, you and Eli and me will go in your truck. The rest of you follow us."

John watched David walk away, glad they weren't riding together. He couldn't get the image of Grady's shriveled hand out of his mind. He started the truck and drove down Lightning Creek Road, turning at Walker's instruction onto a graveled road. After that, Walker rode with his head lowered and his eyes closed. He was so quiet John worried that the head wound was acting up.

"You alright, Grandpa?" he asked.

Walker opened his eyes. "Just thinking, John. I'm the only elder Snake Dancer left. In spite of what you boys have seen, you've got a lot to learn and nobody but me to teach you. There's more to the guardianship than the Ulunsu'ti and the relics that control it. Lots more."

John stopped him. "That's not something I need to know about, Grandpa."

Walker gave an expressive grunt and continued. "You five boys are in for some interesting times, different from anything the ancestors could have prepared you for. But to tell you the truth, I don't think there could be a better choice of guardians. I've got a world of confidence in every one of you."

John tried again to shut him up. "This is all stuff I'm not supposed to know, Old Man. I've already heard and seen more than I want to. So I suggest you wait till I've gone home before you tell the guys about this Snake Dancer stuff."

Walker went on like John hadn't said a word. "There's

Buck. He's always behaved like he was born to keep an eye on everybody in the Eastern Band, or anyone that had anything to do with us. Not much ever got past him since he was just a boy. And David has a greater love of the old ways and knowledge than anybody I've ever known. He'll make sure they live for the children's children. Eli knows every inch of our land and has dedicated his whole life to looking after it. Yona makes sure the resources of the land are protected and used wisely. He and Meredith Wayanettah will have some fine kids one day to keep things going."

The car tires squealed as John rounded a curve. Eli swore, the first word he had said since they got into the truck.

Walker said, "I know you don't want to hear this, John, but you might as well listen. You're the wild card. It's gonna take you a while to accept where you fit in, but the truth is, you don't have much choice. You're already in too deep to get out now."

John said, "You're dreaming, Old Man. I don't want any part of this bullshit."

Walker paid no attention. "Sure, it might take some time, John, but you'll come around. You might learn to like being the Suye'ta one of these days."

John let him know in words that he could never have used if Wren was in the car, that he could forget that idea right now.

Walker leaned back and got comfortable. "Well, you'll have to learn to accept it. Not much you can do about it anyway. John McLeymore, you're the first white Snake Dancer, and for sure the first white Suye'ta.

John gripped the steering wheel and tried not to look at Walker's smug face. He was afraid he would punch it if he did.

Eli picked that moment to put in his two-cents worth. "Yep. We're in for some interesting times, John. Might as well get used to it."

Epilog

Friday Morning

YELLOW HILL

This was about the prettiest day they'd had all year. Sounded like every bird in Swain County was singing its heart out. Under the canopy of hardwoods, newly opening dogwood blossoms gleamed so white it looked like a light dusting of snow on the trees.

John stumbled on a rock and would have dropped the coffin if there hadn't been five other pall bearers to cover for him. Through the trees, the sound of drums called, guiding them to the place where Grady Smoker's body would be given back to the Earth Mother who lent it to him eighty some years ago. Thomas and Eli walked ahead of the coffin. The Choctaw woman, her head bowed in grief, walked beside Thomas. He supported her with an arm around her waist. Eli's mother had already said her goodbyes, then left for her long delayed return to her family in the west. John couldn't help thinking it was for the best. She never was happy on the Snowbird and her melancholy had always been hard on the Smokers.

The Choctaw woman knew the way to the grave. They had come here with her just the day before, to lay her daughter to rest beneath the mound of newly turned earth beside it. John had stood at the casket with Thomas and Eli when they saw the girl for the first time. When Thomas took the Choctaw woman in his arms, it was easy to see she had never left his heart. He had traded love for duty and come home to a wife and son who needed him, but he hadn't forgotten.

The Choctaw woman had pleaded with Thomas and Eli to forgive Grady and Lena for keeping her secret. They had all done what they thought was right. And it had kept Eli's mother from leaving for Oklahoma and taking her son with her. Her grief for Grady made it obvious she had loved him.

The grave lay open, welcoming an old man to his rest. The pall bearers positioned the coffin on the frame that would support it until time to lower it into the dark earth. John lingered a moment to say a silent goodbye then joined the crowd who had come to bid farewell.

A quartet of elder women broke into song. The language was Cherokee, but every one at the grave recognized the hymn and knew the words. *Amazing grace, how sweet the sound.*

Walker Copperhead came forward and laid a hand on the coffin, then turned away to face the four directions, calling on the guardians of each to guide his friend through worlds above to his dwelling place. While he prayed, Yona and David walked among the people with shells of smoking sage. Mourners drew the cleansing comfort of the smoke to themselves with feather fans or bare hands.

Eli returned to Hilda's side. His wife clung to his hand, her blue eyes brimming with tears. Her parents stood behind her, looking uncomfortable and out of place. The deep respect they had for their son-in-law's grandfather brought them here. The young priest from the Episcopal Church in Murphy stood with them to lend support, then stepped up to the grave and read a prayer from his book.

Drums beat a rhythm and a singer took the priest's place. His song was not for the living, but for the journey of the one who walked over to the other world. The Cherokees understood.

The song resonated in John's heart. An image of Grady and Lena, standing together under a giant beech tree danced before his eyes and vanished when the singer fell silent.

Eli and Thomas came forward to add their prayers. They sang them together in the tongue of their forefathers, asking the ancestors to look with kindness on a man who had suffered to right his wrongs.

The empty grave showed no evidence of what lay beneath it. Yona and Walker had come in the dark of night to bury it there. It was the best place they could think of to conceal the replenished medicine bowl and all the rest of Kanagwa'ti's grave goods. There were no safe hiding places in the wilderness anymore. Here, on the grounds of the Baptist church, pot hunters didn't prowl like they did in the old burial grounds. The conjuror's medicine would be safe, until the right person and the right time came along. They had told John all about it, as if he cared what they did with their Snake Dancer business, saying he had a right to know since he was the Suye'ta.

They looked from the grave to the rise beyond as seven riflemen lined up at parade rest. At the command, "Firing Squad. Attention," the riflemen snapped to attention.

"Port Arms." They brought the rifles into position.

"Lock and load," The squad leader called. In unison, bolts snapped back and the first round dropped into the chamber.

"Prepare to fire salute."

"Fire."

Rifle fire cracked in the stillness. Three seconds to reload, then the second volley, and the third. A salute to a fallen hero.

Echoes resounded off the far hills. "Order Arms." The squad brought their weapons to the position of attention. "Present Arms," and rifles snapped vertical before the riflemen's chest.

The squad leader's hand salute signaled a lone soldier who raised a bugle to his lips. The buglers mournful refrain called an old soldier to his final sleep. The final note still hung in the air when the next order came.

"Order arms."

"Right shoulder arms."

"Right face"

"Forward march." The squad marched away over the rise.

The six soldiers who came forward to remove the flag from Grady's coffin, folded it into the tricorn shape. The squad leader presented it to Thomas on behalf of a grateful nation.

They stood in silence then, watching dark suited strangers from the funeral home lower Grady's coffin into the grave.

Thomas and Eli each scooped up a handful of black earth and dropped it in. The Choctaw woman knelt, holding a shiny gold locket shaped like a heart, and released it to fall atop the coffin. A gift she said, that Lena and Grady once gave her daughter. Thomas lifted her to her feet. She buried her face against his chest and let him hold her.

The funeral was over and done, but they couldn't go home yet.

John, and Eli directed the crowd away from the grave, guiding them to a circle prepared in the meadow over the rise. Eli had asked for a give-away. Usually that came later, but Thomas let Eli have his way.

Walker was in the center of the ceremonial circle, blessing the drum with sage and tobacco. John joined him to walk the circumference, consecrating it with smoking sage bundles and prayers, while Grady's family and friends gathered at its outer edge. He felt awkward, performing a ritual better handled by one of the Indians, but Walker had insisted.

The only sound now was the drum. A deep regular rhythm, the heartbeat of the earth. Mourners swayed gently to the healing song of the Mother's heart.

When everyone had found their place, lined around the circle, a different rhythm emerged. The drum thundered and singers raised their voices in an ancient primal song that lifted the Cherokees to another place and time. There, they were one with the ancients who lived here before the white man came, those who journeyed west or left their bodies along the Trail of Tears, or sacrificed to stay behind and preserve the little that remained of their ancestral land. Even with those who had left the community but still remembered who they were. They were Cherokee. Behind closed eyes they gave themselves up to the ache and joy of being who and what they were. One People now, they entered the song, lifting voices that blended and united. It stirred their spirits and called them into the circle.

John felt the call. His feet moved and his body swayed in union with the dancers. Perhaps other white people were standing awkwardly outside the circle, like he would have done before, but now he belonged with his people. Faron was at his side, matching his rhythm. He could feel her there, though his eyes were closed. The dance was a prayer, a covenant and a source of power, and he understood. No longer an outsider who married in; John was Cherokee.

He saw Walker, Buck, and David leave the circle and pride welled in his heart. They would return as warriors. He had looked up to The Cherokee Warrior Society as long as he could remember.

A few more songs and dances, then the dancers snaked from the circle and took their place in a ring around it. Only Eli and Thomas remained inside with the drum and singers. The last deep rumble of the drum hung in the air then faded into stillness.

Through the silence, Eli's voice rang strong and proud. "My grandfather was a warrior. In World War II, he received a battlefield commission for an act of courage that saved his platoon and gave his people another reason to be proud of our warriors. When this was our own land, our people fought to defend it. When America goes to war, Indian people are among the first to go and the first to die, and often the last to be recognized, but our warriors do their duty. Today, my father and I hold this giveaway to honor Lt. Colonel Grady Smoker, a soldier in the American Army. His courage was as great as any hero of the past. His final battle will be sung by only a few, but it will be remembered through all the generations of his children."

The drum came alive, rising with the power and passion of a warrior's dance. Women gave voice to a tremolo that ignited war cries from young men. The circle parted at the eastern side and with great dignity and bearing, Walker danced in, carrying in one hand the totem banner of the Bird Clan, and in the other, his walking stick. He wore the uniform of the U.S. Marine

Corps. A badge on his sleeve proclaimed him a member of the Cherokee Warrior Society. A single hawk feather and a strand of red yarn adorned his long braid. Behind him came others clad in parts of uniforms they had worn in their own service to their country. Army, Navy, Air Force, Marines, a couple of Green Berets. Two elder women wore Army Nurse Corps uniforms from the same vintage as Walker's garb. Women and men alike added something of their Indian regalia to the military dress. All danced to honor a fallen warrior who would no longer dance in their circle.

Clan banners and totems from all the seven clans were lifted proudly above the marching, dancing warriors as they traversed the circle. They formed an arc behind Thomas and Eli and came to a halt.

David and Buck stepped out of the line of warriors, each in uniforms worn during their service in the desert. David laid a blanket before Thomas and Eli, spreading it out on the ground to reveal a collection of items that belonged to Grady.

On a white blanket that lay waiting, Buck carefully placed a tunic and leggings, the ceremonial regalia Grady treasured and wore only on the most important occasions. Lena had made it for him soon after they married. Every bead and feather on the beautifully worked buckskin spoke of the skill and love with which she fashioned it. Today, it would be passed on to the one who would finish any tasks he had left undone, and carry on his place and duty in the world.

One by one, Eli and Thomas held up an article that had belonged to Grady and called out a name. The old Barlow pocket knife he had carried with him for years went to Hilda's dad. He blinked back tears and struggled to maintain his Anglican dignity when he accepted it from Eli's hand.

A turquoise pendant went to Bonnie Locust. She stood straight and proud, lifting her hair for Buck to fasten it around her neck. Hilda's younger brother choked up when he went into the circle to take the keys to the old Pinto. He would be old enough for a learner's license in a few months. With a few repairs and a new set of tires, it would serve him well. The deed to Grady's land went to Eli. Thomas took a quilt Lena had made and laid it across the Choctaw woman's arm. She held it against her breast and cried. An old book of poetry went to John. He leafed through it, noting scribbled comments in the margin that revealed a sensitive, philosophical side of Grady he'd never known about.

When nothing was left but Grady's regalia, Buck picked it up on its blanket and laid it across Walker's arms. Walker signaled with a nod for John, David and Yona to stand with them when he made the presentation. With a lump in his throat, John listened. Walker spoke loud enough for every one to hear, but the depth of meaning in his words was meant for Eli and the four who flanked Walker.

"You stand in your grandfather's place now, son. What he would have done, you must do. What he has forgotten, you must remember. Keep his words to pass down to the generations of his children. Honor his spirit as long as you live and keep your duty to him until you leave it in other hands that you trust to keep it well." Lowering his voice, he continued, "Eli, you are the grandson and heir of the last guardian of the Ulunsu'ti. Until the Suye'ta calls for it, it is in your care. In your grandfather's stead, I will stand with you until I walk over to be with the ancestors. Grady did wrong, but he atoned for his offense in the only way he could. It's up to you to set it right. We'll be with you, Eli."

Walker laid Grady's regalia across Eli's outstretched arms and stepped back and bowed his head. John and the others followed his lead. The clear sweet melody of a lone cedar flute sang the old warrior to his rest.

When the last note faded, the drum took up the slow solemn rhythm of the heartbeat. The Cherokee Warrior Society danced out of the circle.

John looked across the hill where the new grave would be left behind, unmarked. Grady Smoker no longer existed in this world. He silently thanked him for a lifetime of stories that had prepared them to get through the past week alive. Other than Grady's son and grandson, only Walker and Yona had reason to remember where his bones rested.

Yona walked away without a backward glance. Meredith Wayanettah slipped her arm through his and fell into step with him. She wouldn't be leaving until Monday morning, They needed time alone to make the most of her visit home. John was glad he wasn't one of the men who had to work with Yona on Monday. His brother-in-law was always grumpy as hell when Meredith left for Atlanta. They had to keep reminding him that she was doing the right thing for all the right reasons. As smart as she was, she'd make a good doctor, and one day come home to the Eastern Band where she was needed.

Yona waved goodbye over his shoulder.

John watched them go, anxious to leave the cemetery and go home. Back on the Snowbird with Faron and the kids, he could put the last few days out of his mind. Saturday night was coming up, and he'd be singing bluegrass with the boys at the Round House. Life would get back to normal then, or as normal as it would ever be again. And if Kate volunteered to keep the kids, Faron could come along. A night out was just what they needed.

"Ready to go, John?" Faron took his arm. It would be easier if he could tell Faron everything, but he had to keep the Snake Dancers' secret from his wife, if he could.

Walker was up ahead, leaning on his walking stick and looking frail and tired. It made John feel guilty for some of the things he'd said to the old man when he kept hassling him about getting initiated into the Snake Dancer Circle. He had to get it through Walker's head that he had no intention of ever being a Snake Dancer but the tension it created between them hurt. The old man was only doing what he thought best.

John made an attempt to mend the rift. "You want to ride home with us, Old Man?" He clapped a hand on Walker's shoulder.

"Sure, son." Walker grabbed Diamond's arm as the boy tore

past him. "Your son's getting as independent as you are lately. Thinks he can get by on his own without any help from anybody. It'll take time, but he'll learn we're all in this together." Diamond broke into a run, dragging Walker along with him. As usual, Walker got the last word.

Kate said goodbye to Nathan Axe with a brief kiss and left him to join her family. Wren took her hand and stood, looking toward the grave. "Mama Kate, are you sure he's in that grave?"

John waited for Kate's answer, not at all happy with the dark circles under his baby's eyes. The poor kid probably hadn't slept a wink since that morning on Wolf Mountain. No wonder. He'd had a couple of nightmares himself.

"He's in there, isn't he, Mama Kate?" Wren asked again. "The real Uncle Grady?"

"That's just his body, honey," Kate told her. "Grady has walked over to the above world."

"But it's him, isn't it? Not the thing that made him a bad man?" Wren needed to be sure.

"Honey, that bad thing can't hurt anybody anymore. Uktena is asleep again inside the Ulunsu'ti. I think the men know better than to try to use it again. Let's hope they learned something from this." She shot a meaningful glare at Walker.

"Mama Kate," Wren asked. "Why do the men keep that thing? Why don't they just try to find a way to break it and make it go away?" John kept quiet and listened. He had wondered about that more than once.

"You know the stories about the good the old conjuror did with it, and the others before him who controlled it. When it's used in the right way, by the right person, the power of Uktena is good to have on our side."

"Mama Kate, do us women have anything like that. Some kind of thing that gives us power?"

Kate smiled, a faint mysterious smile. "No, Wren," she said. "We don't need it. We do just fine without any crystal."

For the first time in days, Wren smiled. "Let's go home

now, Daddy," she said.

John picked her up and held her like he had when she was much younger. Faron slipped an arm around his waist. Kate went to help Walker try to keep Diamond under control till they got to the car. They were less than an hour away from home.

"Yes, baby," John said. "Let's go home now."

The first white Suye'ta took his family home to the little house on Snowbird.

About the Author

HOLLY McCLURE is the daughter of a Cherokee mother and a Scots Irish father. She grew up in Robbinsville near the Snowbird Community and spent many happy days listening to her dad singing bluegrass and her mom's people telling stories. She now lives on an island off the coast of Georgia but the mountains around Graham County will always be home.

also by
Holly McClure

TWIJTED HAIR

At 108 years old, the Cherokee Grandfather walked over to the next world. He left behind his stories.

One of them told of an ancient holy man who came to warn his people fo the arrival of the first white men to walk these shores. Some believe he reappears when his people need his wisdom.

He reminds us of our heritage, of the stories, songs and sacred ways that keep us strong.

But more important, he warns of things to come.

Twisted Hair brings the stories of his people.

Twisted Hair. Myth, History, Prophesy as the Cherokee elder saw it.

Coming soon from Bella Rosa Books
ISBN 1-933523-16-6

Printed in the United States
124301LV00008BA/103-111/A